THE CHANGED WORLD

MAUREEN O. BETITA

Created with Vellum

Listen to My Immortal, by Evanescence and you'll find Ivy.
Watch Life After People and you'll find The Changed World.

Maureen O. Betita is a maniacal writer with a talent for binding unlikely elements into a book full of adventure.

If you would like to receive updates on her releases and a chance to win cool stuff, sign up for my newsletter, at maureenobetita.com. Your email address will never be shared, and you can unsubscribe at any time.

INTRODUCTION

From
The Book Of Cruz

In the days before time shattered, the earth rolled with billions of people. Many colors, many countries. Much conflict. Cities rose to the sky, holding every luxury imaginable. Humankind knew their place, which was standing upon everything else. Even their kin.

As was written by a great author of the before, "It was the best of times, is was the worst of times."

We, the Cruz, were tolerated. Called aliens, we knew the truth and kept to ourselves, in small communities, and did what we did. We were humans, science supported that fact. Our people came from the same roots, but the Cruz evolved...twisted. Or blessed. It all depended on perspective.

The oldest of us remember how full of noise and distraction the old world was, before it changed. But even their memories grow faint, with the years.

The change swept through the galaxy, a great tide that fed on time. It struck with no warning. One moment, the earth was as it had always been, revolving with simple elegance through the ancient sky. Then the wave intersected that path. Instantly, the planet felt the weight of time. Billions of people aged instantly, then in another second, they were dust. Cities crumbled; the monuments of men were swallowed by nature, speeding by to sweep them away.

Coastlines changed, mountains rose, islands sank and in the span of minutes, the survivors stood, alone. The wave swept past, no doubt moving on to wreck havoc through the cosmos, done with us.

Most of our people were spared. We'd always been few, but our instinct to cluster boded well. In the aftermath, we stood together.

The rest of the survivors had to find each other and begin again, in small villages and communities. With perseverance, they learned all over again how to grow crops, hunt animals, take care of themselves. We did what we could to assist.

It didn't take long for the worst of human nature to rise. A decade? Less? Within a century, misery ruled the land. The visitor had done more than steal history, it left behind altered biology. People aged, but they didn't die. Not naturally. Swords still worked, and axes, and clubs.

And one more thing. Births slowed. And then, they all but stopped.

The survivors needed someone to blame, someone to point a finger at. We were handy. We were different.

In the Changed World, standing out could get you killed.

Or worse.

PROLOGUE

If only this were a nightmare Ivy could wake from. The ground offered no comfort, unyielding and rough, her skin shrank from the ice particles coating the earth. Voices discussed her capture, and how much he would pay them. Distracted by the throbbing in her head she barely heard them, unable to reply, object or counteroffer.

"Pity, she's one of the last. Not many of them left," a gruff male voice spoke. "But her price will see us through the winter."

"Longer, she's with child. He'll pay twice for two," a hard female added, without mercy. "Pity she hasn't had it, we could keep it and just sell her."

"World's gonna be a plain place when they are all gone." Regret painted that voice. Ivy felt a wrinkled hand brush the hair from her mouth. "I remember..."

"Stuff it, old woman! Memories won't keep us fed," the hard voice cut off the memory. "Bind her arms and legs. Denny, you carry her. This is good luck for us, we have to use it!" The orders were obeyed without further discussion. Rough rope bound her wrists, safely enclosed in a bag. They knew Cruz and their tricks.

Helpless, totally helpless. Weak from five months of running, trying to find enough to eat, avoiding the constant patrols as her belly grew and she cursed the unwanted burden. Shelter after shelter came up deserted, nothing but ashes remaining. He'd been merciless.

Her captors bargained well. Ivy recovered enough to attempt talk, but all that accomplished a gag. Fiona, the older woman, tried to offer comfort. The old woman remembered life before the world had changed.

They haggled well and received a high price, she actually didn't blame them. Life was hard. But now she sat, back to the familiar cell. At least he'd been absent. She had two nights of peace. Many of his clan came to stare at her, but no one spoke. She was fed, but sparingly. And her hands were kept loosely bound at her back. She could have freed them, but why? They'd only redo the rope, tighter. Instead, she welcomed the small mercy.

He'd finally arrived and stood, staring at her through the bars. A tall man, broad shouldered, sun bleached hair falling down his back, tightly braided. He bore scars on his face, one she could be credited for. She nearly smiled at the tear at his cheek, her knife would have taken an eye if he'd been a second slower.

He signaled archers to stand ready before ordering the jailor to enter and undo her hands. The jailor hesitated and Ursus struck him.

She tried to smile, even comfort the man, whispering, "Won't hurt you..."

Her arms fell useless to her sides as the binding fell away. She swung them, trying to restore feeling in the long denied muscles. Ursus glared at her, then brusquely spit his demand, "Strip." Ursus, the leader of the bear clan. The brute. The rapist. The murderer.

She wasn't wearing much to begin with. Rags and strips of cloth stolen here and there fell at her feet. Survival was at stake, she didn't challenge him. Sensations slowly returned to her hands, enough to do the job. When she finally stood, naked and defenseless, he gazed at her swollen belly, bearing mute testimony to her state. He'd turned to three of his men. "Call the midwife."

She'd known humiliation, but this as new. Surrounded by men, they gaped and giggled. The midwife trembled, attempting to be gentle, but too aware of what was at stake. Ursus had looked for an heir many, many years, only to be fruitless, as most were in the Changed World.

The midwife leaned back and turned to him. "Due in two months."

Ursus stared at the midwife. "She was in my bed a solid month. This baby is mine?"

"It seems likely, sir," the midwife declared gazing at Ivy with pity. Those gray eyes pierced her soul and sent her to the depths of grief. With a soul-wrenching cry, she rolled to one side and surged to her feet, threw herself at the bars, attempting to see one of the poised arrows take her belly.

Two months, Ursus kept her in that cell. Assigned a young boy to watch her, keep her from harming herself. Young Emmett, a Cruz from the greater jails. One of the few left alive. For months, the big blond man had been systematically disposing of the small group he'd captured, all of them known to Ivy. They were the last of the farmers who resisted his authority. Who took up arms to fight him. The last of her blood family.

Emmett had been frightened, but did his best to help her. If she harmed the baby, Ursus would kill him. In front of her. She did nothing to put the young boy in danger. When the little girl slipped free, she'd refused to look at the infant. "Not mine, his! His!"

Ursus was pleased, and made the mistake of ignoring his two captives, emerged in the care of his daughter. Fiona drugged the guards, took Ivy's hand and led her from the cell. She'd sheltered Ivy and Emmett for a week, seeing strength returned, and told them of the shift in their fortunes. "Rumor comes of a group of

Cruz that sail the seas. They seldom touch on shore, knowing they are a hunted people. Each carries a curse, as you do." She'd transferred her gaze from Ivy to Emmett, "Yours will come, boy."

Ivy closed her eyes, the night of her twentieth birthday, her genetic curse had settled on her. And for too long she didn't see it as a curse. Twenty years later, she knew it as such.

Eternal youth. What a fucking joke.

CHAPTER ONE

The Gathering began simply enough. She sensed nothing beyond the normal risks of exposure. They could be followed when the left, but that was nothing new. Every two years, peace reigned in the old zone of countryside, a place known as Gathering Valley, and thousands gathered to enjoy the amenities of the past. Technologies that no longer functioned elsewhere flourished here, and she wanted a rest. Needed a rest.

Fighting and warfare stayed outside the valley barriers, held at bay by a threat the normally warring population recognized, though none understood it. Troublemakers died, without warning, during the Gathering.

This didn't mean that plots weren't hatched, or nefarious events didn't occur, but nothing came into the open. No one knew where the edge lay between normal and 'get in trouble', consequently everyone took care. The valley opened, played host, then closed and the burdens of outside life returned.

Ivy and Emmett hadn't attended a Gathering in more than a decade. His curse of old memories, striking on his twentieth birthday, generally proved too vivid and as a result they remained in the wild, taking care of each other. Any remnant of former civilization stirred visions in the man. Memories that weren't his howled through him, demanding attention and dividing his soul. If they kept to the wild, the ghosts didn't rise.

But they never strayed far from Ursus' territory. Ivy denied her reasons. It wasn't that she looked for her daughter. Not that, not at all.

Her rapist named the girl Helen. Ivy always remembered her as simply the baby.

After she and Emmett escaped, the young boy tried to talk her into leaving the area. But she insisted they stay close enough to watch and spy on her nightmare. After coming too close to being caught, he finally won the argument and they moved into the relative safety of the mountains.

She tried to move further, to the south or the east, but another lie held her. Ivy dreamt of rescuing her daughter. But they never got close enough to put together a plan. Four years after the baby was born, they spied Ursus from the center of a mercenary camp. Before him road a little girl, bright yellow hair, smiling and laughing with her father.

After that, Ivy abandoned her fantasy. They joined a band of free mercs, as the nonaligned bulk of mercenaries referred to themselves. She and Emmett worked alone, a pair for hire. After all, the girl didn't need to be rescued. Didn't need her mother. Why stay close?

The free mercenaries offered further training and a camaraderie that demanded little in return.

Ivy looked forward to renewing seeing their old comrades, so they took a chance on Emmett's curse, and it appeared to pay off. The streets no longer wandered through the old sections of the village, meaning Emmett didn't suffer from ghosts. The residents had changed just enough that it all felt new.

Ivy glanced about, still hearing the music her grandmother used to hum. Music floated over the village, from the old world.

"Shouldn't be here...but none of this should be here." Her grandmother had shaken her head, but still smiled. She lightly sang along. "Whatever caused the world to change had a strange sense of humor, Ivy."

The soft strum of some stringed instrument, a woman's voice rising above it, drifted down the street. '*...flowers in your hair...*' Ivy closed her eyes. Her grandmother once sang that song.

Ivy still feared it was a mistake to attend. But Emmett was restless and even she had to admit the idea of a real espresso drink haunted her mornings. Her grandmother introduced her to the beverage decades ago, when the Gatherings celebrated what they held in common, not the short period of truce it later became.

For a week they considered themselves welcome. She met old friends and comrades, listened to rumors and stayed away from the neighborhoods where the greater warlords met to talk. Her shields lowered and she started to relax.

At a great masked ball she spied her daughter for the first time. She and Emmett put together elaborate costumes, hiding amidst the upper class. He dressed as a sad clown. She became a debonair man about town, her breasts wrapped tight enough to fool anyone. She danced with women and enjoyed the trick. When she came face to face with Helen, she accidentally jostled a large glass of beer from a bystander and nearly starting a dispute. Apologies soothed his ire, she recovered her equilibrium and looked for that face again.

The girl strongly resembled Ursus. The age was right. Ivy dodged contemplating what it meant, refusing to consider why she wanted to examine the woman closer. She'd gone numb at the first start of recognition. The ache in her heart, the flush to her skin, the shattering at the core of her bones, shook her. The deeply buried fantasy of Helen, trapped by Ursus, treated like a scullery maid, praying for rescue...it sank into the sea of reality. Instead, she saw a beautiful, smiling, well fed, vibrant and thriving woman. Nothing Ivy wanted to acknowledge, but everything Ivy wanted to know. She grew dizzy with the tangle of her thoughts.

A cold clamp seized her heart, slowing its runaway pace, her brain locked into a predatory mode, useful when surviving in the wild. Ivy froze the emotion away, locked it tight. Quieted the fear, rising like a tide and threatening to swallow her whole. If Helen danced here...he had to be close. She would survive, plan her revenge...

Ivy maneuvered around the room until she could request a dance of the young woman. As they spun about the room, she studied the face, and slowly recognized hints of herself. The young girl appeared pleasant, eyes sharp and smile warm. At the end of the dance, Ivy bowed away, avoiding questions and small talk. She needed to find Emmett and leave. The crowd pressed upon her as she swept her gaze about the room.

Ivy's height kept her from spying him for several minutes. A new dance began before she reached an elevated platform. There she gained a few inches and gazed around the room.

The last thing she'd expected to view was Emmett, dancing with Helen. And clearly enjoying himself. Ivy stayed silent as Emmett chatted, laughed. Along with Helen. Ivy faded to the exit. If she broke them apart, he'd know something was wrong. If any one could pick up on what her mind spun with, Emmett would. He'd find his way back to their billet in his own time. Let him enjoy himself. Ivy fled the music, needing quiet. To think.

The familiar coffee shop of her youth stayed open during the Gathering. She stepped in and ordered a drink, sat and tried to process the complex whirl in her brain. Helen was stunning. Her hair a long, bright blond, her eyes... Even masked, Ivy had recognized those eyes. Her mother's eyes. But the plains of Helen's face betrayed her father's legacy, pure Ursus. Ivy had no idea of anything else, save that the touch of her daughter's hand had caused shivers to find a home along her spine. The barista she'd befriended too long ago to remember – the valley denizens showed little sign of change over the decades – sat down across from her and spoke, "Ivy? Great costume. I knew you by your drink."

"Hey, Dave. Uh, thanks." She'd pushed the eye mask away before she'd entered. "Dave...Ursus is here?"

He nodded. "Yes. Though he hasn't been seen in this part of town. He generally stays in the towers section. He saw you?" Dave knew enough of her history to realize this would prove painful.

"No. I saw his daughter. Had to be Helen, she has his face." Ivy sipped at her drink. "I understood he seldom came to the Gatherings."

"He usually doesn't. It's a far distance for him to travel. And rumor has it he finds a month of peace too hard to keep, but I hear his daughter insisted. He can't hurt you here." Dave touched her hand. She curled her fingers away from the comfort, smiling slightly in apology. She didn't need his pity.

"He still hunts the Cruz. He won't rest until we are all dead," she softly said. "Emmett and I must take care how we leave."

"He is a warlord, he is bound to stay the full month. You aren't," Dave suggested the optional departure date. "You have time to create distance. *If* he discovers you are here."

"Someone will sell him the information. We haven't been careful enough." She sat straighter and met Dave's eyes. "I won't be his toy again."

"I know." He sighed. "I remember when you and Emmett stumbled into the valley and the conflict it spurred. But I'm grateful you were allowed to stay and heal. Ivy? I hear rumors of a group of seafaring Cruz."

"I've heard that rumor before." Ivy snorted. "Marauders, bitter men. Few women. I am not a sailor."

"Nor is Ursus and you could learn." Dave sighed as a group of late night revelers came in. "Got to go."

"Yeah, if Emmett comes in, don't tell him I want to leave. I'll talk with him. I'm heading to bed." She finished her drink and stood up. Dave watched out for her. He was a good man, but he couldn't save her. No one could.

The next morning, Ivy woke to Emmett staring at her. She blinked awake and met his eyes. He sighed. "She is the baby, isn't she?"

"You find any of me in her? Where?" Ivy pushed up from the blankets. Emmett still wore part of his costume.

"Her eyes, and she has your toes." He smiled ruefully. "We went for a walk in the garden, she likes the feel of grass on bare feet." He drew a deep breath before continuing, "Her father wasn't at the dance."

"Small favors." Ivy stretched. Not ready to discuss Helen, she asked him, "You get any sleep?"

"No. I've walked the entire night. When I made the connection, I ran from her." He rubbed at his face with a towel, removing the last of the face paint from the night before. "She's what? Nearly twenty."

"You were in attendance...you ought to know." Ivy considered a moment. "She's half-blood, with his hatred of the Cruz, it must gall him." Again, her brain simply shifted gears, avoiding the connection. "Are you going to sleep?"

"No. I want a meal." He continued to change his clothing. The small fabric enclosure they shared contained the only privacy they had. But they had no secrets from each other. Ivy dressed with equal lack of modesty. By mutual agreement, they avoided the topic of Helen. Basics came first. Food.

They left the huge building, pausing at the message boards. Neither expected anything, but sometimes posts contained information about jobs available in the greater world.

They found a black envelope, her name spelled out in a fair hand. Black seldom carried good news.

Ivy grimaced, pulled it down, and turned it over to examine a seal. A bear paw, in red, adorned the back. "Ursus! Fuck it." Her belly boiled, anger rose. While her daughter's presence froze her, Ursus' lit her on fire. Damn, she wanted him dead. She didn't know what she desired from Helen.

Nothing. Nothing!

"There goes anonymity." Emmett sighed. "What's it say?"

She moved away, opening the envelope with trembling fingers and read. Rolling her eyes, she answered him, "Wants to meet me, or Helen does. Leaves the time and place up to me. He'll be present, but this is for her. Wonderful." She looked away, took a deep breath. "Okay. I hoped to avoid this, hoped we'd get away without his notice. Fuck! Someone sold us. What do you think? This afternoon, at the café?"

At his nod, she continued, "I'll let Dave know." She filled out the reply envelope, with a guarantee of a reward for speedy delivery and looked for a handy messenger to send off with it. Only then did she meet Emmett's eyes. "Nothing to do but face it." Her head whirled, considering she could handle Helen's presence if it presented a chance to kill Ursus. Twenty years of running must be enough.

"You're curious about her?" he asked. "I found her pleasant enough, good dancer, good kisser."

"You fuck her?" Ivy asked bluntly. It didn't matter, but if her partner grew attached, it might.

"No, not enough privacy. But she proved suitably amorous in the garden. I have no doubt we would have, if I hadn't figured it out." He shrugged, used to Ivy's forward questions. He'd grown up with her.

"She has the Cruz mark, I touched it, high on her right thigh. But it isn't complete or something. That's when I put the pieces together." He shuddered. "Jesus, I saw her slip from you." His voice sounded odd, but Ivy didn't push for details. The both treasured privacy; his business if he'd wished the affaire had progressed further.

Ivy again shoved any more talk away with a practical observation. "Yeah, you were only nine, Emmett. Probably remember better than I do." Her memories revolved around pain and ache. The voice of Ursus filled her head, threatening to kill her if she hurt the baby.

At least Emmett remembered the miracle of it.

Shaking her head, she led him out to the greater encampment into the built-up sections of town. As they walked, she talked, "Sure, I'm curious about her. But I want to know what he's told her." She smiled bitterly.

"Planning to cut between them? Heady revenge, if it works. But she has to be aware of the basic truth. Too many know of his vendetta," Emmett commented.

"The basics. And if he's smart, he didn't try to shield her, but he isn't always a smart man." She grinned crookedly. "Or he'd never have lost me in the first place, or the second."

"Here, they have good meat pies here." He led her into a corner bistro. "What do you want to do before the meeting?"

"Let's go watch the Holy Roller show." She snickered. "I'd love a good laugh."

Hours later the religious asked them to leave the meeting, disturbed by their laughter. They interrupted a continuing discussion on what the overnight changes to the world meant. The leaders of faith held the same debate at each Gathering. The biggest question? Which religion followed the correct path to heaven? Emmett knew enough to poke holes in nearly every assumption they made. His curse of past knowledge and visions wasn't specific, save for religious philosophy and theory. Those memories went back centuries. And though these recollections didn't haunt him, they realized if the religious knew of it, he'd be considered a valuable commodity. They tried to tread carefully, but found the debates too entertaining to skip.

He'd whisper the original belief in Ivy's ear and she'd reply with a silly parallel. They'd been banned from numerous religion halls.

Humor still foremost in her mind, they entered the café. Ivy knew how to compartmentalize and enjoyed the distraction. With a sigh, she knew the time to deal with Helen dawned. She'd sent a message to Dave that they'd need a table in the center of the café, and why.

The barista spied her and nodded at a smallish round table with a reserved sign on it. He frowned as he came forward. "Is this a good idea?"

"Of course not, it isn't mine," she tossed back. After a pause, she bowed her head. "I know, but it's inevitable and now is a good a time as later. I feel safe here. He isn't reckless enough to try anything in the cafe."

"I have extra staff on, to make certain." He shook Emmett's hand. "I know you watch her back, you sit in or want a good vantage point?"

"He's with me," Ivy interrupted, not letting Emmett answer. She needed him at her side, he often read people better. Ivy knew her vision of humanity was tainted by her experiences. "I'd like plate of cookies? I have enough credit for that, right?"

"Of course." Dave shook his head at Emmett, both well aware of her need for control. "Drinks?"

"Yes, but let him order his," she snickered and sat down. She would not lose ground at this face-off. It had taken her too long to leave the constant nightmare behind. Though a few only faded, never totally disappeared.

CHAPTER TWO

Late afternoon proved a slow time at the coffee house. Few of the tables sat occupied, most customers took drinks to go. She sighed, inhaling the scent of real coffee with deep appreciation. The entire existence of the chain attested to one of the many mysteries the Changed World now held. How they received supplies, even the power that ran through the entire city, remained a mystery. Those who came to Gathering simply enjoyed, choosing to ignore the mysterious aspects.

She assumed these luxuries didn't exist anywhere else. Ivy snorted, took a sip of her drink.

"What?" Emmett asked.

"Oh, considering how little I know. How this place is even possible. I used to ask my grandmother, but she'd only shrug. Said it was likely some arcane scientific art." She met his eyes and smiled. "At least our ignorance doesn't lead to stupid argument. Like what happens at the Holy Roller show."

He snickered. "They are sure of themselves. Each certain of what contradicts the other. I don't know why more people don't attend the meetings. They are entertaining."

"Ought to simply shoot all of them." Ivy looked up at the doorway, watching a brooding man enter the café. She recognized one of the men who'd thrown them out of the hall when their laughter had grown disruptive. "Oops."

When the stern faced man strode in to glare at them, Emmett muttered, "Idiot."

"You two! Stop disrupting the meetings!" He wore a brown robe, bare, dirty feet visible at the tattered hem and a most impressive scowl warped his face. One hand held tight to a fist, white with tension. Those who preached religion played at being meek and mild, but she knew different. Not even his temper would spur any actual attempt to do damage. The Holy Rollers may be unintelligent to her eyes, but they weren't stupid.

Ivy met Emmett's glance and the two collapsed in laughter again.

The preacher snarled. "You're an abomination!"

"No proselytizing in here!" Dave called out.

"I wouldn't even attempt to convert these two heathens." He looked from one to other. A cold smile grew as he spoke again, "Do come back to Montan, we'll welcome you warmly. We always have work for able-bodied non-believers. As firewood."

His tone froze her blood.

Ivy grew somber, understanding the threat completely. Burning witches was rumored to be a newly revived practice in some of the more distant villages. The mercenaries would be meeting later to discuss it. She planned on being there for that conversation.

"You start burning those who are willing to work for your lovely little hamlet and they'll join forces, teach you regret," she countered the threat. "Better get used to standing alone against raiders.

Emmett stood. "We already reported the need to take payment upfront to the guild, or risk being cheated."

"We didn't pay you? Pity, take it up with the city council." The preacher spun about and hurried away, speaking over his shoulder. "Others know of your heresy. You corrupting bitch."

She lifted her cup and took a sip, softly spoke, "Heresy?"

Dave squatted near their table, after setting a platter of cookies down. "Talk to me tomorrow. I'll find out what he's babbling about. Montan?"

"Squatty little place in the mountains to the north. Had a problem with beggars in the forest turning into bandits. Found out later they were victims of religious intolerance, turned out of their homes and possessions confiscated. When the town leaders chased us away for refusing to kowtow to the town's preacher, we led the whole group down to Fairview," Emmett replied. "They were welcomed and given shelter there."

"Yes, we learned a valuable lesson, no matter how cold it is, insist on payment before taking up guard duty." Ivy suddenly went still. "Oh, time for the circus."

"No trained bears here." Emmett softly said, as he stood, subtly moving to her back. She didn't stand, but looked directly at Ursus, all but filling the doorway. He ignored her, eyes darting about the café. Dave nonchalantly went back to the counter. After what Ivy assumed a calculated amount of time at the entrance, Ursus moved forward to the table. Behind him came Helen, and another woman; tall, thin like a rail and dark as night.

Something about the stranger repelled Ivy. She turned her eyes away, her skin crawled, as if her body's heat fled inward. Shaking her head, she shoved the impressions away. This was about Ursus. And Helen.

The warlord pulled out a chair, sat directly opposite Ivy, and met her eyes. "Your curse, quite effective. Haven't aged a day, have you?"

"Only in my heart." She smiled coldly. "While you? My, how gray you've grown, Brer Bear."

"The better to display my maturity, and wisdom," he countered.

"Or at least appear you have them. More likely dotage and dementia." She sniffed, not moving an inch, carrying off a sort of nonchalance that took immense concentration. The drive to kill the man proved difficult to control. She kept her hand from the hand axe at her side by sheer, cold, willpower. Her mind tried to flood her with memories of that bedchamber, his laughter...his body.

A huge man, well muscled. And he'd known how to use that bulk to overpower her, to make her feel tiny, powerless and insignificant. He'd taunted her, whispered obscenities as he violated her body. Promised her an eternity of nightmares. Seeing him brought it back to the present. Her skin crawled with repugnance at his nearness. Her body strung tight as an overdrawn bow, ready to break.

Run! Scream! Kill! Kill! Hide!

She had to control it. Had to fling up a shield, display nonchalant fearlessness. Play dead and wait for another day. A sudden stillness and chill flooded her body at the demand. Self-preservation rose to dominate every other reaction. And she had it, held it.

Emmett must have sensed her iron control, he relaxed minutely, then turned his head to watch the lithe black woman go to the counter and order drinks. Ivy knew Emmett was a keen observer and would later speak to her of useful impressions.

Helen sat next to her father, waiting for the glaring to cease. She finally waved a hand between them. "Enough! Hate each other, I don't care. I want to talk."

"Talk? Why?" Ivy turned to the girl she'd lost nearly twenty years ago. The sudden shift in her emotions startled her. An urge to smile, to hold out her arms, to touch the sculpted cheek... The rush of changing sensation threatened to break the emotional dam. Ivy had to shut it back down. Her voice turned cold, better to show Ursus nothing. Any signs of softness would be used against her. Probably against this girl.

This stranger, her daughter.

Ivy blinked, slowly. "You seem well-cared for. Self-assured, confidant, healthy. What do you want from me? There will be no sweet embrace from these arms." Ivy fought not to shudder when gazing at the girl. Close up, those eyes...no make-up this time, like at the dance. Her mother's eyes stared at her. Her mother, dead by Ursus' forces. Every member of her family, dead by his hand.

Easy to find, her people. They clung together, looked alike, and all carried a green cast to their features. In their hair, their eyes, and skin. They'd never spread themselves out, never tried to fit in. The result? They'd been easy to target and never stood a chance. Ivy shook her head, returning to the present.

"I wouldn't expect that. I've heard of you, all my life." Helen tilted her head. "I don't see myself. I expected some resemblance."

"According to my dear Emmett, we share toes." Ivy reached behind and urged Emmett to take a chair.

"Toes?" Ursus looked perplexed, then snarled at her partner. "Twisted Cruz!"

Helen suddenly blushed, sat up straighter. "Ah. My clown of last night. I thought you quite rude, running away without a word."

"I plead shock, I realized who you were and fled. I witnessed your birth, girl." Emmett nodded. "Who is this?" He looked at the third woman, setting drinks down in front of Ursus and Helen before taking a chair herself.

"This is my bodyguard, Diva," Ursus said.

"You insult the valley, to assert such a need." Ivy eyed the woman. "Odd, similar features to mine, seems to be my darker shadow. Looking for me in another? I hope you find disappointment habit forming."

"Not at all. Diva serves as my advisor and companion. Though she plays any part I want." Ursus glanced at the bodyguard.

Ivy growled, hackles rose. Play?! "Keep such *play* from coming near me, bastard! It was never play, it was horror."

"You were a spoil of war. Others have adjusted and gone on to new lives. Even earn freedom," Helen jumped in. "Diva is clever. She found you."

"Hardly difficult to do. You found me first, sweet daughter. I enjoyed the dance," Ivy countered, throwing insult on the bodyguard's ability.

Helen examined her face and slowly made the connection. "Ah, the silent gentleman. Of course, had to be a woman." She shook her head. “I don’t care. Why didn’t you bend with the storm of my father’s victory?”

This girl appeared sure of herself. Untroubled by the manner of her conception? Ivy refused to shudder. “It isn’t in my nature to bend, regardless of the storm’s fury.” Ivy sighed. “A spoil of war? An interesting interpretation.”

“Only the truth,” Ursus answered.

“Truth? That word from your mouth means nothing.” Emmett’s soft voice carried conviction.

“Consider it simply reality,” Ursus retorted.

“Bah. I was an unwilling captive. From war or genocide, doesn’t matter.” Ivy looked at her daughter. “You were the result. I escaped. You’re grown. Fine, you look healthy and content. What do you want from me?”

Helen drew back. She didn’t appear to have a concrete answer and looked away. “I don’t know. You are half of who I am. I want to know more about you.”

“I’m sure you’ve heard a myriad of things. Pick what you like and disregard the rest. I’m not a captive now, to offer entertainment.” Ivy growled.

“You didn’t want me at birth. You don’t want to get to know me now?” Helen grew pale, but stood her ground.

Ivy refused to acknowledge her daughter’s appeal. “I didn’t want you. You’re his, girl. I can deduce enough from your voice and actions. You appear a dutiful daughter. Loving even. You respect him. I am a curiosity, nothing more. Are you a warrior? You go to battle at his side?” Ivy asked bitterly. “Have you killed at his command? Will you mate at his command? Girl, you’re nothing to me but the child of my enemy.”

“I told you, Helen. She’d have killed you in the womb, if I’d allowed it,” Ursus sounded satisfied.

“I would!” Ivy snarled.

“If I gave you a knife now, would you slit my throat?” Helen softly asked. The red spots on her cheeks betrayed the depth of her wanting an answer.

Ivy observed the fade of color as his daughter – her daughter – absorbed the cold responses. Emmett glanced at her. He felt sorry for the girl, Ivy knew it. She couldn't afford to show pity. Not with Ursus watching. She stared at the face her nightmares wore, refused to show anything. And the black sharp-eyed harridan at his side noted everything. Ivy knew her façade had to stay solid. She had years of practice at showing no reaction.

While Emmett shifted his attention between the two women, Ivy turned her glare from Ursus back to the girl. She met the eyes, gave the impression of considering the notion, then shook her head. "No. It isn't your fault he's a monster."

Ursus grunted his doubt.

"Good." Helen took a deep breath. "What is growing on my leg?"

"What now? A riddle?" Ivy laughed, glad for a distraction. "Do I win a prize if I guess correctly? A mole? A wart? A third arm?"

Emmett snickered, while Helen let a small smile cross her face. Ursus had no reaction, only continued to stare at Ivy.

Helen stood and simply bared the leg in question, turning slightly to reveal the mark. Ivy sighed and leaned closer to examine it, high up on her left thigh.

It was a shapely leg, but no one in the café commented on its baring, Ursus' reputation undoubtedly kept ribald talk from erupting. But nudity held no taboo for the populace.

Emmett tilted his head. "Not...quite..." He turned his face to Ivy's, eyes troubled. "I knew it wasn't..."

Ivy pulled back, interrupting him. Ursus didn't need to know how close the two had come the night before. "It's reversed."

"Reversed? It...oh. I look at it in a mirror." Helen let her skirt close and sat back down. "What does it mean?"

"I don't know. I'm not a diviner." Ivy took up a fresh cookie. "Ask a soothsayer." She nonchalantly took a bite, avoiding Helen's glance. Seeing it close up, the twisted letters of the Cruz alphabet, intertwined and difficult to interpret, filled her with an odd sense of connection.

"It means I'll know a Cruz curse on my twentieth birthday, doesn't it?" Helen asked directly.

"Maybe." Ivy shrugged. "It's reversed." She glanced at Emmett. "Maybe she'll get a blessing instead of a curse? Hardly seems fair."

Emmett likely suspected she was putting on an act to keep herself at a distance. They both knew a reversed curse mark must mean something.

Ursus' unwavering stare got to her, she needed relief from his attention. Emmett provided it, intercepting Ursus' eyes. "Get her to a soothsayer. We don't know."

"Liar. You're Cruz, you know. Tell her of your curse," Ursus ordered.

"No, it's mine to hold," Emmett replied, his tone of voice soft and even, betraying nothing. "You don't order me. I know my family is dead, despite your lies they stood hostage to my good behavior."

Ursus grinned. "Oh, who told you? A mine collapse was out of my control, boy."

"You controlled rescue operations," Emmett hoarsely replied.

She knew he didn't hold her deep hatred for the man, but still wanted to spit at him. His voice took on a calm she knew well.

"You left them buried, alive or dead." Emmett posed, coiled for attack and though he appeared insignificant compared to the bulk of Ursus, he was quite capable of starting something neither wanted to face.

"I don't waste resources." Ursus snorted. "You should thank me. I saved your life! Gave you a new mother, though it looks like you'll be playing father to her, if she lives that long."

Time to stop this.

Ivy gathered the remaining cookies into a pouch and stood, determined to move on before things escalated. "Though this meeting proved entirely enlightening and such fun, I suffer from the need of a long, hot bath. Fine. You wouldn't believe us about Helen's mark anyway. So certain we're lying. Truthfully, I wouldn't tell you if I did know, bastard. Find a Cruz shaman and ask...oh, that's right. You've killed them all! Too bad, didn't know you might need one someday."

She stood and Emmett joined her, moving smoothly to her side. They slipped from the table and out a backdoor before the others moved.

Dave stood in the way when Diva tried to follow, shaking his head. "No public passage this way."

"They are public," Diva snarled.

"No, they are wandering citizens. Only those granted access use the back passages." Dave grinned when the two started, watching them storm from the cafe.

Helen blinked at the barista, curious at the turn of phrase. "Wandering citizens? They could stay? Why don't they?"

"Reasons of their own, I imagine," Dave answered.

"I'm her daughter, what about me?" she softly asked, surprising herself at even the idea.

He tilted his head, showing a real interest in her question. "I don't know. What are your reasons for wanting to stay?"

Something in his tone made her cautious. It hinted at a promise of change. The offer of an unknown. She took a step backward. "I'm not sure I want to stay. I only wondered if I could."

"As you wish." Dave moved back to the counter.

Helen slowly stepped to a table and sat down again, lost in deliberation.

Ivy hurried. She went from street to street, not paying attention to where she was going. Emmett kept pace with her, saying nothing. Finally, she reached a bridge and stopped at its center. She tried to slow her breathing. Emmett waited for her to speak. Slowly, she turned and stared at him. "Reversed?"

"A mistake? Perhaps it meant to develop at the front of her thigh." He shrugged.

"I've seen them upside down, sideways, even split between two limbs. Under the hair, even inside a mouth! But never reversed." She shuddered. "Doubtful it means a blessing."

"No dire omens rose when you gave birth. Fiona read nothing unusual, not even in your abandoning the baby." Ivy flinched slightly at his words. He leaned on the short wall and put an arm around the shorter woman. "You worry for her?"

"For her? Not likely. I worry for how her father will react to whatever it means. I tire of running," her voice softened, filled with weariness. "And seeing him again... I still want to run my blade into his belly. And scurry fast as I can, far away as I can. Damn! He scares me! I hate being scared."

It was an immense thing to admit. She stunned herself by sharing the truth with him. He knew, of course he knew. But they never actually talked of it. He'd been there for her, through the nightmares. More nights than she could count, she'd woken up, his arms around her, softly talking her back from the brink of madness.

And in return she'd taken care of him. When Fiona told him of the disaster at the cave, that the Cruz prisoners had been deep underground and Ursus had simply ordered the shaft abandoned, he'd cried.

Despite all she'd gone through, tears never touched her cheeks. She's always been that way. Emmett lived his emotions more plainly than she, though as he grew to adulthood, pragmatism became his byword. She figured they were mirror images of each other.

Helen was only a young woman. Confused and worried, and distant as the sun from the moon. Ivy knew herself bent, likely to never truly heal. And Emmett was an orphan, despite the "gift" of a second mother. She smiled ruefully, pulling free from his comfort.

She sighed. "I do want a bath. We're due."

"Let's retire to the Bridge Street Baths. They are a little further on." Emmett offered her his arm, this time as a gentleman would. The night approached fast, twenty days of the Gathering to go.

Though she doubted they'd enjoy much of it from here on. Something in Ursus' eyes promised trouble.

The baths proved delightful. Ivy and Emmett paid for a good soak, opting for the communal tub. They scrubbed clean, rinsed and settled into the big tub. Ivy's eyes closed and she purred as the heat burrowed into her bones. Too much of her life was spent in cold climes.

"Is that Ivy? The finest fuck in the valley?" a cherry voice called from the other side of the tub.

Ivy peeled one eye open. She countered with a droll smile, inordinately pleased to see a former lover. "Is that Duran? The biggest...mouth in the valley?"

A great laugh rose at the pause she'd taken. Water splashed about and a brown skinned man pushed others aside to sit next to Ivy. He smiled brightly and winked. "You're the one who shouted loudest last time."

"Yes...well...your mouth was busy." She grinned. "Duran, good to see you."

"Emmett." Duran nodded across Ivy to the young man. "You have filled out. Must be eating better?"

"We had a string of good paying jobs since we last shared camp with you," Emmett nodded.

"I heard rumor you were at Gathering. I need to speak with you, in private." Duran leaned toward Ivy. He wouldn't touch, this wasn't a frolic tub.

She made a face. "Talk? Damn."

"I'm sure I can offer you more, girl." Duran looked away for a moment.

Ivy studied his profile. She remembered first meeting him, ten years ago. Younger, brasher, but always terribly confidant. She'd liked him from the first.

He glanced from the corner of his eye and cocked an eyebrow

quite high. "I know, tonight, late. Have you heard of the Cherok Club?"

"Ah, outskirts of the towers residence?" Ivy sighed, drawn back from the pleasant memory. "Yeah, supposed to be a hot new party club, right?"

"Yeah, with private rooms upstairs. I'll secure us one." Duran leered at her. He aimed a glance at Emmett. "I have news you'll want to listen to."

"We'll come," he answered. Ivy nodded.

They left the tub and Duran whistled. It made Ivy smile. He was a cheerful man, despite his sharp eyes. And often underestimated, due to his cheer. She looked forward to visiting with him later, aware of the heat between her legs at the notion. He had good sources, but she doubted he had any news to delight her, but no doubt he would make up for that lack with his other skills. More bad information wasn't going to ruin the anticipation.

The Cherok Club vibrated with cheer when they arrived, loud and overflowing with revelers. Emmett prowled through the crowds, leaving Ivy to sit at the bar and wait for Duran to reveal himself. She perched on a stool, sipping a cool bit of wine when Diva slid into the next seat, disturbing her calm. The hard muscled arm settled on Ivy's shoulders for a scant second, danced down her spine.

"I don't do women, bitch." Ivy spoke plainly. "Go away."

Diva examined her. "What did he see in you? You have a body only past adolescence, your only curves are from muscles. He likes *women*."

"Yeah, well. Maybe you don't know him that well. Go away." Ivy wanted to ignore the bodyguard, but she had presence. When Diva didn't move, Ivy turned and returned the stare. "Not much of a woman, far as curves go. Grace, and speed, I bet. You sure he likes women?"

Diva grinned. "I know. You know, too!"

"Not by choice. Rape has little to do with preference, anyway." Ivy turned back to the bartender and touched her glass. She wanted a refill.

"He remembers it differently than you," the reply came with a slight delay, as if for emphases.

Ivy gripped the stemware and deliberately lifted it to her mouth. She took a sip, before quickly throwing it in Diva's face. "Go. Away. Now."

"Hey! None of that!" the bartender protested.

"She is pestering me." Ivy set the empty glass down. "I'll leave. If she follows, I will object with more than wine."

Diva licked at the dripping fluid, and smiled. "Good stuff. I'll have a glass, barkeep."

Ivy tossed a few coins on the bar. "Get her drunk." She turned to leave, regretting the hasty loss of her drink.

Duran approached. He put an arm around Ivy and pulled her close. "She bother you?"

"Of course." Ivy rolled her eyes. "But no longer, you will banish her from my brain. I have offended the barkeep and have to leave. We'll find a room somewhere else."

"No, he won't care if we go upstairs." Duran smiled at Diva. "If you follow, I will mind, Ursus' crow. My family watches."

"Hold your family close, Cruz lackey. Ursus seeks new prey. He runs out of Cruz to kill." Diva laughed and turned away from them.

Ivy felt Duran's body tighten, though his expression revealed little. He laughed with deliberation, turned and spoke loudly to Ivy, "His teeth will crack if he attempts to devour the Losanglo!" He waited until they reached the bottom of the stairs to signal his clan brother. He hissed, "You heard? Spread the word to be on the watch. She returns with me, make sure Emmett is kept safe."

Ivy opened her mouth to object and Duran squeezed her slightly, asking for patience. She sighed, not wanting to deal with any of it. His body warmed her, smooth, strong, and his hands - Ivy remembered his hands with fondness. She closed her eyes, knowing she had to speak. "I am not one of your family, Duran. You don't hold command over me."

"I know, girl. I know. But don't be stupid and turn down help when it is offered. Ursus shows signs of restlessness. If his blackbird speaks the truth, we will be hunted together." He pressed her against the wall, eyes locked to hers. "We need each other."

She knew his need, at her belly.

She smiled. "One need at a time. Ursus always threatens one tribe or another. It's the nature of warlords. Losanglos is far. Too warm for his denning."

"Maybe, but his cub has thinner blood." He pushed against her, harder. "This need, first."

Her blood rose as her breath caught. She tilted her head, more than pleased at his ordering of business. "Yes, this first."

He dove at her face, seized her lips with his. Her arms rose to tangle fingers in the dark, thick, hair and he lifted her into the air. She wrapped legs around him and he turned to eagerly make his way up the stairs.

They fell into the room, still engrossed in each other. A clearing voice gave them pause. Ivy stiffened when Duran growled. They turned to gaze at the man standing near the window. "What?" Duran snarled, a hand already gripping a blade, relaxed at recognizing the man.

"She needs to know about the offer. I want to make sure you remember, Duran." The older man shifted his attention to Ivy. A shiver traveled up her back and she wanted to hide in Duran's bulk.

Why?

"Get out, Bosun. I'll tell her, in my own time," Duran replied. "How the hell did you get in here?"

"I go where I want, lobo. I will wait downstairs for an answer." He nodded before turning to the door.

"You'll wait until morning!" Duran called out at the shutting door. He pushed Ivy away. "You shivered. You cold?"

"His voice. I know him?" she asked.

"Not yet." He slid his hand along her neck and pushed the loose shift-like top off her shoulder. "My time. Our time. The morning will wait for an explanation. I want you. I want you around me, now."

She surrendered to the flames his touch kindled and nodded, thoughts of the old man flew from her as Duran cupped her breast.

"Take me, fill me." Her eyes closed when he growled at her words. This night, she would forget the rest of her life. For a little while.

Until the dreams came, again.

CHAPTER THREE

Ivy woke that morning mentally, and emotionally, tired. Her sleep, little as it was, had been full of Ursus. His laughter, his invasion. She'd even found herself remembering Helen's birth. Nightmares weren't uncommon for her, but this detailed bitterness drained her mind. Too much of it lingered, even now.

Her body reveled, in contrast to her mind, wondrous and glowing. Duran slept deeply at her back and she sighed at the peace he brought with him. He was a warrior, like so many in her world, but the ability to incorporate war into his life and not be constantly colored by it, set him apart. And he was a superlative lover. She always left his side feeling cherished.

They'd fallen into bed within an hour of their first meeting. Introduced by one of his numerous cousins. To the Losanglos, everyone was a cousin, she'd finally realized. He'd touched her cheek with a dirty finger, smiled and called her chica...she'd slapped him. And he'd grinned, snatched her hand and pressed a kiss to her palm. And her insides had melted.

Letting out a deep breath at the memory, she carefully slid out from the sheets and quietly began to dress. The early light of dawn filtered through the curtains and she needed to find Emmett.

Duran's voice startled her. "Running out on me, chica?"

She turned. He gazed at her, comfortably reclined on his side. The sheet had slid away, leaving him mostly uncovered. A hand rested near his slightly erect cock, one finger lazily stroking up and down the impressive length. A surge of lust rose in her and she smiled slightly. "Trying to lure me back to bed?"

"Of course, mi corazón." He raised one eyebrow. "Why not?"

"Because I don't want to hear what the man, Bosun, wants you to say. I don't want to make any decisions right now. He was determined...and pushy! To linger here waiting for two seasoned mercenaries to enter? He's lucky he didn't end up with a blade in his belly." She shook her head. "My instincts say he's trouble. I'm sorry if you'll lose a finder's fee or something of the like." She smoothed the tunic down her front. It fell bellow her belly. She reached for her pants, unconcerned with the reality of Duran's monetary motive. Everyone had to eat.

"Chica, I don't give a fuck about my fee. It isn't always about money, you know. Get over here. Have pity on me, it's early," he coaxed.

"Not about money?" The idea intrigued her, despite her intention to steer clear of the information. Duran tugged at his impressive erection, now at full mast and licked his lips, crooned some nonsense in Spanish at her. She stepped close enough to be reeled in.

He gathered her onto the bed and rolled over atop her. So much taller than she, Duran carried more muscle, more bulk. He could easily force himself, but gentleness ruled his touch, even when being insistent. He gathered her hands in his and held them above her head. And he filled her, fast and furious. As he pumped, a constant litany of Spanish poured from his mouth. When he wasn't kissing her, he sang into her ears. Words of passion and praise and thanks filled her, as surely as his cock.

She lost herself under him, and she cried out when three orgasms swept through her, one quickly following the other. Her brain shut off and she lay, panting while he paused. He smiled down at her. "You ready to listen, now?"

She fought to catch her breath, eyes slowly finding focus. He was still like an iron bar inside her, she could feel him flexing. She gasped, "Your...fee?"

"No, chica. Bosun offered money, of course. But I want you to listen because what he offers you is more valuable than money. He offers you safety, chiquita." Duran brought her hands, still tight in his, to his lips, where he kissed them.

How could he stop and talk? She could barely form a sentence!

She swallowed again. "Safety? How? From what? I have new enemies? None can promise me safety from Ursus."

Patiently, still buried in her, he continued, "Bosun represents the Cruz who fled to Lina, the island off the south coast. They settled there more than twenty years ago, built a fleet, recovered in numbers, grew strong." He paused when she narrowed her eyes. And waited.

Ivy's heart had frozen at the phrase *twenty years*. A silence roared in her head, followed by a fury rising from her heart. "Twenty years? Twenty years? When my family died? When my home burned? When Ursus wrecked havoc...they ran? They were enough to take an island? This is the safety they offer me? NOW? Not good enough for my family?" She struggled to get out from underneath him. "Let me go! Let me go, Duran!"

"No, you listen to me." He held her, the first time in her memory he used his strength to overpower her and it wasn't in play. After a moment, she quit fighting.

He shook his head. "Jesus, stop! I'm having a hard enough time concentrating on this! Stop! I'm not the enemy. I don't know why some were left. You have to ask him. He probably knows. I've stepped ashore there, chica. Been to Lina. It's like this valley, it holds things nowhere else does. Not as much, but more than the rest of the Changed World. The Cruz, most aren't pure blood. Like you are. Like your family. They are more like Emmett. He has actually family there."

"Shit." She looked to the side, fighting to think without anger. What family would mean for her partner... If a chance existed for Emmett to be with blood relatives, she wouldn't stop him. She couldn't. The memory of the emptiness on his face rose in her. The deep lines that sorrow carved remained, even after twenty years. She took a deep breath, Duran shifting to allow it.

Damn, he was perverse to do this!

Haltingly, she spoke the only truth she knew, "Bosun should talk to Emmett. I don't want to go. I don't want to hide on an island. I know that look in Ursus' eye, Duran. He'll be coming after me. An ocean won't keep him from aiming for me. I know him."

Duran released her hands and sat up, sliding free of her body's warm welcome, grown chilly in the last few minutes. She untangled herself as he watched. "Ursus threatens everyone, Ivy. Not only you."

"Yes, but for me, it's personal. For the rest, it's only blood. Blood and money, land and produce. Slaves. She's the only child he has, and I gave her to him." She met Duran's eyes. "He wants more. He's always wanted more. Taunted me with it..."

Duran grimaced. "He means to take you? Again? Force more children from you?"

"He has always wanted more children. Always the focus of his pursuit of me. I believed, for a while, he'd give it up. But no. It's in his eyes, last night. His hands, on the table, flexing..." She shuddered. "He attempts to lure me with Helen. He looks at her with hidden loathing. She isn't enough, Duran. I bet he's never stopped trying, with other women." She wrapped arms around her knees, amazed at how much she'd absorbed from the coffee house meeting. "And now this island wants me? What timing? Does Ursus know about Lina?"

"He has recently become aware of them. But the full secret of who they are has been kept quiet." Duran closed his eyes. "Children exist there, Ivy. Not a great many, but more than everywhere else I've ever been."

She shuddered, imaging rare Cruz children and what Ursus'

knowing of them would signify. More slaughter. Or the rest of the world would steal them. The hunger for children grew stronger each year, because few were born. "I won't give him more children, mine or anybody else's. I won't go. If he knows about them, he'll find them. He'll steal a fleet, he'll pay someone to betray them. I won't take the chance." She met Duran's eyes. "I'll die first. And he'll die with me."

He nodded. His dark eyes grew sad as he spoke, "I understand, but will you listen to Bosun? Ask your questions, chica. I've been to Lina, you belong there."

"I belong on Lina? What makes you certain, Duran? And how did you see it? You're not a sailor." She shivered and he pulled a blanket over her shoulders.

"We read the writing on the wall. Our local warlord, Genesee, grows old. A fight will erupt when he steps down. The protection he afforded us fades already. Ursus has visited, three times. Each time, he leaves a legacy of bitterness behind, along with unrest and jockeying for power. The Losanglos look for shelter, for allies. The formidable San Gabes will not stop Ursus. We're learning to sail, chica. There are other islands, not only Lina. The Cruz have promised to assist, if we are stealthy." He smiled slightly at her. "We won't run, but we won't leave our families vulnerable."

"Like mine?" she whispered. "We didn't realize..." She closed her eyes at a growing suspicion...was she the price of their help?

He reached forward. "I know. None realized how ruthless and mad Ursus is. What have you heard in your decades of wandering the frozen mountains? Haunting his borders?"

She shrugged. "Not much. Rumors of viciousness. Fables. Nothing seemed real. Whenever we ventured toward the coast, we found too many burned hamlets, too many dead. No survivors to tell who, or why. The religious slowly gain total control of the mountain towns. They know only lies."

"Ursus was likely responsible. He looks for something, sending out spies, searching for certain herbs, plants. He orders the ruins from the past explored, searching. He kills witnesses and recruits the religious. Many live at his stronghold now." Duran lowered himself to the bed. "I don't know everything. I'm not the leader of the Losanglos."

"Why isn't there more talk?" she wondered, growing more comfortable with the conversation leaving her personal fears. She set aside the unease rising at the words *herbs, plants*. Later, she'd figure it out later.

"Fear," Duran simply answered. He yawned. "Don't run away from help, Ivy. You have many friends, many allies. You are admired."

"Admired?" She snorted. She turned to gauge the sun coming through the window. "Friends? Allies? They betray me, or they sell me. Or he finds them and kills them. I am not safe to admire."

"Ivy." Duran's hand strayed to her leg, under the blanket. "Ivy." He sighed. "Don't be blind. Ivy, chica, so soft. Fuck me, Ivy. You owe me."

She shook her head, laughing. "Owe you? Take care what favors you give me. He kills those who do me favors." But her words were lightly said. His hand traveled up her leg, robbing her of the ability to make the threat serious. She sighed and bent to kiss his pierced nipple. She lightly bit the nub and giggled. "I'm not safe, macho."

"Thank God." He pushed her head downward and she gamely allowed it. His proud cock waited for her. She nipped at the bulbous tip before licking away the salty flow dribbling down its length. He moaned as she began to assault him. Where gentle words of love and praise had fallen from him before, now he cursed and cussed, hissed and growled. He grew stiffer in her hands, against her lips and she smiled.

"Cabrón!" he sputtered before manhandled her legs, posing her above his mouth. He hauled her away from sucking at his balls and began his own campaign. She melted over his tongue, poured out her praise in copious moisture, abandoning attempts at winning his surrender. She sprawled, head at his belly, riding wave after wave of sharp pleasure.

He took a deep breath, before pushing her to sit up. "Take me, chica. Ride me."

With a moan, she slid down his body, following the path to his eager cock. His hands at her hips, he provided a saddle she clung to. Her grip tightened on his knees while he bucked and thrust upward into her. He seemed hell bent on making her cry out once more. Before he was done, he pushed her away, knelt and filled her again, shifting her grip to the footboard of the bed. Roaring, he went suddenly still, before a great shudder gripped him. One hand slid down to where they met and Ivy cried out, one last time. They both slowly collapsed onto the rumpled covers.

Within minutes, Duran began to snore. Ivy smiled as she carefully moved off the bed. She dressed, aware of his gentle rising to watch her. She turned, he watched her with barely open eyes. "I will talk to him, Duran."

"And move to our camp without argument. I won't pester you about agreeing to anything. Only come, to be safe." He yawned. "We will make it difficult for him to track you."

"Safe? With you? I won't get any sleep," she teased.

"Who needs sleep?" He chuckled, before fell back to snoring.

"You, obviously." She snickered and left the room, still smiling. She paused at the top of the stairs, hoping Bosun wasn't still downstairs. Her agreement to speak to him didn't mean she'd search him out.

At first, she believed luck was on her side. The downstairs reflected what had obviously been a raucous party the night before. A few workers milled about, gathering glasses and wiping away at spills. They kept their voices low and moved easily. The light was sparse and she missed the older man, sitting to one side near the front door. She turned to the exit, pausing to speak to Gabe, one of Duran's men, about Emmett.

"He's got a room next door." The man whispered, one hand shielding eyes from the bit of light. He didn't look well. "He agreed to move, already gathered everything and gave it to Jacinto..."

"He's with Jacinto?" she softly asked, taking pity on his hangover.

"No, some other chica came wandering in, late," Gabe replied. "Duran?"

"Snoring. I'm getting some breakfast." She prepared to exit when a throat cleared and she froze. "Damn."

"I said I'd wait, Ivy." Bosun stood and gestured to the chair across his small table. "I won't take long."

"Fuck." Ivy snarled, before dropping into the chair across from where Bosun nursed a cup of something hot. "Okay, Duran said you represent the Lina. Want me to come to your island. No."

"Not even a visit?" He smiled slightly.

"A visit, right. And no boat to get me back to the mainland? Oops!" She snorted.

"Ship, Ivy. Boats are small and not the safest way to cross to Lina." Bosun eyed her. "Why do you consider it a prison?"

She thought a minute before replying, "One trap for another. Ursus will hunt me. I won't go, Bosun. I won't draw his attention to them. Even if such a sanctuary was denied my family when needed. I'm a better person than those who left mine to die."

"No one understood how deep his hatred ran. Your father believed there would be time," Bosun answered.

"How do you know what my father believed?" She nearly spit at him. "Hiding on Lina!"

Bosun sighed, looked to one side of her. He looked distant, maybe recalling a deeply buried memory? "Ivy, I knew your father. I knew your grandmother better. I didn't understand why she fought coming to Lina. Why she convinced your father..."

Ivy surged to her feet. "No. No! You! You blame him! I don't believe you!" She'd adored her father, she remembered a gentle, loving man. This stranger wasn't going to get away with blaming him.

He seized her arm before she could slip out the door. "No. You must listen. We know he will come for you. He must not find you, must not sire more children. You know the signs, his intent. We watch him with our spies! Let us hide you! He will not know where you went. Not all the shamans are dead. I do not lie to you, Ivy. I knew your grandmother...I loved your grandmother."

She froze, her lungs suddenly too tight to allow breath. Her head spun, hints coming together. Her eyes met his. "Bosun. That isn't a name...it's a ship's rank... What is your name? Your given name?"

"You already guessed, right? You resemble your grandmother very much..." He smiled slightly, shook his head. "Of course." He waited for her to nod and eased his hold on her arm. "Please... listen to me."

This man, this man was her grandfather? The man her grandmother called a coward? A man who couldn't face a daughter, wanting a son? The man who abandoned her? She'd always said he'd died. "Fuck you! My family is dead!" She jerked her arm free and surged out of the bar. He didn't follow her.

"That went well," one of the workers commented.

"You manage the coffee house, David," Bosun replied. "What are you doing here?"

"I work where I'm needed. She is my friend. I'm not the only one keeping an eye out for her. You believe she'd be safe on Lina?" Dave sat down, wiping the table lightly even as he did. Old habits die-hard.

"Safer than wandering the mountains. The cold increases, the snowfall is heavier every year. The villages will be starved out. He'll offer too much, they'll sell her. We won't."

"She doesn't know that," Dave commented. "She's been sold once, she's suspicious. And she doesn't like the ocean."

Bosun examined the barista's bearded face. "No, she doesn't. Do you know why?"

"Yes. And no, I won't share it with you. That is her story to tell, not mine. She has reason. Old fears find deep roots when planted by those we love," Dave cryptically answered. "Some two weeks are left to this Gathering. Ursus is bound to stay the rest. She must leave, soon. Or never leave."

"You offer her sanctuary," Bosun observed. "But he would know where she was. And find a way to force her out. We seek to hide her better. Until he is dead."

Dave tilted his head at Bosun. "How many die of old age? How is your health, Benjamin? You wait for natural causes to take Ursus? You'll wait a long time. The balance isn't free. Longer life, fewer children."

Bosun stared at Dave. The valley dwellers never revealed much to those who visited. What did it mean? Slowly, Bosun's shoulders sank. He accepted the truth. "We'll have to kill him."

"Someone will have to kill him." Dave stood up. "It will likely be her. You can't protect Ivy from destiny."

Bosun closed his eyes, not wanting to believe it. Not wanting to accept it. A tear ran down his cheek and he sighed. When he lifted his gaze again, Dave was gone, and the bar ready for new customers. He slowly stood, back bent. He needed time to deliberate.

Ivy ran down the street, not wanting to consider what her heart told her. Family? She had family? An internal war drove her far from the Cherok Club.

Finally, her brain took control of her flight and stopped her. She leaned against a wall, catching her breath. It didn't matter...it didn't matter what identity he claimed. She kept reassuring herself, and slowly the bitterness of her grandmother faded away. The woman had done more to raise Ivy than her mother.

The story her grandmother told lay buried in her heart. Benjamin Sols.

"Coward! Coward! He ran from that baby girl, ran from you mother. Always ran!" Grandmother Rosa would spit when she spoke of him.

Ivy was masterful at compartmentalizing. She slid the memories away and stood up straight, reigning in control of her emotions and these revelations. There would be time to work it out later. Right now, she needed breakfast and to find Dave, find out if he'd heard anything new about the charges of heresy. Yes, she'd deal with that problem first.

And later that day she'd be part of mercenaries meeting. Her mental list helped establish balance. A nearby open café beckoned to her and she strolled into it.

Ten minutes later, she enjoyed a hot repast of fluffy eggs and crunchy bacon. Her belly settled with the possibility of a surviving blood relative, carefully considering how the idea made her feel.

Blood relatives were precious to the Cruz. They were, or had been, clannish, and proud of their heritage. Even before the world had changed. They seldom married outside of family connections and when they did, were particular. She knew Emmett's family had reconciled to outside blood. Her family never had.

"Ah, the bitch I wanted to speak to," Ursus' voice insinuated itself into her ear as he slid into the next seat. She started and tried to get out the other side, when Diva took that chair. She froze, hand clenched on a dull butter knife. "I'm not going to stick you, Ivy. I want to talk, relax!" He grinned.

"Talk? Fine, move away from me, your stink ruins my breakfast," she bravely answered. The trembling in her legs proved difficult to control, but she was determined not to let him know how she shook at his proximity.

Diva snorted. "Crazy little Cruz! That isn't breakfast! There are no pancakes."

"Fuck off and die." Ivy knew her banter wasn't terrible clever. She didn't care, only wanted them to move away. The mental exhaustion of earlier returned with a vengeance. Seeing him brought back the nightmare, squatting at her back, sending shivers up and down her spine.

When he settled into the chair across from her, Ivy turned to lock eyes with Diva. "You. Move. Now." She'd find some control. Somehow.

"Oh, yes. That's right, you don't do women." Diva snickered and slid to a seat kitty-corner from Ivy.

"Order food, Diva," Ursus directed. When the black woman was gone, Ursus studied Ivy's face. "Have a good night?"

She steeled herself to reveal nothing. Curling her toes until they verged on cramping provided some distraction. Gave her something to focus on other than the growing panic.

"Small talk? You want small talk?" Ivy shoved the last bit of egg into her mouth, no longer tasting anything. The trembling had eased and she let the butter knife go. Instead, she drew her small throwing ax and set it next to the plate, her fingertips brushing it lightly. She'd rather have her larger, but it proved cumbersome, save in battle.

"No. I want to know about my daughter's curse." He leaned back. "I was trying to be polite."

"Trying. Yes, that's you." She shook her head. "I don't know anything about Helen's curse. I have no reason to lie, as amusing at that might be. I don't know what it will be. I don't know what the mark's reversal means; I don't even know when it will come to her. I don't remember when she was born."

"She'll be 20 in ten months. Isn't that when the rest of you..." He paused and smiled. "The remaining Cruz find out their curse?"

"Usually," she answered, refusing to rise to the bait of how few he'd left alive.

Silence greeted Diva's return. Ivy stared at Ursus, grimacing. He gazed back at her, but he grinned. Ivy broke the impasse. "You find her curse amusing."

"No, only dwelling on memories." He winked and Ivy gripped her ax.

"Memories are the only thing you'll ever know. Touch me again, and you'll die." Ivy pushed her chair back, nausea clawing at her throat. "Well, it's been..."

"No, not yet. I don't believe you, regarding Helen. She is mine! What did you do, lay a curse on her?" Ursus glared.

"Me? You credit me with being able to lay a curse?" Ivy actually laughed. She reached for a glass of water, it might ease the urge to vomit. She studied him over the rim as she drank. Carefully, she set the glass down, determined to be steady. "If I could lay a curse, it would be on you. Something wonderfully dire and deadly."

"Isn't having this beast as a father curse enough?" Diva snickered, touching Ursus' face. "This bitch isn't going to say, even if she knows. We'll need leverage."

Ursus tapped his finger on the table. "Yes."

"Leverage? I have no family left, monster. And you can't use Helen against me, I don't give a damn about her. You've killed all my friends. Good luck finding someone or something. Use nothing to find nothing. I don't know what her mark holds, bastard." Ivy stood. He must never know how his words chilled her. "I would wish you luck, but what I truly wish you is death."

"Duran," Diva hissed, loud enough to reach Ivy's ears.

Ivy turned, a smirk on her face. "A fair fucker, and you would target him for that? Certainly, your jealousy will become legend." She left the café before another word could reach her. She casually turned back toward the nightclub, to warn Gabriel. Duran was a new target. A hand rested at her belly, trying to ease the turmoil. Would he believe her? That Helen could not be used against her? Did she believe her own words?

Every thought of Helen came with Ursus, like a dark shadow. She couldn't help but make that connection; hence nothing but an empty ache filled her heart. The girl viewed her as disposable chattel. Ivy couldn't blame her. She'd left the girl to be raised by that monster. If Helen knew nothing but lies, the fault lay with on her. And it was too late to change anything...

Duran's eyes shot open soon after Ivy left the room. Falling asleep wasn't part of the plan. He stared at the ceiling, studying the water spots, wondering when it had actually rained in Gathering Valley. Never rained during Gathering. He sighed.

Ivy always brought out a protective streak in him. He realized this when the bargain had been struck. The Cruz on Lina wanted Ivy off the mainland, and the help they offered to trade was important to the Losanglos. He wanted his family away from Ursus' reach. He also wanted Ivy, wanted to help her. If she'd let him.

This deal was a double-edged sword. If he succeeded, Ursus would target Duran's family in retaliation. No doubt of that. Ursus had a reputation for vengeance when crossed. And everyone understood he wanted Ivy.

A large bounty rested on her head, announced a few months ago. She hadn't found out about it yet, from the way she acted. He wanted to tell her, but she was paranoid enough already. And no one would attempt anything while in the valley. Let her enjoy the little bit of freedom she had left.

He'd get her to Lina, for her sake and for the well-being of his family. Climbing from the bed, Duran dressed, determined to hunt down Emmett for a good long talk. He liked the young man, respected him and admired his streak of loyalty. He'd turned down offers to join other mercenary groups. Groups that didn't want Ivy. Oh, everyone acknowledged she was a fierce fighter, but she also proved disruptive to moral.

Her jumping from bed partner to bed partner resulted in jealous fights. Duran chuckled, he'd fight for her. She was worth fighting for. But he appreciated it wouldn't impress her.

He turned to the bed, ready to leave. With a rueful smile, he lifted the pillow and inhaled. Damn, she smelled good. He dropped the pillow, and returned down stairs.

Gabe looked up at him, raised one eyebrow. "You missed the excitement. Looked like Ivy was going to tear Bosun a new one."

"Damn, I wish he hadn't interfered. I'm supposed to be

working on her, not him!" Duran snorted in disgust. "Probably got her bitch riled and now she'll be twice as hard to convince."

"Emmett already agreed to help move the camp. Before he snuck upstairs with a bed partner of his own." Gabriel nodded toward a table where coffee waited. "He took a mug and sits over by the window. Was up about ten minutes after Ivy. I understood you wanted to talk, asked him to stay."

"Thanks, coz." Duran loaded up a mug and turned to search for the younger mercenary. He paused, keeping out of sight, watching for a few minutes. *Does not look happy.* Duran took a sip of his coffee before moving over to pull out a chair and face Ivy's partner.

"Heard you found company last night," Duran opened the conversation.

"Yes. You have good spies, Duran. Gabe asked me to wait. When did Ivy leave?"

"Been about thirty minutes. I'm glad you agreed to move camp, Emmett. I haven't told Ivy, but Ursus has put a price on her head. He doesn't seem to be spreading the offer too wide yet."

Emmett rolled his eyes and sighed, looking like he'd been sucker punched. "Fuck. She's always certain of it, and now she has proof. She'll find out, Duran. You can't hide it from her. Who has he made the offer to?"

"He's spreading it through the foothill villages. He is aware of where you two wander. Not sure how you managed to make it here without running into someone trying to collect." Duran smiled up at an attractive woman who set a plate of pastries on their table, "Gracias, bonita."

"De nada!" She replied with a tile of her head. "Davey said to take good care of you."

Duran chuckled and commented to Emmett, "You two deliver his baby at some point?"

Emmett seemed to consider the question a moment, a puzzled expression crossed his face. "You ever see any children in the valley? Figure they must face the same problem as the rest of the world."

Didn't answer the question of why David favored them...

"Never spent time on it, Emmett."

"Why you want to talk to me, lobo?"

One thing about Emmett, he was direct. Ivy would dodge and weave to avoid uncomfortable topics. Not this man. Duran set his coffee down. "I need you to trust me. I want her safe, away from this bounty. Away from that madman."

"I trust you, Duran." Emmett lifted his mug up and gazed into the steaming brew for a minute. His eyes met Duran's and he sighed. "As much as I trust anyone."

"Not as much as you trust Ivy, and I get that. You believe I want to keep her safe?"

The Cruz man took a minute to nod. "I'm not sure why, but yeah, I believe you want the best for her. But you two may not agree with what is best for her. You're the first man she's ever bedded more than once."

Duran sat back, oddly touched at that revelation. He looked away for a moment, it didn't matter. She not only needed to be on Lina for her sake, but for the Losanglos. Even for this man sitting across from him. Bounty hunters wouldn't hesitate to use him to lure Ivy.

With a chuckle, Duran winked at Emmett. "Well, I am gifted."

Emmett snorted. "Yeah, I'm sure that is it. I didn't know about the bounty, I only discovered how determined he is to get her back last night." He tilted his head, as if deciding whether to stay more.

Duran had to convince him. "There are Cruz on Lina, off our coast. They offer refuge to my clan. They want Ivy."

"We've heard of them. Why do they want Ivy now? Why the rush?"

"I imagine they've heard about the bounty. They haven't forgotten Ursus. And it's well known that his greed looks toward the southern reaches."

"You believe they have spies in his compound?" Emmett sighed. "It might explain it..." His back straightened and he turned his gaze directly to Duran. "My bed partner last night was

Helen. She shared information, about how badly he wants her mother."

Helen? Duran shuffled that tidbit about. "You believe she came for...you? Or information?"

"Both. I'm not stupid, Duran. We met at the masked ball, and connected before we identified each other. Of course she wants information, she's scared about the Cruz mark she's got on her leg. Hell, she may not be able to admit it, but she's scared of her father. She does admit being leery of Diva. Blames Diva for her father's obsessions."

"Helen has a Cruz mark? Damn, that must drive Ursus crazy. She's not only his." Duran considered the complication of Helen's attention to the situation. "Diva... None of us have discovered much about her. She's from the far north. She's been sighted all over Calif, for years. At least it's assumed to be her. She is quite distinctive. And she is disruptive. Tried to join the free mercs, but we rejected her, after a two-month trial. All she did was stir up trouble with bitter gossip and rumor."

"According to Helen, when she joined Ursus...he grew cruel, even to his daughter." Emmett took a deep breath. "He's been raping women for decades. Treating them as he did Ivy, trying to sire more children. Helen suspected, but he did attempt to shelter her. Until Diva. Seven years ago, he began bragging about it. He also began to distance himself from his daughter. As she matured, the Cruz blood began to manifest. Her hair has the green tint."

"Well, you two did more than fuck." Duran considered the information. He'd be sure to pass it on to Taki, the current mercenary captain.

"I don't believe she has anyone to talk to," Emmett quietly stated. "She wants Diva dead. Wants Ivy to do it."

"If Ivy gets close enough to kill Diva, she'll take out Ursus first."

"That's what I told her," he replied. "She's a good daughter. Believes separating Diva from her father will return him to what she wants."

Duran shook his head. "He never was what she believes."

"She's reaching that conclusion, but slowly." Emmett paused. "I like her. Ursus tries to pretend that he is a good father. Perhaps he was, once. We met with him yesterday."

"That's what Ivy meant about his hands...she met with him yesterday." A sudden understanding came to him. "I did not know that. Why and where?" Duran leaned forward.

As Emmett explained, Duran's face betrayed nothing. Once the meeting in the coffee house was done with, Duran comprehended why events moved faster than he'd anticipated. "Emmett, the Lina Cruz want more than Ivy."

Emmett waited.

Duran reached over to touch Emmett's hand. "You have family on Lina. And they want to you to join them."

"Family?" Emmett's voice broke slightly, his eyes widened. "My...family died in the mines."

"No, your cousin Alfie. I've met him. Looks a lot like you."

"Alfie? No, he died. They all died." The shock on Emmett's face was heartfelt. "Why...? No, if they were alive, they'd have contacted me!"

"They didn't know you were alive, Emmett. He didn't tell me the entire story. The Cruz are close-mouthed about clan business. I'm not clan. I saw him, and the resemblance is uncanny. He had to be your relative. I mentioned your name and he...he threw arms around me, laughed, cried..." Duran shook his head. "He's demonstrative for a Cruz."

"He isn't full blood. Neither am I." Emmett blinked back tears of his own. "Fuck. I'm not alone..."

"You always had Ivy, Emmett. More than a lot of others can claim," Duran softly reminded Ivy's companion.

"Yes. No. That's not what I meant. Of course, I had Ivy. But despite what Ursus insinuates, she was never a mother to me. Not even a sister. She's full blood Cruz, Duran. You understand what that entails? She doesn't...she can't..." He shook his head. "Never mind. It's impossible to explain."

"I met full bloods on Lina, Emmett. They are different. She's more human than those I met!" Duran grinned crookedly.

"Cruz are human." Emmett stared at Duran. "It's a lie that they aren't."

"I didn't mean...forget it. Emmett? I don't care what stupid people say. I don't care what the religious spout off about the Cruz being less than human. We're people and not many of us survive. This fighting about bloodlines is useless. For the Cruz, for all of us."

"My father said the same." Emmett sighed. "I apologize. Damn. Alfie is alive!"

"And he has children. You're an uncle."

A wide smile grew on Emmett's face. Duran raised his mug in salute.

"I need to find Ivy. Tell her..."

"I told her you had family on the island, but I'm sure she'll be glad to hear the particulars."

The two continued to talk for another twenty minutes.

When they parted, an agreement had been reached. They would share information, keep an eye on Ivy and those who watched her. Emmett left to facilitate moving the camp while Duran agreed to get a message to Helen. She would be able to find them. And a way would be made to keep lines of communication open.

CHAPTER FOUR

Ivy didn't find Duran, nor did Emmett find Ivy, until the mercenary meeting. She arrived late, as the location had been changed, to a larger hall. That's what happens when you miss a dozen Gatherings. She squeezed in through the crowd, made up of rough men who took advantage to stroke or touch. She ignored them, intent on finding Emmett. The actual discussion hadn't begun, just the normal jostling for position that always occurred at these things. She made it to the edge of the attendees and gazed around. But didn't see her partner. Duran spotted her and winked from across the room. He sat with the Losanglos.

It was a huge place, rectangular in shape. The bar squatted in the front room, waiting for a break in the proceedings. The benches were only along the longer walls and stepped to allow everyone a good view of the short table where the meeting leaders sat. The rest of the crowd sat on the floor, or stood in a loose ring. There were separate groups, as like called to like. Ivy didn't fit into any particular clique.

The benches were full, gossip and rumor running through the throng. She stretched, trying to see the faces in the back. Emmett was tall, she ought to be able to see him.

"Need a hand up?" A burly man to her right offered a foothold, binding two hands together. "Who you looking for, Ivy?"

"Ebain, thank you! Looking for the boy I walk with, man now." She set her foot in the makeshift stirrup and balanced with her hands at his shoulders as she scanned the crowd. A ribald comment was thrown at the proximity of her sex to Ebain's face and he laughed.

"Not worth the bite!" he bellowed.

"I wouldn't bite you." She smiled down at the big man.

"I wasn't talking about you!" He winked and she shook her head, not being able to find Emmett. "Don't worry, he'll be here." Ebain set her down as the room quieted some.

The meeting began as Commander Taki called them to order.

Ivy listened, fighting to keep her mind focused beyond the events of the morning. Rumors were brought forth, some dismissed, some verified. Complaints were heard, most left to be settled between the opposing tribes. A few were ruled on by the three who ran the meeting, voted in earlier in the Gathering.

There was a lull and Ivy got Taki's attention with a shout. He rose to the challenge. "Ivy? What is your bitch?"

She snorted. "Ah, the rest have complaints, I have a bitch?"

"Shut up and get to it, woman. The bar is waiting!" Taki grinned at her.

"Emmett and I ran into problems at a puissant little settlement in the mountains, called Montan. They promised pay, didn't. And drove us out without provisions when we pushed for it. Met one of their preachers yesterday, threatened us with fire if we return." She looked around the room. "I hear of burning witches, what of it?"

No one tried to answer, but many looked angry. Some nodded with approval, she imagined at the topic being raised. At least, she hoped that was why they nodded.

A cutting voice came from a group to Ivy's right. "What spell did you cast, Cruz? That they threatened you with fire?"

Ivy turned to gaze at the one-eyed mercenary who'd spoken.

She grinned. “I don’t curse, Bill. I am cursed. There is a difference, you idiot.”

“I heard different.” He snarled at her, one hand rising to brush at his scared face. Rumor had it he’d been given that by a Cruz woman he’d tried to rape.

“Oh, she’s cursed, no mistaking that,” Duran drawled.

Ivy stepped forward, onto the open floor and swayed her hips as she sauntered toward Bill. “Want me to curse you, Billy? Or you had enough of *curses*? Want to try for totally blind?”

He grimaced at her. “I’m just saying...what did ya do to deserve burning, bitch?”

“Nothing, Billy. Ask for pay? Nothing anyone else here wouldn’t do!” She looked around at the faces watching her. And spotted Emmett at the outer edge, looking pale. She nodded minutely at him. Too many gazed at her with anger. She held her head high and nearly shouted, “They start burning those wanting to be paid...who is next?”

“Put Montan on the list of those who stand alone,” Taki stated. “Anyone else know something about burning?”

“I’m finding myself on fire.” Lisle, a Vallaeen joked, crooking a finger at Ivy. “I have a place you can sit, Ivy.”

“Lisle! My long lost love!” Ivy slid toward the group of women mercenaries. “We’d set the room aflame.”

“Yes, but it would shut her up,” Duran said dryly and the room erupted into ribald joking.

Ivy let herself be hauled next to the Vallaeen, who put an arm around her shoulders and whispered into her ear, “Talk to me later about burnings. They don’t want to address it publicly.”

With a nod, Ivy sat down next to Lisle, waiting for the meeting to die down. For another hour, the talk went back and forth. There was concern over the power the clergy were beginning to assert. And rumors of assorted alliances the warlords were forming. “They making it hard to be a free mercenary. Pushing on groups to sign on with them. Specially that Ursus,” a wiry man from the north coast spoke up.

"Ursus hates free folk," Ivy murmured, more to herself than to anyone else.

"Specially free women," Lisle agreed, standing with a shrug. "What about the grabbing of Shamans? I hear complaints by three villages of their Shamans going missing, huts in disarray, injured left half-treated...not what the Shamans do! This just ain't a wandering drive thing, these men and women are being taken."

As usual, a rise of arguing voices greeted the new topic. Taki finally restored order and asked if anyone else had news of that sort to report. Two other added similar stories. Taki sighed. "This needs to be investigated..."

"Why? We ain't police! If they pay, we'll look. Otherwise, let 'em do without!" a deep voice shouted from the back.

"Easy for you!" Emmett shouted back, "You travel with a Shaman! What of the rest of us? No one is immune to injury! Ain't just the villages needing healers."

"Good point, Emmett. This is why we'll look into it. Make sure they aren't simply answering some mystic call and be back." Taki nodded. "Anything else? No? We meet once more, two days before Gathering ends... To the bar!"

Ivy stood with the rest and turned to Lisle. "Since when do we meet twice?"

"You missed a lot of Gatherings, Ivy. Decided six years ago to meet twice. Gives everyone a chance to bring up what they forgot at the first meeting. You really threatened with fire?" The tall mercenary looked around the room, even as she spoke.

"Subtly, but yes." Ivy sighed. "Billy serious? I deserve fire?"

"You know Billy, he thinks all women are witches." Lisle smirked, leaning closer. "Too many are talking that way. I'm meeting up with Taki in a few days, I think some of the warlords are infiltrating the free mercs, sending in agents to push sentiment their way. Some of the foothill groups are spouting about long-term alliances, rules and laws...and punishment. Stuff we all don't want! Or didn't."

"Bullshit." Ivy snorted. "We aren't free if we're under long term contract. Where did the Shamans disappear from?"

Emmett shoved into the women, reaching for Ivy's hand. "Sorry I was so late."

Ivy just squeezed his fingers in acknowledgement as another Vallaeen replied, "Jibbon, Sonora and Colom."

Emmett blinked. "We worked those, two years ago."

"Yup, all of them. Talked with their Shamans, too." Ivy shivered. "Fuck. That bastard."

"Ursus? You think Ursus is behind this? Ivy, you always think it's Ursus." Lisle snorted. "Why?"

"He's been looking for me." Ivy stepped back, her mind spun, connections made. Lisle was an ally. Ursus killed her allies... Moving fast, she slapped the tall amazon mercenary, surging at the woman. She hissed. "Stay away from me, he kills those who help me." Lisle stopped her fellow warriors from grabbing at Ivy. Emmett hauled her back. The two women stared at each other. Ivy's eyes pled for understanding, and the Vallaeen got the message.

"A simple no would have sufficed, bitch." Lisle laughed and turned away from Ivy. "Let's leave the cock lover alone. Her hands are too small to offer me anything more than a bee's slap."

Ivy slowly relaxed in Emmett's arms. He whispered, "That was taking a chance. Assaulting her in the mercenary hall."

"Sure, but now everyone knows we aren't friends. I wasn't struck down, the valley knows what I was doing. And now he'll leave them alone." Ivy closed her eyes. "We need to leave."

Soon." Duran appeared at her side. "You suicidal? Getting the Vallaeen all pissed at you?" He spoke to be overheard.

She shrugged. "Fuck 'em. Where the hell did you go?" Her hand leapt out to punch him, but he caught her arm before the fist landed.

"Honey cunt, no foreplay in public!" He laughed, then winked at Emmett and swept her over his shoulder, slapping her ass as he carried her out of the hall. She heard him remark to Emmett, "I'm already on his hit list, she doesn't have to make a play at hating me. Dave has news regarding some heresy charge?"

"Coffee!" Ivy shouted at Duran's ass, it being what was before her.

He swatted her again. "Demanding wench... Coffee!"

Emmett laughed and played into the charging call. He lifted his arm and swept through the bar crowd. "Coffee!" They swept from the hall into the street, behind them followed Duran's family, ensuring his back was covered.

Ivy waited until they were clear of the hall before demanding Duran put her down. He laughed and she calmly cleared his coat away from his ass, leaving an area covered only by a single layer of clothing. And she bit him. Hard. He yelped and tossed her down, setting a hand on the injury. "That was nasty! What I do to you?"

"Wouldn't put me down and I got tired of conversing with your butt." Ivy brushed herself off and stood. "He's already targeting you? He make it plain?"

"I'll tell you over coffee. Coffee! I could be quenching my throat with beer! What do you have against beer?" He nonchalantly glanced around the streets, noting his cousins keeping watch.

"Nothing. You want beer, there is a bar across from the coffee shop. I want to talk to Dave, you know that." She turned and began marching away.

He chuckled and caught up with her. "Too bad your never-ending line of credit doesn't extend to the bars. I'd have to marry you then!"

She just blew a raspberry at him. No one married anymore. They fucked, they sometimes chose to live together...no one married.

Entering the familiar coffee house, she paused. Helen was there, talking with Dave. The naturally pale girl was nearly white. Ivy saw her grimace at seeing her mother, before glancing beyond Ivy to smile slightly. Ivy followed that glance and saw Emmett, eyes locked with Helen.

"Shit," Ivy muttered, then resolved to ignore the two. She found a large table near a wall and sat where she could watch the door. Dave patted Helen's hand, as the rest settled down and he approached. After a moment, Helen followed him.

"I need to talk with you," she spoke to Ivy.

"Why not look for me at the merc meeting? Why here?" Ivy was curious.

"My father doesn't need to know I'm looking for you. And I'm not allowed to spy on the mercs," Helen replied. "May I sit?"

"Such nice manners." Ivy shrugged. "Sit, don't sit. I don't care. Have your say and move on, I want to talk merc business. And you're not allowed, dad being a warlord and all."

Helen sat. "I'll make it quick. I love my father, but I'm not blind. Up until seven years ago, he was content with what he had. Yes! He was content. Doesn't mean he put down his sword and took up gardening. But he was working at consolidating, not expansion. Then that...then Diva arrived. It's her fault."

"What's her fault? That he's a murdering bastard? He's been that far longer than seven years, girl." Ivy took a drink from Dave and sipped at the caffeine, sighing with pleasure.

"I don't care about your opinion. I care about his sanity." Helen leaned closer, her voice was softer. "Listen to me! Set aside this hatred for me and just listen!"

Ivy studied her. No one else said a word. Ivy's lip twitched, undecided on smirking or frowning. "I don't hate you. Have your say. Then go away."

"I know they saw you this morning. I know they threatened Duran. I overheard them a few hours ago. Talking about when you were in his bed again. And she said something, something that is just wrong. So wrong!" Helen shook her head.

"I don't imagine that is so uncommon..." Ivy began to joke.

She stopped when Helen grabbed at her hand and hissed, "You were drugged, right?"

Ivy's breath caught. She froze, remembering, for just a

moment. Words, taunting words...a bottle of something, something vile.

Helen took her silence as confirmation. Duran cursed softly and leaned back. Emmett closed his eyes, no doubt putting pieces together. He'd heard her nightmares often enough.

But none realized the shock traveling through her.

The fair-haired girl stared at Ivy. "You were. Against all covenants, he did it. Found some desperate Shaman and paid for some drug, some herb, some bitterness to give you... And I was conceived. I suspected as much."

"So what? So what?!" Ivy yanked her hand away, the sudden flood of memories painted her voice sharp as the recollection grew pointedly into focus. "He wouldn't care about the covenant! Proved it! Whatever it was...it was the last of it. He taunted me with it, there would never be a way to prove what he did...forced his way into me and I couldn't fight. Couldn't put two thoughts together! Said he hoped it killed me...thought it had. So!?" There was more, Ivy knew there was more, but her mind slid away from it. Memories too slippery to hold, too sharp to grasp. Why had she forgotten it?

"So, she's found more for him. Found some Shaman to help her put it together. They were gloating about it! I heard them!" Helen shuddered. "Drugs! The one rule the Changed World lay down."

"Testify against him," Emmett softly said. "You heard him, you heard her. You are as guilty as they are if you don't bring this to the village elders."

Helen wiped at an angry tear. "No. I won't. I want her gone. I want her dead. Without her it wouldn't be a problem. He wouldn't be considering it. It's all her!" She glared at Emmett. "You can't force me."

"Then what do you want?" Duran asked. "Why tell Ivy?"

"She has to get away. Or stay! Dave said you could stay, both of you. So, stay! If you leave, he'll find you. He'll break the rule." Helen tried to get through to her mother, who just stared at the tabletop. "Or kill her! Stop her, find the Shaman and stop him!"

"Kill Diva." Ivy appeared to be considering it. Her eyes lifted, slowly. The shock of sudden remembrance faded. "Gladly. She gives me a chance, she's dead. All right? Is that what you want to hear? But, dear daughter, he'll die, too. I'll kill him. Don't fool yourself into thinking you can bargain with me. Give me one, expect me to let the other go?"

Helen pulled away, looking at the other two men. "She'll die if she goes after him. You'll let her?"

"Let her? There isn't any stopping her, girl." Duran shrugged. "She's owed. He used drugs."

"You thought you'd just scare her away?" Emmett softly asked. "You don't know her. All you've done is fan the fire, Helen. Leave."

Redness bloomed in Helen's cheeks. She threw the chair back and stood. "You're fools! He's right, you're all suicidal fools!" She stormed from the café, nearly knocking into Dave as he brought over a platter of cookies. He straightened the chair and looked at the three somber faces, one at a time.

He noted Ivy was crookedly smiling. "What's the joke, Ivy?"

"Oh, I am, darling Dave. I am." She blew out a deep breath. "What have you learned about the heresy charge?"

Dave was silent for a moment, frowning as he sat down. "You two haven't been careful enough."

Ivy had been chewing on a bit of cookie. Revelations could wait for another time. She burst into a loud fit of laughter, spewing crumbs all over the table. Dave calmly pulled out a small towel and wiped them away as Ivy fought for control of her voice. She finally managed a few words, "Who? Us?" She looked at Emmett. "What's enough?"

Emmett snickered, then grew somber. "About what, Dave?"

"Your curse," Dave softly replied.

Ivy grew instantly still. "Oh. Shit. They know? Suspect?"

Duran wisely stayed silent, just listening.

Dave nodded. "Suspect. They've twisted it, of course. But the gist? They want him. Some to shut him up, others to exploit. One of the more exuberant preachers talks of converting him. Or he'll be burned. And you, as his corrupt teacher, you're for the stake. Period. You walk into the wrong township and it's over."

"Well, that's just great." Duran smiled slightly. "Lina is looking better all the time."

"Lina would be a good alternative." Dave paused, "To burning. Or worse." Dave took the chair Helen had vacated, sat to converse with Duran. Emmett leaned in; trying to understand better what was going on.

Ivy surged to her feet, and paced, arms tightly wrapped around her torso. She knew they watched, even as they consulted with each other. But she couldn't help herself. The nightmares Emmett knew about weren't always of Ursus. She'd told him of the burning she'd seen once. The stench of it, the glee of the mob, the screaming. The thought of Emmett, tied to a stake, made her nauseas. Bad enough, the things he'd heard from her, about her month of captivity. Why did she ever tell him?

"He tied me, eventually. Always had chains on, but I used them to hurt him. Until he just tied me flat, stretched." They'd been sitting at a fire. He'd been fifteen when she'd finally told him details. Not about how she'd escaped. Because she'd forgotten...now she knew why.

It was the one rule everyone knew about. Set out for all of them, in the first year after the change. Several valley dwellers wandered among those who were left and spelled it out. "No mind altering drugs. No mind-altering herbs. Alcohol is permitted. If you find pills, destroy them. If you are discovered using drugs, to escape your hardships, to ease your nightmares, or against another, we will find you. And you will die. No appeal, no rational, no excuses."

They'd made their point, entering houses and farmsteads where a few held out, often in a drugged haze. The tallest of the villagers would empty pockets, find pills or needles. They were collected and the users died. Horribly, gibbering, twitching and thrashing in pain.

When it was over, directions were given to the Gathering Valley, where every two years some respite from the hardness of the world would be granted. Stories circulated, of those who ignored the one rule. And died. Not always at first, but they were always discovered.

She'd never told him how she suspected a drug was used on her. For fear he'd leave her, fearful that the Villagers would find her and judge her, whether she'd been willing or not.

So many pieces fell together with Helen's news.

They kept whispering, while she mulled it all over. Back and forth, between the thought of her being tainted and a mob, with lit torches...

"How did Ursus...?" Emmett murmured, then looked at Dave. "Did you know?"

"Know what?" Dave asked, "The three who man the kitchen at the Religious Hall let me know about the heresy discussion." Emmett shook his head. "Then what is it you think I know? Or don't know?"

Duran set his hand on Emmett's shoulder. "There is no proof. You lay the charge and they might hold you accountable for falsehood. Be careful. A shunning could be worse than having the clergy after you."

Dave glanced up at Ivy, still pacing. Duran knew the villagers were extremely intuitive. Not all were the enforcers, in fact, few were. Dave appeared to deflate as a sudden sadness filled his eyes.

The barista quietly spoke, "There was no proof. It was suspected. I am not one of the valley enforcers... If she had fled here sooner, she would have been tested."

"And held accountable for taking drugs. And executed," Duran hissed. "It happened before. We all know that!"

"Yes. But not anymore. I can't discuss it. I did what I could." Dave stood, leaning closer. "You bring me proof, and he'll be dead."

"You hear of any Shamans meddling with drugs? Trying to recreate what is gone?" Emmett pointedly asked what they both wondered. And feared.

"No. You heard a rumor?"

"Yes, a rumor." Emmett wouldn't look Dave in the eyes.

"Tell me." Dave prepared to sit again.

"No. You valley dwellers no longer go out into the world. Where we live. I won't risk an investigation without more information. You'll stumble about and it won't just be the clergy who wants us dead. Duran is right, a shunning is the best we would face." Emmett stood and went to Ivy, stilled her pacing and held her.

Duran studied the pair of them, closer than many who actually shared bloodlines.

She wrapped arms about him and held tightly. Bosun entered the café. Ivy saw him enter, and fear soared into her, for Emmett.

Duran knew she was scared. He saw the glance she shot at Bosun and the nod. His cousin had taught him to read lips, so he knew what she said. *For Emmett.*

She'd go to Lina, good.

Emmett was looking at Duran and didn't see Bosun enter the room. He signaled to the Losanglos. *I'll help. Lina. For Ivy.*

The couple clung to each other, an agreement made without words between them. For two separate goals. Why didn't matter, Lina would offer sanctuary.

CHAPTER FIVE

The campaign to see Ivy and Emmett safely from the Gathering took days to plan. She resisted taking part, all but pleading with them to let her go on her own.

Her concern, regarding Ursus finding one more reason to target Duran, fell on deaf ears.

"Our encampment is large. Lots of opportunity to confuse and divert his agents," Duran argued back. "He knows I'm an enemy, Chica. Knowing we fuck isn't going to make that worse."

Dave would continue the search for rumors and related how Bosun had disappeared from the valley altogether.

"You place your people in danger, Duran!" Ivy protested. They weren't listening to her!

"My people know what they are doing. Genesee tried talking with the San Gabes, trying to convince them against an alliance with Ursus. He failed." Duran leaned closer. "I told you before, we aren't going to fight, Ivy. We're going to leave. Not all agree, but enough. Those who stay will fade into the rest of Calif, or die. Lina wants you, we help them, and they help us."

Ivy stared at him a moment, a sense of disappointment at the reality of his true motive. But she'd do the same. Most would. She squashed the ache in her heart with an appreciation of his practical reasoning. Ivy was a temperate woman, she rode the thoughts to a harsh conclusion. “Running from him, eh? We’re the ticket to paradise?”

The expression on her face was one of derision; she couldn’t hold that back. They were running. Her family had stayed. And died defending what they thought important.

Duran simply nodded, ignoring her disdain. “I don’t care how you justify it, Ivy. Believe whatever you want to.” His gaze, hard as flint, bored into her, as if daring her to say more.

She admired his control.

Emmett shook his head, interrupting the building tension. “Ivy, we won’t be there forever. He’ll grow complacent, more corrupt. We’ll have a chance to kill him.”

Ivy took a deep breath, swallowed the wash of emotions that threatened to burst through her. Fine, she knew the truth. “Duran, I apologize. We’ll remain in your camp. But I won’t stay penned up.”

“No, I wouldn’t ask that. But we’ll be a second set of eyes, Ivy. If you wander, we wander, keeping you covered. Ursus has broken so many covenants, there is no guarantee he hasn’t found a way around the village safeguards.” Duran leaned back. “Apology accepted.” He grinned. “I look forward to your nights.”

She snorted, battling her inner demons at his earlier words. She distracted herself with a foray at Emmett. “You’re seeing Helen.”

“Yes,” he kept his reply simple. “Going to lecture me?”

“No.” She chuckled. “Just be careful. We don’t know what her curse will be. And our luck, it will be some uncanny ability to track or read minds or some nonsense her father can use to find us.”

“She wouldn’t help,” he flatly stated.

“Uh huh, keep telling yourself that,” she replied. “When did this start?”

“None of your business.” Her companion lifted an eyebrow at her.

“Oh, fine! Just be careful that monster doesn’t decide his

precious daughter needs to be protected and makes you his primary target instead of me." Ivy drained her cup and snagged a handful of the cookies. She pushed her chair back. "What now?"

"We fuck, sleep, eat...drink," Duran dryly replied.

"Oh, in what order?" She stuffed a cookie into her mouth and loudly chewed.

"Why don't you choose?" He stood. "Let's find you a good billet."

Emmett gathered the remaining baked goods and they followed Duran from the café. They faded into the large Losanglos encampment. Duran made sure his desire for her constant sexual attention was loudly understood to be the reason he'd insisted she move.

She played along. Better the rumor claim they were simply lusting after each other than she was running, to hide with the Losanglos.

The Gathering continued as before, Ivy actually finding some peace, relaxing with Duran's people. She saw little of Emmett, but Duran assured her he was under watch.

They sprawled in the sun near a small lake, at the outskirts of the Gathering streets, as he lazily informed her, "Emmett is careful. He and Helen meet often, but aren't seen meeting."

"Great. Any sign that monster knows?" she asked, acutely aware of his hand stroking from her shoulder to her ass. The playing at lust was proving rewarding, she mused. This much public touch would have earned a real glare from her grandmother. But when the world changed, thoughts of moral values, shyness about nudity, even public sex changed. No one cared.

It was nice to feel the sun on her back, as well as his hands.

"No. His little pet lingers at our camp border, when she isn't strolling about with Bill and some of the other malcontent mercs."

He leaned closer and licked at the sweat pooling at the small of her back. "You taste so sweet."

"Camouflage," she murmured. "Damn."

"Yeah, damn." He bit the cheek of her ass. When she yelped he held her down. "I owe you, bitch."

He rolled atop her, pinned her easily. She feigned a protest as he slid between her legs, deep into her welcoming heat. He rocked inside her, her voice faded away.

Damn, he was growing quite fond of keeping her diverted. A man could settle down easily with such duties. Live happy, lazy and satisfied.

They were often found about the camp, entangled. Having her total attention was something he grew used to. He didn't leave her side, save for when she was deeply asleep, to meet with his family as they ironed out the plan to see her away. Not all of the tribe agreed on his actions. But enough to keep the rest from interfering.

They awaited a message from Bosun. Dave eventually delivered a note, that Ivy's grandfather had gone ahead to set down the ocean escape route. It was accepted that Ursus would chase them. He might not be allowed to leave, but he had enough allies to send after them. They would be ready.

He didn't lie to Ivy regarding the danger, but he didn't dwell on it either. His focus was the woman beneath him.

The scent of green grass filled her. She opened her eyes to the blades beneath her, and Duran's strong hands at each side of her face. His body strained inside her, pulling and stretching her to an exquisite degree. She inhaled the strong green odor and groaned, "I always...pay...my debts!"

Her body rode the rush of his desire and the two went limp, panting. He kissed her shoulder. "I know you do."

As he slowly eased free of her, she stretched, then rolled to face him. "I don't want Helen, am I unnatural?" She wasn't sure where that question came from. Sure, it had been floating through her brain for days. Every time she thought of the girl, the tug of war filled her. Between wishing she could hold her and shaking at the very idea of touching her. Helen looked too much like Ursus. She hadn't counted on that. Not in all her wildest fantasies.

"Of course you are," he was honest. "With this world so tight with children, all of them are precious. But you were made so by Ursus. The blame isn't on you."

She blinked, considering. "Will she ever understand that?"

"I don't know, chica." He smiled slightly at her. "She's your daughter, what do you think?"

She snorted. "Hell. No one should understand! My daughter? She doesn't look like me, she doesn't seem to have any part of me, Duran. But, it isn't only looks. I wish I wanted her...I wanted to want her!" She sat up, wrapping arms about her legs. "It shouldn't be something anyone understands. I don't." She sighed. "If she hurts Emmett..."

"Emmett isn't stupid," Duran stated. "Ivy, I've seen Helen grow up. Periodically, I'd see her. She isn't an innocent, and she is right. Ursus changed when Diva began whispering in his ear. Not that he wasn't always a bastard, but she strokes the blackest part of him into action."

"I have permission to kill her." Ivy mused. "Oh, if only the opportunity would present!" She looked out at the lake. "When will we leave?"

"Soon." Duran pushed her back to the grass. "Soon."

She let herself be diverted.

Three days later, she watched two women, dressed as alternate Ivys, climb aboard horses next to disguised Emmetts. Duran took her hand. "We'll be on foot for several hours."

"What happens if he catches them?" She thought they weren't very good decoys, but it was dark and might work.

"Should the chase grow close, they will discard the disguises.

Be simple lovers looking for privacy." He shook hands with each of them. "Luisa, Gerri, take care. Jenna, Thad...ride hard."

"Good luck." Both couples replied and then urged the horses along divergent paths.

Ivy looked at Duran. "I'm ready. Where is Emmett?"

"He'll meet us at the edge of the valley," Duran replied. He took her hand, made sure his pack was secure on his back and pulled her along. Back where they usually billeted, another couple loudly fucked. All part of keeping spies confused.

They met Emmett on the road less than two hours of riding out. It became plain how many agents Ursus had looking for them, slowing their progress. They ducked into some greenery at the sound of galloping horses behind them. A group of six rode by as if pursued by demons. Duran whispered in Ivy's ear, "Bill."

"Bastard," she hissed back.

He pulled them deeper in the trees. "We'll cut through here."

"Who were they chasing?" Emmett softly questioned.

"Jenna and Thad rode this way. They'll hear them in time to get away." Duran shook his head. "He's reacting faster than I would have thought. And with less discretion."

"And you think I'm unreasonably aware of him?" Ivy snorted.

Duran smiled wryly and they continued through the night. Ivy shot glances at Emmett, worried at the sense of sorrow he appeared to carry. His brows were pinched, his eyes red and shoulders hunched. This wasn't the staid young man she'd known for years. Ivy wanted to curse Helen.

She kept her counsel for the rest of the night. When they reached a rocky bluff containing a hidden cave, she tried to pry. "Emmett? Gods, don't tell me you care for that chit?"

He glanced at her. "You'd care if you'd let yourself get to know her, Ivy. Diva hates Helen. And Diva is a wicked enemy."

"Well, sorry we couldn't take the poisonous bitch out before we left. Maybe next time. I'm sure Helen can take care of herself. She's done fine till now." Ivy dismissed the concern with a grimace.

Why don't I feel more?

Emmett stared at her, then shook his head. He rolled to his side and was soon snoring. Ivy rolled her eyes at Duran, and took to her bedroll. Duran watched both of them and wondered at how deeply Emmett had involved Helen in their plans. He'd have to ask the boy when he woke.

Hours later, Ivy came awake in a flash at the sound of angry words. She sat up, her hand on her ax, to see Duran holding Emmett by his throat against the cave wall. Emmett quit struggled and met the Losanglo eyes.

Duran hissed, "If you put her in danger...!"

"I wouldn't," Emmett choked out.

"Duran, let him go," Ivy kept her tone of voice level, almost bored. "He wouldn't."

"He shared too much," Duran replied, easing his grip but still kept the younger man to the wall. "He underestimates your daughter's survival instincts."

"You think she'd sell us for his favor?" Emmett's body betrayed his fury at the thought, deadly still, save for a small tremor at his right hand, near where his blade rested.

"Of course she would," Ivy spoke up. "She isn't stupid. Well, maybe not for his favor, but for time to save herself? Yes. I would."

"I don't believe you," Emmett said.

Duran let go of Emmett completely and turned to stare at Ivy. "You wouldn't."

"Okay, I wouldn't, but at least you two are done with the display. What's to eat?" She threw the light cover off. "And exactly where are we going?"

"We have horses waiting for us later today. Bosun sent word, the *Windsong* will be waiting for us at Hidden Cove," Duran replied.

Ivy looked at Emmett. "Mean anything to you?"

"Hidden Cove is on the edge of San Gabe territory. What is the *Windsong*?"

"Passage to Lina," Duran answered. "Here." He tossed them both apples.

Ivy shivered at the thought of the ocean. She didn't care for salt water. But she'd keep them moving, for Emmett. The residents of Lina would have to settle for only one extra Cruz, instead of two.

———

Hidden Cove was ringed by a rocky precipice, leaning out over the sea, a foaming beast far below. Ivy nearly lost her nerve at the path he led them. Partway down the cliff face, he pointed to a cleft in the rock. "Cave, with provisions to last until the *'Song* gets here."

She crawled on hands and knees into the dark opening, and huddled in the dark. Duran stared at this method until Emmett diverted his attention from Ivy's distress. "Where would a ship wait? It's all rock and crashing waves."

"They have a way." Duran held Emmett at the entrance. "What is wrong with her? She hasn't said a word since we saw the Pacif."

"She doesn't like the ocean." Emmett shook off Duran's hold. He paused. "How big will the *Windsong* be?"

"Big enough to hide in if the ocean disturbs her."

Duran reacted to Emmett's snarl. "I don't know how to tell you. I'm not being stupid about it."

"Great."

Emmett slid into the cave. Duran paused, wondering what the hell was going on. He entered the cave to see Ivy huddled in Emmett's arms.

"How long will we have to wait?" Emmett's grip tightened each time a wave hit the rock below. And Ivy shuddered.

Duran answered as he lit a small torch, "Days, likely. We'll set a signal each night to let them know we're here. It can't be seen from the bluff, so if we're tracked this far..."

"Isn't likely," Ivy muttered. "I need to sleep."

Emmett nodded, shifting about until his back was to the wall, Ivy all but using him as a mattress. His arms settled over her again. She took one of his hands and clung to it, near her face.

Duran couldn't help but be aware of her reaction. He'd never seen her scared before. This was a situation he wasn't ready for. How would they get her to the ship?

He inventoried the provisions, searching for an answer while Ivy slept fitfully in Emmett's embrace. They'd reached the cave in the early morning, after a night on the road. The horses had been set free a little more than a mile from where they rested, just before the cliff path. Duran knew they would wander back to the interior fields, eventually make their way back to their keeper.

As Ivy fitfully slept the day away, he kept an eye on her. She seldom stayed still for long, but clenched at Emmett, or whimpered, twitched. As the sun finally approached the horizon, Duran prepared the signal lamp. He'd seen Emmett fed, but the young man wouldn't release Ivy, despite Duran's attempt to take over the watch.

"I can hold her, you've barely slept," he'd offered.

"I can sleep when she wakes. She needs me right now."

"What is wrong with her, Emmett? I need to know." Duran crouched near them, speaking softly. Emmett just shook his head. It was frustrating.

Maneuvering to the rear of the cave, Duran cursed under his breath, "Damned Cruz!" There was a trickle of water from a stream flowing through the cave, starting at the deepest part. He refilled the water bottles and sat, thinking. When the pounding of horse hoofs broke through his contemplation, he started. He'd thought it was the ocean, but he realized it was above them. He heard a shout to dismount. He looked around, wondering how he was hearing this. A waft of breeze from a crack in the ceiling answered his question.

He listened carefully.

"Fucking horses! Can't catch the damned things! Why did they set them free? No way down that cliff face!"

"You searched it thoroughly?" Duran recognized Diva's voice. "He'll skin you if they slipped away!"

"I'm no fool, I looked. Just rock and broken ground. If they tried, they died on the rocks below." Ah. That was Billy.

"They had a plan. Don't make sense to use so many diversions to just commit suicide at the ocean." Diva's voice faded some. "I will look in the morning."

Duran grinned, she'd look and if she weren't careful, she'd end up broken in the surf. That path was a trick devised by the best of the Cruz. If she didn't know the right way, she'd fall. That would be a nice answer to a problem...

"We camp!" Bill shouted out.

Nothing more was coming through clearly, Duran snickered as he turned back to the front of the cave. Just then, Ivy gave a harsh cry, nearly a shout. He froze as he heard Diva bellow out for the troop above to be quiet, she'd heard something. He scrambled to Emmett who was helping Ivy wake up.

Duran bent down. "Hush! We have company above."

Ivy blinked, instinctively struck out at Duran for lurking above her. He bit his tongue as her hand gripped his inner thigh, too close to his balls for comfort. He hissed, "Ivy! Danger! Be still!"

Her grip eased up as she recognized his voice. Emmett tilted his head, whispered, "I hear nothing..."

"Back of the cave, go quietly," Duran peeled Ivy's fingers away as Emmett moved to the rear of the cave. "Damn it, woman! I need those."

"Sorry." She tried to clear her throat without sound. He handed her a nearby water bottle. She took a sip.

"There is plenty, Ivy. Drink all you need," he spoke directly to her ear.

"Who listens?" she asked as she reclaimed the bottle, drank more.

"Trackers. Diva and Bill, I don't know how many more," Duran answered.

"Shit. She's here?" Ivy looked pleased. "I can..."

"No, you can't." Duran peered at her closely, the last of the sun's rays slipping through a turn in the cave to paint her face. She looked pale, but still deadly. "You cannot risk this sanctuary."

Emmett returned. "It's all right, they are searching the tree line. I'd say there are six of them." He still spoke softly, and cautioned the others to follow his example. "Until they leave. This cave acts like an echo chamber."

"Never thought they get this close." Duran sighed. "Ivy, what is haunting you about the Pacif?"

"Fuck off." Ivy pushed him away and stood, stretching.

"No, not right now." He yanked her down by her ponytail. "I need to know."

She stared back at him. "And I need to eat. It won't be a problem, Duran. Feed me."

He snorted. "You stubborn bitch. And next time you shout in your sleep? They won't be fooled into the tree line again."

"I won't sleep," she retorted.

"Tell me, damn it," he demanded. "I can be trusted, Ivy. I have to know you can make it down to the ship without falling to your death." He saw her shudder at the thought and seized on the reaction. "This is a strategic need. Tell me, I have to know."

She wilted slightly, and then sighed. "Let me eat. Then I'll talk."

He relented, believing she would keep her word. The three chewed the stale bread and dry cheese. He revealed a small bag of cookies Dave has sent and Ivy smiled, no doubt enjoying the barista's thoughtfulness. Allowing her some time to thoroughly wake up, he lit the signal lantern and showed Emmett where to place it, just outside the cave.

"It cannot be seen from above?" Emmett glanced above, to take note of the overhang some ten feet above them. "They are so close."

"No, they aren't. Not really. That stone is partway down the cliff face. They are another twenty feet above that," Duran reassured.

The night was advanced when he faced Ivy again. Emmett said he would stay at the cave entrance. He'd seen little of the sea and found the moonlight on the water soothing.

"Ivy, why does the sound of the waves disturb you?" Duran sat across from her. She looked up from the idle doodling she'd been doing on the sandy cave floor and sighed.

"You know, when the world changed...some things were fast. Some were slow," she began.

"I've heard it." He nodded. They still kept their voices down, even though Emmett had stuffed the crack with rags left by past campers. They had to be careful.

"My grandmother..." Ivy closed her eyes a moment. "She told me how the ocean rose and swallowed nearly all her children. She'd taken my mother to higher ground to clean up from a day at the beach. Mama was three years old. The day went from a sweet time in the sand to her worst nightmare. Mama was the youngest of eight, Duran. Three boys and four girls died that day, along with everyone else on that beach."

"I've heard how the ground sank." He sighed.

"Grandmother said the sea reached for her. My grandfather was joining them, climbing down from an even higher bluff. He saw the water recede and screamed at her to climb. She was torn..." Ivy shuddered. "He bellowed at her, ordered her to climb. There was a rocky protuberance; he was balanced on that when the ground began to shake. She reached him, gave my mother over and turned to save her other children."

A tear ran down her face. "She told me how the world went mad. She could hear the screams from below as the water rushed in, howling... 'It's a rabid dog,' she said. 'The ocean is a mad thing, greedy and always hungry...' It ate her family. Her husband wouldn't let her try to save them. The water rose as high as they perched, the cliff coming apart around them. But the rock...its roots were deep, and it held. The sky...it went black, stars appeared through the froth and spray..."

Duran shuddered, her voice was hollow, yet it conveyed the misery and fear of that day. He swallowed. "I've heard of no one that survived the ocean's rise."

"They did. She cursed him, for not letting her help the rest. My mama didn't remember it, too young for it to stick... But Grandmother never forgot. When the light returned, their world was gone." She met his eyes. "I hate the ocean."

Her face grew even grimmer. "The rock they were perched on was surrounded by water. Land was in sight, but far. He forced her off the rock, tied my mother to his back, and pushed his wife into the water. She wanted to stay, was terrified. He couldn't make it and come back for her. She nearly drowned."

"Damn, no wonder she never forgot." Duran reached for Ivy, but she skittered sideways, out of his reach. He studied her a moment. "You never intended to get on the boat, did you?"

She looked away. "I don't know. I don't know if I can..." Sighing, she acknowledged the weakness. "But Emmett can. He has to go. Make sure he does." She stood. "I always avoided the coast. The smell of salt water makes my belly ache. I want your word, Duran. Emmett will reach Lina."

With a sigh, Duran nodded. "You have it." He didn't say the rest aloud. *So will you, Ivy. So will you.*

The troops above them left the next day, after a deadly attempt to make it to the oceans' edge. Duran perched where he could see them, and saw two men tumble down to the rocks below. Diva ordered the rest back and they returned to searching the forest.

Ivy slept fitfully, rising at sunset more ragged each time.

Three days passed and she grew restless and angry. Emmett was patient, engaging her in endless games in the sand. They played battle games, each time seeing Ursus defeated in an alternate history of what really occurred. Meanwhile, Duran continued searching the supplies, scattered throughout other small caves on the bluff. He found what he wanted in the furthest.

The night a light blinked back at them from the water, Duran answered, they would be ready the next evening. He returned to the cave to find Ivy had fallen asleep. Emmett glanced at him, arms cradling the small woman. "The sea is quiet tonight. She just drifted away."

"Good, she'll need her strength, but let me have her Emmett.

I...want to feel her." Duran was stripping away his shirt, making it clear he would tolerate no argument.

Emmett glanced at Ivy, then nodded and eased her into Duran's care before walking to the cave entrance to watch the sunrise.

Duran propped himself up on an elbow and watched Ivy sleep. The scant light from the candles painted her face with shadows, kinder than the sunlight. Ivy was worn. Still young and beautiful, to most who looked. He could see the sorrow life had rained on her. He sighed, fingers stroking her face, easing down to lightly caress her breasts. "Ivy," he whispered, "Ivy, wake up mi chica. Wake up, I want to fuck you." His voice was casual, his expression was not.

She moaned and turned her face toward him, "Wha...?"

"Ivy, you randy slut, cielito lindo, bonita...let me in," he crooned.

Ivy blinked, shifting closer to him. He undid the buttons of her shirt and began to seriously play with her breasts. He bent, closer, brushing his lips along her jaw line as fingers danced closer and closer to a nipple. He pinched one of the peaks just as he reached her lips. She arched and he seized her with more fever. From one breast to another, he took her in hand, stroking, tugging, and teasing. And he kissed her without stop.

Finally, he rolled atop her and his lips left hers, to wander down her body. The perfect breasts he had toyed with, he now devoured. One kiss and lick after another followed as his hands journeyed to her drawstring shorts, loose for sleeping. He pushed them lower until he could kick them away with his feet and pinned her with his body, as she admitted to being totally awake.

He set her on fire and out of her mind. When his lips weren't kissing, he crooned. Spanish words. Some she knew, some she didn't. But there were spoken with passion, that was all that mattered. He paused as he moved lower, and bit her belly. It was fast and sharp. She began to object and he stilled her with two fingers sliding into the inferno at her center. He stroked and plunged and the sting of his teeth disappeared in a wash of sensation.

When he finally surrendered to her lure, their eyes met. She began to speak and he thrust harder, driving the words away. He drove her, lost with desire. He rode her soft, then hard, his adoration clear to any who could see. Who would see.

They both laughed as his assault saw them tremble, falling from the world into each other. He sprawled atop her, unable to speak for several minutes. He felt moisture on his cheek and quickly wiped it away before she was aware of his tears. He gracefully slid from her, then turned her so that she was cradled into the comma of his body. He kissed her hair. "Mucho gracias, señorita. Sleep, chica. Sleep. I will hold you..."

She snuggled into his warmth and comfort, and let herself acknowledge a harbor that kept her safe. She pressed her lips to his arm and drifted away.

Later, he revealed his find. Two bottles of clear liquor from the world before. He drank nothing, and carefully watered Emmett's rations. Ivy was given it straight.

She was more than willing to get drunk. Tired of the cave, of the dust and the constant reminder of what lay outside the cave, she dove into the drinking games determined to lose. And she did, finally succumbing to a mind numbing state of drunkenness as the afternoon waned.

Emmett sighed. "The only way to get her down the cliff?"

Duran nodded. "Yes. I can carry her now. They will be waiting as the sun sets. She's out?"

Emmett lifted her head from where it rested on her chest, peered under her eyelids. "Thoroughly."

"When did you catch on?" Duran began to gather up Ivy's pack.

Emmett took care of his as he answered, "I saw you adding water."

"Damn, thought I was better at sly of hand." Duran handed her bag to Emmett. "You can manage both. She's a bit of a woman, but I'll need to be ready in case she stirs."

"What of yours?" Emmett asked, adding Ivy's pack to his.

"I'm not going," Duran quietly answered. "Never meant to. I have things to do... Family to gather. Bosun will be there and take care of you."

"You led her to believe you were going with us." Emmett straightened.

"And she led you to believe she was going to Lina," was Duran's calm reply. "We all lie when it comes to protecting those we care for, qué no?"

Emmett froze, looked down at Ivy, snoring with increasing volume. "Oh. For me."

"Sí." Duran took a torn up rag and began to tie Ivy's hands together at her wrists. Emmett bent and helped him bundle her onto his back. He followed Duran carefully down a path he could only discern foot-by-foot. They were moving from slippery rock to slippery rock when the small raft came into view. He offered no objection when he was assisted aboard, taking Ivy from Duran and holding her tightly.

He met Duran's eyes. "She is going to be royally pissed at you."

Duran grinned. "I will look forward to fighting with her again." His smile faded as he glanced down at Ivy. "Take care of her. Mi corazón..."

He turned and began to climb back before Emmett could react to his words. Or even understood them. Perhaps one of the sailors would translate them. Emmett heard the emotion, understood how deeply Duran cared. Even without know thing the word.

CHAPTER SIX

Ivy softly moaned. The vise around her head left room for a slow pound between the spikes of pain. Slowly, she grew aware of the soft covers around her, under her lay a soft mattress. She opened one eye. A small room, deep in shadows. She sat up very slowly. "Duran?" The sound of her own voice drove a spike through her head and she groaned. "What the fuck was that stuff?"

A soft tap came from somewhere. She saw a movement out of the corner of her eye and reacted with the swiftness of the hunted. In the unfamiliar place, the move didn't go as she planned. She stumbled off the bed and fell in a heap of covers. A shaft of light invaded the cabin. "Miss? Are you all right?"

"Who the fuck are you? Where the fuck am I?" Ivy groaned. "What the fuck did I drink?"

A soft chuckled was the first answer. The door was closed as the rest of her questions were addressed.

"I am first mate Johnstone. This is the *Windsong*. I don't know what you drank, but there is water near the bed if you are in need. The bathroom is here."

Ivy looked up to see a slender man gesturing toward an open door. She rose with some difficulty, felt her stomach begin to heave and dashed for the door, barely making it in time. The first mate poured her a glass of water helping her recover from the trauma of a massive hangover.

Soon, she was sitting at the edge of the bed, wearing a soft white robe and sipping water. Johnstone sat next to her. She met her reflection in the mirror and grimaced. Now she understood the movement she'd seen.

Her own reflection, gods.

Her companion told her some light food would be available soon. Her belly felt hollow, but she wasn't altogether certain of filling it. Nevertheless, she nodded. "Good, might help. Where is Duran? And Emmett?"

"Your companion is huddled in the closet behind you," Johnstone answered. "He appeared to be in distress, we let him be."

"Closet?" She hurried to the odd door. Johnstone showed her how to open it. She did so slowly, then knelt. Emmett was turned away, curled up tightly in the small space. He was sweating, she could smell it. "Shit. Leave us alone," Ivy ordered the first mate away. He left without argument.

Slowly, she convinced Emmett to relax, to let her help. She sat on the floor as he huddled with his head buried in her lap. "Oh, Emmett. It's the ghosts?" She stroked his head.

He shuddered even as he nodded, and took a deep breath. She knew he was attempting to anchor himself in her presence. She had taught him this. And she began to hum one of the lullabies she remembered from her childhood, ignoring his clutching or how he buried his face at her crotch. It had been like this since his curse hit him.

It had been raining, and cold, the night his curse revealed itself. Huddled under the jagged remnants of what must have been a huge bridge, he'd shivered. He'd been tracing a worn metal plaque with his finger, asking her about what it meant.

"One thousand nine hundred and fifty seven whats?' he asked.

"I think it was a year. They counted years before the change." She'd shrugged. "When it was erected? How many died building it?

I don't know. You cold still? I can build the fire up more, the smoke isn't going to give us away in this downpour."

"No, I'm fine." He'd started, eyes jerking upward to where the span broke off. "You hear that?"

She'd tilted her head, listened carefully, "Hear what?"

He'd suddenly screamed, then covered his ears, ducking down as if something were attacking them. His face screwed up tight, his eyes closed and he trembled like a caught bird.

Ivy cursed, "Your birthday today, boy?"

"I...I don't... Loud! The lights! Don't you see the lights, moving so fast? Up there!" He'd pointed above them.

"Fuck." She'd gathered their gear, kicked the fire out into the rain and took hold of him. She'd hurried them away from the ruined bridge. She'd had a distant cousin who saw and heard conversations from the past whenever near ruins. But for him, it was whispers. This proved much worse.

Emmett could see and hear the past. They'd lost the shelters the scattered remains of a civilization long gone provided, until she taught him some control.

The next decade proved hellish. His curse continued to strengthen. He didn't just hear them, he saw them, all at once. She tried to help, but it was too much. Her grandmother has said the world before held more people then the needles of a pine forest. He couldn't fight that many ghosts, no one could. As the scattered remnants of the past crumbled, the ghosts faded.

Trapped on this ship, he couldn't get away, damn it.

A soft knock heralded some food.

It was nearly an hour before she managed to coax Emmett into taking some of the toast left for her. Then he drank, and slowly, he relaxed enough to sit up. He kept his eyes closed until she touched his face. "Look at me, Emmett. At me. Not at the ghosts. You know they don't matter, they don't see you..."

"So loud," he hoarsely answered. His eyes were bloodshot and haunted.

"I bet." She sighed. "What a strange relic to survive so pristine. You know where Duran is?"

"Didn't come, Ivy." Emmett shivered. "I'm sorry. Tricked you."

She growled. "Bastard."

"You...you were going to leave me!" he sobbed and dove at her again.

She rocked him. "I'm sorry, too. I guess I deserved the trick. We're...we're at sea?" Ivy looked around the room. "Fucker. Why didn't he come?"

"Said..." Emmett clung to her. "Said he had things to do. Family..."

"Next time I see him, I'm going to make him regret this." Ivy snarled. There was a tapping at the door. "What?" Ivy shouted, cursing as Emmett shuddered again.

"Miss Ivy..." Johnstone entered the room. "Ah, you got him out of the closet." He shook his head, then knelt on the carpet. "Master Emmett, would you like more food? Water? Drink? How can we help?"

"Go 'way," Emmett's voice was muffled.

"He just needs privacy," Ivy answered. "Get me some pillows from the bed. How long are we going to be...until Lina?"

"Another night and day," Johnstone answered. "Are you sure there is nothing we can do to help him relax? I know it's strange, but it's just a room."

"It isn't the room," Ivy snapped at him. "He isn't a backcountry idiot, scared of trappings from the past. It's his...curse."

Emmett looked up, glancing about the room. "Ghosts." He shook and sheltered his face again.

"Ghosts?" Johnstone looked perplexed, then sighed. "Oh, this was a luxurious cruise ship, full of passengers, constantly changing. He sees them?"

"Sees them, hears them...all at once," she answered, upset at revealing so much. "Damn, none of your business!"

"I don't mean to pry. We are aware of Cruz curses. His is a cruel one, I am sorry. There are no newer areas of the ship. Once on Lina, I will suggest he is settled in the newer part of the settlement." Johnstone stood. "I'll bring more food and water. Will you stay with him for the duration?"

"What do you think?" Ivy snapped back. "Apologies. He has family on Lina."

"Yes, miss. They wait for him." The first mate strode to the door. "Would music help? We have several musicians who could play for him."

Ivy thought a moment. "What do you think, Emmett? Remember the thunderstorm outside that broken city? It helped..." She fought back a shiver, that had been a haunted place, not just broken. They'd found food, still edible. The change didn't strike evenly. It appeared only a few years since the people had disappeared.

Emmett nodded minutely, pulling Ivy away from those memories. It had been unnerving, to see dolls, children's toys...overgrown with vines and moss. Because the storm provided distraction, she'd been able to gather canned goods that saw them through several lean weeks.

She turned toward Johnstone. "It's worth a try. Thank you."

"I'll see to it." He closed the door softly behind him.

Within the hour, the room held two men with guitars, filling the cabin with soft music and soothing voices. Relief filled her as Emmett slip into sleep. She eased herself away, saw to his comfort and rose.

A woman near the door softly spoke, "I am Mary. Can I help any further?"

"I need to walk, see that I am sent for if he wakes up." Ivy tugged the robe off. "Where are my clothes? And sandals?"

She gestured at a small stack of clothing, not shying away from Ivy's nudity. Ivy dressed and followed Mary out into the corridor. She blinked. "Everything is so white!"

"Easier to keep clean," Mary answered. "It is growing dark on deck. Do you want to get some outside air?"

Ivy shuddered. "At sea. No. I can...no, don't want to see the ocean. Just walk. How far can I walk?"

Mary gestured to a plaque on the wall down from the cabin. "This is a floor plan of the *Windsong*. These are the exposed decks." She pointed out areas Ivy could stretch her legs but remained secluded. "We have a small gym, but it has windows."

"No windows," Ivy replied, not admitting she didn't know what a gym was. She met Mary's eyes. "I have an aversion to the ocean. Okay?"

"Okay." Mary nodded. "The captain would like to meet you. If you stay to these areas, I will see where he is available."

"Yeah, sure, fine." Ivy stalked off, head down. Her brain was finally able to shuffle the last few days around and make sense of it all. Duran's betrayal rankled her. What did it mean that he stayed behind? She did understand the pull of family, but his family already knew what he was doing and according to him, were already preparing to leave for Lina. Why did he need to be there?

Ivy growled, considering the trick of getting her so drunk. He knew she didn't intend to board the *Windsong*...he said he'd see Emmett was safe. Damn! She slammed a fist into the wall. Emmett and the hauntings. She hadn't seen him so deeply affected in years. He needed to get off this boat.

She turned to make another round and nearly ran into a tall man. He reached out to steady her and she slapped his hands away.

"Excuse me, Miss Ivy."

"Ivy! Just fucking Ivy!" she snarled. "Who the hell are you?"

"I'm Captain Leonardo." He bowed his head. "I'm sorry I wasn't able to welcome you aboard personally, but you were incapacitated. I understand."

"Drunk. I was dead drunk. Thanks to that rat bastard, Duran!" She backed up to look into the captain's face. He was nearly two feet taller than she was. "How the fuck could you leave him behind?"

"There was no leaving him behind, miss. He wasn't scheduled

to return to Lina this trip." The captain's face revealed nothing to her.

Her eyes narrowed. "Wasn't scheduled to return? When is he scheduled to return?"

"I'm afraid ship's business isn't yours, Miss...Ivy." He gestured down the corridor. "I have a dinner being set for us. I understand your companion isn't available."

"We'll be at Lina..." She thought a moment. "Late tomorrow?"

"Yes." He urged her to walk next to him.

"Then you leave again, for the mainland. When?" She allowed him to escort her. Dinner sounded like a good idea. Her stomach was finally settled from the drunk Duran had thrust her into.

"Again, Ivy. Not your business." He tilted his head at her. "Do you insist on knowing the business of those who inhabit Gathering Valley?"

She considered for a moment, then grinned. "Sometimes. And sometimes, they actually answer. I have no intention of remaining on Lina, Captain. Emmett has family there. I don't. I have no family."

He didn't answer, just continued along the length of the ship. Eventually, he ushered her into a large room, scattered with those she assumed were crew. The captain led her to a corner table, separated from the rest by curtains. He pulled a chair out and she sat down, knowing how to behave in civilized company.

"I've seen the plans of the ship. But admit I couldn't follow this trail." She looked around. "I thought ships were more...why can't I feel the ships move?"

"We have excellent stabilizers," he answered. "This dining room is located amidships, above the waterline."

"Above the waterline?" She froze, staring at the curtains around their table.

He observed her closely. "I understand you have an aversion to viewing the water. We have curtained this table off for your comfort."

Ivy took several deep breaths, her hands slowly unclenched at her thighs. With a supreme act of will, she met the captain's eyes. "Thank you."

As they ate, the conversation wove back and forth regarding Lina and what she and Emmett could expect when they made port. "It is one of the only coastal cities to survive the change. The entire island was unaffected. Save that the populace was gone. We discovered it while searching for somewhere to dock. From the older maps this ship carries, it gained a great deal of land from the change."

"You were at sea..." She shuddered.

"Many ships were at sea. As far as we could tell, we were the only one to make the transition," he answered. "That is all I am willing to tell you."

"Yeah, like Dave." She sighed. "Lina...is that the island or the city?"

"The island. The port is called Avala. Much of it changed, but not all. The Cruz have flourished there." He poured her another glass of wine. "Are you certain you have no family there?"

"I am certain," she answered, unwilling to face the reality of Bosun being her grandfather. She didn't lie, Bosun was back on the mainland, as far as she knew.

The meal was sumptuous, she supposed. She had little experience with rich foods. "What do you know of the situation on the mainland?" she asked as they finished dessert.

"I know it is a violent place, where the strong rule." He leaned toward her. "I understand one of these strongmen pursue you."

"Yeah, that is my understanding also." She looked away. "Duran intends to see his family settled on Lina. With the *Windsong*'s help?"

"I don't know, but there are many other islands available. Several very close to Lina. We were the only ship to survive the change, but more were built after." His eyes were boring into hers. "Ivy. Join me tonight."

"All right," she answered. Her anger at Duran was still boiling inside her. They weren't a couple. She could fuck whoever she wanted to.

She thought. Until she found herself shaking as Captain Leonardo caressed her. He didn't press, just held her and rocked as the night passed. It was oddly comforting. She woke up in the room with Emmett, angry all over again, at both herself and Duran. Emmett was asleep, head buried in her side. His eyes were swollen, and he periodically shuddered. But at least he slept.

She spent the day pacing the hallways.

CHAPTER SEVEN

By the time the *Windsong* reached Avala, Ivy's body constantly twitched. No amount of walking the hallways soothed her. The lines about her mouth deepened. When she felt the ship ease into a slower speed, the sound of a motor changing pitch, Ivy hurried into the room. Emmett had again taken refuge in the closet, but was handling himself better.

"Emmett? Come on, now. I think we're coming into port. I can't face the outside without you." She coaxed him awake, helped him stand. "Keep your eyes on me. Don't let me fall, Emmett."

"What a pair we are," he muttered.

"Yes, a pair of idiots. When did Duran tell you he wasn't coming to Lina with us?" she asked, determined to focus on a distraction.

He took a deep breath. "At the boat. He lied to you. You lied to me."

Her gaze faltered. "Yes. Who did you lie to?"

"I didn't."

"Well, fuck you. Too damned pure, aren't you?" She tried to joke. "Emmett, I couldn't let you stay. Not with the Holy Rollers looking to burn you. I've seen them, seen what it's like when they are in control. I'd crack if I had to see that, Emmett. I'm sorry."

He choked slightly as he replied, "I wouldn't see you in his grips again, Ivy. I remember how it was. I came to Lina for you."

"Ah, now I know you're lying! You came for your family... though I know it was more than that." She shook her head. "God, we're all liars."

A light tapping came on their door. "Ready to disembark in fifteen minutes."

Ivy caught the crewman in the hallway. "How do we disembark?"

"Ma'am?" He looked confused.

"I was unconscious. How do we get off the ship?"

"Oh, a small zodiac," he answered.

Ivy rolled her eyes and turned to speak to Emmett. "You know what a zodiac is?"

"No. But we came aboard on a motorized raft," he answered, eyes locked on her face. She figured he still saw and heard the ghosts, but he only had to hang on a little bit longer.

"Okay, that must be what a zodiac is." She sighed. "You want to look out the window there and see what time of the day it is?"

Emmett eased over toward the curtained opening and gazed out. "Late afternoon. It's partially cloudy."

"Wish it were dark," she muttered.

"I think I can get us to where we came aboard." He tottered slightly. "I need food."

"Let me get you a glass of water." She saw him drink and even peeled a piece of fruit to eat. Then they ventured out of the room. A crewman escorted them to the stern, where the ramp was. Ivy shook as the scent of the open water reached her, haunted by Grandmother's voice, all but screaming in panic at her. Emmett tightened his grip on her shoulders. It helped.

As humiliating as it was, she couldn't face the deep blue water. She buried her face at his shoulder as they were helped into the raft. The trip was quick, and they climbed out to solid ground to meet the shadows of the island's peak, growing to swallow them. The port of Avala faced east, she surmised, clinging to any factual tidbit she could use to drive away the ocean at her back. Ivy looked up at a city of colorful square houses. They ran up the slopes from the bay in a very picturesque manner.

Ivy stood, growing steadier as she ignored the water lapping at her feet. Emmett suddenly fell to his knees. "Linc?"

Striding toward them was a man that had to be related. Ivy smiled and moved aside. The two men embraced, Linc pulling his cousin up from the sand.

"I thought you were dead. You never came back, then we were caught! Father thought you'd been taken by Ursus to keep from warning us!" Emmett smiled. "I remember you...and Alfie? Bosun said Alfie was also here."

"You were just a little boy. Alfie is visiting the interior." Linc turned and grabbed at Ivy. "Thank you for keeping him safe."

"Safe? He kept me sane." She smiled. "Take care of him, Cousin Linc." She backed away to give them privacy.

"No, you must come with us." Linc took her hand, pulling her closer. "We have a welcoming party at the house. Please, join us."

She sighed, catching sight of Bosun striding toward them. She pulled free of Linc and hurried to meet him, astounded at his being there before them. She immediately lit into him. "Duran! You left Duran, you doddering idiot! The only one who knows where I am! Ursus will hunt him down, kill his family, capture him, torture him! Kill him! Whose stupid idea was it to leave him there! Get him here!"

Bosun stared at her. "Duran isn't with you?"

She froze midst her tirade and suddenly deflated. "Oh, shit. Bosun...we can't leave him there. I know Ursus, he won't give up. How soon can we get back?"

"I...I don't know. I will talk with Captain Leonardo. Ivy, please. Stay, let me do this." Her estranged grandfather pled.

"Hell, no." She turned back to Emmett. "I have to go, Emmett. I can't leave Duran...he doesn't understand how driven Ursus is."

Emmett glanced at Bosun first, then looked at Ivy, and nodded. She was thankful he wasn't going to fight with her.

"Tonight, come to the party." Linc stepped in. "It isn't every day we welcome home a member of the family."

"Yes, please," Bosun urged Ivy to join the two men. "I'll come after I talk to Leonardo."

Ivy let herself be carried away between the two cousins. Bosun watched her walk away, seeing her grandmother in the tilt of her head. He waited for them to be out of sight, before signaling to George, at the zodiac. They spoke for a few minutes. Bosun then left to meet with the Lina elders.

Ivy watched Emmett slowly open himself to the reality of so many surviving family members. She sipped the wine, nibbled on the food and observed it all. He was obviously overwhelmed. His face had never been so open with acceptance. Her heart warmed at seeing him so surrounded. Memories of good times with her family were so faint, but watching him brought them to the surface, sweet memories.

Her father told good stories. Her mother would recite poetry from the world before. Her curse had been a gentle one. Her grandmother would sing, leading the family in rollicking songs about places and people long gone. Ivy asked about them once and her grandmother muttered something about unions and protests.

Linc sat down next to her, watching Emmett bounce a baby on his knee. "We have children here. Not as many as before, but better than the mainland."

"I can see that." She smiled at the little girl who brought her a piece of cake. "Thank you, chica."

"What does chica mean?" the waif asked.

"Little girl," Ivy told her, then yawned. "I fear the ship wasn't restful, for either of us."

"We will take care of him," Linc assured her. "Bosun's home is around the corner. There is no view of the Pacif, so it should prove easier for you."

"Who told you of my affliction?" she sharply replied. "They gossip from the ship?"

"No, it was assumed. Bosun is not fond of the ocean either. I can escort you when you are ready. Emmett can join you, or stay here." They sat and watched the rest for another hour before Ivy requested directions.

Linc walked her to Bosun's door. "I'm sorry he didn't join us. He may be home or still in discussions with the *Windsong*'s crew."

"I'm sure I'll see him in the morning." Ivy wandered the house, touching small items she assumed her grandfather treasured. She wanted to speak with him, but didn't know the town well enough to go out looking for him. She settled on a couch in the main living area and eventually drifted to sleep.

Bosun never came.

Ivy snorted as Emmett brushed at her hair. "Ivy! Wake up...Ivy..."

"What?" She thrust his hand away, jerking awake with anger. She glared at him. His hair was in mild disarray and his eyes were bright, watery. He was trying to grin at her, swaying.

"You're drunk!"

"Maybe, some," he admitted. "Ivy, I understand why you lied. Because I did, too."

With a deep sigh, she looked around the room. The early light of dawn had lifted the shadows. "Where is Bosun?" she asked, not wanting to deal with Emmett and lies.

"That's the thing." Emmett sat on a footstool, near the couch. He sniffed. "When you said...said you had to go back...I nodded?"

She peered at him. "Yeah."

"I lied. He stood behind you, signaled he'd go, you'd stay. I agreed with him." Emmett bowed his head. "I...I got it. Why you lied."

"Okay." She patted his hand. "Okay. I get it. But I'm still going."

"Uh, no, you're not. He's already gone. He came by Linc's and left this." Emmett held up an envelope.

Ivy snarled, grabbed the envelope and shot to her feet. "No. The *Windsong*, I have to get to the ship!"

"She's gone," Linc spoke from the doorway.

Her curse was potent, Linc backed away as she dashed at him. Out to the street and down the slope, she raced until she could view the bay. There it was, clear, blue and empty. She sagged. "Fuck. Trapped."

"You're not trapped," Linc answered, following her.

"Fucking lot you know," she snapped back. "Should have known, couldn't trust that rat-faced bastard."

"Your grandfather?" Emmett joined his cousin. "Why didn't you tell me?"

"Tell you what?" Ivy's lips twisted in anger.

"That he was your grandfather," her companion answered. Then yawned.

"Because I wasn't sure I believed it. Not sure I do, even now! Who the fuck told you?" She turned back to the house, realized she still held the envelope and ripped it open. She read the single page it contained.

Granddaughter, I will do this for you. I failed your grandmother, I failed your mother. I will not fail you. I will bring him to Lina.

It was signed Benja. Ivy crumpled it up and let it drop to the pathway. She focused on Linc. "How do I get off this fucking island?"

He studied her. "You are much like him. Stubborn. The *Windsong* is the only ship that regularly sails between Lina and the mainland. They have no schedule, we don't know when she will be back."

"You live on a fucking island and no one else has a boat?" Ivy shook her head. "I don't believe you."

"There are fisherman, based at Flounder Point, but they do not venture far. And Trader's Port has some smaller boats. But none that cross the water this time of year. There are only a few months when it is safe to do so," he answered, bending down to retrieve the crumpled paper. He handed it back to her. She grimaced but shoved it into her pocket.

"Trader's Point? Which way?" She glanced up at the sky, attempting to get a fix on the compass points.

"It's four days journey to the north, along the coast. But no one can help you there, Ivy." Linc watched her pace.

"Why a Trader's Port? What's wrong with this one?" Emmett asked curiously. The drink he'd taken was keeping him from focusing on Ivy's anger.

"Those who are willing to trade with us are not welcome here. Because of the children. If the mainland knew about them it could be risky. So they are restricted to Trader's Port, where there are no children," Linc answered.

"Very smart of you." Ivy began to stride back to the house, to fetch her bag. "I'll head out now. Bosun can't do this alone. He doesn't know Ursus like I do."

"You can't. The Elders Council have called a meeting tomorrow. If you want, I will see you have a guide afterward. There is a map at the village center, it will help you familiarize yourself with Lina." Emmett's cousin sighed. "Go back to the house and make sure, Ivy. Bosun is quite capable of taking care of himself. We know Ursus well."

"Not well enough since you've run without killing him first," she shot back the retort as she walked away. "Elders Council, fuck."

Emmett yawned again. "She's right. Basically. We've been running from him forever, and it never stops. Unless he's dead. Maybe it will stop then."

Linc put an arm around his cousin's shoulders. "Come on, Em.

You need to sleep. She knows the importance of the Elder Council, right?"

"I guess so. Her family was very traditional. Never married outside the Cruz. Unlike ours." Emmett rubbed at his eyes. "Take me to her, I'll make sure she stays."

"No, you sleep. We'll watch her." Linc assured the taller man.

She sat, smoothing the letter on her thigh. A council meeting. Damn. She hated those things. Memories of her grandmother fighting with the rest rose in her head. They were always so careful. Never wanted to actually do anything, just wait. Always, wait. She had no intention of waiting.

But she also remembered how clever they were when it came to getting their way. She'd have to be smarter.

She got up, wandered around the small house. There was another family living on the lower level, their entrance ran next to the southern wall. Bosun kept very little. She touched a shell, placed carefully on a shelf. It reminded her of one her grandmother kept. With a sigh, she turned away.

The family downstairs brought her a meal. The oldest woman carried it up. "We care for Bosun. Told him we'd care for you." Her old face wrinkled as she smiled at Ivy.

Ivy had been taught to be courteous to the elderly. She offered the woman a chair. Then sat and shared the small kettle of tea with her.

"They call me Prima." She winked at Ivy with eyes of clear blue, shot with green. Her white hair also held a trace of green. Ivy recognized signs of a non-pure Cruz breeding.

Prima winked again. "My father was a Losanglo. Mama broke all the rules by marrying him."

"I bet she did," Ivy replied. "Do you break rules?"

"Sometimes." The chuckle was dry. Ivy poured her more tea. "You break rules, girl?"

"Whenever possible," Ivy admitted. "Why does the council want to meet with me?"

"To find out if you'll obey the rules!" She cackled again.

Ivy grinned, liking the woman.

"Oh, I guess that makes sense. Does Bosun follow the rules?" Ivy asked.

"Not usually." Prima's smile faded. "He obeyed your family council and lost you. Lost everything."

Ivy tilted her head. "What do you mean?"

"Ah, that's his story to tell, girl. You finish the tea and breakfast. Spend the day getting to know Avala. I'll see you at supper." She rose with some difficulty, but appeared to draw strength from standing. Prima left the house without need of assistance. Ivy ate half the food, wrapped the rest in a large napkin and tucked it away. For later.

She wandered the village, watching it wake up. The children were a delight, running all about the cobbled streets. Ivy completely understood why they protected them from the mainland. She'd seen homesteads burned and the rare child stolen by those jealous of offspring. Turning a corner, the bay was revealed to her. With a shudder, Ivy forced herself to gaze out at the expanse of blue.

Her breathing quickened, a chill ran up her arms. The water swelled, and rose, threatening to swallow everything. She shut her eyes, shook her head, looked again. The vision, deeply implanted by her grandmother, lost some strength. But to her eyes, the water was still a malevolent thing. She turned away, arms wrapped about her chest.

"He didn't like it either," a little girl spoke from Ivy's side. "I'm Elena. Linc is my father."

Ivy wiped at the cold sweat on her face and forced herself to reply, "Hi, Elena. Linc is a lucky man."

"Do you have any children?" The girl reached for Ivy's hand and pulled her down the street. "There's a fountain..."

“Oh, thank you. Children? No, no children,” Ivy lied. Easier to lie than try to explain about Helen.

“Oh.” Elena’s brow wrinkled. “Is Emmett your husband?”

Ivy smiled crookedly. “No, Emmett isn’t my husband. I’m too old for him.”

“No, you’re not!” Elena protested. “You’re pretty, like my cousin, Betts.”

“Well, thank you, Elena. But trust me, I’m older than I look. I knew Emmett when he was your age...eight?” Ivy tried to turn the talk to the little girl.

Elena snorted. “You were kids together?”

Ivy sighed. “No. Is that the fountain?” She pointed at a splashing ring of water, with three youngsters frolicking in. “Isn’t it a bit cold to be all wet?”

“Not yet, but it’s getting colder.” Elena sat on the fountain edge, waiting for Ivy to wash her face. Ivy did so, getting splashed by a little boy. She retaliated and in a matter of minutes they were all soaking.

Ivy laughed. Elena beamed at her, watering dripping down her legs, pooling at her small feet. Elena giggled. “See?”

Ivy pulled the hair away from her face and grimaced at the three boys laughing as they ran away from the water carnage. “Elena, your daddy said there was a map of the island?”

“Yeah, I can show you.” Elena jumped up with the energy of eight years, pulling Ivy from the fountain.

At the map, a wooden carving that faced away from the ocean, thankfully, Ivy studied the island shape, tracing the roads with her fingers. She settled on Trader’s Port. Elena watched. “Oh, we never go there. The path is high above the water. The seabirds nest there and sometimes they dive at you.”

“I thought you never go there,” Ivy asked absently.

“We don’t, but we walk the path sometimes. It’s steep and it used to scare me,” Elena admitted.

“Steep, above the water.” Ivy sighed loudly. “Any other way?”

"Through the center of the island, to the other side and back." Elena showed Ivy. "But that takes more than a week."

"What about cutting over here?" Ivy cut across an empty area of the map.

"Lots of hills, rocky. Have to climb, and no path." Linc's daughter shuffled her feet. "It's lunch time..."

"Oh, well you better get home to eat. I'll be fine. Thanks for showing me the map, sweetie." Ivy smiled as the little girl trotted away, turning to wave before disappearing around a corner. The map wasn't very useful, but it was better than nothing. She noticed an entire section appeared to have been added at one point. Perhaps the addition from when things changed. Ivy pulled the slightly damp note from her pocket and made a rough sketch on it. There was no real sense of scale, so she had no idea how far anything was. But Linc had said Trader's Port was four days walk. Elena said the other route took more than a week.

But Ivy could walk very fast. And she had no intention of sitting through a council meeting. She returned to Bosun's house and set about gathering her bag. She took all the fruit in the house, the bread and every edible item she found. Then she walked to Linc's to check on Emmett.

He was nursing a hangover and glared at her, a hand at his head. "Why did you let me drink so much?"

"What? I'm in charge of your drinking habits?" Ivy glared back. "Your family let you drink too much, not up to me."

"I saw you earlier, didn't I?" Emmett closed his eyes, swallowed.

Ivy pushed a glass of water closer to him.

"Yeah, idiot. You let Bosun run out on me." Ivy snorted. "Not going to fight with you, Emmett. You looked good last night, with all of them. They'll be good for you."

"Linc told me...the cave in? There was an opening at the back of the shaft and that's how so many got away. Not my parents, or sister... but the rest." He took a deep breath. "Ivy? What are you going to do?"

She looked away, not wanting to lie. "Get to know Lina, I

guess. Try to find a way off. I owe Duran a nasty hangover." She turned back to him. "You stay with Linc and get to know your people, Emmett. I'll be all right."

Linc's wife bustled over, handed Emmett a steaming cup of something aromatic. "This will help. Will you join us for dinner tonight, Ivy?"

"No, Prima is bringing me something. I can't be rude." Ivy paused. "I'll ask her if she minds." Her mind had considered, the more food the better for traveling...

It was past midnight when she slipped away from Avala. Her pack was stuffed with items from Prima's dinner tray and leftovers from Linc's wife. Ivy had good night vision and made use of it, cutting across the rougher terrain toward Trader's Port. The meeting tomorrow would go on without her.

CHAPTER EIGHT

The route Ivy took to Trader's Port proved a rough one. There was a great deal of steep climbing, and she found no water. She rationed her food, drinking very little. The weather remained mild, and clouds kept the sun from being too oppressive. The nights were lonely, without Emmett near by. But she would not regret. He needed his family. She needed to protect Emmett, protect Lina and kill Ursus.

She didn't sleep well, but stayed up, studying the stars, attempting to figure out where she was in comparison to the mainland. And she considered how to get close to her nemesis.

Perhaps she should have stayed and met with the elders. But her memories of the loud and contentious meetings her grandmother attended made the idea less than appealing. She had no patience for the elders talk. They had run from Ursus. They had left her family to be slaughtered. Nothing she wanted to hear from them.

The island wasn't inhospitable. She'd talked to a few sailors on the *Windsong* and knew there were no large predators to worry about. No big cats or wolves. No bears.

She shivered.

Emmett would be pissed, but he'd be with family. Time for him to be on his own, anyway.

It took Ivy six days to reach Trader's Port. She surveyed the port from an overlook. Alone, she fought her ocean phobia. If she didn't look directly at the water, but focused tightly on the buildings...it still appeared to heave and move unnaturally, but she was able to move beyond the babbling fear. She'd seen the water several times as she'd traveled, and knew it would now be a constant companion. And she was determined not to be crippled by it.

A crunch of rock behind her caused her to start. She shot to her feet and spun. A man held up hands, showing he meant no harm. "Easy, girl. I'm not here to hurt you."

Slowly, her breathing returned to normal. She swallowed, took her hand from her ax, spreading her fingers wide to illustrate her peaceful intentions, and nodded. "Sorry, I've been alone for several days and a bit jumpy."

"You heading for the port?" he asked. "Oh, I'm Trex."

"Trex, I'm Ivy. Yes, I was hoping to find a ship to take me back to the mainland." She sighed. "The *Windsong* stranded me at Avala."

"Stranded you? That don't sound like Captain Leonardo." Trex strode past her. "Well, follow me, I'll take you the safest route down. Why did you come overland? Quicker by the coast path."

"I don't like heights...over water...and was told the coast path contains many," Ivy explained, stepping closely after the friendly man. He was taller than she was, but that wasn't uncommon. Most people were. His hair held the green tint of the Cruzan, but his eyes were blue. She had to step quickly to keep up with his long strides. She tried to slow him down with conversation. "Are you a port resident?"

"Yup, but was visiting my cousin inland, at his goat ranch." He hefted up a bag. "Fresh meat and some goat cheese."

"Ah, I saw a few small holdings, tucked away at the foot of slopes," Ivy commented.

He glanced over his shoulder at her. "You didn't stop?"

"I don't know them." She shrugged.

"Don't matter, Ivy. We take care of each other here on Lina." He peered at her, pausing to examine her closely. "You're pure, aren't you? Those eyes, your skin..."

"Supposedly," she answered, not put off by the study. "And I'm older than I appear."

He suddenly grinned. "Ah, you're *that* Ivy! I hate to tell you, dear lady. But there won't be a passage to be had to the mainland for months. But come anyway and meet the pirates of Trader's Port."

"Pirates?" Ivy tilted her head with surprise.

"Well, the merchants from the mainland consider us pirates. We have what they want, and we are shrewd bargainers. We don't sail all that much, the water still holds too many bad memories for most." He reached out to take her hand as they maneuvered around a steep drop off. "You're not the only one who avoids steep places."

She didn't reply, just accepted his help. When they stood at the worn road, leading through the center of the port, she thanked him. "I am not used to the kindness of strangers, Trex. Thank you."

She prepared to stroll out on her own when he stopped her. "No, come to my house, try the cheese. Time enough tomorrow to begin badgering the captains to risk their boats. You won't succeed, Ivy."

"I have to try." She let him take her to a small apartment above a tavern. He left the meat with the tavern owner and led her to his spare rooms.

"You look tired. Use the bathhouse behind the tavern, eat, and sleep." He showed her where he stored the bread and cheese. "I'll ask around for you."

She'd noticed how her appearance at the tavern had caused a pause in the conversation. She had no doubt by tomorrow, her business would be known. But that would spare her explaining.

And she was exhausted. A bath sounded impossibly lovely. She nodded and began to strip her weapons away.

She knew he watched, saw her youthful body. Did he see how tired she was? The years of living rough in the foothills, hoping to see her daughter? The times she starved? Froze? Her body communicated twenty, her spirit? Decades more.

She set her weapons down. A pair of double-headed axes, strapped to belt. A short blade and a small dagger, best for throwing. She removed the slingshot and bag of stones. And lastly, her big ax. When you're not the largest warrior in a fight, the ax brought everyone down to size. No one seemed to carry weaponry on Lina. She must appear odd, to be so prepared for battle.

With a smile, he left her, pointing out a drying towel. "There is soap in the bathhouse." He hurried back downstairs.

Ivy bathed undisturbed, slipped back to Trex's rooms and spread her blanket on the floor. She woke to find her host had placed a second blanket atop her. And left a bit of cooked meat on the table for her.

She spent over a week in Trader's Port, making friends and answering questions about the mainland. But none were willing to risk the sailing the strait. Three captains took the time to explain to her that they did not sail ships like the *Windsong*, they were only decades into learning the nuances of the sea and were careful. She was invited aboard their ships and could see they were speaking the truth. Their vessels were nothing like the big sailing ship.

It was grating. She was blunt concerning her worry about Duran, who several had met.

One shared with her his news, "I spoke with a mainland captain two months past. He said he'd been approached to ferry a group of Losanglos to the Chan Islands, south of us. I don't know when they were going. Some were there already, setting up a place for the group to settle. He was worried at attracting Ursus' attention."

"He should be. Ursus doesn't take escaping from his influence lightly." She sighed. "But he told you?"

"He knows we're not speaking to that bastard." The captain growled, then grinned. "They may not like how we bargain, but they know we will never trade with Ursus. Information or anything else."

"I hope they are as steadfast," she murmured.

Stillness settled over the group. One raised a cup and drained it, then softly spoke, "Ursus has no ships. No sailors. He has taken no port town...we would have time to stop him. Ships burn. The mainland knows we would not hesitate."

"I hope it is enough." Ivy leaned on Trex. "I'm sorry, I don't mean to spread fear."

"From what we hear, you have every right to be suspicious. Of Ursus and those he might influence," Trex answered, setting his arm over her. She hadn't accepted his invitation to his bed, but enjoyed the simple physical contact. She'd told him of Emmett, left at Avala to connect with his family. Trex thought her a fool, but a well-meaning fool. She smiled, recalling how he'd said Emmett would come looking for her.

"It isn't just Ursus' influence I fear. He uses torture, and...other banned techniques." She shuddered.

"We be ready, Ivy. If he thinks to take Lina." An older woman leaned closer. "I won't speak of our preparations, but they are ready."

Ivy met the light green eyes and nodded. "I have appreciated the hospitality, but I have to try the fisherman's village. See if any will risk the strait."

"Fishermen know the currents best, but don't hold out hope, Ivy." Trex kissed her head. "We'll see you with provisions and a better map. I'll attempt to smooth things over with this Emmett when he shows up."

She left the next day.

CHAPTER NINE

Duran prepared for another cold night on the run. He gazed at the rickety village, light flickering through makeshift window coverings, desperate for one warm night. One refreshing mug of beer, one hour before a fire. Was it too much to ask?

He'd known Ursus would be after him once he'd surfaced from seeing Ivy and Emmett off. In fact, he counted on it. While Ursus and his henchbitch, Diva, sought him, the Losanglos moved to the Chan Islands. His family would be safe. Ivy was safe.

But he was bone tired. Diva never let up. She hired every discontent mercenary she could find. The she posted a bounty on his head that would tempt the angels - while Ursus looked for Ivy.

With a shiver, Duran decided to take a chance. This was a bitter edge village, about as far into the mountains as was possible to go before meeting the sheer granite cliffs that bared the way further east. Duran led his pursuit this way, knowing they would likely slow down, believing him trapped. But the Losanglos had a way down. Treacherous, but it worked. One hot meal would help him prepare for that desperate descent.

He stood by the door, peering into the lit room. He saw no one he knew, no one he thought would recognize him. Bending slightly, he shuffled into the room. None commented on his presence. He sat at a small table, near the smoking fireplace. The room smelled stale, but it was warm. The mattered more.

A lame serving girl approached him. "What were you wanting?"

"Anything hot to eat. Anything cold to drink," Duran replied gruffly. He sniffed loudly, coughed and rubbed at his leg as if it were aching. He wanted any descriptions of his state to include infirmities.

A platter was brought over to him, a bowl of steaming stew. He could see the grease floating on the surface and his mouth filled with readiness. He'd lived lean for weeks, eaten raw food over and over again. This was nectar. He barely kept his hand from trembling as he took the spoon in hand. After a moment, he gave up and simply lifted the bowl to his lips.

Gods. It was divine. Hot, greasy, full of chunks of meat, bits of vegetables. He didn't set the bowl down until it was empty. He pounded his chest and beamed at the serving girl, staring at him. "Another?"

"Yes, sir!" She seized the bowl and scurried away. Duran turned his attention to the cold tankard of beer. Two minutes later, he leaned back and gazed at the ceiling. He hadn't been so content since the cave with Ivy. Turning his thoughts from that melancholy memory, he sighed. The heat of the fire on his back was blessed relief. Though all the scrapes and cuts were waking up.

He spoke to the server as she handed him a second bowl of the stew, "You have baths?"

"No, sir. But there be hot springs down the slope, in Vixenville." She took his empty tankard. "Another?"

"Yes." He reached into his pouch and paid for the food. Taking up the fresh bowl, he began to eat it, this time using a spoon.

As his tankard was coming back, the door opened from the outside. And this time, it was someone he knew. Duran dropped the spoon and lifted the bowl, hiding his face behind it. He swallowed, knowing this was his last hot food for the duration.

Bill, the mercenary who had joined up with Diva, examined the room. His eyes barely registered the ragged looking man at the fire. He directed the two men with him to circle around the room, searching the kitchen and hallway to the outhouse. Duran bent lower, grunting over the bowl.

A moment later, Bill was standing next to the fire, ignoring the man eating the stew. Duran made sure a small amount of the stew remained, and with deliberation dropped the bowl on Bill's foot. The man glanced down and cursed at the mess on his boot tip. He struck at Duran, who fell to the floor, whimpering apologies. He scurried to the door and slid out into the cold, as if driven by fear.

Bill wiped at his boot, snarling at the ineptitude of mountain people. He doubted Duran was here. The man was too smart to be trapped. But that black bitch was certain the trail led here.

The serving girl approached, looking confused. She held a tankard and appeared to look for someone to serve it to. "What ya looking for, girl?" Bill snarled

"The man who ordered this, where did he go?" She blinked.

"He..." Bill paused. "He left a paid for drink!? What did he look like?" Bill grabbed the girls arm, wrenched the tankard away from her. "Well?"

"He was cold, he huddled. He was cold...dark hair." She tried to pull away from him. "Let me go!"

"His name!?" Bill growled.

"He didn't say." She yanked her arm free. "Least he was polite. He smiled at me."

Bill's eyes narrowed, then he grinned. "Smiled, did he? Big smile?"

"Nice smile. Big smile," she shouted at him as she hurried for the kitchen.

Bill downed the pilfered drink and shouted out for his men. They hurried to his side. He pointed at the taller one. "You, get down to Diva. He's here. Jero and I stay, push him down to her. He's looking ragged, tell her to search any who come down the path."

Mot nodded and headed for the door.

Once outside, he turned, trotted down the side of the tavern and was yanked into the alley. A knife slipped across his throat and he fell, silent.

Duran hauled the body deep into the alley. First, he stripped the coat free and took it for his own, then pushed snow over the body. The water flask, the bag of coins, a large knife, all were tossed into his knapsack.

Duran waited in the shadows. Bill and Jero exited together, more than an hour later. Bill directed Jero one way, he went the other. Jero died as swiftly as Mot. Duran then turned his attention to Bill.

At the top of the barely there street, Duran faced the half-blind mercenary.

"Still think she cursed you, Bill?" the Losanglos softly said.

"She cursed you, Duran... You're walking dead," Bill hissed back. "Where is she? Tell me and we'll let you go."

"No you won't. I know the price on my head. I know you're lying." Duran hefted up the knife he'd taken from Mot. "Mot knows...knew...steel."

Bill looked about the deserted street. He drew a deep breath and Duran threw the knife. Bill shifted and the blade took him in the shoulder instead of the chest. Bill shouted, amazingly loud, "Bounty! Help! Bounty!"

Duran stood a moment, then grinned. "You're dead, Bill. I ran the blade through the outhouse and all the Shamans are dead. Enjoy dying." He turned and dashed into the forest, toward the cliffs.

Bill shivered, even as several villagers entered the street. The treacherous mercenary pointed toward the cliff. "Bounty...catch him!"

They gazed into the forest and nodded. As one led Bill back into the tavern, the other three followed the path into the forest. They were poor and bounty could keep them alive.

Duran hurried through the forest. He was searching for the split pine he'd been told of. Near a gaping crevasse he found the tree. He leaned over the inky black opening. The whiteness of the snow contrasted with its maw.

Shit.

Taking a deep breath, he counted the steps from the pine, east toward the cliffs. At seventeen he searched for the hidden step. And found it.

The path down those steps, to the hidden rope ladders, and further down, proved harrowing. His hands bled before he closed in on the floor of the valley. He could hear the river below him. This area wasn't meant as a winter route, but he had no choice. He prayed the river wasn't too high.

His legs trembled as his feet hit the rock. He collapsed, gasping, tucking his hands into his armpits. Huddling, he simple cursed, though he knew it was a waste of energy, "You bitch, I hope you're warm, well-fed and tucked up next to some friendly man." He shook his head, "No, no friendly man...wait for me, girl. Wait for me."

It took him over an hour to find the cave. Once there he unearthed the provisions set aside for a time of need. He lit the tiny fire, and sat, staring into the flames, wondering what that spitfire woman was doing at that moment.

He didn't call her his woman, even in his head.

Another month passed before Diva caught him.

CHAPTER TEN

Ivy wandered the interior of Lina for months. She found the fisherman's village, but they also refused her request for passage to the mainland. They welcomed her, fed her, spoke of the scattered settlements across the interior. She spent a week there, and left knowing how to find water. First time through, she'd missed the small ponds and deep springs, sheltered from the heat of the sun with clever camouflage.

The herders, keeping an eye on the goats that provided so much of the meat the islanders ate, often sighted her. She helped out now and then, unaware that they keenly watched her. Messages were sent to the harbor regarding her safety.

She dreamt of Ursus only to wake sweaty, holding back screams. Each time that happened, she moved. It was the end of the fifth month when she wandered into a camp of old women.

Her grandmother once spoke of the custom of old women, going out on the full moon to whisper secrets to each other and celebrate rituals only they remembered. Ivy gazed at the seven women and sighed. She would never know such a group. Over forty years old, but she'd never be a crone. Forever young was a bitter curse to hold.

"Stop gawking, woman. Come, join us. We have a rich rabbit stew boiling. And bread fresh from the harbor bakeries." One gestured at her with the invitation and a place was opened for her to sit with them around the fire.

With a sigh, she surrendered to the inevitable. One did not disobey old Cruz women.

At least, not in person.

The smell of the stew was rich and her stomach cried out in hollowness as she sat. One of the women thrust a mug in her hand. "Drink! Tonight you'll get answers, wandering soul."

"Answers? I don't want answers, I want off this bloody island." She swallowed the foamy draft and gasped. It was ice cold, rich and nearly a food item all by itself. "How...?"

Two of them women cackled and Ivy cut off her question. Old women magic wasn't something to question. She sat still and listened as they told stories to one another. This was the wisdom of the crones and she relished it.

One of them began a ribald story about an old lover and before she knew it, Ivy was laughing so hard she wiped tears from her eyes. Another chimed in with an even dirtier story. The night grew dark, the fire roared higher and higher into the sky. Ivy drank each time her tankard was filled.

It was very late when the fire was allowed to die down to embers. Ivy fought back a yawn, realizing she had been dozing in her seat. She carefully set the tankard down, preparing to rise and find a spot to spread her bedroll.

"Wait. We have a gift for you, Ivy. A gift of wisdom you sorely need." One reached out and took her hand. Another rose and left the fire for several moments.

"I don't want a gift, thank you. Your company has been rewarding enough. The last few months have been lonely ones," Ivy admitted. Her eyes blurred with sleep. Her free hand was seized.

"But you need this gift, girl. Here, Elspeth is back with something to help you sleep without dark dreams," the woman directly across from her smiled as she spoke. "Drink it, Ivy."

A cup was held before her. She drew away; even mildly drunk she was wary. The two on each side of her held her tight. The cup was pressed to her lips and with resignation, she opened her mouth. To sleep without dreams of Ursus would be nice...

The woman behind her emptied the bitter drink into Ivy's mouth and held her head back until she's swallowed it all. Immediately, her head began to spin. She fell forward and was lowered down until she found herself held by the woman on her right. The rest cleared an area around the fire and began to sing, to chant and dance. Ivy fought to keep her eyes open but eventually lost that battle. She fell asleep to the sound of their singing.

And woke to the sound of creaking rope and slapping sails. A vision of the *Windsong*, settling anchor rose in her. And she knew they were back. She shook her head as she sat up. There was no camp around her. No signs of a fire. But her mouth still held the remnants of that cup.

She spit and climbed from the bedroll. Months of wandering left her with a rudimentary feeling for where she was and how far away Avala lay. She had to move fast, before those bastards left again without her.

———

Duran woke to the sound of the anchor chain being lowered. His head ached, as did the remainder of his body. They'd treated his injuries to the best of their abilities. But some things were never going to be the same.

He groaned as he sat up, taking care with his bandaged hands.

"Don't try to walk, Duran. I'll get enough help so you won't fall," Bosun spoke from the shadows.

"This Avala?" Duran hoarsely asked.

"Yes."

"Ivy is going to kill me," Duran morosely commented. "Should have taken me to one of the Chans, to the Losanglos colony."

"Then Ivy would kill *me*. She isn't going to be angry at you, not when she sees you."

Duran heard Bosun climb to his feet and walk to the bed.

"She's sees me and she'll go after him. Don't let her run off half-cocked." Duran swallowed, fighting not to be sick again.

Bosun brought a cup of water to his lips and he took a sip. It felt so good going down. He hoped it stayed down.

"This ship isn't going to take her back into danger and every captain on this island knows not to go against the council orders that she is to stay put." Bosun opened the door at a gentle knock. Several men entered and began to prepare Duran to go ashore. It would take that many to see he wasn't injured further.

"She's going to kill me," Duran muttered, angry at his own infirmity.

Bosun sighed. "No, she's going to kill Ursus and his bitch, Diva."

The trip off the ship proved excruciating, but Duran didn't care. He'd thought of her, through the pain they thrust upon him. He'd see her soon. Even if she was pissed at him, even if she spit on him, screamed...it didn't matter. He'd see her and know she was still safe. He'd argue the finer points later.

Ivy ran the entire way. She'd risen with more energy then she'd felt in months. And she used it. Keeping an eye on the angle of the sun, she crossed the hills, jumped the gullies, just kept moving. And her anger grew with every step. She'd been trapped here, tricked here! She was getting off this fucking island if she had to swim.

She ran through the night, slowing down to avoid injury and continued the next day. It was mid-afternoon when she crested the lip and looked down at Avala. Sails furled, the *Windsong* sat as she'd seen it in her dreams. Ivy took several deep breaths, readying herself for the battle ahead.

And she descended to the city's edge.

A voice hailed her at the first row of homes, mostly abandoned. She spun on her heels and turned to see Linc, perched on a wall. He held up a water bag. Her hands trembled as she reached for it, taking a long drink before handing it back.

"Thank you." She managed manners, barely.

He nodded at her. "I was told you were likely to pass this way."

"Told? By who?" She glared at him. "How is Emmett?"

"A dream of crones said to wait for you here. Emmett is fine, angry with you for avoiding him. He's down at council hall, discussing the news Bosun brought." Linc sealed the bottle, set it at his side, studying her. "You look worn."

"Thank you," she replied sarcastically. "I have to go."

"They won't take you, Ivy. And you need to get to Bosun's house. Duran returned with him, but..."

The voice faded as Ivy hurried away. Duran was here? She was going to tear him apart.

The few people out in the afternoon heat stepped out of her way as she came roaring down the path. She aimed for Bosun's home, ready with accusations and demands. She threw the door open and stood, staring.

"Ah...is my gentle dove here finally?" Duran's voice sounded odd, as if he were drunk.

The woman blocking her view moved aside, turning to look at Ivy, concern in her face.

Ivy gaped, shocked silent. All the anger fell to her feet, rooting her in horror. He was a mess. She stared at his face. An eye patch perched jauntily over his left eye, bruises colored the rest of his face. His lips were blistered and swollen; his nose had been broken and now sat off center.

Ivy tried to make a sound, but couldn't. He smiled at her, his teeth still perfect. And she cracked, falling to her knees. He was reclined, feet resting on a footstool. Her eyes traveled down his body, bile rising in her throat.

Bandages covered his chest, but she could see marks of burns and bruises down his arms. A light cloth covered his crotch. His legs were vivid with the sign of healing flesh. Cuts and burns riddled his thighs, disappearing under the cloth. Ivy crawled close enough to see the bottoms of his feet, the evidence of burns and beatings evident there also.

His hands were completely covered in bandages; she couldn't tell what was done to them. All the while, he just grinned at her.

"I'd rise to me feet, mi paloma, but..." his voice faded, his body grew lax.

The woman at his side spoke, "He just ate and took his afternoon draught. He's going to fall asleep soon. I would have held off if I'd known you were so close."

Ivy slowly met the woman's gaze, pulling her eyes from Duran with effort. "What...? Who...?"

Duran managed to reply before a soft snore signaled his fading. "Ursus...his bitch, Diva. Helen...helped me 'scape..."

Ivy found her feet again, spun for the door. Linc stood there, blocking her exit. He held his hands up. "This will be answered. But you can't..."

She pushed him aside, staggered out into the streets and fell to her knees; throwing up the water he'd given her, an eternity ago. He followed her.

"I don't know the whole story. Bosun thinks he spent over a month in Ursus' cells. He got him out of there, with Helen's help. It took too long to get him to the coast and here. The eye is gone, had to be removed. The rest? He'll recover. But it's going to be slow."

Ivy wiped at her face, a cold sweat covering her body. The weariness of two days running fell on her. "His...his hands?"

"Nothing broken. Seems they kept their torture to burning, beatings and whipping. The skin of his back is apt to be sensitive for years." He glanced up as the woman who'd been caring for

Duran stepped next to them. "This is Winter, she's the most talented of our healers."

Ivy gripped Linc's hand to get back to her feet. She studied Winter before speaking, "He...his head?"

She blinked, and then nodded. "Ah, his head is fine. Nothing lasting, save for the eye. Your...Bosun got to him just in time. He talks in his sleep and has said enough to understand. It was close." She took a deep breath. "I need to get back to my family. There is food in the kitchen. Fresh provisions are brought every morning. He's ready for a good wash, if you are up to it when he wakes. He can walk, but it's slow and he should keep standing to a minimum."

Ivy stood, stunned, uncertain of what she was hearing. Then Winter turned and walked away.

"Wait!"

Linc urged Ivy back into the house. "She hasn't left for two days, Ivy. Your turn."

Before she could say another word, the door closed behind her. She was alone with a wounded man who needed her. She drew closer to Duran and stared, unable to think of a word to say. He slept.

Pulling a stool close, Ivy sat. And waited. When he began to dream Ivy wished she could cry.

He mumbled, cursed, even joked, reliving the torture. He never pled. Ivy stood it as long as possible, and then moved to brush at his face, trying to ease the memories. She didn't know where to touch, afraid of hurting him, even with the lightest touch. It worked and he calmed. She used a single finger, stroking his brow, an ear, wherever no bruises hovered. The heat of the day was gone when his eye flicked open.

"Ivy?" He tried to clear his throat and she put a finger to his lips.

"Yes, you bastard. I'm here." She tried to smile. "Winter said you were ready to bathe. The sun was strong today, the water should be hot."

"Not as hot as you, I bet." He winked, then grimaced.

She didn't reply, just shook her head at him, then set about helping him get to his feet. He stumbled and held tight to her as she led him to the outside shower. The wrap at his waist fell and she let it.

There was a bench near the showerhead. It rested on a long pole, but she could detach it and direct it by hand. She led him to it and paused. "I have to get all the bandages off, Duran."

"Yeah, I know. It will hurt. Who cares?" He shrugged, wincing as the bandages were stripped away and set aside.

She growled at the state of his back. "Jesus, you're going to have scars to shame the devil. You bastard...what the hell happened?"

"I got caught," he simple stated. "It happens."

She sighed and took the showerhead in hand. He hissed as the water hit his back, but then relaxed, actually leaning until his head rested at her thighs. "You're getting wet, Ivy."

"Don't you brag about that? How I always get wet for you?" she teased.

"Yeah, that's true, mi corazón," he all but whispered. "God, I missed you."

She looked down at his bent head, the wet hair glistening in a massive tangle. "You should have come with us."

"He would have known you'd gone to sea. He knows about Lina. Doesn't know about the *Windsong*... I led him away, gave you a chance."

"Cost you an eye. What else?" she demanded to know.

"Pain. Just pain." He tilted his head up and met her look. "Helen found me. Guess Daddy blabbed. Damned good woman. Brought Bosun to me. Just in time."

"In time for what?" she asked.

"In time to save my balls. Ursus was done. Diva was just getting started." He groaned, fell against her again.

She trembled at the surge of fury that roared through her. She played the water against his back. Then took up the soap and worked up a lather, and began to wash his hair. "I'm going to kill her, Duran. I'm going to kill them both."

"Good."

Neither spoke for the rest of the shower. Ivy saw him as clean as she could without causing more pain and then stepped back, removed her wet clothing and began to wash herself. The water was growing cold, but it didn't matter. All that mattered was his watching her. She'd freed his hands. Each finger showed cuts, burns, and were swollen to the point of uselessness. His nails had been torn away from several. It took all her willpower not to surge to her feet and scream at the damage. The only blessing? None were gone.

She stood, combed his hair free of tangles, allowing him to inhale at her belly as she did so.

"Ivy?" he spoke into her skin.

"Yeah, Duran?" She braided his hair loosely.

"I don't regret lying to you."

"I know. Good thing you're so beat up, or I'd make you regret it." She grabbed at one of the towels the neighbor left and set it across his shoulders. "Where is Bosun?"

"Down talking to your council, I guess," he answered. "Easy, Ivy. It's getting better, but..."

"What the hell did he use? No, don't tell me. I don't really care." She lightened the touch of the towel. Looking back to the kitchen she saw Prima watching her through the window. The old woman smiled, waved and pointed toward a table.

"I think dinner is here, Duran. What does Bosun do that they all take such good care of him?" She wondered aloud.

"No idea. You gonna wrap the bandages again?" he asked as she helped him stand.

"No. Looks to me like they are ready for air. Can you sleep without a drought to help?"

"I will now." He grinned at her. She held to his wrists as they returned to the house. A basket sat at the center of the table,

Prima was pulling out items. The scent of freshly baked break filled the room. This time Ivy groaned.

She fed Duran carefully. "Why the hell did they leave your teeth alone?" she finally asked.

"Said they wanted you to know it was me by my smile." He lifted his hands, studied them. "He wanted to break my fingers. Pull them off. Diva talked him out of it, said they'd preserve better if he waited." He chuckled, slowly curled his fingers. "Just bruised and burned. She liked to use embers."

"Stop," Prima ordered. "You'll give her nightmares."

Ivy stared at the old woman. Then, in unison, she and Duran began to laugh. Prima glared at the pair of them until they stopped. She left soon after that.

The pair sat and just stared at each other for several minutes. Duran broke the silence. "They aren't going to just let you leave. And I'm not going to be healthy enough for months. You'll have to wait."

"I've already waited long enough," she replied. "You should have told them where I was. He doesn't have any ships, doesn't know how to sail..."

He shook his head. "He has coastal territory now, took two harbors in the last five months. He'd find a fleet. He already has plans to crush Lina. He and Diva bragged about destroying the island by cutting off trade. He'll find a way to send troops once he knows you were here."

She didn't know what to say so she changed the subject. "Are the religious still intent of Emmett?"

"I have no idea. Oh, I killed Bill."

"Good. I hope it was painful." She rose from the table. "I am so tired."

There was a pounding on the door. Before she could reach it, it flew open and Emmett stormed in. He nodded at Duran, stopped before Ivy and just gazed at her. "Don't ever do that to me again. I deserve better from you. What are you going to do about Helen?"

Ivy blinked, confused by the fluttering topics. She shrugged. "I don't know. Thank her next time I see her?"

Emmett snarled, fists clenched, and then took a step back. He pulled a chair up and sat down, stared at Duran. "You didn't tell her?"

"He didn't tell me what?" Ivy stopped Duran from answering. She yawned, terribly exhausted.

"Helen is pregnant with my baby," Emmett spoke solemnly. "We have to get her away from Ursus."

Ivy simple fell to her knees. She bent, hugging her belly. The shock of it simply knocked her down. Pregnancy was so rare. Of all the women to succeed, her daughter?

"You sure it's yours?" she finally spoke.

"She told Bosun I was the father." Emmett left the chair and knelt in front of Ivy. "He'll kill my child."

"Does he know it's yours?" Ivy whispered.

"She won't tell anyone. He is still looking for a Shaman to decipher her mark. He pretends it doesn't matter. But when the baby is born with Cruz traits? He won't stand for it," Emmett all but pled. "Ivy, we have to help her."

"Why didn't she come with Bosun and Duran?" She took his hands. "Maybe she doesn't want to come."

"She said it wasn't safe. Bosun tried to convince her," he replied. "Ivy?"

The plea shot to her center. It found a home with the unspoken dream of rescuing her girl.

Ivy reached out and pulled him into her arms. "I am glad to see you looking so healthy. I'm sure your family took care of you. I'll figure something out, Emmett. I promise."

"She still has three months to go. There is time to formulate a plan," Duran added. "Let her sleep, Emmett. Look at her. Come back tomorrow."

"The council wants to meet with you, soon," Emmett told her.

She let him go and sat back on her heels. "Fuck them. I'm not stupid. They are keeping me from leaving. The wind shifted and the traders still found excuses not to take me to the mainland. I'm not a council toy!"

"If you refuse to see them, to talk to them, nothing will change," Emmett pled.

She snarled, but agreed to the tactic. "Hell. Not tomorrow, Emmett. I need a few days. I feel stretched too thin."

He examined her. She'd put on a shift after the shower, first wrapping a light piece of fabric around Duran's waist. Kneeling on the floor, it did little to hide her gaunt frame. He reached out and touched her cheek. "Didn't you eat?"

"Never. I lived on air." She pushed away and got to her feet. "I'm going to bed."

Duran stayed in his chair. He felt stronger, just seeing her did wonders for his stamina. He wanted to get into bed with her. Watching her saunter away, a sarcastic retort at her lips, simply made him hungrier for her. He met Emmett's eyes. "Tomorrow, lad. Or the day after. I don't know if I can, but I plan on keeping her in bed tomorrow. You've seen her, she's here, she's thin, but she's here."

"You'll do it. Don't hurt yourself, Duran." Emmett stood, then held out a hand and helped the man to his feet. He stood, a trifle unsteady. He looked toward the room where Ivy had gone, took a breath, and a step. Then another. On his own, he left Emmett.

She sprawled on the bed, face down, still wearing the shift. Duran grunted as he sat on the edge of the bed. "Move over, bitchy woman. Tortured man needs room. And get that dress off."

Ivy snorted into the covers.

He poked at her with his elbow. She rolled over to look at him. "You are so full of shit. No fucking tonight, you idiot."

"I might surprise you." He sagged. "Or not. Ivy, I just want to feel you next to me. Chica, mi corazón, let me on the bed."

She sat up, touched. Tossing the simple dress to one side, she helped him remove the loin cloth and slide between the light blankets. She looked down at him. “I saw the marks on your cock, Duran. And your balls.”

“Yes.” He flexed his hands slightly. “The fingers are better.”

“Talk to me, Duran.”

He took a deep breath. “Yes. It was hell. She laughed. Doesn’t mean I can’t fuck you. Might hurt, but that would just make it interesting.”

Her hand clenched at his side.

He knocked her arm away where it propped her up and she fell against him. “There is nothing more to say about it, chica. Sleep. Just touch me, let me feel you next to me sleep. We’ll keep the nightmares away.”

She settled in the crook of his arm. He felt her tension drain away as she grew lax. She was warm. He stared at the ceiling, pushing the memories away. And finally slept.

CHAPTER ELEVEN

Duran woke, aware of his cock. It was painful, but delightfully so. Ivy had sprawled across him as she slept. Her thigh rested at his cock, her hand at his belly. And his body reacted. He welcomed the pain, blessed the desire that still burned bright.

The dawn light was faint so he knew the night had been peaceful. Neither of them had risen with nightmares. He stretched slightly, heard her sigh and settle more firmly on him. He didn't know if it was possible, but he wanted her. Despite the pain. He knew what caused the hurt, the skin was stretching across the damaged tissue. Blood pumped into his cock and woke up everything, good and bad.

He moved the arm tucked under her and very slowly, he eased her atop him. She weighed nothing. She hadn't been exaggerating at living on air the last few months. She'd never been more than a wisp, but now she was past the point of slender. He'd lost weight, but nothing compared to her. Ursus had seen him fed, wanting him strong enough to think he could fight the torture.

Ivy shifted slightly, waking up. Her legs sprawled across him, teasing his erection with the hint of pubic hair. She raised her head. "Are you insane?"

"Yes," he answered, pushing his hips up to nestle in her heat. He could feel how wet she was. She'd been nestled up against him, no doubt dreaming of other mornings. He had no qualms of taking advantage of that. Just a little bit closer...

She set her head down and sighed. "Aren't you hungry?" she managed to speak around a yawn.

"For you, chica. Been too long." He set his hands at her back and pushed her downward. "You're killing me, woman. Have mercy."

She resisted, spoke directly to his chest. "Only if you stop moving. I don't want you to open up any of the scabs and bleed again. I mean it, you move. I leave."

"Shit." He nodded. "Fuck me, Ivy."

"Garbage mouth." She sat up and slid down to surround him. He hissed and she stopped. "You alright?"

"God damned teasing bitch..."

"Ah, that's the man I know." She rose on her knees and swiveled her hips. "If I get off you and see blood, I won't touch you again for weeks. Until I know you're..."

He flexed his butt muscles and she nearly melted. He felt the heat swell out of her, her knees tightened. In the faint light, he saw her nipples draw up into hard nuts. He lifted his hand to touch her and she slammed it back to the bed. "No moving! Stop that!"

"Then move, you frigid bitch!"

She glared down at him, but followed his direction. She rode him with a driven gentleness that drove him mad. He moaned, words spilling from him like rain. He knew dozens of passionate phrases in Spanish and he used them all. Not only was it habit, but they were true. With her. He knew she understood most of them. And the language made them easier for her to accept. She didn't like soft words. He knew the Spanish left her the illusion of not understanding him.

He felt her contracting around him, milking him from the base at his balls to the slit at his tip. She trembled, right at the edge. He flexed his abdominals, though it hurt like hell. And she lost what control she held, falling forward on him. He gripped her ass and slid her up and down his ready cock. With a roar he filled her. The pain was intense, his fingers tried to cramp, his hands burned. And none of it mattered.

The fire burned all of that away. He gasped, holding tightly to her. The sweat they were both coated with made the room chilly. She shivered so he pulled a cover up over the both of them.

"If...if you bled," she murmured a threat.

He kissed the top of her head. "I always bleed for you, mi corazón. Always will."

The two of them drifted back to sleep.

———

They stayed to the house for three days. He grew stronger and she added meat to her bones.

She stood at the kitchen, watching Duran shower. He was recovering fast. She felt more at peace than she had for months. But in the back of her mind, she knew Emmett waited, Helen waited. And Ursus still lived. She removed the bread Prima had left them, setting it to the side.

A shaft of light fell on Duran. He was a beautiful man, despite the damage done in Ursus' dungeon. She smiled as he pulled his head back, into the water. Lust rose in her to a level she didn't know existed. Then he turned away and she saw the eye patch come free, dangle in one hand. He would not let her see under the patch.

She's seen all the bruises fade; the lashes turn toward a simple scarring. But he kept the ruin of his eye from her. She clenched the fruit in her hand, unaware of the juices spurting out from her hand.

"I will avenge thee, Duran," she whispered. The start of pain at her heart surprised her. She knew the rush of passion, the fire of desire. But this was different. He bent to scrub at his feet, still needing the bench to do so and she gasped. The awareness of his vulnerability and what that meant to her, rose to fill her senses. Her heart raced, her breath quickened, her hands trembled.

A sudden clarity entered her mind. She loved that man. Was in love with Duran. She didn't want to leave him ever again, but she had to. She would protect him. He would not walk back into that dungeon... It would be razed. There would be no safety until Ursus and Diva died. Only then would the nightmares end.

She forced the realization away. Wiping her hand and disposing of the fruit pulp, she abandoned the meal preparation and left the house. She needed to talk to her grandfather.

Bosun waited for her in the street. She didn't know how he knew where to be. She didn't care. He listened to her simple request and nodded. She returned to the house, knowing he would do as she'd asked.

Duran waited in the kitchen, looking concerned. She forced a smile onto her face before speaking, "It is time for me to face the elders. Emmett has been patient."

He sighed, then nodded. "Give me another month and I'll be fit to lift a blade again." He flexed his right hand, grimaced. "I need to start practicing."

"Your depth perception is likely to be off, Duran," she calmly stated, all the while plotting to see him out of danger. He still moved too slowly. And would for weeks. Diva may have kept Ursus from breaking bones, but the damage done was still deep.

Early that evening, she left Duran and walked to the council house. There she faced nine elders. The captain of the *Windsong* was there, and he spoke of the new Chan colonies, full of transported Losanglos.

A man from the Trader's Port talked of the few trading ships coming to port, "Three of our ships have returned, nearly empty. The ports have been warned off from doing business with us. For fear of Ursus' vengeance. It could be a rough winter."

Ivy sat through these reports, taking it all in, storing the names of the frightened cities, shuffling the information to place how far

Ursus' influence had spread. She studied the maps Bosun had brought her, familiarizing herself with the coast.

"Ivy. You are ready to speak to us." One of the elders smiled at her. "I am Telsa, one of the island's Shamans. We have waited a long time for you."

"I don't know what you want to hear from me. What you thought I could tell you that Emmett couldn't." Ivy shrugged.

"How were you originally taken by Ursus?" The youngest woman in the group asked.

Ivy swallowed her shock at being asked that. She stared at the woman who had spoken. "Why the fuck do you want to know that? What does it matter? It's history, decades old!"

"Did he seek you out in particular, Ivy? Or was it chance you fell into his hands?" Telsa spoke softly, "We do need to know."

Ivy shot to her feet, began to pace, her mind whirling. This wasn't what she expected. Finally, she stopped and stared at Telsa. "Why do you need to know? Tell me that first."

He sighed and one of the more blunt women answered for him, "Because we need to know if he was following a prophecy blindly, or with direction. Was he looking for you or did he rape every woman he captured."

"Prophecy? I...I was part of a prophecy?" Ivy felt her blood rise. "Shit. Pure shit. You're all so fucking caught up in all that nonsense! Religious mumbo jumbo. Crap! He was angry. I'd been harassing his lines for months. He methodically killed all my men, turned two by promising to let them live and they betrayed me. He killed them anyway. There was no stupid prophecy!"

"I wish that were true," Telsa stood, talking as he walked to her. "I should know. I started it. The promise that a Cruz woman would give birth to his death. Another twisted an answer for him. If he were the father, his death would turn away from him."

Ivy shook her head, drew away from the old Shaman. His prophesy? He started the boulder down the hill? Killing everyone she knew? She nearly spit at him, "Pain, all you've brought to us is pain! All of you wise men and women! Before Ursus killed them all,

I talked with the children from Brekly. They saw the world's doom coming from the stars. It was a stellar phenomenon that twisted the world, broke the back of time. No religion! No wrath of God! No fucking prophecy!"

"That is true." A woman with grey hair trailing to her feet stood. "I am Sammie. I knew many of the Brekly scientists. But that doesn't matter, Ivy. The truth doesn't matter. What is believed matters. Ursus believed the lie and took you. He also believes his death still comes from you. He'll seek you out. As he ages, he grows more determined."

"Oh. Yes. Bringing me here was such a good idea!" Ivy snarled, "Right to the last colony of the Cruz. I can't believe you were so stupid."

"They did it for me, granddaughter." Bosun stepped into the light. "They owe me and I wanted to save you."

"You can't save me. No one can save me. His death did come from a Cruz woman. My mother. I'm going to kill him. Send me back to the mainland. Save yourselves and let me go," Ivy demanded.

"We're formulating a plan, Ivy. You won't go alone. He has to be stopped, and it is time we stopped him." Sammie walked to Ivy and touched her face. "I knew your mother. You look like her in so many ways."

Ivy broke and ran.

Duran looked up when the door flew open. Ivy stormed in, red in the face and obviously angrier than he'd ever seen her. He held up his hands. "I didn't do it."

"Fuck off! You didn't do anything, it's that shit council. Stupid questions, stupid planning! Anything but action." She rubbed at her eyes. "I have to get out of here." I feel like I'm going to crack open."

He snickered. "I'll help."

"Help what? You can't help anything right now," she softened her voice. "No, that isn't true. You do help me, Duran."

"Oh, don't go all soft on me, bitch. Let's ditch them all and head for Trader's Cove," he winked as he spoke.

"They won't take us," she answered.

"They might take us to the new colonies. It's a start." He struggled to get to his feet. One of his feet still pained him a great deal. They'd argued about having the healer come by again to check him out.

She took the decision away from him. "I'm getting Winter. You can't go anywhere until we can get that foot better," she spoke as she turned and left him, still partly sitting.

At the street, she paused. Telsa strode toward her. She growled at him as he held his hands up.

"I am sworn to help you, Ivy," he stated.

"I..." she paused, tilting her head at him. He could be useful. She saw Emmett's other cousin, Alfie, and waved him over. "Duran needs to see Winter again. One of his feet is growing painful again."

"I'll see to it," he stated.

"All right, how can you help me, Telsa?" She gestured at a bench in the shade of some spindly trees.

They talked for hours. Winter came and went, directing Ivy that Duran's foot needed to be wrapped for several days and he needed to stay off of it for a week at least.

"How'd he take that news?" she asked.

"Unhappy, but reconciled," Winter replied. "I left ointment to be used after each cleaning."

"I'll see to it," Ivy reassured her, then turned back to Telsa. Winter left them and she continued the discussion.

"I don't believe in magic, Telsa. How do you intend this to work?" she asked.

"It isn't magic. It is part of my curse and how I have learned to use it," Telsa explained. "You are already gaunt. We wrap your breasts, cut your hair, keep you dirty and my curse will do the rest. Ursus still wants answers to Helen's mark. He isn't going to turn down a Cruz Shaman walking straight into his compound. Once there, we'll use whatever opportunity we find, or make opportunities."

"And how do we get there? You have influence with the *Windsong*?"

"No, I have a boat of my own and the knowledge to sail us there. Conditions are favorable right now. You know the mainland and can lead us to Ursus once we reach land. We have to move quickly, Ivy."

She bowed her head, thinking.

"What is your curse?" she asked quietly. It wasn't something a polite Cruz asked another.

"I can hide in plain sight, Ivy. A sort of not-notice talent."

"No invisibility?" She looked hopeful.

"No, more of a blend-in talent. Trust me. Some mild disguise and I can throw it on you enough that no one will remark on you at all."

Ivy rolled her shoulders, took a breath and asked, "When, Telsa?"

"Tonight. There is no moon, the tides are right. We can be gone before the council comes looking for you. Will you take Emmett?"

She thought about it for over a minute. He would be so angry, but unlike Ursus' people, the religious zealots were everywhere. And looking for him. "No. I can handle his anger. But the religious are still searching for him and they are everywhere. Ursus is enough to deal with. One foe at a time," she whispered. "What time?"

"Two hours past midnight. Follow the coast trail north of the city. Bring nothing, Ivy. Just you, no weapons. He knows your weapons."

"I know how to infiltrate, Telsa. I'll be there." She got to her feet, sighed heavily.

It was a hard decision to make, but it was hers. It was time to end this game.

She went next door and obtained a small amount of the herbal sleeping mixture Winter had been giving Duran, using the excuse of nightmares. Then she set her facial features into calm and returned to her warrior.

He sat in a chair, an expression of introspection heavy on his face. She sighed. "Winter told me. I'm sorry. We'll go to Trader's Cove when you're better. I can avoid the council. They aren't going to force me into anything. She say why it worsened?"

"Just used it too much. The left was more severely injured to begin with. I'd hurt it slightly while on the run from them before capture." He examined her face. "Why were you so pissed before?"

"One of the council admitted to spreading a false prophecy. One that set Ursus on the path of raping Cruz women. He apologized!" She growled and shook her head.

"Why would anyone do that?"

"I suppose he simply thought it a threat Ursus couldn't address. A Cruz woman will give birth to your death? One of his religious asswipes told him the way around it was to be the father of that child. Twisted, torn, taken over..." She snorted. "I guess I'm the only one that got pregnant, so I became the focus of all of it."

"I'm sorry. The religious mess everything up." He wrinkled his nose. "And Ursus uses them brilliantly. Did the council talk about Helen?"

"I don't know. I left. Just so much blathering!" Ivy strode to where he sat and bent to examine the newly wrapped foot. "I hear she left some ointment?"

"Yeah." He reached out to touch her hair with a gentle hand. His fingers were still swollen, but he simply used a light touch. Duran was a thoughtful man to begin with. Ivy closed her eyes, enjoying the interlude. What was ahead of her would be difficult enough; she wanted some softer memories to take along.

They ate a light meal, then retired to the bedroom. There, Ivy wandered his body for hours. She lingered at his lips, healed more than the rest of him. The taste of him, dark and deep, made her strong. His prick still held the marks of Diva's fire. Ivy licked, kissed and suckled him there with more care than she'd ever shown another human.

He prayed into the night, aware of something changed. He asked her and she denied, "I just feel sorry for you, fool. Shut up."

He murmured and she maneuvered herself so that she was above his lips. That shut him up as he savored her, using his strength to pull her down tightly over his face. It nearly undid her. She fell atop him, after a screaming climax. He manhandled her until she sank around his cock and then flipped her over.

"Duran! Don't...your foot!"

"I'm on me knees, woman. Shut up." He threw himself into her, a desperate claim. Duran strove to hold her still, fucked her hard and fast until she all but beat against his back. He found himself and softened his attack. Lowering his face to her breast, he sucked at her nipples, pausing to savor her excitement.

At last, they both lay sedate. Ivy climbed from the bed. "I'm going to get some tea."

He lay back, gazing at the ceiling until she returned. She brought him a cup and helped him drink. He had no inkling that she'd slipped the draught into the tea. He set the cup down and eased back on the pillows. She curled up, her head at his chest. As she felt the sleeping medicine take him down, she whispered straight to his heart.

"Mi corazón...my love... I wish, I wish, I wish..."

By two o'clock, she had made her way through the town, found the northern path and met Telsa. He took her to a small boat and they left for the mainland. With her, she packed the bandages left over from Duran. It took them three days.

When they reached the coast, at a small harbor named Pine Point, they cut her hair off, shaving it down to the skull in several places. She rubbed dirt into her face, arms and legs. And let Telsa push his curse onto her. It felt wrong. Her skin itched with it, but she let it be.

They headed north for Ursus' territory. Within a week they were collected by a patrol and hurried to the compound.

CHAPTER TWELVE

Duran woke that morning full of misgivings. The small house echoed with quiet. He had a slight headache and his mouth parched. He quickly realized his sleep had been too smooth to be natural.

"Ivy!" No answer. He swung his legs off the bed and paused. He saw her small satchel in the corner. Her ax sheath hung from a hook, the blade intact. Carefully, he worked his way to the outer room. No one there.

He swallowed a sense of dread, all but hopping to the door. Winter walked toward him with a crutch in her hand. She hurried, chastising him for trying to walk. "I told you yesterday! Here, use this if you must move about."

He took the crutch, his eyes still searching the street. "Have you seen Ivy this morning?"

"No, but she is seldom seen out on the street. Why?"

Emmett hurried toward them. "Where is she? The council wants to discuss how to stop Ursus."

"I don't know where she is. She dosed me last night. Her kit is still here," Duran answered. "I have a bad feeling, Emmett. Why would she dose me unless she wanted me out of way? She's done something stupid." He thought about how she'd eyed his wounds, the hard look in her eyes. That little witch lived for vengeance. And Ursus fueled that, again. With him.

They both turned to look down into the bay. The *Windsong* was still in port.

He should have found that reassuring, but he didn't.

By the end of the day, they knew she'd gone. Telsa and his boat had to have been her passage. The debate on what to do began.

Emmett moved into Bosun's house. Ivy's grandfather returned and they plotted, ignoring the council, drawing the *Windsong*'s captain into their confidence. A plan formed.

"No matter what the two of them do...they'll need an escape route ready. If they are caught, they need to be rescued." Bosun was practical. "I can find them. I can find anyone."

"Why did it take you so long to find her? Twenty years?" Emmett asked bitterly.

"I wasn't looking. Thought everyone was dead." Bosun sighed,

"Shut up, quick bickering," Duran growled at them. "Who the fuck cares? You can find them; the captain here can get us away from the mainland and any pursuit. I have allies and family scattered everywhere. We've been keeping an eye on Ursus for years now. Emmett, the religious are looking for you. I'm not sure it's safe for you to come."

"Like hell! I am not staying put! She's my partner. Helen is carrying my baby. Don't even consider leaving me. I'm going!" Emmett glared at Duran.

The Losanglo snickered, admiring his spirit. Growing up with Ivy as a mentor had twisted him into a real fighter. "Fine. But you better curb that curse, offer no clue to your identity."

"And you, that foot. How will we move fast with you gimping about?" Emmett poked at Duran.

"I can move fast on a crutch and we'll get horses." Duran studied Emmett as if preparing to strike him. He had her mouth, too.

"You two, knock it off," Bosun calmly intruded into the mutual glaring contest. "Quit blaming each other for her sneaking off. You want to save her from this folly or just beat the shit out of each other?"

Duran curled a lip at Emmett, but a lift of an eyebrow signaled his willingness to ease off.

Emmett sighed and took a step back. "I can't believe she did this to me again."

"Yeah, I was owed. Don't know why she's being such a bitch to you," Duran agreed.

"She must be very determined to cross the strait in Telsa's small boat. She was terrified on the *Windsong*," Captain Leonardo ventured into the fray. "That comes from either deep love or deep hate. Not from a desire to piss anyone off."

"No, but that would be icing on the cake for her," Duran chuckled. He sobered. "We will work together, no fear of dissension, Bosun. I want her back. I'm not done with her in my bed."

"You'll never be done with her, Duran. It's apparent." Emmett shook his head. "Obvious enough that Ursus thought he could use you to draw her into his clutches. He underestimated how far you'd go to keep her safe."

"He underestimates most of us. Good." Duran didn't address Emmett's first comment. He knew it was true, but he held out little hope of the situation ever changing. He'd had the strangest dream the night Ivy left him. Thought he'd heard her speak of love.

It had to be a dream...

Despite their determination, it took more than two weeks to mount their offensive. The council convinced Leonardo to hold off leaving until more could be sent. In the end, seven climbed aboard the *Windsong*. Armed with the best the remaining Cruz could put together, they left for the mainland. The *Windsong* lingered near the coast, as Bosun used his gift to see them as close as possible before landing. His curse was an actual blessing. He always found what he sought.

The ups and downs of Cruz curses mystified Duran. So many ended up totally useless, like Emmett's but then there was Bosun's... the most practical he'd heard of. Ivy and Emmett thought they were so careful with the boy's curse, but he'd deduced it years ago. Not so hard when they refused to enter ruins that held useful provisions.

Many of the more northern coastal communities had never seen the *Windsong* and wondered at the ghost from the past, floating just out of reach. It was another week before Bosun said they were as near as they were going to get.

Duran studied the map, pointed to a small cove. "There, I know a family there that will help. Where will you wait, Captain Leonardo?"

"We will move out of sight of land, head south then return. How long do we patrol, assuming you are successful?"

Bosun looked at Duran before speaking, "Give us two weeks. Then head for Hidden Cove, where you picked her up originally. It is a good place for survivors to take refuge. As for past that? I don't know. Use your best judgment."

The seven waited until dark to move to Peter's Harbor.

Ivy and Telsa traveled together well enough. She babbled constantly on the trip over, attempting to keep her nervousness at bay. She did not like being on the ocean or how close the water was to the sides of the boat. It was unnerving, making sleep fitful and short.

Telsa not only listened, he worked to engage her in distracting discussion. And so she learned more about what the break in time meant.

"They scientists at Brekly saw it coming, as you know. They couldn't tell for certain if it would hit the earth. They saw it pass the outer planets, some were left untouched, and some appeared to instantly age. One became a sun, another burnt out to nothing. They could do nothing. So they waited."

"How horrible," she whispered. "The rest of the world just kept living, they never told anyone?"

"They weren't sure what they were seeing. The debate raged behind the scenes, until it was too late. Not that telling the world would have made a difference."

"For my family, the world simple changed..." She let the thought hang.

"For some it happened that way. For others? A terrible thing. I spoke with one man who saw everything around him instantly age and shift. People around him simply turned to dust. Buildings fell, faded, the land moved, weather sped past him. Years sped past him. But none touched him and he never understood that. No survivor understood why he or she was left untouched. Which is how the religious made such inroads."

"Perhaps if the scientists had spoken of it, the religious wouldn't have risen to such prominence?"

"Or they simply would have roared louder as the phenomenon headed for us. It is the nature of religion to take advantage of confusion to recruit believers. They offer comfort. It isn't always about politics, influence and survival." He glanced at her.

She snorted. "That hasn't been my experience. But I do know others who are content in their belief. Who don't hammer at those who don't share them. The Cruz have seldom shown a need for any religious belief."

She found it interesting to discuss all of this. Her grandmother knew much, but shared little. And what she did share reeked of bitterness. The only parts of the past that Grandmother revealed with joy had been the music. But she'd shared little enough of that. And aside from making observations about the few sanctuaries, never speculated about why they survived.

"But what is Gathering Valley? Or the *Windsong*?" Ivy asked.

"I don't know. I think they are places where the time-break

skipped. A sort of place between the world of what was and what is. I asked one of the tenants once and he agreed that was as good an explanation as anything else. He didn't know why they had electricity, food, water...all the comforts of the old world. They simply did and always would, he thought." Telsa kept her thinking of anything but the water just outside the boat. The depth of his knowledge regarding the valley wasn't his to share. He told her what he could.

Once they reached the shore, the conversations ceased.

He apologized as he cut her hair with deliberate harshness. The long hair fell in tangled strands. She'd thought of braiding it and tucking it away. But it didn't matter and was too dangerous. Instead of being upset as the weight disappeared, she just shrugged. Once they'd made land, she shut up. Fighting the overwhelming fear and buried hope took all her energy. She was walking back into his den. Where her daughter lived. But also housed a chance for vengeance, to extract pain for the horror she'd lived.

When they were picked up by the patrol, Telsa introduced her as a mute boy, frightened of most everything. Ivy took to the part with careless abandon. Telsa's curse served them well. The soldiers barely took note of her.

When they reached the compound, they were shoved into a small room and told to wait. They fetched Telsa eventually, took him to meet with Ursus and examine Helen. He'd been blunt when the patrol found them; he was the Shaman with the answers Ursus sought. Ivy kept to the small room, only wandering out to haunt the kitchen. She made herself useful and scouted for a good knife.

She didn't see Ursus or Helen. Diva visited the kitchen often and sat with the cook, telling stories to curdle the blood. Before he'd lost a leg the cook had been a singularly bloodthirsty soldier for Ursus. With an odd culinary talent.

Ivy held herself from sliding a knife into Diva's back. She wanted them both and she could be patient. Instead, she listened, huddled in a corner gnawing on a heel of bread, living the lie Telsa had given her.

The Shaman often met with Helen. Telling Ursus he needed to get to know the woman to assess the mark on her thigh. Ursus kept busy coordinating a plan to march through the SanGabes to reach the Losanglos. He dined with his daughter and Telsa, but spoke little.

Telsa shared whatever he learned with Ivy. "He drinks a great deal. And I don't like how he studies his daughter. There is an unwholesome look in his eye," Telsa whispered to Ivy as they cuddled together at night. A week had passed and the cell they were given never grew warm.

She simply nodded, signaling her understanding him.

"She knows who I am, and why am I here. She doesn't know you are here. She thinks Emmett sent me to take her away. She insists she won't go."

Fool, Ivy mouthed.

"She loves her father, but she isn't a fool. She is worried about this new campaign and she hates her father's advisor."

Diva!

"Yes, but not just Diva. There are three generals, for lack of a better word. They are a determined as she to shed blood. And they look at Helen with hunger."

Ivy shrugged.

Telsa suddenly froze. His body stiffened so much, Ivy reached out to touch his head. His gaze snapped to hers. "That is the way Ursus looks at her. She is in danger, Ivy. Who better to give him more children if you are out of reach?"

Ivy grimaced, closed her eyes a moment, remembering something she'd overheard earlier that day.

About when it would be safest to add the ingredient to keep her from dying?

She thought they'd been talking about the latest women Ursus was keeping in his bed. But why would they worry about a safe time to poison a woman? Did they mean to poison Helen?

She moved her lips next to his ear and with a bare breath, whispered her suspicions. It was hard, she hadn't spoken in weeks. He nodded.

"Poison but not kill...why?" He sighed.

She shook her head, not knowing.

"Did they decide on when?" he asked her.

Ivy tapped on his chest three times.

"What meal?"

She drew an 'S' on his chest.

"Supper in three days. I will announce my deduction then. I believe he will clear the chamber, he doesn't trust any to know. I will propose you serve since you are mute."

She nodded in agreement. Soon, it would be over soon. And she'd either be dead or he would be. And Diva, she would kill Diva, avenge Duran's pain. She left the rest to Telsa. If they survived, they'd get away.

"You know?" she whispered. "Her mark?"

"For the most part. It is confusing." He sighed. "You have been left alone?"

She nodded.

"See if you can learn anything more in the kitchen." He always held her close, often stroking the bristle of hair growing out from the near shearing of two weeks earlier. Never sexual, he just seemed to find comfort in holding her. She assumed he carried a lot of guilt over how his stupid spouting off to a young Ursus set all of this in motion. She wasn't above using Telsa's guilt to further her goals.

She fell asleep feeling his curse seep deeper into her. It exhausted him, but it didn't matter. She had to be safe to deliver the blow. He'd survive.

Three days. He had three days to win Helen over completely. Her daughter knew the secret passages out of the compound and would see them to safety. He had to convince her to accompany them. Ivy figured if he didn't she'd just grab her. Might be difficult, if the girl balked once her father was dead. By Ivy's hand, but it didn't matter. If Telsa was right, the only way that girl would survive sane was if her father died. And if the cost meant losing any chance of connecting with her daughter? Ivy would pay that. Despite what the girl wanted, Emmett's baby wouldn't be born here.

The next few days saw Ivy all but haunting the kitchen. The few who actually noticed her just assumed she was starving and let her be. She did help out, proving she could carry heavy loads and obey orders. She curled in the cold fireplace, rocking, when Diva entered. The rest of the staff was absent. Ivy closed her eyes and listened.

"Her cup, the one with ivy painted on it." The cook pointed to a tray with an odd assortment of cups on it. Remnants from before the world changed.

"I'll take care of it," Diva stated. She glanced down where Ivy huddled. Ivy kept her breathing even and deep, feigning sleep.

"Use that boy to serve. If poison is suspected, he can take the blame. It will be fast. She's strong and will carry more children."

With that, Ivy understood. The poison was to kill Emmett's child so Helen would be free to conceive another. By the man Diva chose. Ivy kept her temper, stone cold determined to stop it all.

The cook kept close track of the knives. But there would be cutlery at the dinner.

The next night Telsa found her in the kitchen. "Boy, you're needed to serve the warlord tonight. Just take what the cook gives you and follow the guard to the room."

Ivy nodded, keeping her head down. They would be ready.

The meal began easily enough. Telsa actually sat with Ursus, Helen and Diva. The room was clear of everyone else. Telsa made it plain that Helen's curse must stay private or he would not speak of it.

Ivy took entrees from the cook into the room, set it down and stood to one side. Until they were done. The cup pointed out to Diva days earlier was still waiting, intended for an after dinner bit of drink. Ivy had seen Diva whirl a liquid into the cup hours before, even paint the lip.

A stilted conversation stuttered on and off as they ate. Helen was pale, and did little more than push the food around her plate. Ivy noted the swollen belly and wondered how she was so certain the baby belonged to Emmett. But there was no choice but to believe the girl. She would know who shared her bed.

Diva bid her to clear the dishes and bring the drink tray. "And lock the door behind you when you return, boy."

Ivy swallowed her rage and followed orders. She'd managed to sneak away a single knife, tucked into the bindings for her breast, just in reach of her hand, tucked into the small of her back.

As she walked down the hallway, she considered Ursus. He didn't look well. The last few months had not been kind. Ivy thought he had gained every pound she had lost, and more. His nose was red, his cheeks flush, and his skin had an unhealthy pallor to it. But his eyes were still keen. And she had no doubt he still carried speed. She would not underestimate him.

She'd noted how Telsa had kept hold of a knife. They had worked out the night before how he would hold one as she took the other. Who would be the first would be determined by opportunity. He had warned her to expect a drain of the curse that kept her hidden, needed to keep the room secure.

She returned with the sturdy tray. It held a heavy clay carafe, with a large handle, and three cups. Diva directed her to pour the drink. Ivy deliberately spilled the hot drink all over Diva, so that the woman soared to her feet, cursing. Ivy ducked her head, appearing terrified. She still held the carafe. When Diva turned back to the table, disgust plain on her face, Ivy saw Helen raise her cup to her lips, a sly grin on her face. No doubt she'd enjoyed seeing Diva drenched.

Ivy screamed, "No!" and struck Diva across the head with the carafe. It shattered and Diva tottered. "Poison!" Ivy pushed the black woman aside. "It will kill the baby!"

Helen threw the cup away as Diva spun to confront Ivy. The

curse fell and Ivy stood straight. And she struck at the woman in front of her, using the broken handle, still in her hand. It struck as true as a knife would have, slicing Diva's face open from one cheek, across the nose, taking one eye with it.

Ivy grinned. "For Duran!" she hissed.

Diva spun away, blood splashed along the floor. Ivy followed up with the sturdy tray, smashing it down on the back of Diva's head. Ursus' agent collapsed to the floor and didn't move again.

Ivy stood over her panting, then looked up to see Telsa, a knife at Ursus' throat. Helen gazed at her father. "Did you know?"

"Know what?" Ursus was strangely calm.

"That she planned on poisoning me?"

"You believe that crazy bitch?" He glowered at his daughter, then at Ivy. He winked.

Ivy saw red and took a step closer, the tray still in her hands.

Helen moved between her mother and father, her eyes darting between them. "How did you know about the poison?" Helen addressed her mother.

"She hid under my curse and was in the kitchen when Diva plotted with the cook to serve you the abortive," Telsa answered.

"Why?" Helen again addressed her father.

"I don't know what Diva was planning." Her father stayed perfectly still, the blade at his throat.

"I saw how you watched her prepare to drink. You lie." Telsa quietly stated. "Helen, you have no reason to distrust me. I have been honest with you in all things, save the presence of your mother."

"Why?" Helen's voice broke with uncertainty.

"So he could free you to bear a child of his choice. Likely, of his," Ivy managed to hoarsely state. "Telsa saw it in his eyes."

Helen staggered, a hand went to her belly. For a moment, the Shaman was distracted and Ursus struck. Telsa fell to one side, gasping as Ursus rose to meet Ivy's charge.

All her life, she had waited for this chance. To thrust death into the man who had tormented her. She threw the tray and Ursus easily deflected it. He didn't bother to draw a weapon, he simply threw himself at Ivy. He was larger, but Ivy was balanced better. She darted to one side, Ursus staggered, nearly tripping on Diva's sprawled legs. He kicked out. "Stupid bitch." He glanced down at his dying lieutenant.

Ivy danced toward the large fireplace, drew her blade and beckoned at Ursus with her free hand. Helen ran to Telsa and helped him stand.

Ursus smirked. "Well, now you can return where you belong. Under me, on my bed. I want a son this time, Ivy."

"No," Ivy managed to state. "You die this time."

He laughed. He moved faster than Ivy thought possible. She barely made it to one side, thrusting at his back with her blade as he drew past her. One leg, still in his path, saw him twist and her blade missed. He fell.

Ivy landed on his back with her knees, her hand gripped his hair and pulled his head up prepared to slit his throat.

"No! Please!" Helen shouted.

Ivy paused. For the first time in her life, she heard a daughter's plea and listened. The trembling of her arm, her gasping breath, the adrenaline rush of being so close to her life dream...stopped by a woman's simple plea. Ivy tottered.

Telsa studied Ursus when Ivy lowered the blade, suddenly aware of the lack of fight in the figure beneath her. "I think he's dead."

"What?" Helen staggered over to her father.

Ivy looked down at the monster and dropped his head. He was still. They rolled him over. He had fallen onto the corner of the hearth. Blood covered his face and his forehead was unnaturally dented.

Helen set a hand at his chest. "He's breathing."

Ivy found it hard to catch her breath. She staggered away, leaning on the wall. The knife dropped from her hand.

Telsa knelt next to Helen. "No one can survive that blow. He may be breathing, but he is dead. Let him go, Helen. He meant to destroy you."

"I...I don't know that!" she sobbed.

"I do," Ivy whispered.

A pounding on the door interrupted the silence in the room. Telsa threw out a hand at Ivy and she felt his curse fall on her again.

He took Helen's hand. "Will you deliver us to death?"

She called out, amazingly collected, "Gero! Break the door down! Hurry!" Next, she pushed Telsa toward Ivy. "Let me explain it all."

The door shook, and then crashed into the room. A huge man rushed in, holding a short sword in his hand. Helen took control, rising to her feet. Her shirt was covered in her father's blood. She gestured at Diva. "That bitch. I never trusted her! She attacked me! My father tried to intervene, but he fell! He hit his head... That boy struck her down..."

Gero knelt down to feel Diva's pulse. "She's alive...Ursus?"

"He's alive, but barely. Drop her in a cell and get help for my father. Get those two to their room. Thank you, boy," Helen wiped at her face, smearing it with blood. An escort took Telsa and Ivy back to their room. Ivy curled up into a corner, the shock of it too much to handle. Telsa sat on the bed, attempting to plan further.

Ivy kept repeating in her head. *Alive. Alive. Not finished. Fuck. Fuck! Fuck!*

It had all happened so fast. She couldn't keep it straight in her head. Always, she figured the details would stay fresh in her head. The memory of sliding a knife into his gut and yanking it upward. But it didn't happen that way.

She shivered, unable to relax. Muscles cried out for her to let go of the tension. She couldn't. Telsa left the room, summoned by Helen and Ivy simply sat, staring at nothing.

He returned after some hours and attempted to get her onto the bed. She didn't cooperate, simple sat, clinging to her knees. He laid a blanket around her and didn't push. The next morning, he left again. This time, two men entered the room; ignoring her they began to search.

"Ingra said he sketched the mark down on a tablet, kept it with him. Made notes."

The other grunted, lifting the light cot up and searching under it. "No where to hide stuff in this room. Think he still has it with him?"

"Maybe." The first speaker glanced at Ivy, but his eyes shifted away, as if he couldn't focus on her.

"It's going to take some persuasion to get the truth out of him. Decide whether she's worth keeping or too much trouble." This was the one with part of an ear missing.

"Oh, I'll keep her. Least for a little while, till I'm done with her." The taller one loaded his comment with so much innuendo; Ivy fought the urge to growl.

"Fine, you take her, I'll take command," Notch-ear shot back.

"Like hell! I'll take both!" Tall-man stood and glared at his partner in the search.

The other backed off slightly, shaking his head. "Let's see if she survives the baby dying first. And find out from that bastard Shaman what her mark means."

"Diva didn't dose her." Tall-man paused, "Ah, once the brat is born? I say we see how green it is first."

Notch-ear tossed the pack he'd been searching through to the floor. "I say slit its throat anyway. Or...use it to keep her in line. She is his daughter and the troops set great score on his fathering a child. And now she has a child. Let's do it that way. Make her choose. You or me."

The other considered the idea. Ivy could see neither would live up to whatever agreement they came to right now. Treachery lay all over their faces. But Tall-man nodded, held out his hand. They shook on it.

"We tell her tonight, make sure she knows there is no way out." Notch-ear spat on the floor.

They left without making comment on Ivy's presence. She shivered, Telsa must have thrown more of his curse at her than before.

When the Shaman got back, Ivy managed to haul herself out of the stupor long enough to relate to him what she had overheard. He nodded. "She's going to see us out of here before dawn...now she'll have to come with us."

CHAPTER THIRTEEN

Ivy's feet no longer registered the rough path. Her eyes couldn't focus. Helen led the way down a trail to a gate, set in a thick hedge. Her daughter had been arguing with Telsa since they'd left the buildings behind.

"No. I don't care..." Helen's voice stopped as the gate swung open. Emmett grabbed her. He swept his other hand up to keep her quiet, drew her face upward so she could see who held her.

Ivy just quietly snorted, not terribly surprised. But glad it hadn't been an enemy, she was too fucking numb to react.

Emmett removed his hand from Helen's mouth, letting it settle on the mound at her belly. Ivy slid to one side and saw it all. Saw Helen smile slightly. "Take them. Get them out of here."

Not a chance in hell.

"Bring her. She's being stupid," Telsa stated.

"I can handle Buckler, Gero and Jango," she hissed.

Emmett studied Telsa. "Where is...Ivy?"

Ivy knew the curse was effective, but Emmett couldn't see her?

"I have her covered in my curse. I can't focus to remove it right now. Helen, those two mean to use Emmett's baby to manipulate you. They have more men at their command. Hell, your own cook agreed with Diva's attempt to kill that baby." Telsa kept his voice low. The wind sheltered them, but sharp voices would carry. "Come with us. Once your curse is revealed, I fear you'll be useless to them."

"Tell me what it is before you leave," Helen requested, still stubbornly determined. Ivy waited for Emmett to handle the situation. He did.

The young man sighed, and before Helen could protest, he had her hands bound together, and a gag at her mouth. He bent to meet her outraged eyes. "I will not lose you, this baby, or Ivy. If Telsa says there is danger, there is danger. Don't be stupid. Come with us. We'll talk as we run. If you convince me, we'll set you free."

He gave her no chance to reply, simply swept her into his arms and the fugitives faded into the forest. Ivy approved and followed, all but unnoticed by Bosun and the others. Only Telsa, who swept an arm around her, trying to offer her shelter from the storm, appeared aware of her at all. She wondered where Duran was, hoped he was still on Lina. This weather would be hell on his foot.

They were camped the next night when the lookout rushed into camp. "There's a huge force marching this way. Lit torches, scouts out front!"

"Fuck!" Bosun cursed. He thrust Helen and Ivy onto a horse, gave Telsa the reins. "Get the hell out of here! Felton, Dano...take the other horse and bait a new trail. I'll meet Durn and stop him leading the rest into a trap! Go!"

Telsa unerringly took off. Ivy held tightly to Helen, who had shown a stubborn streak and kept attempting to return to the compound. She claimed to believe the threat as real, but maintained she could handle the two generals. They kept her wrists bound and she was never out of sight.

Ivy had said nothing during the argument. Telsa's curse continued to make it difficult for the others to even register her presence. Helen appeared to see her mother clearly. But Ivy still wouldn't talk, she wasn't sure she could.

At least Telsa had mentioned Duran, so Ivy knew he waited with fresh horses along the escape route. That must have grated! To be left with horses. But his foot had been a problem.

Ivy simply didn't want to talk. The arguments and discussions meant nothing to her.

Ursus, alive!

She focused on her failure to see the bastard dead. And Diva. She planned how to use this curse of Telsa's to get away from the rest and return to the compound, finish the job.

If only she weren't so cold.

Hours after they had split up, she became aware that the forest had changed from oak to redwood. She shook her head, that wasn't possible. Telsa took them a path she didn't recognize. And she knew all the paths. When she saw a pair of great stones ahead of them, she blinked. They were too far from Gathering Valley.

But as he led them through the stones, the shadows of the familiar buildings rose. Ivy gripped her daughter's hands, turned her head. "Helen!"

Her voice, barely above a whisper, didn't stir the half-sleeping woman. Ivy pinched the flesh of her wrist. "Helen!"

"What?" Helen spoke softly, awake now.

"Some odd...magic. Don't step outside the path Telsa leads. Danger!" Ivy remembered when she and Emmett had stumbled through this gate. Nearly dead from the giving birth, desperation drove her and Emmett on a path they weren't aware of. And so they'd found Gathering Valley when it should have been shadowed.

It had sped her healing, but what would it do to a pregnant woman?

Telsa paused, the horse looked interested at a shadow to the front.

"This is not your time, Telsa. Why are you here?" A voice spoke from the dark.

"My need is great. We seek shelter until our forces gather, nothing else."

"Who is with you?"

"Ivy and her daughter, Helen. Helen carries Emmett's child. Ursus is dying and we are pursued by those full of ambition, seeking to seize her and take his lands." Telsa summed their situation up concisely.

"Ivy?" Dave stepped into the light, holding up a lantern. He blinked at her, shook his head then grinned as he focused again. "Nice, Telsa. She's covered in deception. Follow me, do not deviate." He turned and led them through the streets.

Ivy fought not to look at the buildings. She knew this place distorted time when the Gathering was absent. The tenants managed it well, but it was perilous for the rest. Dave told her in detail over twenty years ago about it. When she was invited to stay.

Helen leaned closer, whispered, "What is the danger..." her voice faded. "Why do the buildings lean...?"

"Time is out of place here." Ivy tried to keep it simple. "Close your eyes, it's catching."

"Catching?" Helen shuddered, then Ivy felt her bury her face against her shoulder.

Good. Safest that way.

Ivy kept her eyes on the horse's head, gripped the mane and just waited. Dave would find them a place to shelter.

Finally, they entered a small courtyard. A fountain splashed water in the center. He helped both women down as Telsa tied the horse's reigns to a post and fed it a handful of oats. Dave promised more hay for their mount. Ivy bent and untied her daughter's hands. "I'm trusting you here. You saw the streets, don't wander, Helen. Or that baby could grow beyond you in a moment." Why had her voice returned? Had to be the valley's influence...

Dave nodded. "She is right. Stay here. I'll clear a path to see you ahead of your pursuers."

"What of Emmett and the rest?" Helen asked, rubbing at her wrists.

"I'll scout around the valley and find them. Bosun will sniff us out." Telsa drank deep of the flowing water and smiled. "Always choice water."

"You know what to watch for." Dave nodded at Telsa, then left them to the courtyard.

Ivy hauled the rations off the horse, watching Telsa straighten with a hand at his back. "You should rest," she hoarsely said, coughing slightly.

"And you should stop worrying about his not dying. He's dead, Ivy. No one could shake off that blow."

"He's strong!" Helen tried to defend her father. At the glance the other two threw at her, she sighed and turned away. "I know, he is a terrible man... I know."

"What he planned for you was evil, not just terrible," Telsa stated.

Before Helen could offer retort, the shaman stepped from the courtyard. Helen surged after him, but Ivy caught her, threw her toward the fountain. "You will kill yourself and the baby! Stay here! Fight with me!"

"You don't fight, you just ignore me," Helen sighed. Then she sat on the fountain edge, bent and washed her wrists. "I don't need to be tied."

"Yes, you do," Ivy cleared her throat again. Her voice grew no stronger as the hours passed, remaining locked in a whisper. She wondered if it were part of Telsa's curse, to keep her from betraying herself with words.

Helen fell asleep, which Ivy was grateful for. She didn't know how she felt about her daughter and the baby she carried. The cry of '*please, don't*!' still echoed in her mind. If she'd ignored those words...if she'd used that knife, there would be no doubt.

Why did she stop? She didn't want to give a rat's ass for Helen. She'd given her over without a second thought.

Oh, what a lie.

If only she could believe it, perhaps her life would have been easier. No, she'd abandoned her baby to be raised by a monster.

And she would forever pay for that. As long as Helen didn't pay, it just didn't matter.

Though the truth of it included no choice in the matter. But if she believed that... No, she'd been useless. Hadn't even tried to protest.

Ursus took the baby without a backward glance at the bleeding woman on the cell floor. Ivy considered it a fair trade to the lax security that saw them able to escape afterward.

Ivy studied her hands. There was still a trace of Diva's blood under the nails. So tired...

Dave entered the courtyard. With a glance at Helen's sleeping form, he bent and took Ivy's hand. He whispered, "Take this knife. Telsa is in trouble..."

Ivy rose without hesitation. She knew the valley dwellers didn't interfere with outside affairs. But they could observe and share information. She followed Dave a convoluted path to another pair of smaller stones. He led her out of the valley, to a small clearing. A fire roared at the center, over a dozen men sat around the fire, drinking and telling nasty jokes to each other.

Across the clearing, Telsa stood, tied to a tree. Two men continuously punched him, pausing to ask questions. Telsa stayed silent, ignored them. Ivy skirted the light of the fire to make her way to the two bullies. She paused at the bloody bundle thrown carelessly to one side. She bent. It was Dano, dead.

She closed his eyes, stilled her heart and stood. A knife was buried in Dano's belly. She pulled it forth. Two knives, two to take down. Just then, one of the brutes turned away from Telsa and walked to the fire. A small fight broke out as he snatched away a bottle and drank.

A great howling came from the far side of the fire. This had to be Dave's distraction. The men rose, all attention away from the prisoner. Ivy slid up next to Telsa and slit the rope holding him to the tree. She threw the other knife with deadly precision and the other tormentor fell. Ivy all but carried Telsa from the ring of fire. Within moments, Dave was there to help her.

And they faded back into the time distortion of the valley.

Helen woke up to find herself alone. She sat a moment, and thought about what to do. She set a hand on her belly. Seven months along and the baby was a quiet one. She seldom felt a kick, though he appeared to be swimming at times. When Emmett had touched her belly, she swore there had been a surge toward that hand. It was so strange. The midwife who had overseen her birth spoke to her often about what to expect, but the fear still lingered. So few gave birth, so the process was a lonely one.

Her mother had done this in a cell. With one lone boy keeping watch. The midwife visited once a week. "Your mother had to held down when I was fetched to examine her. It weren't a happy place for her. That boy did a good job at keeping her calm. But she fought me, every time."

It was a hard truth for Helen to hear, but hear it she did. And heeded the truth of what her father had done to her mother.

"Is it true? That he would have done the same to me?" she wondered aloud. The only answer came with the bright sound of the fountain. She stared into the water, remembering how her father changed after Diva came. The water caught the bit of light in the courtyard and in that glitter the truth of the memories filled her. A single tear trickled down her face. He had always been a monster. He simple wasn't a monster to her.

She jerked to her feet, looking for some shelter from this harshness. The bitter cries of the women he would chain to his bed filled her. Their accusations rang in her head. With a cry, she sought escape. The strangeness of the dark buildings, tilting oddly, didn't stop her. She dashed down the alley they had entered through.

"Stop," Telsa gasped.

Dave eased him down as Ivy paused. She turned back. "I can tend him back at the courtyard!"

"He isn't going to make it to the courtyard," Dave replied.

Ivy threw her head back, ready to scream her frustration.

Telsa gestured at her, from the cradle of Dave's arms at the forest floor. "Ivy."

"Oh, shit. Telsa. Did they catch Emmett and Felton?"

"No, they went ahead to get Duran and more horses." He drew a sputtering breath. "Helen...her curse."

"Yes?" Ivy leaned close. A hand rose to brush at his grey hair. It trembled.

His eyes drooped, his voice faded as she bent till her ear touched his lips. He whispered a phrase, then went limp.

Dave eased him further down to the ground, closed his eyes, and sighed. "Ivy, we must go. They aren't far behind us. I'm sorry."

She let him help her up and followed him back into the odd entrance to Gathering Valley. Where they found Helen, in desperate straits, her belly huge. Ivy rushed to her. "What the fuck?"

"Meyer, what happened?" Dave asked the woman holding Helen's hand.

"She wandered, a time stream touched her. This baby is coming, now," Meyer replied calmly.

"Helen! Why didn't you listen?" Ivy proved all but useless. Her frustration that Helen had done this to herself left her with energy. But pacing and cursing wasn't helpful. Meyer and Dave assisted Helen and delivered her son.

Dave thrust the little boy into Ivy's hands. "Take him. I have to get this bleeding stopped."

Ivy held the baby away from her, what to do? He gave a lusty scream and she instinctively held him close. He was a big baby and extremely unhappy. Ivy surged to her feet again, started walking and talking, "Easy. God, what a big boy you are. Your father will be so surprised... I..." She gazed down into the greenest eyes she'd ever seen. The hair was long, and thankfully not blond. She searched the features of the new life, praying there would be no sign of Ursus.

She saw nothing of the bastard. He looked like Emmett. She sat near the fountain, wetting a corner of the blanket and letting her new grandson suck at the bit of wet. He calmed down and fell asleep.

Ivy found herself drifting away, unable to think past the warm bundle in her arms. The water soothed her, the hurried sound of Meyer and Dave, huddled around Helen faded away.

"Ivy?" Dave touched her arm. "She wants to see him."

Ivy shook her head, rousing herself. She held the baby out to Dave, who simply stepped away, forcing her to rise and go to her daughter. Helen looked tired and confused. "Is he all right? It's too early..."

"No, he was ready. Remember? You touched an unstable time ribbon. He's big, fine..." Dave urged Ivy to kneel next to her daughter.

Ivy handed the baby to Helen, who gazed at him, awestruck. For the first time, Ivy really looked at Helen. She was thin, pale. Ivy could see the Cruz in the tint of green at the girl's wrist veins. She was careful with the baby, stroking his cheeks.

"What is his name?" Dave asked her.

Helen blinked. "I don't know? What would Emmett like?" She asked Ivy.

"Emmett?" Ivy sat back on her knees. She thought about the boy she'd known since before Helen was born. "Emmett...his father was called Indego. His brother was Jerome. Your father killed them. Honor them."

"Jerego. This is Jerego," Helen smiled as she named her son. Meyer showed her how to feed him.

"When will Telsa return?" She settled down, cradling the new baby.

"He isn't returning. The men chasing us caught him and killed

Dano. We got there too late to save Telsa." Ivy stated matter-of-factly.

"Emmett?" Helen caught her breath, grasped Jerego's little hand in hers.

"Telsa said he'd gone ahead for Duran and horses." Ivy couldn't keep her eyes open any longer. She slid down the short wall she'd been propped up on and instantly fell a bare level of sleep. The tiny bit of her brain that remained aware listened.

Helen gazed at Dave, who was gathering up the debris of helping her give birth. "How will they find us?"

"You'll find them. And Bosun is with them. You can't stay much longer. Sleep and gain strength." Dave smiled softly at her. "Helen. He will be welcome here. And I heard the soldiers talking. Your father is dead. He woke up briefly, named Ivy his killer. Said you belonged to who killed her. They will chase you. You've proven to be fertile."

Helen bowed her head.

Dave left them resting. Helen wiped at the tears on her cheeks, then gazed at her son. "Jerego...you'll never know him. And I think that is best. Your father is a good man. We'll be fine," she cooed at the baby, who slept on peacefully.

The reprieve from running lasted another six hours. Dave roused them. "There is an exit from the valley near the rest of your party. Hurry!"

Ivy climbed to her feet; the weight of weeks without enough sleep left her buried in weariness. But she took up the pack without a word.

Helen peered at her. "Why isn't the curse fading?"

For a moment, Ivy thought her daughter meant the curse Telsa had told her of, not the one he'd pushed onto her. Ivy shook her head and looked at her arm, saw the thin wire of a boy and shrugged. Telsa's words made no sense and she refused to even attempt to figure them out.

"Bosun will know." Dave beckoned. "Come. Stay close and hold to each other.

Meyer showed Helen how to strap the baby to her chest and so leave her hands free. And the four left the courtyard. It was a long walk, through the whispering streets, full of oddly leaning shadows, even in the light of day. They had to leave the horse, unable to traverse this path safely. Helen let her hair fall in front of her face and held tightly to Ivy's hand.

Ivy maintained her silence. When the cobbles turned to a dirt path, the light changed. Helen braved a look around, relieved to see trees surrounding them again. A light fog filtered through the greenery. Dave paused, and then pointed Ivy down a rocky path.

Helen raised her free hand to wave and Dave faded into the fog.

Hours later, the two literally walked into the camp. Helen sagged against a tree, trying to catch her breath. Ivy led a punishing pace, knowing the new mother wouldn't dare cry for mercy. They needed help and fast.

Felton looked up from the fire and beckoned at the two of them. "Emmett is hunting rabbit. Bosun said you'd be here soon... where is Telsa?

Helen glanced at Ivy, who said nothing.

"Telsa is dead," Helen sighed and answered. She stumbled as she pushed off the tree. Felton sprang to his feet to help her. Ivy stared into the fog-darkened forest, standing, ready to dash away.

Helen touched her arm. "Ivy, come...the fire is warm."

Ivy turned a blank face at her daughter. There was never any time. For just a moment, Ivy's eye rested on the newborn head, cradled in Helen's hand. And her eyes softened, but the moment passed quickly.

Ivy shifted her pack and turned toward the trees.

"Wait!" Helen cried out as Ivy dashed back the way they had come.

But Ivy didn't get far. A familiar set of arms grabbed her, hauling her back toward the fire.

Duran looked around the camp. “Who is this boy and where is Ivy?” He held tightly to her, not realizing who he held. Ivy would have laughed if she’d had a voice.

“You’re holding her,” Helen replied. “She’s still covered in Telsa’s curse, it hides her.”

“Ivy?” Duran held his captive out and tried to see it. Not until her eyes met his did he believe it. “Well, fuck. That’s how you did it, eh?”

Ivy still didn’t answer. He grinned at her. “Ah, speechless with pleasure, honey muffin?”

Ivy grimaced.

Duran let her arm go and draped his arm about her shoulder. Ivy quick stepped to the side and Helen called out a warning, “Don’t let her go!”

“Why?” Duran reached out and snatched at Ivy before she’d gone a step too far.

“She’s acting strange. Stranger...” Helen closed her eyes. “I think she wants to go back and finish. Diva was injured, but hasn’t died yet.”

“Not without me, my dove,” Duran spoke to Ivy, shaking his head. “Give it up. I’ll tie you to me. Though you are a remarkably ugly boy and my reputation will suffer.”

“What is going on?” Emmett tossed three rabbits to Felton, glancing around the clearing. He saw Helen and then the baby. He sagged. “Not mine? Born already?”

“He’s yours,” Helen quickly reassured her lover. “I got lost in Gathering Valley. Dave said I touched a time ribbon and suddenly...he grew and here he is.” She looked down at the face of her son. “I called him Jerego. Come, hold your son, Emmett.”

Duran tucked Ivy under his arm again and held her tightly, watching as Emmett picked up his son and held the baby up. The resemblance was uncanny.

“My reputation will never recover, eh, Ivy? Ugly boys, grandmothers...” Duran pushed her ahead of him. “The horses are tied up at the boulders we passed. Bosun?”

"Not back yet," Felton replied as he set about skinning the rabbits.

Emmett held his new son tight and just gazed at Helen, reaching out his free hand to stroke her cheeks. "You were lucky. Lost in Gathering Valley? How did that happen?"

Again, Helen glanced at Ivy, waiting for the woman to answer. But Ivy said nothing.

Duran found Ivy's silence interesting. He watched her as Helen took a deep breath and replied, "Ivy and Dave left to help Telsa and I got scared... It was my fault. I'd been told not to leave the courtyard. They returned in time to help me give birth. Telsa is gone. Oh, Emmett! He didn't tell me what the curse was!"

Emmett sighed. "We'll deal with it when it rises. At least two months closer now. You need to eat, you look exhausted."

"How can we take the time to camp like this? Aren't they still looking for us?" Helen asked.

"We're days ahead of them, thanks to the valley," Duran stated. He eased down onto a blanket, hauling Ivy down with him. He looked at her. "Just settle, bitchy woman. Bosun should be back soon."

Once Ivy allowed herself to give up, sleep caught her before the rabbits were done. Duran roused her enough to feed her, then lay down himself, an arm protectively holding her against him.

Helen rested in Emmett's arms, Jerego snuggled between them. Felton waited for Bosun.

CHAPTER FOURTEEN

The next morning, exhaustion and a sense of unknown filled the group. A shaft of sunlight fell through the tall trees as Bosun roused them. They erased all signs of their stay and began a slow walk toward the coast. Duran sat on one horse, Ivy in front of him. She still refused to speak.

Bosun had returned sometime in the night and shared news with them as they broke camp. “I found a soldier's camp three days to the north of us. Their security was lax and I got close enough eavesdrop.” He repeated what Dave had told Helen. “Ursus is dead. Two of his generals hunt for Ivy and Helen.”

“I told you that.” Helen sighed. “I am a prize.”

“Yes, but the third general? He stays with Diva, who has taken on the chase.”

Duran had to clamp hold of Ivy, who tried desperately to get away at that news.

Bosun continued, “Evidently, her face is all but destroyed. But Buckler counts on her to help him take over Ursus' command. The other two, Gero and Jango, depend on seizing you.”

Helen shook her head. “Wait. Three days behind us? How did you travel so fast?”

"I skirted the valley. If you know how to use them, the time distortions are walk able. It's risky, as you discovered," Bosun eyed her as he spoke. "One thing at a time. Get you to safety. Diva is determined, but her injuries are slowing her down."

"Why is Telsa's curse still holding Ivy?" Duran asked.

Bosun studied his granddaughter a moment, then he grimaced. "She won't let it go, I would guess. Leave it for now. We have three days to reach the coast, board the *Windsong* and leave Ursus' generals to tear each other apart."

Those days held no rest. Duran had to hold Ivy constantly. On the second night, he forced her out of the firelight. He limped to a small area and sat, dragging her down to face him. The moonlight made it easier to focus beyond the curse.

"Ivy. We both know you could slip away. You could trip me up easy enough, this foot isn't done with me yet. But if you do, I will hunt you down. I will drag myself after you. You will tear Emmett apart, Bosun is an old man and tired. Quit fighting me. We have to get Helen to safety. I know, girl! I know what you are thinking! I want her dead, too."

He examined her face. "Talk to me. I know you can talk, tell me how it felt to see him at your feet." He tried everything to coax words out of her. Insults, jokes, and memories...nothing worked. She wouldn't speak.

He slapped her and she reacted. Her mouth opened, but then it shut. A blank look shuttered her face. He sagged. "Chica, what am I going to do with you?"

She turned her face away. He forced it back to him. "You leave me no choice, chica. You're being tied to me. I know a knot you won't be able to slip out of. Bosun has spent several years sailing and he's been teaching me." He hauled a length of rope out of his pack and did as he'd threatened, chatting all the time, "He felt it would assist with bettering my hand coordination. It is." Ivy didn't attempt to stop him, barely registering she was hearing him at all.

They picked up the last of their group and two days later reached the cave at Hidden Cove. Ivy assisted Duran in walking the trail, she even helped to unwrap his foot once in the cave and tend to it. But he wasn't fooled, the rope stayed. He knew her well enough to assume a show of concern masked waiting for an opportunity to get away.

Not going to happen.

He had her, and he kept her. His need to hear about the blood, about the battle made him patient. News of Diva's ruined face made him smile, but he wanted details.

His craving for Ivy remained paramount. She wasn't going anywhere.

They waited five days for pick-up. Ivy refused to speak, though she continued to help Duran. She would hold her grandson once he was placed in her arms, even smile down at him. But she didn't speak. When the *Windsong* arrived, the group cautiously made their way down to the waiting zodiac.

Ivy balked at the raft. She shook her head, pulled at the rope. She shook, even bent and vomited her last meal. Duran hauled her into his arms, where she beat at him.

"Ivy, sweetheart. I know it is hard. I know, but I will stay with you," Duran crooned to her.

She took a deep breath, pulled away enough to look into his eye.

"Not...done!" she choked out. Her voice sounded like a rusty nail being pulled out of rotten wood.

"You are for now. We are for now. Bosun is right, let them sort it out. With luck they will tear each other to shreds, making it easier to come back and kill her." He paused and lowered his voice, "I want her dead, chica. I'm not forgetting."

"I...now!" She tried to insist.

He shook his head. "No. It's a wonderful disguise. But she knows it and you are weak, starved, tired. Revenge isn't worth the risk. Later. Later when it is a better bet."

She struggled and he simply picked her up, handed her over to

Bosun, already in the raft, then followed. The last of them stepped aboard and the zodiac turned to the ship. Ivy huddled between the legs of Duran and Bosun, shivering.

Duran kept a hand at her shoulder. He studied Emmett, watching her partner of twenty years. Duran waited for some discussion, but the lad seemed too disturbed. It must be hard to watch the strong as steel Ivy be so frightened. One of Emmett's arms kept Helen close, even as she held their son. Fortune had changed so much in the last year. Ivy always appeared tough and strong, but the weeks of nursing him unearthed the fragility that lay in her heart. As often as she watched his nightmares, he knew hers as well.

Helen stirred, catching sight of the *Windsong* for the first time. "Oh! How beautiful!"

Bosun answered her wonder, "One of the few relics left that function outside the disturbed time zones."

Emmett shuddered, then turned to Helen. "You need to know. I see ghosts of the past, Helen. That ship is full of ghosts for me. I hear them, I see them...all of them."

"How many could that ship hold?" She gazed at him, trying to understand.

Again, it was Bosun who explained, "That *Windsong* spent years, full of passengers taking pleasure cruises. Helen. Thousands of ghosts."

She blinked, shook her head, then took hold of his hand. "Emmett. I'll be there. So will Jerego. We will help you bear it."

He sighed, squeezed her hand then looked at Ivy. "She has always been there for me when we had to walk through haunted places. Singing helps, small places, kept dark, they all help. Ivy?"

Ivy just shook.

"I don't understand. Is she ill?" Helen laid her head on Emmett's shoulder.

"She doesn't like the ocean," Duran kept the explanation simple. He met Helen's eyes. "Don't ask more."

"Do you know?" Helen challenged him.

"Yes. But it's up to her to tell you or not," Duran calmly answered.

Emmett kept silent, undoubtedly preparing himself to do battle with his curse.

Duran insisted Ivy be left with him. He saw her to a small interior cabin and blocked the door with a chair. He sat and studied her. The knot undone, she scurried to the opposite corner of the cabin and glared at him. He grinned.

"You and I are going to bath. Mary showed me how the shower worked on the way over. And you smell worse than I do. Admit it, Ivy. That sounds good, doesn't it?" He coaxed her out of the corner slowly, as one would a wild animal.

He used the rope to bind the chair to the door, then sat her on the bed. She'd given up the glare and simply went blank again. He stripped the rags off her body, tearing them to pieces. It was easy to do. He threw them into a pile. He grimaced, then sighed. "I wish I could see you, Ivy. You have to let go of this curse. It isn't yours. Bosun said it would exhaust you."

She didn't appear to register his words. When he began the laborious job of stripping away his clothing, she turned to help. Gently, she removed the bandages from his foot and examined it. To Duran's eye, it was looking better. The days aboard the ship, in this small cabin, should see it much improved.

She helped him get into the bathroom, made sure he didn't fall. He held tightly to her, knowing this was a prime time for her to attempt escape. But she didn't try. She seemed to appreciate the shower as much as he.

"Perhaps I've overlooked ugly boys all these years," he joked as she scrubbed his back, taking care with the rough, newly formed scars.

When he closed his eyes, he knew it was Ivy. The hands were hers. He knew her touch. His eye told a different story.

He turned to help her wash and met that partially bald head. He shuddered. "Your hair. It is gone, isn't it?"

She said nothing. He sighed and simply helped to wash what was before him. Once they were both dried, he pulled her into his arms and directed her to the bed. He turned the light off. In the dark, it was Ivy. This night wasn't for sex, it was for deep sleep. The *Windsong* sailed into the ocean. She had no place to run to.

Hours later, Duran woke and she had left the bed. He sat up, listening. And he heard her. Whimpering? Carefully, he searched the room until he found her, huddled in the closet, shaking. As he drew her into his arms, he felt wetness at her face.

He traced the tear on her cheek.

"Thought you couldn't cry, Ivy. I remember you telling me years ago that you forgot how to cry," he whispered. "Oh, chica. Mi corazón...girl..."

She jerked away from him, kicked out as he tried to take hold of her. Her angry breath filled the closet. In the struggle, one of the doors came off its track and fell with a crash. Ivy was fast and determined, but Duran proved stronger. He finally held her still.

"Well, fuck me, Ivy. I'm all sweaty again and I didn't even enjoy it. You bitch."

She tried to bite his arm and he forced her face away from any vulnerable area.

"Why, Ivy? Why fight me? I am not Ursus. I am not your enemy, girl."

"I'm...not a girl," she hissed, coughed.

"Ah. That pissed you off enough to speak?" He chuckled. "No more fighting. I'll let you up. No biting, no hitting."

"Yes," she whispered.

He eased off her gingerly, climbed back onto the bed. A faint light lit the room from a crack under the door. He could see her stand up, then sit on the corner of the bed. He leaned on the headboard and waited.

She coughed a great deal. Then, instead of continuing the argument, she curled up at his feet and fell asleep. She obviously wasn't ready. He'd wait. He threw a cover atop her and lay down, thinking.

She was right. She wasn't a girl. She might appear a girl, but she was a woman. He was forty-eight years old. She was nearly the same. He understood the need to be fierce. She looked so young, so nubile and soft. How does one combat the affects of never aging? And make your way through the trials of a working mercenary?

He fell asleep contemplating her life from a new perspective.

She woke to feel Duran's arms holding her tightly. Sometime in the night, he had shifted about, covered them both and taken her into his arms. She felt safe, for nearly a minute. Then it all came back again. She pushed his arm away and stood. He rolled to his back and yawned.

"Out." She pointed at the door.

"We're at sea, you know. No where to go." He stretched and squinted. "Damn, still an ugly boy." He set a hand at a morning erection and winked at her.

"Drop dead." She cleared her throat again. It felt like the thousandth time. Something about the curse struck at her throat.

"Why you want out, chickpea?" he asked her.

"Emmett. Food."

"I'm sure Helen is taking care of him, but..." He held up his hand in response to her grimace. "I'll set you free. You need something to wear."

He climbed from the bed, turned on a light and searched the partially destroyed closet. "I'll ask Leonardo if I can work on repairing this..." He tossed her a light colored bit of fabric. "Must be some remnant from before. You'll look funny, wearing that..."

She snarled and held the garment up. It was a light yellow, covered with some blurry sketches of fish on it. She slipped it on as

Duran untied the door and moved the chair. She darted out of the room before he could say anything else to her. Glancing back, she saw him standing in the doorway, naked. A look of exhaustion on his face.

Not watching where she was going, she ran into a woman in the corridor. Untangling from each other, Ivy realized she knew her from the last time aboard. Of course, they probably never changed, like Gathering Valley.

She pointed along the hall. "Emmett?"

"Let me take you to their cabin." The woman took her up a deck to a door. "I'm not sure they are in." She knocked, waited a moment, then opened the door. Ivy pushed her aside and entered, going straight to the closet. But Emmett wasn't there. The room was empty.

"Where?" Ivy grabbed the guide. "Where?"

"If you'll stay, I'll find them." She carefully removed Ivy's hand from her arm and hurried away. Ivy sat on the corner of the unmade bed and worried. Ten minutes later, Helen entered.

"You're up. You and Duran slept most all night and half the day away," Helen sounded cheerful.

"Emmett?" Ivy's patience reached its limit.

"He's on deck. Once the sun rose, I coaxed him outside. If he focuses on the water, it's easier to ignore the ghosts. It's a lovely day. Bosun is with him, and Jerego. I can take you to them." Helen held out her hand.

Ivy jerked away, turned and faced a wall. "Outside?" she whispered.

"Bosun told me you were on a tiny boat with Telsa, this one is so big...it isn't going to sink." Helen tried; Ivy could admit that the girl made an effort to win her over.

Shaking her head, Ivy left the room. She needed food. Her instincts concentrated on the basics. Emmett. Food.

Duran found her in a galley far below the waterline. She sat on a stool, chewing on some bread. He snatched a plate, served himself items from those she had scattered on the table and sat.

"I saw Emmett outside, he's fine. Still shaking some but when he holds that baby, he solids up," Duran commented.

Ivy just sighed.

"Helen told me what she remembers of the fight. I want to hear it from you, Ivy. Helen couldn't tell me much about how badly you injured Diva. I want to know. I have a right to know."

Ivy swallowed the last bit bread and turned to look at him. She cleared her throat, took a sip of water and cleared it again.

"I...I struck her with a heavy clay pitcher. It..." she swallowed again, "...shattered and sliced her face. I got one eye, Duran. I had a small knife." She smiled at the memory. "She bled...half her face sliced open. But tried to get up. I broke the platter over her head. Thought she was dead. Should have..." she coughed, "...made sure!"

"Helen said she should have died. Got her eye? Good. I get the other one." He drew a breath. "You and Telsa had a good plan. We'll come up with one just as good. Without the ugly boy stuff."

"Not ugly!" Ivy protested.

"You can't see yourself. Ugly." He shook his head.

She coughed again. "Why am I...so hoarse?"

"It isn't going to get better until you let go of Telsa's curse," her grandfather interrupted.

The pair of them turned to see Bosun in the doorway. "The sun is going down and Emmett wants to see you. The bright light on the deck helped, but he'd gone back to the cabin for now."

Ivy pushed him aside as she hurried from the galley.

He called out to her, "He wants to *see* you, Ivy. Not this boy you wear!"

Shit! Like she wanted to feel this constant itch. As she climbed the steps to the Emmett's cabin, she tried to shake the disguise off. She paused to stare at her hands, fighting to remember her hands, her arms. She saw a mirror and stopped to stare at herself.

All that stared back was a blotchy face boy, with hair sticking out at strange angles, face sunburned.

She turned away from Emmett's door and went to the cabin Duran shared with her. And crawled into bed.

CHAPTER FIFTEEN

Duran opened the door, tired of searching. Tired of her stubbornness. His foot hurt, his head ached and arguing with Bosun had left him confused. Ivy had disappeared. Leonardo assured them she had to be on the ship, an alarm would have sounded if she'd fallen overboard and no rafts were missing.

"Shit," he cursed as he flipped on the switch by the door. He didn't register her presence at first. She sat on the edge of the bed, staring at a mirror.

"Ivy?"

"I can't find Ivy," she whispered.

He took one step out of the cabin and shouted, "Found her!" Then he slammed the door shut in the face of Bosun. And ignored the knocking.

He removed his shoes, tossed them into a corner and slid up behind her. He studied her reflection. He still saw the boy disguise, but knew she was there.

How the hell had Telsa done it? His uncle once said the Cruz weren't cursed, just physically gifted. How did he gift Ivy with such a disguise?

Wrapping an arm around her narrow shoulders, he softly spoke, "I see Ivy. I see Ivy in your eyes."

"I don't." She coughed. With a twist, she faced Duran. "Why... why don't I feel different?"

Tilting his head, he blinked. "Different than what?"

"All my life...I have hated him. Even before he caught me. After..." She shuddered. "After, I lived to kill him. Now, he's dead and...and..."

"And you don't feel different." He stroked her face. "A long time to hate, that isn't going to be easy to let go. Tell me how he died, woman." He kept his eye on hers. He read them, wiling to finally let go? To finally let him in? "Yes, woman. I do know you are a woman, not a girl. I know how old you are."

She tried to duck her head down, but he held the chin up.

"I won't call you *girl* again, I promise. How did he die?"

She took a shaking breath, then began, "Quietly. He died quietly, in a bed."

He shook his head. "No, he died when you struck him. It just took a few days. Helen said he struck Telsa and dove at you..."

"I avoided his rush. He was fast, but clumsy. When he..." She coughed and cursed at her throat, "Fuck this! He turned and came at me again. Bare hands. I had a blade. I tripped him and he struck the corner of the fireplace ledge and didn't move. I fell upon his back, took his hair in my hand, drew his head up...had his throat under my blade..."

He saw her eyes dilate, her nostrils flared. She licked her lips.

"Then...Helen pled. I...I hesitated. If he'd moved...if he'd tried to get up... But he didn't. It was over?"

For only the second time since he had known her, twenty years of friendship and more, a tear trickled down her cheek. With it, the façade of boyhood began to thin. Her chest rose and fell quickly. He could hear her struggle for each breath; he heard her teeth ground together. One hand rose, trembling.

Her voice squeezed out through the struggle. "It was over?

No...no blood. No tearing. No slicing. No...dying eyes..." She touched her cheek. Her eyes fell to look at her fingertip, the tear glistening in the whirls. "I...! I...! Can't be done!? Can't be...over!?"

Her dark eyes, so green Duran felt as if he gazed into the heart of every forest in the world, shouted at him with pain. He felt a tear making its way down his cheek, a sorrow for her so keen it made him want to cradle her inside. This woman, so slight, so fragile, so powerful. He wanted her to be his to defend. To claim, to protect.

He said none of this. His tear spoke for him.

Ivy's mouth opened wider than he thought possible. Tears erupted as her voice returned. She cried, keened a sharp bitterness held back for twenty years. It made his heart ache. She fell back from him and screamed at the ceiling. He could make out very few words...

"...tied me! ...Hit! Bit! ... Tore inside...! Heavy...bled! Over and over and over and over..." Ivy curled up into a ball, sobbing, shaking with fury and grief. The boy was gone. A woman ranted and railed against the injury done to her, the violence and terror of that month, over two decades old.

Duran fell against her, drawing her into the curve of his body and he cried with her. Opening himself, he offered her everything to make it plain; he was there with her. He would always be there for her.

Somehow, he found her mouth and poured the truth into her. His lips met hers. And she devoured him. They tore at each other, tears mingled, cheek-to-cheek, even as he ripped the yellow dress away. His need drove him to push, but some bare bit of sanity remained and he let her lead. She rose above him, placing his hands at her breasts as she slid down to encase him in heaven's very heat.

She still sobbed, shook even as she rode him.

He took such care. Her thinness frightened him. Her breasts such a bare memory of what was, he could feel every rib, her hips bones ground at him. Her softness replaced with stretched skin over a bare frame.

His cock didn't care, didn't know her as anything but the ultimate home. The explosion he'd waited for took him outside of anything he'd ever known.

She screamed as she came, fell against him, panting. Her shaking slowed, her breath evened out. And she fell asleep atop him. He held her, pledged to make her wait to kill Deva, until he was with her. They'd do it together. No matter what.

Outside the cabin, Bosun sat on the floor, head cradled in his arms. He'd heard her screaming, heard enough to know she'd reached crisis and surfaced. He gradually climbed to her feet and went to tell the rest she had returned. Telsa's blessed curse was gone.

———

His arms held her, his chest rising easily at her back. Ivy clung to his forearms, listening to him breath. He'd cried with her! She'd always known Duran wore his emotions on the outside, but to see tears for her? This closeness unnerved her. She could admit her heart was involved with this Losanglos, but she had never taken his words of care seriously.

Not really. Had she hoped? Wanted to believe? Could she trust this?

She had to now. His breath changed as he shifted positions.

"Duran?" she whispered.

"Hmmm?"

"I don't want to go to Lina."

"Okay." He propped himself up on one elbow so that she rolled to her back. He gazed down at her. "Options?"

"I don't know. But Lina? It...they just...don't understand. Helen will be there. I know she isn't him. I try to see her and not him, but it's so hard. Emmett has his family. Now he has Helen and Jerego. I'm not...not ready to settle like that," she tried to explain.

He tilted his head then nodded. "Ah. Not ready to settle because she isn't dead yet."

"Yeah, I guess." That sounded right to her. "I need to train. You need to recover. We need to plan."

"The Cruz on Lina have been peaceful too long. I agree. Okay... Let me see if Leonardo will take us to the new settlement on Chan. I need to see my cousins. There is work there, building." He smiled down at her. "And regular contact with the mainland."

She shuddered. "Emmett needs to live without worrying about me. To take care of his son. They kept me prisoner, Duran. I don't care if they thought they were keeping me safe...Lina kept me prisoner!"

"You let me keep you prisoner?" He bent and took her lips with his. She knew he teased and didn't worry about his chaining her down. His was a sweet kiss that built to a promise before he lifted.

He loomed above her. "We'll kill her, Ivy. If you want, we'll travel to hell and kill Ursus again. We'll take the ones who killed Telsa and Dano."

"Duran... You know me so well." She'd almost told him she loved him. But she couldn't, not yet. They talked for hours, outlining the work he needed for recovery of stamina, balance and aim. He wanted to feed her constantly and promised good meals from his aunts.

The news unnerved Emmett. He tried to convince her to come ashore, but she refused. He came to their cabin at the end of the next day. They'd reach the port of Avala before dawn. He held his son, Helen stood at his back. Duran let them in. "Ivy is in the shower."

"She's back to herself, Bosun said." Helen urged Emmett into the room. "Just hold to Jerego, Emmett." She turned to Duran. "Holding the baby helps with the ghosts."

Ivy strolled out of the bathroom, a towel draped loosely over her shoulders. "Curses always distance themselves when infants are nearby."

Emmett gasped and took a step toward her.

She took a step back. "What?"

He pulled the towel away from her. "You are so thin! I knew the months on Lina were lean...but!"

She jerked the towel back from him and grimaced. "I know. Duran keeps feeding me every hour on the hour. I will get better. I'm not going to Lina."

"You have to...you can't go back to the mainland!" Emmett protested.

"I'm not going to. We are going to the Chan settlement. Leonardo will take us. Boats sail between Trader's Port and Chan. I already told Bosun. I'm not going to discuss this." Ivy strolled to the closet and pulled out a pair of lime green shorts. "Why in the hell did they wear shit?"

"What if we need you?" Helen asked.

"Send a message." Duran made a face at the baby, who gurgled at him.

"Come with us, sail to Chan in a few weeks. I need to see you... Ivy?" Emmett buried his face in the baby's hair.

"No. You don't. You have done fine for months without me. Emmett." Ivy took a deep breath and moved close to Duran. "You have Helen. Jerego, your family. I need Duran to help me. I need to learn how to live knowing Ursus is dead."

"Oh. And I remind you of..."

"No! You were the only good thing I knew. You held me when I woke screaming. You kept me sane. Shut up, Duran!"

He stifled a laugh but then rose from the bed. He met Emmett's eyes. "Trust her with me, Emmett. We'll take care of each other."

Helen had taken a step back at hearing Ivy's words. Ivy wasn't stupid and realized her words likely wounded the girl. But the reality of Helen hurt. The dream of her, of the little girl who needed to be rescued, had been a lie. Emmett was the only good thing she knew. She took a deep breath and considered her past.

With a sigh, she reached out a hand for Helen and touched her arm. “Take good care of him. He was mine, but now he is yours. I trust you with him.”

Helen nodded. Their eyes met for a scant few seconds. That was all Ivy could handle. She looked away first.

CHAPTER SIXTEEN

Seven months passed at the Chan settlement. Duran's family welcomed the pair, handing them tools to help build homes. Ivy found it restful to simple get to work. Duran's relatives held a feast the first night, asked about his injuries and cheered at hearing Ursus was dead.

His two aunts fussed over Ivy and promised to keep her fed. They spread a bedroll under the sky and Ivy studied the stars, placing Lina under one. They went to work the next day.

Her weapons arrived from Lina, sent by Emmett. They took an hour each morning and a second hour each afternoon, drilling. Duran regained total use of his right hand by the end of a month, and improved every month after regarding his depth perception problems.

Nothing really changed, but the steady work and calm running of the settlement eased Ivy's nightmares. They faded in intensity, though she still found tears on her face with little provocation. But she also laughed more and with greater freedom.

One day Bosun brought over more ointment to help with the continued healing of Duran's foot.

He requested Ivy take a walk with him that day.

"Did Telsa tell you what Helen's curse was?" he bluntly asked.

"Oh. Yeah. Strange. Didn't she pass that birthday...uh...last week?" Ivy gazed out at the ocean. She did better with her water phobia every day. The Chan settlement perched on bluffs above a sandy bay. The tide rose too high to build near the water, so they chose the bluffs along with the many small valleys that spread off of it.

She looked down at the two ships from Trader's Cove that had come in that morning. Another two, from the mainland, were spending the day before moving on.

"She did, but nothing of significance rose. They kept watch, but nothing. Or her curse is very subtle." Ursus studied her. "You look good."

"I am good. What Telsa said made no sense." She paused, remembering his gasping words, *...hers like yours, but reversed... If she wins... she'll be a pollinator...* Then he'd died. She repeated this to Bosun. Ivy shook her head. "Just nonsense! A pollinator? She would assist in crop growth? He'd intimated that her curse would see her pursued. Has she shown any talent with plants? No, too early..."

"Usually those who carry a plant curse find themselves drawn to green things. Helen doesn't show any sign of that."

"Has her mark changed in any way? The elders checked it at all?"

"It appears darker, but none can discern what Telsa saw."

"Well, I don't know. He appeared to find it ominous, but perhaps Avala tempers it. Or the schedule is wrong and it hasn't manifest yet. Touching Gathering Valley might have thrown it off." Ivy shrugged. "I don't have any answers. I admit, the idea of my curse, reversed? That sounds ominous."

He sighed. The two paused and turned to look inland. The Chans had an established forest, larger game, and more water than Lina. Ivy had been told about the debate the Cruz council held about settling here or on Lina. They decided on Lina as a safer refuge. The mainland was visible from the Chans. They wanted more distance from the rest of the world.

Ivy studied him. He took a step back and she grinned. She must look fierce. He shivered.

She chuckled. "I unnerve you, grandfather?"

"Yes. You do. I don't know what to say to you. What you need from me."

"I don't need anything from you. I am...thankful you brought Duran back. That's really all I have to say." She locked eyes with his.

He took another step back from her. "Someday, I hope...you will ask me about your grandmother, about when I left and let me tell you my story."

"I know your story. You wanted to flee to Lina with the rest. She didn't. She was stubborn, and she died, along with the rest of them. Fighting for what she believed in." She didn't wait for his response, simply turned and left.

An hour later, she practiced blade work with Duran. She wielded her sword fiercely and the two shouted insults at each other even as they sparred. She'd gained weight, her color was good. Her hair was growing back in and looked a shaggy mess.

That night, Ivy picked a fight with Duran and stormed away. She stayed away for nearly a week, eventually returning to work as if nothing had happened. Duran didn't pursue it; he understood the fight had nothing to do with him.

Five months later, she discovered he'd been warning off any other Losanglos men from approaching her for company. The effort actually touched her, though she attempted to protest it. He laughed at her, and continued to the dining hall. She followed, studying his strut. He appeared almost cocky about her accusations. He no longer limped, he'd regained muscles and the sun had baked him a wonderful shade of brown. His fingers were nimble again, and the scars on his back faded in the sun.

She never tanned, despite the sun. Her Cruz blood saw her remain lighter than the Losanglos. Though she had noticed her hair showed a greener tint than it had before, especially where Telsa had shaved it close to the skull.

She sat across from him at the narrow table, chatted with three of his cousins. The older Losanglos came in later. They were eating goat, as always. She grew tired of goat, but they thrived on the island. A shaft of light illuminated the edge of the table. One of the cousins laughed at a joke and leered at Duran, putting an arm around Ivy's shoulders.

Duran simple smirked. "She too old for you, Wes."

"Maybe you're too old for her, Duran. She needs a young buck to keep her busy after you fall asleep!"

Ivy chuckled, then met Duran's eye across the table. He winked at her as he answered his cousin's challenge. "She'd chew you up and spit you out, boy. Ivy is a woman. She's not like the girls you're used to. Besides, she snores."

Ivy chuckled, shook her head and gazed out the open door to a sliver of ocean in the distance.

"He exaggerates, you aren't too old for us." Pallo, at her other side, jumped into the conversation. Turning to her, he spoke with earnestness, "He just doesn't want to share you."

"Damned straight. Get your hand off her leg, boy," Duran spoke casually, but with authority.

"What if she wants to share?" Wes asked.

"What gallant cousins you have, Duran." Ivy pushed Pallo's hand away and removed Wes's arm from her shoulder. "To pay such compliments to a woman old enough to be their mother."

"That's a lie!" Pallo protested.

"Oh, but it isn't. Appearances are deceiving. Look into my eyes, Wes...what do you see?" Ivy's face was less than a foot away. He studied her face and she sighed. "No, my eyes."

Wes shifted his focus and gazed into her eyes. She saw the mystification gathering on his face, the hesitation. After a few moments, he backed away a little bit and then turned to look at Duran. "They are a beautiful green, but..."

"Confusing?" Duran stood up, held out a hand to Ivy. "Come on, bitch. You've tormented the youngsters enough."

"If I'm a bitch, and you're my only lover, what does that make you, Duran?" She laughed as she joined him in leaving the hall.

He put an arm about her shoulders. "I guess that makes me a dog lover, eh?"

"Too bad there are so few dogs left..."

The young men watched her from a distance after that. It was peaceful, knowing her strangeness had at last been acknowledged. As well as Duran's holding of that strangeness.

A group of grey-hairs approached her some days later. She set her hammer down and greeted them.

"Come join us tonight at the autumn fire."

"Me?" She couldn't have been more shocked.

"Yes, tonight. At the beach. Moonrise."

They left her without another word. She swallowed her nerves and turned to see Duran at her side. "Why do they want me? Last time I joined a bunch of crones at a fire, they showed me the *Windsong* back in port."

He shrugged. "I don't know, Ivy. Our crones aren't like Cruz crones. Our magic is milder. Go, enjoy yourself."

"Fuck." She found it difficult to concentrate on the frame they were building. Chan had decided they needed a bar. Duran had been asked to run it but had declined, saying he still had business on the mainland. When he returned he'd be happy to discuss it. They did understand and left him alone about it.

That night, Ivy walked down to the beach to find a good-sized bonfire lit. The moon hadn't risen above the bluff, so the sand was still in shadow. Six crones sat on large logs, set up near the flames. One rose, and addressed her, "Ivy, come sit next to me."

She bowed her head and did so, aware the rest were examining her closely.

"We understand your curse keeps you young."

She nodded. "It keeps my body young."

"Ah, there is a difference. You still age, you still know the length of your days. You accumulate wisdom..."

Ivy snorted. "Well, that last is debatable."

None of them laughed. A hand touched her knee. "How many years have you walked our Changed World?"

"Forty-eight," she answered.

"Your body has shown no sign of the passage of time?"

Ivy shrugged. "I bleed every few months. I gain weight, I lose weight, I scar. I carried a child for nine months." Her eyes closed. "I grow tired. Duran says my eyes show my age. I've gazed at myself in the mirror and I don't know what he sees but I trust that he sees it."

"He grows older. How long have you known him?"

Ivy thought back to when she'd first met Duran, a summer campaign not far from Gathering Valley. To clear those attempting to control the pass to the Gathering. He'd made her laugh. She'd escaped from Ursus three years before. "Ah. I was twenty-seven. I have known him twenty-one years."

"He thought you younger?"

"He knew of my curse. I don't know what he thought." She met the eyes of the woman studying her. "Are you worried for him? I don't see his age. I see him. He sees me."

The woman who had asked her to sit down smiled. "His reputation is enhanced with you at his side."

Ivy sneered, the hair at the base of her neck rose. "You think him so shallow? I've known men that only wanted me for this body. Not Duran!" She stood; ready to walk away no matter how much she longed to actually belong. "Why did you invite me here?"

"Ivy, please sit down. No one means to insult Duran. It is simply the truth. His reputation is enhanced because of you. His association with you also puts him in danger. But that isn't why we asked you to come. We realized that we make the same mistake of men, who see you only for your figure and appearance. We are sorry."

"You are a woman of maturity."

"And wisdom."

"We wish to invite you to the woman's fire and celebration, every full moon."

Ivy put a hand to her heart, aware of its sudden loudness. She swallowed the momentary anger of before and took a deep breath. She sat again, suddenly uncertain of herself. The fire crackled loudly. The moon suddenly shown down brightly, looking huge against the bluff.

"I...I am honored." Ivy stuttered. "I never thought I would be... included. I will never be a crone...?"

"Of course you will, albeit without grey hair and wrinkles, but there is more to the wisdom of age than that."

"We understand you and Duran still seek vengeance on the woman who took his eye. We have some news to share from the mainland. Gero and Jango are dead. Buckler has risen to command what is left of Ursus' troops. They are less than a fourth of what they were. And what is left is tightly bound to the religious. The mercenaries have done poorly during all the bickering and fighting. Their ranks fell as they choose sides. Though a new leader is attempting to carve what is left into a permanent force.

Ivy's eyes grew sharp. "Any news of Diva?"

"She rides with Buckler. Her face covered with a veil. She leads the religious factions, Ivy."

"Fucking bitch. That figures." Ivy growled. After a few moments of silence, she rose. "I am honored to be invited to the women's fires. If Duran and I succeed, we'll be back and if the invitation is still open, I will take part. For now, we must plan our return to the mercenary camps. Thank you."

Before they could reply, she dashed away.

The women said nothing for several minutes. "Do you think the mercenaries will accept them back?"

"Depends on this new leader and how valuable the prize Diva has put on her head. They will be careful."

"Let us hope so..."

Two more months passed as Duran and Ivy drove each other to

hone the skills of battle and stealth. They discussed a plan and prepared to return to the mainland when the ships sailed again.

He arrived without warning. No ship came into port, as the seas weren't permitting easy sailing yet. That wouldn't return for another month. The storms roared as they had for two months. No one was out in the cascading rain. Ivy and Duran returned from a successful hunting trip, dropping off haunches of venison to several families. They headed for the small hut they occupied, ready to dry off, eat and crawl into bed. As soon as the ships returned, they were leaving for the coast. Trained, rested, recovered, they were ready to go after Diva.

They entered their hut to find him.

Ivy saw him first, froze in the doorway. "Who is there?" One hand rested at her ax, ready.

Duran stepped to the other side of her, his knife already drawn.

"I come from Gathering Valley. You are summoned to a hearing." He sat at one of their two chairs, hands at his side and made no threatening move.

"A hearing?" Ivy moved so the light from outside shone on the stranger. "Who are you? Who sent you?"

"How the fuck did you get here?" Duran tossed the two steaks on the table, strode to the banked fire and stoked it.

"I am Michael, a Guardian of the Changed World. Charges have been made of drug use against Ivy of the Cruz. You will come to Gathering Valley to answer these charges." Ivy noticed only his eyes moved, observing her reactions. She bet he could read much from how she responded.

"I have been charged?!" Ivy appeared shocked. "Me?"

"Who made these charges?" Duran's back had gone rigid for just a millisecond, then he bent to gather a skillet and some spices.

"Diva of Orly. Gathering takes place in three months. You will come and face these charges, Ivy." He stood up, slowly.

Ivy studied his face. She stood nearly a foot shorter than he, yet gave the appearance of equal stature. She didn't flinch at his gaze, showed no sign of fear or guilt. She simply nodded. "Fine. Gathering Valley. Three months. I'll be there."

"We'll be there. So, you want some steak?" Duran turned to the man. Ivy watched as he set the guardian at ease. They were men and women, untouched by time, but basically just men and women. And they talked just like everyone else. Michael presented a chance for information. They wouldn't waste it.

She put aside the shock at being charged with drug use. Something they'd discuss later, once the messenger left.

"Thank you, that would be pleasant. I am not a judge. I am just an envoy." He sat back down as Ivy stepped away. "I first went to Lina."

"The ships aren't sailing right now. How did you get there and then here?" Duran kept his tone light and conversational. Ivy pulled bread from the trading bag along with a handful of greens and root vegetables. Duran suggested she change into dry clothes then it would be his turn.

She nodded, and ducked behind a half wall to dry off and change. Her hair had grown long enough to be tied back and dripped water all down her back.

Michael knew she'd be listening, but raised his voice. "I saw Helen on Lina. I advised both she and Emmett to come to Gathering. She will find answers there." She noticed he didn't answer Duran's query regarding his mode of travel. Yup, he might call himself a simply envoy, but he was more than that. He was one of the inner circle.

"Answers to what?" Ivy came around the wall, a loose shirt leaving her legs bare. She rubbed her head with a towel.

He watched her, feigning a nonchalance that was almost real. "You might consider visiting them and traveling together. The religious still seek out Emmett. General Buckler would take Helen, given a chance."

"What is troubling Helen? Her curse finally rise?" Ivy sat down, careless with the amount of flesh she showed the messenger.

"Helen touched an unstable time ribbon. It is causing her trouble. It is possible the valley can see it better."

"What is it specifically?" Ivy stared at him.

He tilted his head at her. "You do not age. Perhaps this is why the ribbon touched her as it did. She is your daughter."

"What do I have to do with what troubles her?" Ivy snarled, her patience growing thin.

"You do not age. She does. Every month she gains a year. I spoke with them. They didn't understand it at first. Finally, one of the elders deduced why the sixteenth of each month saw her rise slightly altered. Only on the *Windsong* is she safe. They have lived aboard for the last two months."

Ivy looked away, thought for a moment. "Only on the sixteenth? Or constantly?"

"They are scared to experiment. She stays aboard all the time. Emmett returns each night. When ashore, if he is touching her when the curse falls, he shares the year. It's very unusual."

"This isn't related to her curse! Telsa told me, it had nothing to do with age!" Ivy snorted. "Nothing to do with me. Just the time fuck up."

It could be. Not that bit about a reversed curse. That was too cruel!

"You know the nature of your daughter's true curse?" Michael asked with curiosity.

"None of your business," Ivy growled.

"How is the baby?" Duran asked to break the tension.

"To all appearances he is flourishing. Avala is doing well."

"What of the mainland? We hear little remains of Ursus' great kingdom." Duran turned the steaks, tossed in the few vegetables, put a lid on the skillet and sat at the table, pulling Ivy onto his lap.

"True, but what does remain is tightly bound. Buckler and Diva use the religious to set a lure to the mountain villages. The weather grows cold, crops fail. And they spread rumors of a threat from the north. A threat Ursus kept at bay."

Ivy grimaced.

Duran thought a moment. "Diva of Orly? Orly is to the north? Is she an agent from Orly or a traitor?"

"We aren't sure," Michael replied.

"So, you'll let her walk the streets of the valley, sew discord..." Ivy snorted.

"The Valley is open to all those stranded by time. We take no sides. You once found refuge there due to a service you performed. But if you are found guilt of drug usage, that will not matter."

"What service did you perform, Ivy love?" Duran asked. He'd always been curious.

"Emmett and I saved Dave from a savage boar. He was injured. I was still recovering from Helen's birth, the three of us managed to enter the valley. Dave knew the way." She paused, then addressed Michael, "Why a hearing? Always thought you who wandered could tell by simply looking at a person?"

"Not when the purported usage is over two decades old."

Ivy jerked from Duran's lap. She spun to stare at him. "Two decades old! He...!"

Duran slapped a hand over her mouth. "Sounds like they are visiting history, honeypot. We know the truth of it. And Helen knows... You have witnesses to testify to the truth. And when this is done with, we kill her."

She quieted, nodded her head and he dropped his hand.

"Now, dinner is ready."

When they woke the next morning, Michael was gone, leaving no sign he'd ever been there.

The tides turned a month later.

Ivy huddled in the bow of the trader's ship, longing for the feel of solid ground again. When sailing, she suffered. Duran sat nearby, keeping a hand on her wild hair. He glanced down at her and frowned. The bright light from the sun revealed how greenish the new strands were. It was bothersome and would make it harder to blend in as they moved toward Gathering Valley.

He had walked with Michael, the evening of his visit, asking whether the valley was guaranteeing their safety when traveling. Michael had shaken his head. "No. Our concerns don't embrace your enemies and how you avoid them. Or don't."

"And if our...her...accuser dies before the hearing?"

"The charge still stands...and there will be no opportunity for cross-examination. I would recommend you travel with a large group. What remains of the Losanglos would suffice."

"Sure, if they aren't tempted by the price on her head," Duran replied, eyeing the tall man at his side. "Most of my allies now live here. We are a contentious clan. The Valley mind if I lie about dire consequences of interfering in our travel?"

Michael turned a charmed eye on him, winked and shook his head. "We also have no concern regarding lies. Use what you need. All we want is for her to arrive and subject herself to testing."

"And if she had no say in whether drugs were used on her or not?" Duran turned to block Michael. "If she were unaware of their use?"

"It's been charged before. She must be prepared to subject herself to intense questioning. To be open. No dodging, no refusal. Such a defense is hard to prove." Michael reached out to touch Duran's eye patch. "You both have reason to wish Diva dead. And that will be used against you. Some of the valley find it difficult to interpret Gabriel's laws with any mercy. Some look to do just that. It will depend on who triumphs."

"Who will defend her?"

"David. And I will oversee the hearing. We have petitioned Gabriel to come. You believe that would be beneficial?" Michaels' voice carried a mild warning with it, but also some hope.

Duran paused, spun to gaze out at the dark sea. "Gabriel set down the laws the valley follows. I have heard of his first foray into the Changed World. He fucking killed over fifty people. An entire settlement!"

"They not only refused to obey the law, but had a hoard of pills that could kill. They bartered with them. It was a harsh lesson. He has been traveling since. Rumors speak of his growing tired of the strict interpretation. It would be a gamble."

"My uncle said Gabriel cried as they died. Hell, yes. We are gamblers. Bring him on." Duran sighed. "And Diva deserves death. Not just for my torture...but I will leave that for the Gathering."

He recalled that conversation as he comforted Ivy. And he wondered about Gabriel, about Helen and what Ivy had in mind regarding her daughter. She'd spoken of using this twist to see herself aged. He understood but worried. Ivy seemed to appreciate his referring to her as woman, and the invitation from his elders, to sit at their fire, touched her. But he caught her studying his bits of gray hair one day. Some things couldn't be changed. He'd accepted that truth years ago. But this spitfire woman? She accepted nothing.

CHAPTER SEVENTEEN

Avala hadn't changed. Ivy and Duran paused at the overlook, having left Trader's Port several days earlier, to catch their breath. The *Windsong* sat placidly, sails stowed. It appeared brilliantly white against the deep blue of the harbor.

Ivy's belly growled.

"I told you to eat before we packed up camp," Duran teased her. "Now everyone will know we are here."

"Yeah, go sit on a stump." Ivy shoved him to one side, clearing the trail ahead for her to lead.

"If it keeps growling they'll meet us with pikes and swords, thinking a wolf is stalking the streets." He snickered as she sauntered away from him. Tilting his head, he admired her ass, back to its rounder aspect. The split skirt she wore just reached her knees, and he liked the new pair of leather sandals she'd bartered for at the port. She looked good and knew it. She knew he liked it. He knew she knew...it was a good bit of knowing going on.

Shifting the pack on his back, he followed her toward the cluster of white buildings, whistling a new melody Trex had taught him. Anything to distract him from thinking about Ivy and Helen. She had something in mind, and he wasn't sure it was a good idea.

His uncles had talked about the damage the time disruptions caused. He recalled meeting a woman who'd survived the change. She still shook at the memory of watching her baby age ten years with every breath it took, only to die and turn to dust in her arms. Ivy had no business messing with whatever touched Helen. But she didn't agree.

Ivy heard the song and smiled slightly. He'd been working on creating a dirty version of the sweet song. It had made last night's campfire entertaining, once he'd quit fighting with her about Helen.

Forty minutes later, she set her pack down on the patio that fronted Bosun's home. Duran sat his down, next to hers, then stretched. "We could have made this last night, Ivy."

"You're just spoiled by having a bed, lazy man." Ivy peered in through the window, then tapped on the glass. "I think Prima is here..."

The old woman opened the door. She blinked at the pair of them, and then nodded. "Ah, Michael got to you."

"Yes, but we were planning on coming before we headed to the mainland anyway," Ivy lied. They hadn't included a trip to Avala in their plans. But she figured acting a concerned parent bought them more goodwill than admitting to never giving it a thought.

Prima snorted, then stood to one side. "Bosun! Your vagabond granddaughter is here, with her worthless sidekick!"

"Sidekick? I'm more than a sidekick!" Duran complained. "She's my sidekick." He turned to look at Ivy. "What the hell is a sidekick anyway?"

She shrugged. "One of those before terms that survived. Someone to kick in the side when bored?"

"Someone to stand at your side and prop you up whether needed or not," Prima explained. "Usually mildly annoying."

"Oh, then it must be you," Ivy snickered.

"Must be, you're much more than mildly annoying," Duran stressed the word 'mildly'. Ivy shot him a glare.

Bosun entered the room, Emmett followed, holding Jerego in

his arms. He smiled at Ivy, walked straight to her and deposited the baby in her arms. "Helen will be glad to see you. Michael tell you about her complication?"

"Yup," Ivy cooed at the baby. "You're getting so big! Looks more like you everyday, Emmett. Here, you take him." She dumped him into Duran's arms, her eyes locked on the basket of food Prima must have brought earlier. She began to rummage through the contents. Biting into a fig, she chewed noisily.

"Michael didn't give us specifics, Emmett." Duran held the baby easily, letting one of his braids fall forward to provide the boy with something to chew on. "How many years has she gained?"

"It's hard to tell. Winter thinks it began eight months ago. Eight years. Tomorrow night is the next."

"Where is she? She doesn't have to stay on the *Windsong* all the time, does she?" Ivy finished the fig and bit into a chunk of bread. "Why can't your family make better bread, Duran?"

"Fuck off, Ivy. Bren makes good bread; you're just a snob. What about it, Emmett? She have to live on that ship?" Duran took a chair, settling the baby on his lap.

"Yes. She is too frightened to attempt setting foot on land." Emmett pushed the basket to the side and wrapped arms around Ivy. "It's good to see you, no matter the reason. You look so much better."

Ivy sighed, letting herself relax in the familiar scent of the man who'd seldom left her side for twenty years. She set the bread down and returned his hug. "You look good, too. Easier to put on weight when not running, right? Especially when you don't have to eat Bren's bread."

She easily stepped away and resumed her attack on the basket.

From the corner of an eye, she noticed Bosun watch the interchange, a slight smile on his face. Ivy was aware of his presence, but chose to ignore him. She appreciated his making a home for Emmett and Helen, completely acknowledging his doing so relieved her of any responsibility toward the two. She figured her grandfather owed her. Let him pay it off with her daughter and leave her out of it.

"So, if she's on the ship, the time warp doesn't touch her? Are you sure it works that way?" Ivy took several figs over to a bench against a wall and sat, continuing her breakfast.

"According to Sammiel the *Windsong* holds it from her. Michael said it might be reversed at Gathering Valley." Emmett picked up his son and nuzzled the baby's long braid of hair. "She is terrified to hold Jerego. One night...the first time it happened, we were touching and I felt it sweep toward her. She said my face aged for a moment, before she pushed me away. What if she were holding the baby, Ivy? Or if she were pregnant? I haven't touched her in months."

"Oh, shit. Didn't think of that," Ivy murmured. She glanced sideways at Duran, who grunted.

"Told you it wouldn't work." He grimaced at her. "You've proven you're fertile."

"What wouldn't work?" Emmett looked from one to the other.

Bosun laid his head back, closed his eyes. "Thought to find your true age, Ivy? Your curse would find another way to haunt you."

"Might have bought her the time to get to the valley with us," Ivy replied. "I won't be tasked for seeking some end to my face not matching my soul."

Duran laughed loudly.

She shot a look of ire at him but he continued to chuckle. He met her eyes and whispered, "But it does...pure sin, sweetness. Pure lust and sin."

"Ha! What you see, buffoon." He winked at her, let his eyes fall to her breasts, she turned slightly away, as if offended. No one was fooled.

Emmett sighed, determined to regain control of the conversation. "She knows she'll likely gain a year on the way to the Gathering. It doesn't matter, as long as we stop this once we get there."

Ivy stood up, walked over to Emmett. Staring directly into his face, she stated baldly, "You shouldn't go. We can take care of her, but you are still sought after by the religious. Stay with your son."

Emmett blinked once, then he simply laughed at her. Without bothering to reply, he left the house, cradling the baby as he did so.

Prima shook her head. "Not a chance in hell he'd let her go without him. You ought to know better. He's heading out to the *Windsong*. If you want to see her, you ought to go along." The old woman snatched the basket from Ivy and stormed from the room.

Bosun took a seat. He took her hand and held it tightly. "You have lost much by leaving him, by refusing a chance to get to know her. And remained away. She understood better than he did."

"What was there to understand?" Ivy snatched her hand away. "I don't...! I can't...! No! Fine! We'll all march to meet Diva and her troops, driven by religious fever. They can twist Emmett, use Helen against him. Burn me, finish off Duran..." She choked and with a curse, left the house.

Duran grinned crookedly at Bosun. "She doesn't understand herself. Killing Ursus was supposed to make it all better. It didn't. She still hurts, still has nightmares. Now this charge of Diva's, that she used drugs? Willingly? It's never going to go away, old man."

"Does she love you, Duran?" Bosun asked.

"It doesn't matter. It doesn't seem to be enough. We have to finish this, see Diva dead. Set her free. Trade pain for pain? She's remembering things, from before. And Diva is there, in her memory. That bitch holds the key. It will tear Ivy apart if Emmett risks himself...and falls?" Duran bent over, put his head in his hands and groaned.

"Does she *love* you?"

"I don't know, old man! I don't know..." Surging to his feet, Duran looked out to the courtyard shower. "I'm going to clean up. She'll come back for that, if nothing else." He hurried outside, shedding clothes as he did so.

The questions stirred up thoughts he'd fought to bury. That she would never be able to leave Ursus behind. That she couldn't move past it. He's dead and his ghost haunted her now. Haunted both of them.

Ivy paced down by the water, eyeing the dock where the *Windsong* was tethered. Come nightfall, they'd move the ship out into the bay further. From what she understood, distance from land eased Helen's monthly anniversary. She saw Bosun strolling onto the dock and headed toward him. She could stand the dock, even if it did make her shiver.

"You seem to be doing better with the ocean, Ivy. I know it isn't easy for you," he ventured a comment.

"She used to curse you and the ocean with the same breath," Ivy replied, not looking toward him at all. "Then she'd wake up a night, screaming out in fear at the memory of the waves smashing her life to pieces."

"She couldn't have saved anyone. It was miracle we survived. She wasn't looking downward, as I was. Ivy, they were gone before the waves swept over that beach. Time turned them to dust."

She turned and studied his face. So many shadows passed over it. Ivy wondered what she didn't know. Grandmother only cursed when talking about this man. He'd never said a nasty word about the woman. So far.

Ivy paused. "I know you had no choice but to push her into the water. To make her swim... Why didn't you wait, let her calm down? She said you ignored her tears."

He turned, gaze met hers, eyes wide. "The water was still rising. We had to move while it was rising, to help us make land. She wasn't crying. She froze. In total shock and denial... I chose life and your mother. I didn't push her, Ivy. I left her. She finally came after me. For weeks she cursed me, swore at me for taking our daughter and leaving her. Then she took your mother and left me."

Ivy blinked. Took a step back, then caught herself realizing how close that step took her to the edge of the dock. "You left her?"

"What else could I do? What would you have done? Once she let your mother slip into the water..." He tilted his head at her. "You didn't know? I turned back to her after surveying the new shoreline and saw my baby girl sinking. I dove in, managed to haul her back to the rock. Then I tied her to me and left for shore."

A shudder ran through Ivy. She sagged to her knees, hugging herself.

Bosun knelt down, facing her. Good thing he didn't try to touch her, Ivy wanted to hit someone. "I didn't blame your grandmother for hating me. But to let go of Rosalie? She was mumbling... '...all gone, all gone...' I couldn't reason with her. She slapped me when I climbed back to the rock, tried to push me off, wouldn't take the baby back. She went mad, Ivy."

"Oh, shit. She...she couldn't forgive you because she couldn't forgive herself." Ivy focused on Bosun. "So, it was all your fault. Always your fault."

"Always my fault. Yes. I tried to protect your mother, but the new council closed ranks and I fell outside. Jero and Ozbi kept on eye on things. Said once I left, your grandmother stopped blaming Rosalie for everything that went wrong. I stayed in touch through the Gathering." He stopped talking as Ivy shook her head. "I know this is all new to you."

"I remember Ozbi. I remember him standing up to Grandmam about my father. Just before Ursus stole our harvest." With a sudden jerk, Ivy regained her feet and hurried away. Too much to think about. Too much to digest. She moved, fast.

Ivy shut out the words of her grandfather. The past was the past and she didn't want to visit there. That far back took her to the woman she was before Ursus ripped her life to pieces. When she'd thought of a life outside of killing. And running. And nightmares.

She stopped before boarding the *Windsong*. The nightmares were supposed to go away once he was dead. They didn't. They just changed. She didn't relive the first captivity anymore, her nightmares took on a new life. Now, Ursus' rushing her didn't end with him near death of the floor. Instead, she froze. He laughed. Killed Telsa, raped Helen then stalked her, taunting, "You'll never be rid of me, Ivy. I am the wound that will never heal, bitch."

And she would scream, and scream and scream. Only to wake with Duran holding her tightly. And she'd cry. She hated crying. But once that dam had been breached, he saw her tears too often. Only Duran. But she still hated it.

She despised still being scared of that monster. She'd been told he was dead. Did she believe it? She kept waking to hear Diva in her head...whispering. The words were too faint to be deciphered. But the tone? Evil. Triumphant. Gloating.

Ivy felt strong. Her body held muscles from all the work on the Chans. Her fighting skills were the best they'd been in decades. Her mind? Her sanity had never felt so fragile. Perhaps because she'd been so far from anything resembling a normal life for too long.

Shaking her head with determination, she climbed about the ship.

She stalked about the lower deck. Crewmembers darted out of her way. She found her daughter in a sunken bar area. Ivy didn't realize it was Helen until she came around to view her front. The changes were shocking.

Ivy gasped, then quickly turned away, breathing hard. The golden hair looked dry, brittle. Her face showed lines of fatigue. Obviously, the quick aging had been brutal.

She would not cry! She'd cried too much since Ursus was dead! Slowly, she straightened her back, and turned to face her daughter.

Jerego sat on her lap, sucking on a bottle.

Ivy swallowed and blinked. Helen sighed and looked down at her son. "I lost the ability to breast feed him after the time curse swept over me."

"I'm...I'm sorry. I never fed you...that way." Ivy's answer sounded forced, she didn't know what to say. She took a chair and sat. Emmett reached for one of her hands. Ivy let him take it and then spoke, "I didn't realize. Of course, you must come. We will demand a cure from Gathering Valley. Michael insinuated it was possible."

"Jerego will stay here with the wet-nurse. I can face one more year here, but then we must hit the road." Helen stated. "If we leave immediately after, we can reach the Gathering before the next one sweeps towards me."

"Well before it. We'll need the time to negotiate with the valley." Tears kept trickling down her cheeks, despite her best efforts to stop them Emmett took his free hand and wiped them away. "Why now?"

"I don't know. It broke when Tesla's curse broke." Ivy brushed his hand away. "I don't have time for tears!" She addressed Helen, "Michael said the *Windsong* keeps the aging at bay... But you look like hell. The last few before the *Windsong*?"

"The *Windsong* held them away, but sometimes, when I step to the pier... It's as I feel them, even if I don't show them. I don't know what will happen once we reach the mainland. There seems to be no rules with this curse." Helen trembled. "My father did not face such drastic changes as he aged. It must be due to the all at once."

Ivy seized Helen's hand. "I take the next wash. I have them to spare. I know Duran fears what would happen if I were pregnant. I'm not pregnant and I will not fuck him again until this is done with. I have years to spare." She darted a look at Emmett. "You will not tell him of my decision. She has to be strong to make the trip. My curse will battle with time."

"I won't tell him, but he'll know." Emmett replied.

Helen sighed. "I don't know what to say. Thank you. I won't argue. How are you so certain of not carrying another child? It happened once."

"Because I knew when it happened the first time. I'd know if it happened again." Ivy squeezed her hand, and then released it. "If you had been raised as a Cruzan woman, you would know how to monitor your body that way. Duran doesn't know all my secrets."

"Can you train me in Cruzan secrets?" Helen asked.

"No, but others here can." Ivy rose to her feet. "I will talk with Leonardo about leaving quickly. We can take to land directly after the sixteenth day and lose no time." She looked at Emmett. "You have been keeping up your training? Teaching her?"

"When I could. My cousin has shown me hunting techniques that will help us move undetected. Helen is slow, Ivy. But she has skill."

Ivy took a deep breath and studied Helen, "You'll need to work as much as you can on flexibility. When slow, fluidity helps in a fight. You fought with... Ursus, didn't you?"

"Yes, from the back of a horse. This is different, but I'll be ready." Helen kissed her son's head. She and Emmett sat, cherishing some peace while Ivy left in search of the *Windsong*'s captain.

Two days later they were under sail.

Ivy sat with Helen on the sixteenth, watching the ship fight with the year time seemed determined to sink into Helen. The woman struggled as she slept, her skin twitched and the room wavered around them both. But the ship won and Helen eventually settled back down into a sleep. But she didn't look rested the next day.

Ivy took Emmett aside. "The *Windsong* wins, but the battle is a hard one. It's why she gets no rest. You keep Duran away as we reach the coast. In fact, I go ashore with Helen first. I'll carry her."

"You have to tell him." Emmett stated.

"No, I don't. He'll figure it out. He's already pissed I'm keeping him at a distance. Let him be pissed. I'm not going to argue with him, and that's all he'd want to do."

He closed his eyes and leaned against the wall. She studied him a moment. "Emmett, quit worrying about me. Or Duran. This is for her. I...I know I owe her. Okay? I know it. I hate it and I resent it, but I know it. I should have gone back, stole her away. Saved her from that monster. I didn't. I pushed her away, I welcomed being free of her. This is something I can do and not endanger our mission. Duran would fight me."

"You wanted to go back, Ivy. Don't forget that. I don't. I was terrified you'd drag us back into the stronghold. All those insane plans to steal Helen away. None could have worked. You always wanted...until the day you saw her laugh with her father. Then you gave up, only then." He studied her face.

"But I didn't go back. I didn't try. I just hurt and let it hurt. And let that monster touch her, raise her, laugh with her. Those giggles should have been mine!" Ivy paced, arms wrapped about herself. She should have tried. She never actually tried. And she could not forget that.

Emmett began to say something more, but Ivy stared him into silence. He took a deep breath. "What will he do when he realizes you've turned him away from this decision? Ivy, you put your relationship in danger."

"It's mine to do so. Not yours. Yours is on that bed and back in Avala. Get it?"

He swallowed, and slowly nodded. She slipped from the room.

Tensions rode high in the ship as they approached the mainland. Duran growled at everything, or stayed silent. Emmett would chatter as if filling up the silence.

They gathered supplies and piled them at the stern of the boat, waiting for the gangplank to be lowered and the raft prepared. Ivy glanced over at him with a sharp look and he bowed to the inevitable. Snapping his fingers he grabbed Duran. "I forgot the water skins. I can help with the zodiac if you'll get them?"

Duran grumbled, but stalked to the upper decks. A moment later the boat was ready, the plank lowered. Helen trembled as Emmett helped her into the raft. She grasped his hand tightly as he kissed her.

Ivy took a seat next to her, pausing for one last word with Emmett. "He's going to be more than growl. Don't let on what I'm doing, Emmett."

"I'll handle him. Go!" Emmett helped push the boat totally

into the water. A small engine roared to life and they quickly left the ship.

He watched them as they grew smaller. He could make out the shoreline as the ship bobbed up and down. Duran threw the skins down. "What the fuck?"

"They'll come back for us." Emmett turned to look at Duran. "She isn't pregnant. She said she'd know."

"Yeah, well all that mumbo jumbo of the Cruz females don't mean shit in this world. If it did, he'd never have made her pregnant. Helen doesn't look good, but she can hold one more year..." Duran's eyes narrowed as Emmett paled. "What the fuck is going on?"

Emmett swallowed. "She lied to me again and I believed her."

"So? She lies well." Duran studied the slender man's face. "What is she doing? What is she doing?" He grabbed Emmett's arms and shook the man.

Emmett closed his eyes a moment, thinking. He ignored Duran's threats, reached into his heart. She did lie well. And not just to him. He took a deep breath. "No, I believe her, Duran. When Helen touches the shore, the years held back will fall on her. But Ivy is going to take them."

"You God damned idiot!" Duran began throwing off clothes and before Emmett could stop him, he dove into the water and began to swim. He'd never make it in time.

CHAPTER EIGHTEEN

Ivy began peeling off her shirt as they drew closer to the shore. Helen followed suite. They'd discussed this, knowing a skin-to-skin contact would be best to ensure Ivy took the years. There would be nine of them. Ivy shoved the shirts into one of the packs and turned to look Helen in the face.

"I'm strong and I want to carry you on my back. This is going to work as I touch the earth or not until you do?"

"Me, I think."

"Then you keep your legs up until I say so. I want to make sure my footing is good and we don't end up totally soaked." Ivy turned away.

"Are you sure?" Helen knew her voice was hoarse. "You don't have to do this. You don't owe me anything..."

"I damned well do! And I want this. You don't get it...I want this! I'm being selfish." Ivy looked at the shore, a small smile on her face. "I want to see some difference. You're young, you think being young forever would be wonderful. I thought that once." She met Helen's eyes again. "It isn't wonderful. It's a real curse."

"I don't get it. But...I'm glad you're cursed, Ivy. Because I want to see my little boy grow up." Helen paused, "I am thankful, even if you do this for you and not for me."

"Fine. Just so we're straight." Ivy stood up slightly as the shore drew distinct. "There, that spit of sand." She pointed and the pilot steered them calmly. He'd made no comment as they'd bared their breasts. Or asked to be taken ashore first.

The raft hit sand and he set the engine to idle. He tossed the packs far above the tide line and waited as Ivy stepped out first. The water was knee high. This was a calm cove with small rivulets instead of large waves. Ivy found firm footing and turned her back.

Helen took a deep breath, shook her hands quickly, as if throwing off the fear, then she climbed to Ivy's back. The girl was slender, Ivy could do it. She didn't bend under the added weight. Her back and narrow waist gave adequate holds. Helen wrapped arms around her shoulders and grasped her own wrists. Ivy helped her guide her legs, grasping her at both knees, getting a firm grip on her. And then she stepped to the dry land.

Helen buried her face in Ivy's short hair.

"I'm scared," she whispered.

"Think of Jerego," Ivy replied. "You are too skinny. You better be able to fight, Helen."

"I will," Helen shivered as Ivy stopped.

Was that a shout from the ship? Helen tried to turn her head, but Ivy distracted her. "Now, slowly ease your feet down..."

Ivy bent as Helen's ankles were released. Slowly, she straightened her legs and slid them behind her mother. Her bare feet skimmed the sand and Ivy drew a tight breath. She jerked them up. Ivy abruptly squatted and both feet thumped into the sand. Ivy shuddered and set her hands on the sand.

Helen swallowed, and then tried to pull away. Ivy reached up and grasped her wrists, holding her still. "No...not yet."

The raft left the shore and headed back to the ship.

"Ivy? M...mother?"

"Oh. Fuck..." Ivy drew a deep breath and shuddered again.

Helen wrenched her hands free and stood. The sudden realization of how much better she felt saw her smile, but a groan from Ivy chased that happiness away. She quickly went to her knees and pulled Ivy up.

Ivy blinked at her and sighed, "Feels so good..." To finally feel something different, something her soul knew was natural. A shift in her skeletal frame, a loosening of the skin, she flexed a foot, aware that it had widened, minutely. So attuned to any changes...it was divine. Then she folded into the sand, unconscious.

Helen cradled her, "No! No! Ivy! Mother? No! Wake up, wake up!"

The girl's voice came from so far away...

Helen held her as the raft returned, a wet Duran and a frantic Emmett hurried to the pair.

Duran hauled Ivy out of Helen's arms and examined her. The changes were slight, but when a woman hadn't changed in twenty-eight years, it shocked. Duran drew a finger down the subtle line between her eyes, down her nose to lips, where a slight smile lingered.

"Oh. You bitch..." He sighed.

While he held Ivy, waiting for her to wake up, Emmett examined Helen.

"It's like you never went through any of it!" He stood back, clearly surprised. "She has all of them?"

"I feel so different. All of them? Why?" She blinked as pulled her close and wrapped arms around her. She shivered. "Why is she unconscious?"

"I think she's just asleep. You selfish witch! How could you let her do this? How could you risk everything, just to lose a few years?" Duran snarled at Helen. He turned his ire at Emmett, "And you! Stupid bastard! What were you thinking?"

Emmett pushed Helen behind. "This wasn't about a few years. It was about making sure Helen could make the trip. Ivy wasn't pregnant, she wanted it!"

"So damn sure she wasn't pregnant! Fine. What about her loss of skill? We've been training for months! She's faster and stronger than she's ever been. Well, she was! She hasn't known age in twenty-eight years. I'm the only one who thought about how this was going to affect her? You're all idiots!" He turned his attention back to Ivy, finally totally awake.

She looked at him, eyes weary. She sighed.

At a whisper, she asked, "Still want to fuck me?"

"You are so fucking stupid, woman." Duran let go of her and she floundered to keep from going flat. One elbow caught and she leaned crookedly on it.

She winced. "That hurt. Then it just felt right. Really strange." She fought to get to her feet, reached for the pack and hauled out her shirt.

Duran has stalked off and stood, feet in the surf.

"Ivy, how do you feel?" Emmett asked her directly. "Did you hear what he said? About your training being lost?"

"Yeah, I heard him. We have time to tighten things up. I'll be fine." She threw on the shirt, making sure Helen got hers. For a moment she focused on her daughter. "You look as you did before...how many did I get?"

"All of them, I think." Helen gingerly touched her breasts. "They feel heavy, as if I still have...milk?"

"Better wrap them tightly, in case you are lactating again. It was the only thing that helped me after we got away," Ivy advised. "There's likely some bandage materials in Emmett's pack."

"I'll get them." Emmett shook his head. "Ivy, you have to talk to him."

"Why? Won't do any good." She shrugged.

"Try."

With a deep breath, she walked toward Duran. He turned, glared at her.

Ivy snorted. "Yeah. Didn't tell you. You weren't with her the night she held another year off. If I hadn't done this, we'd be carrying her right now. I know, you don't believe I could be so certain I wasn't pregnant. Cruz do have secrets. Duran, I had to do this."

"No, you didn't. Or, if you did... You should have told me. Convinced me."

"Oh? I could have convinced you?" She snorted in disbelief. "No fucking way."

"If you'd told me all of it, I'm not stupid. *We* would have worked it out. But no, you had to do it alone. When are you going to see that you are not alone!?" He glared at her, his face naked with more than anger.

She read pity there, and sorrow and worst of all, hurt.

Ivy boiled with confusion. She opened her mouth, ready to spill out derision. Then her heart went to war with her head. Her head spun.

Duran spoke softly, "That what you want, Ivy? To be alone?"

"No," she whispered, arms tightly wrapped about herself. "No." This time she looked up at him. She swallowed. "No. I don't want to be alone. I can't do this alone."

"Ah. You just want me to help you win."

"No! No, Duran! That isn't what I meant. Shit." Ivy stepped closer to him. "I know I need you. Shit. I don't want to need you. It's just me, Duran. It's just me..."

He stared at her. He had to know how difficult that small admittance was. She waited to see if he got it.

"Duran. Okay, I should have tried to explain."

"Yeah. All right, fine. It's done. She does look better. I don't know what you've lost. Let's see." He left the ripples of water and strode to a pile of driftwood. Seizing up a long branch, he stripped it bare then broke it over his knee

Ivy stood back, knowing what he was up to. He tossed her one of the lengths and then attacked her.

Emmett and Helen spun as the sharp smack of striking staffs filled the beach. Helen surged forward and Emmett stopped her.

"No, they are sparring." He watched carefully as Duran appeared to beat Ivy to the sand. The woman he'd known since childhood went down on one knee and bellowed as Duran rained down blows at her outstretched staff. Then with a lightning swift strike, she swept her staff down and around, knocking Duran flat on his back into the sand.

He rolled back to his feet to come at her again.

She lifted one hand, panting. "I give! I give!"

Duran jerked to a halt, watching Ivy closely.

She came to her feet with an effort.

"You are right," she gasped. "My stamina is down. But I'll get better."

"You're still fast." He reached over, took her staff. "I'll keep these and we keep working."

"Fine." She watched him walk away. With a wincing shrug, she moved over to Emmett. "We'd better get going if we want off this beach before dark."

"Maybe we should camp here tonight," he suggested.

"Uh uh. We'll need fresh water by tomorrow. Duran says there's a creek the better part of a day inland. We get some miles in now, be easy to make it in time to rest longer there." She shrugged her pack to her back, slipped her sturdy sandals on and trailed Duran into the forest.

Helen and Emmett followed silently, nothing else to say.

As she walked, Ivy tried to put her thoughts in order. The months on Chan saw the ability to blank out what haunted her fade. The memories had grown vivid, even during the day, and actual thoughts of the future. The work helped, but whenever a quiet time appeared, she found herself looking at Duran and wondering if she could stay with him for the rest of her life. Did she want to?

He would be chatting with friends, laughing and she'd look up from whatever task she'd taken on and want to smile. Want to walk to him and set a hand at his strong back. This was more than lust, though lust ranked high in her deliberations.

If thoughts of Duran didn't intrude, she'd remember her family, all killed by Ursus. All but this grandfather she wasn't sure she wanted. The stories her grandmother told about him wound around her. If she let go of Grandmam's hatred, would it be betraying the old hag? She'd never really approved of her granddaughter. Once she'd grown up, they'd argued a lot. But the loyalty was still in place.

Each morning, she woke lost in the memory of being raped. And swore she heard Diva's voice, encouraging Ursus, explaining what the drug would do. Why hadn't she remembered that before? Was it real?

Ivy shook her head, tried to concentrate on the path before her. The added years saw her step a bit heavier and lose her breath faster. It annoyed, but was nothing that couldn't be trained away. They had a month to get to the Gathering and she'd be back in top form before they arrived.

Duran marched them for several hours, but darkness finally brought them to a halt. They camped in a sharp valley; the ruined bit of a great bridge spanned the gap hundreds of feet above them. She'd looked at Emmett, then at the bridge and he'd shrugged.

"It's far enough away. I'm fine."

Helen set about lighting a small fire as Ivy gathered wood. Duran and Emmett hunted. They were gone a long time.

"Aren't you worried?" Helen asked as they sat close to the fire.

"No, nothing here that would offer them problems. Duran's foot is totally healed, so he won't fall or anything. They are probably fighting somewhere. Or worse, discussing what to do about me." Ivy snorted. "Idiots."

"You toss insults about quite freely. They worry about you."

"I worry about me, isn't that enough?" Ivy rolled her eyes. "Worry doesn't accomplish anything. It just distracts from what needs to be done."

"Words of wisdom from my freewheeling mother," Helen chuckled. "Thank you for taking the years. They settled on you easy enough, why was it so hard for me?"

"You hadn't earned them," Ivy replied with a shrug. "I don't know! I wanted them, you didn't?"

"Why would you want to age? I honestly want to know!"

Ivy poked at the fire for a moment, ran a hand over her hair, leaving it ruffled even more than it already was. She took a breath. "Duran."

"Duran wants you to be older?"

"No, I want to be older...because I should be older! I should carry as many grey hairs as he does. Back at Chan, the young men poked at him, tried to win me away. It started out fun. It became tiresome. At Gathering, it didn't matter. Saw each other every few years. But now? Ursus is dead and soon Diva will be dead. We'll probably go back to Chan..."

"You want to stay with him and have it appear right." Helen shook her head. "It is right, who cares what it looks like?"

"I care. I want to be what I am. Forty-eight years old. I just do! What if you'd kept aging, without the exhaustion and wear? What if you passed Emmett, became an old hag while he was young and vital? Your son sees an old woman at his crib?"

"That is different, I'd leave him too soon... Oh." Helen nodded. "He leaves you. Slower but still. All right."

"He take care of you? Ursus?" Ivy asked after several moments of silence had passed.

She looked into the fire as she answered, "At first. I always saw him. He showed off for me. Did silly things, like riding a horse backward. Taught me how to use a sword. But it faded once he saw you in my hair."

"Humph. You hate me for that?"

"No! Well, shit. Yes. At first. But not for long. I owed you my life. I knew how rare children are. I used to tell myself the reason my father took so many women to bed was because he wanted me to have a sibling. He did it for me. I realized one day how sick that was. Actually saw a woman being dragged into his chamber. She screamed so loudly."

"You once said I was just a spoil of war and should have bent to his desire."

"I lied. No, I know that is the truth. You were a spoil of war.

But the rest was a lie I told myself. I tried to love him." She swallowed, obviously uncomfortable. Ivy had been hard, but she needed to know. Helen seemed determined not to cry. A rustle from the wood behind her signaled the men returned.

Duran took a seat next to Ivy, who began to skin the three rabbits they'd brought. Emmett appeared a moment later. He sat down and sighed, "Found another ruin. More complete. Too many ghosts."

"What did you do?" Helen took his hand.

"Collapse, I hauled him free but they followed or something. Had to go far out of the way to shake them," Duran replied. "We'll need to find a different route than I'd planned."

"I think it was an ancient roadway." Emmett shuddered. "I got used to not seeing them."

"Strange, how some ruins are so gone and others are still recognizable," Duran mused.

"The time changes struck unevenly," Ivy offered up. She smiled slightly. "One time I found a big house, still furnished. They had some lovely stuff before the world changed. A fountain was in the back and a garden that was exquisite. I swear, the dirt looked like it had been newly turned, a small hand trowel sat near a scattered pile of dust. No rhyme or reason to how it hit. I went back years later and the walls had fallen in, the garden taken over by vines."

"You take anything from it?" Helen asked.

"Some cloth, a few knives. It felt like it waited. Spooked me. Usually we find a house like that, we stripped it of anything useful. There were a few in our territory. Used to roam with my cousin..." Ivy's voice faded off. She tossed the rabbit skins into the bush behind her and quietly set up a stick to hold the meat while it cooked.

The night closed in around them. Emmett held to Helen's hand while Duran and Ivy avoided looking at each other.

It took five nights before they fought to a fever pitch.

CHAPTER NINETEEN

She held him off each night. Pleading exhaustion the first night. The second the camp was small and there was no privacy. The third night she kept watch, then pressed him to take the second half, claiming Helen and Emmett had done enough that day. The fourth she simply said no when he reached for her.

That fifth night Duran snapped at Helen. When Emmett rose to defend her, the two men actually came close to blows. Ivy returned from hunting and bellowed at both of them to knock it off.

"You aren't mad at me." Emmett slid his glance at Ivy. "Take it up with her."

Duran snarled, but turned to glare at Ivy. "He is right. Come on, we're taking a walk."

"No, we aren't. I just took a walk, we walked all day, and yesterday and the day before. I am not taking a walk." Ivy tossed the small deer toward Emmett. "Little bugger took me on a steep chase."

"Walk." Duran spread his arm, blocking Ivy from the fire, attempting to direct her back into the trees.

"No."

"You bitch. Fine, you want to have it out here?"

"Call me a name? That's the best you can come up with? What's got up your ass, Duran?"

"You, always you. I'm giving you a chance to convince me, Ivy. Don't you want to take it?" He pulled his arms in and folded them, still blocking her from the fire.

She pushed past him and sat, took a drink from the flask. "Convince you of what?"

"Convince me that it's necessary for you to take Helen's next year from her. It's why you're pushing me away each night. You're already planning on it." He grabbed at her hair and hauled her upright. "Aren't you?" His voice rose in volume.

"Maybe!" she hissed back. "Let me go!"

Helen glanced at Emmett, confusion on her face. "I can take the next year. I think it will help dry my breasts up. Make it easier when we get to Gathering Valley..."

"See? Never even asked her, did you?" Duran pulled Ivy higher.

Ivy snarled and spit in his face, twisting in his grip to swing a leg into his side. He grunted and she followed up with another. Soon, the two were wrestling on the ground. Ivy punched and kicked, while Duran blocked, trying to pin her down with his bulk. He finally succeeded.

Ivy panted, trying to heave him off. There was no chance. He just studied her furious face. "You said next time we'd talk..."

"I did not!" she spat back at him.

"It was understood."

"You don't understand! You can't understand!" She quit struggling and closed her eyes. "I don't want...! I can't... Explain!"

"Yes, you can. I'm not stupid, Ivy. Don't treat me like I'm stupid." Duran waited a moment, then slowly began to ease off of her. "No more fighting."

"Thought you wanted me to keep training." Ivy pushed herself up, brushing mud from her hands.

"Nice try. We both know you'd fall in close combat with someone my size. Survival comes from not letting anyone get that close." He spit, trying to clear the dirt from his mouth. "You find a stream like I said?"

"Yes."

"Come on, let's go clean up." He turned without waiting for her agreement and stalked away from the fire.

She sagged.

"Go on, this will take time. You're filthy. And make some noise as you come back." Emmett looked at Helen. She snickered.

Ivy snorted. "If you take that year, you can't fuck him now."

"She isn't taking the year. I will. It won't be much to me and I can't get pregnant," Emmett sedately replied. He eyed Helen. "Don't argue, I've waited long enough. And your breasts are already showing signs of drying up. You don't need it."

Ivy left them debating the issue; sure that argument wouldn't result in the same messy situation as hers had. She followed the faint game trail down to the stream Duran had remembered. His recall of terrain always had impressed her. She and Emmett generally kept their roaming to the foothills and out of the coast and inland valleys.

She found the stream and looked about for him. Hearing a slight whistle, she followed the watercourse to a soft bend. A friendly stream, it gleamed in the moonlight, bare ripples betrayed some rocks and it smelled of clouds and sparkling air. She took a deep breath, looking up from the water as she came around the bend.

He stood thigh high in a calm pool. Her mouth instantly watered, lips parted and she nearly moaned. His bare back gleamed as water dribbled from his hair. A broad back tapered to a narrow waste and on down to thighs, thick with muscle. The water followed a path her hands knew well. In the tempered light, his scars disappeared.

Ivy understood the reaction lust carried. She'd bedded a great many men without thought of deeper issues. Duran did more than see her belly sink, nipples grow taut or heat build at her thighs. She felt an inferno of physical need, but even more than that. She longed to hear his voice croon in her ear, meet his eyes gazing into hers. She delighted in hearing him laugh, watching him cook, even play with the two children living on Chan.

Pausing to watch him, she shook her head. She didn't want this. He was going to be hurt, disappointed, angry. And she...

No. She refused to speculate further. Thrusting the thoughts away, she let her gaze roam up and down his body. Without volition, she walked toward him.

He turned and smiled at her, one hand dropping to rub at his belly, drawing attention to his ready cock. He knew. She tried to resent that, but couldn't. So what? He knew the power his body held. Nothing she hadn't made plain to him, she wouldn't fault him for being attentive.

He gestured to where his clothing lay, tossed far enough to be safe from the stream. Ivy stripped off her shirt as she drew near, aimed for the pile but missed. He laughed, rescued it from drifting away. With a chuckle, he wrung the water from it then proved his prowess with a perfect throw to the dry pile.

Getting out of her trousers proved a problem. She fell on her ass, cursed as she jerked them free of her feet and left them to join Duran. He hadn't moved, just watched her.

"Chica. Being dirty bothering you, eh?"

"Yeah, dirt. Right." She strode over to him and stood, chest to chest, barely an inch between them. She gazed up into his face. Moonbeams bounced off the water and played on the side of his face. His teeth gleamed.

"Wanna fight some more?" he taunted.

"No." She grasped his cock, watched closely as his eyelids dropped and the smiled broadened. He drew a deep breath as she ran a thumb over the tip, deliberately teasing him. The muscles at his belly tightened.

"You don't fight fair." His voice sounded husky, nearly growling.

"I'm not fighting. I'm fucking." She moved side to side, brushing at his chest with her aching nipples.

"Not worried about getting pregnant?" He raised a hand, set it at her hip, pulling her closer, trapping her hand between them.

"Never was mine. That was your worry."

"No, chica." He bent, kissed her eyelids then whispered, "My hope."

Oh, shit. She fell against his chest fully, trying to breath. "Duran?"

"Yes, Ivy." He held her snug up against. His cock still stiff, one hand still roaming up and down her back.

"I don't...know..." she tried to say *no fucking way*. Tried to deny him that hope. And couldn't.

He drew her face up to look directly into her eyes. "I do know. One day, in our future. *Our* future. I am not running away. And I'm not letting you go. You're mine, Ivy. And I'm yours."

His words drove straight to her heart. And they scared her.

Duran seemed to sense that fear. He smiled. "Together, chica. No one can stand against us. No one."

She took another breath while he waited.

"What if..." She stopped as he shook his head.

"Nada. Nothing is going to drive me away. I love you, Ivy. I need you. I want you. I've waited long enough."

"They might find me guilty," she admitted to him. "She might win."

"Never."

His declaration took root. So certain, so determined! How could she fight with that? She smiled. "No one's gonna stop you, eh?"

"No one. Not even you."

"Loving me isn't easy, Duran."

"No shit. And loving me? Easy?"

"Yes," she whispered. "Very easy."

"Good." He bent his knees, grasped her thighs and lifted her up. She wrapped her arms around his shoulders, spread her legs and welcomed him. They kissed and she lost herself in his strength and desire.

It was dawn before they returned to the camp sight.

Twenty days later they neared Gathering Valley. There'd been no further arguments. Duran and Ivy took every opportunity to practice at fighting. Ivy encouraged Helen to hone her skills while Duran took on Emmett. They would be ready for anything.

Emmett cursed softly after spending a third day seeking a way into the valley. Ivy snickered. "They aren't ready?"

"We're a week early."

"They aren't usually so strict about the timeline. People used to arrive early all the time," Helen stated.

"It's because of Gabriel. He's there and he's a stickler," Duran explained. "We'll just have to wait."

"We..." Emmett's head snapped to one side.

Ivy saw, grabbed at Helen and threw her to the ground, covering her. "Shhhh!"

Duran ducked behind a large boulder as Emmett slid up to a broad tree. The sound of horses grew louder. The four froze.

Several voices grew distinct.

"I think the trail was false. They didn't come this way. I doubt they are even here yet..."

"Basha knows how to read a trail. We just missed them. Probably already tracked back since the valley ain't open yet."

"I'll get back and let her know..."

"I'll set up sentries. We'll catch 'em... Can't eat dirt..."

They rode away still talking.

"Idiots," Duran hissed. "If they'd been on foot and quiet, they'd have had us."

"Good thing they are idiots. We should have been more on guard." Ivy helped Helen back to her feet. All four moved into the shadows of the boulder to hold council.

"They are right, our stores aren't going to last until the valley opens," Emmett began. "We can't hunt while being hunted."

"Sure we can. Snares." Helen replied. "And we eat light."

Duran shared a glance at Ivy. "We can eat light. But we need more water."

Ivy thought a moment. "What about where the Mercy River leaves the valley. It's half a day to the south. We can skirt the valley edge..."

"Not all of us. That is one of the most popular entries. Emmett? You said your cousin taught you to move without sound. You get the water. Ivy can set snares. I'll keep watch."

"I'm not useless. I can help," Helen complained.

"You keep track of the stores. Inventory them and make sure they will last if Ivy can't bring more home." Duran offered. "You know how to light a smokeless fire?"

"Of course. I traveled with my father," Helen replied. "Where do we camp?"

"Remember where those three large boulders formed a partial cave?" Duran asked Ivy. She nodded.

"Good idea. I thought I saw mushrooms near there. There might be rabbits in the bit of meadow we passed..." Ivy looked thoughtful. "We have to be invisible." She swallowed and looked directly at Duran. "Her. Diva?"

"Seems likely." Duran sighed. "Can't risk it, gir...woman."

"No, I get it. It can wait." Ivy agreed.

The four paused; the easy part of their journey was over. They spent several hours returning to the boulder cave. Emmett gathered the nearly empty water bottles. They shared what was left, then he departed for the river. Ivy prepared several snares and saw them set up in likely spots to net results.

The nights were cold without a fire. They only risked enough to take the raw from the rabbits. Ivy and Duran practiced no more, content that they were ready for battle. Several times, patrols came close and they overheard a great deal of who was aligned against them.

The Holy Roller elite traveled with Diva. They assisted in convincing the small holdings near Gathering Valley to ally with her. Several of the mercenary groups were now part of the entourage. When she served as Ursus' bodyguard, she'd been considered tough but lazy. Now she was merciless. Rumor had it she was determined to recapture the length and breathe of his kingdom, lost during the internal struggle for power.

The religious viewed her as a savior. Ivy nearly burst into laughter the day she overheard that bit of nonsense. As the day the valley would open grew closer, the patrols increased until all the four could do was huddle in the boulder shelter and share what little remained of their stores.

"You think your everlasting credit will still be in place with Gabriel there?" Duran whispered in her ear. "I have a great thirst for beer."

She silently snickered then turning her head, she whispered back, "Don't you always?"

Emmett slid close. "Tomorrow is the sixteenth. I'll take the year, but she could cry out."

Ivy nodded. "We'll keep close. Muffle it. Day after tomorrow, the valley opens. You ready to face the Holy Rollers?"

"Of course." He slid back to hold Helen. They'd been playing a quiet game with colored stones, doing what they could to pass the time.

Duran simply entertained himself by meddling with Ivy, sliding hands beneath her shirt and teasing her breasts. It tortured him as well, but he counted it a good distraction from the peril around them.

That night was extraordinarily quiet when Helen's curse fell upon her, without warning. Emmett felt her shiver and reacted swiftly, wrapping himself around her.

He hissed, "Ivy!"

She'd been keeping watch and bristled at his breaking the silence. Until she turned and heard her daughter's sharp cry.

"Shit!" She threw herself at the shadows just as Duran rolled and covered the pair with his larger body. Ivy left him to it, her attention going to the greater forest. Had the cry been heard?

The three in the back of the shallow cave shifted, she heard a mumbled curse from Duran, but the sharper cry wasn't repeated. She gazed out into the shadows cast by the gibbous moon, straining to hear anything different.

An hour later, she saw a shadow pass between three trees, followed by three more. They made broad circles, coming closer and closer to the cave. Duran slid up next to Ivy, watching as she did.

He leaned close and all but breathed the words into her ear, "We can take them. Slit throats to keep it quiet."

She nodded then gestured toward the back.

"Fine. She's awake and he's asleep, recovering. Thinks we lost track of the days at sea."

Ivy sighed and then the two of them moved from the cave entrance. She kept her blade hidden in her sleeve, wanting no reflection to betray her. Her first victim made no noise but a sigh and the dripping of his blood on the leaf litter. She slid him to the ground and stalked the next. This one she held off on. Her knife slid into his neck, but didn't slit through.

"How many?" she hissed.

He shook his head and she nodded. "Very well." Without a qualm, she killed him. A soft footfall at her back saw her wheel, ready to strike when a beam of moonlight revealed Duran. He carried both of his prey.

"Moving them," he whispered.

She nodded and bent to search the man she killed. Duran returned as she cleaned out the first scout, taking several weapons and a small bottle of water before Duran carried him away. The next day the noose drew tighter.

They didn't move from the shadows, barely daring to breath.

Near midnight, they were found. But the force surrounding them didn't close in. Ivy used a throwing knife to kill the one who announced their discovery. Since none knew how many more blades she held they kept a distance from the shadows.

Duran called out for truce.

Ten minutes later, they heard Diva speaking. "Should have traveled with your allies, Duran. This time I'll have your balls as a coin purse. Take them."

They couldn't see them, but heard the rush toward the cave and prepared to go down with the maximum amount of carnage.

The great clang of a bell signaled the valley opening, just as a figure jumped from above them and raised his sword. Only to fall twitching to the ground.

"No weapons will be raised in Gathering," Dave stepped from the darkness, torch held aloft.

"They are outside valley borders!" Diva protested.

"The borders are ours to establish. They are within the valley, as are you. Permanent truce is enforced, Diva of Orly. Do you contest?" Michael made his declaration loud, it rang above the trees. Then he joined Dave. Together they walked confidently to the cave.

Ivy stood up straight, Duran at her side. She'd already sheathed her blade. Emmett packed the rest of the weapons while Helen gathered their packs. Without fear, the four followed the two Guardians through the group and into the comforts of Gathering Valley.

CHAPTER TWENTY

"Why are they waiting?" Ivy sighed as she lifted the decadent coffee drink and took a sip. The intense sweetness on her tongue nearly brought a moan from her throat.

"We are at their call. Who knows?" Emmett broke one of the cookies in two, handed half to Helen, half to Ivy.

"At least the Holy Rollers won't come in here. Thank you." She took the cookie. "Where is Duran this morning?"

"Meeting with the mercs from Losanglo. Seeing if we're welcome in the first meeting. Since we haven't done any work this last year. Well, you haven't." Ivy smirked at Emmett. "Lazing about on Avala. At least Duran and I have been working."

"They don't count construction as merc work," Emmett didn't rise to her bait. "All four of us could claim guardian duties."

"I think that's the path Duran wants to take." She eyed Helen. "The religious been shadowing you?"

"Everywhere we go. They yell at us in the streets, but the merchants won't let them into the shops, so there is always shelter. They get bored and move on."

"What do they yell?" Ivy looked up as Dave stepped close. "Any news?"

"Nothing new. They are watching, just be patient. I brought these, new pastry." He set down a platter. "Cheese and sausage."

"Damn, that sounds good." Ivy reached for the stuffed croissant.

Dave smiled and hurried away.

"Well?" Ivy wiped at the crumbs as she again glanced at Helen. "What they say?"

"Same as they usually do," Emmett answered. "I'm a heretic. Want to know where the baby is. Accuses you of killing the baby." He held up his hand, ticking the villainies off, finger by finger. "Offers of redemption if I'll come with them and tell the truth. Even those who just plead with me...wanting to know if they are saved."

"Fools. No one is saved, we're just here." Ivy thought a moment. "Why would I kill the baby?"

"Because it was Ursus' grandchild." Helen calmly stated. "Why don't you go out more?"

"I don't trust myself if I see her." Ivy waved Dave back over, ignoring the idea that she'd kill the baby because of Ursus. "Michael said you were going to defend me from the charges."

"Yes." Dave wiped at the table. "Once they announce the trial we'll have sporadically monitored meetings."

"Monitored? Why?"

Dave addressed Helen, "To assess honesty. We won't know when the monitor is watching. They'll look for stories not lining up."

"A good liar can fool them?" Ivy asked.

"Unlikely."

"You don't want to hear anything until then?" Emmett reached over and took Ivy's hand. "Will she be alone with just you?"

Dave tilted his head at Emmett. "If she requests a support witness, she is allowed it."

"I want to be there. She is my mother, these charges address the time of my conception." Helen reacted to Ivy's snort. "You *are* my mother."

"You think I forget?" Ivy rolled her eyes and pulled her hand free. "It's my story, girl. You were incidental. Neither you or Emmett were there at the beginning."

Emmett objected, "I was there! Four months of you carrying her, I was there. When he gloated, you ranted. You had nightmares; you talked in your sleep. Hell, you screamed in your sleep!"

"Months after my alleged drug use," Ivy retorted. She held up her hand, talking about it all just muddled her thoughts.

Were her dreams real? Was Diva present?

She sighed and turned to Dave. "Enough. Can they monitor whether dreams are truth?"

The gentle barista studied Ivy. "Only if you believe them truth."

"Not much use then. Of course I believe them."

"Do you? Or are you afraid they aren't true?" Dave smiled crookedly. "I am not the expert, but they will make certain before judgment. I have no doubts."

Ivy found herself touched to the core. She took a trembling breath, then nodded. "Thank you, Dave."

He bent and pressed a kiss at her forehead. "De nada. I am not your only ally, Ivy." He looked over at the door, "Duran! What would you like to drink?"

"A beer?" Duran laughed. "Whatever is coldest and sweetest, Dave. Gracias!" Ivy snickered at him; they didn't serve beer at the café.

He walked over, pulled out a chair and grinned, "We're in. Buckler is out."

"He wanted into the meeting? He's a general for a warlord. He isn't allowed." Ivy shook her head. "There was a question?"

"He's enrolled a good third of the mercs into his forces. Former mercs. That came to a head today. It isn't a merc force. As he claimed. We, on the other hand, have been working as guards to a secret colony, all four of us. So, we are in." Ursus sat. "I arranged a private bath. We won't be badgered like last time." He set his arm over Ivy's shoulders. "Sound good, chica?"

"Yup."

Ivy rolled her eyes as he examined the three of them closely.

"You all look gloomed up. What is it?"

"Just impatient with no progress of this entire trial fiasco," Ivy replied. "And nothing on our request regarding Helen's time infection."

"Is that what we're calling it now?" Duran grinned.

"That is what they are calling it," Emmett answered this time. "We got that out of Dave."

"There isn't a big hurry. I have time..." Helen snickered, "... while we're here."

Dave set a large frosty drink down in front of Duran and he gleefully fell on it. Ivy leaned back and rested her head on Duran's broad forearm; aware of a tiredness she wasn't familiar with. But it felt good. Different. Different was good.

She felt Emmett tense, his foot lightly touching hers. Opening her eyes she followed his glare to the doorway. "Who is that?" she asked, keeping her voice casual.

"Buckler." Duran glanced over his shoulder. "Must have had me followed."

"Why? It's no secret we like it here." Ivy stood and simply stared at the hulking man. She hadn't recognized him. Two years ago he'd been thin and wiry and kept his head shaved. Now he was bulky. Muscles ran up and down his arms and his legs like great ropes. And he'd let the hair grow. Barely long enough for a tail, most of it fell forward to his neck. A very thick neck.

"Can we do anything for you, General?" Ivy called.

He eyed her sharply, snarled then laughed. But not a merry laugh. This was full of derision and contempt. "You can die, bitch."

"That isn't terrible polite. What I do to you?" She pushed her chair back and sauntered toward him. He wouldn't harm her, less he be struck dead.

When she was well within the reach of his arms, she stopped. "You've done well since Ursus died. Want to thank me?"

His neck grew taut, fists gripped tightly. "Left me with that black tiger. An injured tiger, the most dangerous type."

"You allied with her," Duran snickered.

"She wants you dead, woman. More than Ursus ever did. Every order she makes comes down to you. You need to die. And we'll move on." Buckler spoke distinctly.

"Sorry, not my intention to die. I'm not going to make it easy for you. You don't like how she's wired, you kill her. Set yourself free." Ivy shrugged, turned her back on the general and returned to the table.

He stepped after her, stood looking down at all of them. "Helen, I am glad to see you survived. And the baby?"

"None of your business," Helen replied, coldly.

Buckler took a deep breath, then pulled up an extra chair and sat, not quite at the table, but near enough to address the four. "I have a deal to propose."

"Hmmm. From Deva?" Duran asked.

He shrugged. "Ivy, you leave the Gathering. Alone. Run, get away from the trial. She'll withdraw the charges, I'll convince her that chasing you down ourselves will prove more satisfying. The other three can leave, unmolested. We'll even hold the Holy Rollers back from chasing the boy."

Ivy snickered. "Oh, my sacrifice to keep the others safe. Your word that they'd be safe? Not a chance in hell. I'm no martyr. I'll take my chances with the valley. So will Diva. Once the charges are proven false, she's the one who will be punished. You ought to like that, Buckler. Then you can take over the ragtag remains of Ursus' holdings and make them your own."

Buckler's face betrayed nothing.

"Ah. That is the plan, Ivy love," Duran chuckled. "He doesn't want you to run either. He knows the charges are false."

"Doesn't matter. She'll find a way to twist it. She don't care if she goes down, long as you go with her." Buckler stood quickly, the chair fell away and crashed to the floor. "Very well. It won't be long, Gabriel is back."

He turned and stormed from the café.

Helen shuddered, "He didn't used to be so angry. Always clever and sneaky. But not so angry."

"Wonder what she's feeding him. That much change in a body can't be natural," Emmett commented, lifting his drink to take a sip. "When's this bath set up, Duran?"

"Not for you, boy. I set up a private tub." Duran lifted one eyebrow.

"Well, I guess it will be private for four. Not going to let you be so selfish." Emmett set his cup down. He turned to Helen. "Stay with Duran. Without me or Ivy, you could be unmolested."

"Other than the taunts of allowing my mother to eat my baby," she sighed.

Duran drained his cold drink and let out a long burp. Ivy slapped him on the arm and he laughed. "Room in the back. I'll tell Bibo to keep the rest out once we're there."

The chance for an unmolested bath saw the four put away the food quickly. Ivy and Emmett took the back ways, while Helen and Duran went directly down the street. They were delayed by the religious, attempting a blockade down the street from the café. Linking hands, they stood in the way.

Duran studied them, one by one and simply hauled Helen into his arms, and walked through them, dragging several nearly ten feet before the hands released. He turned to look back at them. "Fools."

"Where is Ursus' grandchild?" The question rang out into the street. Several visitors stood and watched. It was always a show when the religious took on a cause.

Duran snorted while Helen regained her feet. Taking a deep breath, she called out, "Why do you care?"

"All life is precious." A man in an orange robe took a step toward her. "We worry that has been forgotten." He had a kind face, eyes that didn't communicate fanaticism.

Helen tilted her head at him, considered an answer. Then she softly spoke, "Ursus' grandchild lives, flourishes and is safe."

"Liar!" Another man in red pushed forward, raised a staff as if to strike her.

She stood calmly as he dropped to the street, clutching his throat. The orange robed priest nodded at her. "Thank you for answering. Children are so rare, no matter their source, they are treasure." He turned and several people left with him.

Helen commented to Duran, "They aren't all lunatics."

"No, but they let the lunatics run the crowd. He turned away, left. Didn't stay to dissuade or convince the rest to leave off the harassment." He knew the orange robed, they refuse to take physical action of any sort. They do know how to defend themselves, if attacked, but that's the only time they use the skill. He remembered working for them once.

"That just means he is intelligent. Knows better than to beat his head against rocks." She shrugged. "I am a treasure?"

"I'm sure Emmett would defend that statement." Duran paused, took Helen's hand. "Your mother knows the truth. Even if she cannot say it. I know what is in her heart, Helen. And there is so much regret over the time she lost with you. Time she'll never know again."

He saw Helen swallow the sudden wash of tears, squeezed her hand and let her gently pull free.

They entered the bathhouse to find Ivy and Emmett already soaking in the steaming water.

As the four left for the night, Michael intercepted them, to announce the hearing would begin in four days.

He asked Ivy, "Who do you wish to call as witness?"

Before Ivy could respond, Duran interrupted, "Does she have to say right now?"

Michael smiled at Duran. "You know her so well. No, when you have decided, let David know and he will take care of it." He gazed at each of them for a moment, his eyes lingered on Helen and with a slight shake of his head, he blinked, looking puzzled. She began to speak, but he turned away and was gone.

Ivy watched him leave, wondered why this sudden acceleration of the process. What happened to the questioning Dave said she'd go through? All the years of skulking in the woods left her with good instincts. This news meant more than her trial neared.

After Michael left, Ivy turned to Duran. "I don't see what the rest of you could contribute. It's my truth that has to be defended, my job to do that."

"I know what I heard in my father's compound," Helen stated.

"I know what you called out in nightmares," Emmett spoke softly.

"I know you," Duran replied. "No making up your mind tonight. Speak to Dave. Tell him what the three of us have to contribute. Promise me this, Ivy."

She stared at him, at war with the impulse to deny them a role in the forthcoming drama. Turning away, she gazed out the window, arms crossed at her breasts.

"We are your family," Emmett all but whispered. "Do not reject us."

Shit. She pictured her grandson, playing on the streets of Avala... He needed his parents there. What if they never left this valley? What if...?

Duran stood at her back, not touching her, but his warm breath, familiar on her neck, offered comfort. So certain that this tide would turn for them. Diva would be caught in her lies, her machinations. Ivy wanted to believe this also. Needed to believe this.

She sighed. "I promise. I will speak to him."

Duran wrapped his arms about her, easily picked her up and carried her to their bed. He crawled in against her and held her, all night. Even as she wrestled with the nightmare again, hearing Diva's voice on the edge of everything, promising Ursus a son, promising Ivy would succumb, grow compliant.

When she woke, there was no sign of sleep on her face.

The merc meeting began the next day with shouting, arguments, cursing. The usual thing. Ivy sat next to Duran, an expression of boredom on her face. Emmett did not attend. Though Duran had won the argument for the three of them, Helen was still on the outside, daughter of a warlord, her loyalties weren't proven yet. Emmett preferred to remain at her side

Shock ran through Ivy as she realized how few the merc had dwindled to. They didn't even fill the room. She fended off the glares, holding tightly to an unconcerned demeanor. Duran shouted good-naturedly at his distance relatives, sitting with the Losanglos contingent.

One shouted back, "What? You a married man now?"

Duran just laughed loudly, one arm draped over Ivy's shoulders.

Ivy snorted. "You should be so lucky."

"I am lucky."

A hand slammed down on the broad table at the front of the crowd and at last they settled down to conduct business.

"Any claims against a fellow merc?" the man leading the meeting bellowed out.

"Against Duran for killing Bill!" a lean man across the empty floor shouted out.

"Bill hunted me, he got what he deserved, so did Jero and Mot," Duran calmly replied. "Never been an issue for claim. They weren't working merc then, signed up with Ursus."

"Ursus could hire mercs!"

"No, as a warlord, if you sign with him, you're troops. Why else is this hall so fucking empty?" Ivy shouted. "You sign with a warlord, you're troops!"

"Duran is right, matter settled," the head table ruled.

"Ain't right, we all take warlord money!"

"Difference in taking money for a one time job and sticking with them, sleeping in barracks, eating their gruel," Parrotte growled, slamming his hand down on the table again.

"Duran won his argument by citing bodyguard work with a hidden settlement for the last year. What's the difference?" One of the Losanglos spouted off. At Duran's glare, he raised his hands, "Just wondering!"

"Working for a settlement isn't working for a warlord." Parrotte shook his head. "Can't you keep your friends from fighting with you, Duran?"

"I'll kick his ass later," Duran snarled.

Ivy stood, the room quieted as she patiently waited. All knew she faced a trial by the valley dwellers. She turned and surveyed the room. "Anyone ever find out about the missing Shamans?"

A shuffling of feet filled the hall. Then Lisle answered. "We Vallaeens found a group of them, near death while we worked a job in the far north. Got them to safety, though we lost one. The remaining three were wrecks. Left them with a small township near the coast."

"They say anything to you?" Ivy asked.

The remaining mercs went deadly silent as Lisle answered.

"Vague warnings of an invasion. Honestly, Ivy, they made no sense. They'd been abused. Whips, chains, burned, cut...the one that died had been emasculated."

Duran looked up, tilting his head. "Any blinded?"

The Vallaeen studied his face a moment before answering, "Yes. The same one. Who did you? And what else are you missing?"

Ivy snorted, a suspicion taking form in her mind. Michael had said the charges against her were made by Diva...of Orly.

"I wonder where Diva learned her techniques." Duran wondered aloud. He faced Lisle, "She didn't finish with me, sweet cheeks." He winked as she laughed.

"Invasions aren't our business, unless we are hired to repel them!" A voice in the back shouted above the chuckles.

"Be our business if there is no business because of it!" Ivy shouted. "Idiot!"

"You killed the only man able to muster a defense! You part of this invasion, fucking Cruz!?"

The shouting in the room grew in volume.

Ivy shook her head, commenting to Duran, "Maybe we deserve an invasion."

"Speak for yourself, woman." He stroked her short hair, considering the repercussions of the news as the room erupted into argument.

Parrotte left the front table and strode to where they sat. He squatted, studied Duran's face, "Diva did this to you. She worked for Ursus, honed his hunger for vengeance and cruelty..." He turned his eyes on Ivy. "Why would the Orly fear you?"

Ivy began to laugh, and then saw the wheels turning behind Parrotte's eyes. He nodded as her laughter died. "Think about it, Ivy. I'm going to petition Michael for the trial to be open air. We all need to hear this. And they need to hear our suspicions."

"Gabriel won't allow it," Duran softly replied. "He doesn't bend rules."

Parrotte grinned, his eyes still on Ivy. "She ain't the only one the dwellers owe."

Before they could respond, he shot to his feet and shouted the room back to quiet.

Returning to his table he stayed on his feet, surveying the ragged mercenaries. He spoke without shouting, "We are all facing extinction. At this rate, the warlords will divvy up the rest of the Calif, waste effort spitting at each other, and leave the townships to dwindle. A ripe time for an invasion. Our Shamans are gone. The bit of magic the Cruz carried is all but gone. We were rich once, even after the world changed..."

The stare of the mercs didn't stifle Parrotte at all. He crossed his arms. "We are treading water as the flood rises. And we don't know enough. Forces bigger than we know are on the move. Get out, listen, talk. Don't argue! Talk to each other. We meet next at this chit's trial." He pointed at Ivy. "You want to keep living free, make sure to attend."

"Parrotte, they won't let us in," Lisle sounded confused.

"Then we'll break in," Parrotte raised an arm, fist clenched.

"She is one of us and we are the merc council! Whether she is guilty or not, we have the right to bear witness!"

Duran thrust his fist into the air, echoing Parrotte's call, "We are the merc!"

The men and women surged to their feet, fists rose. Some dirty, some wrapped in bloody bandage, some missing fingers, black, white, brown, all united. "We are the merc!" roared to the ceiling. The noise was deafening. Ivy sat, astounded at the change. She looked at Parrotte, who returned her stare without blinking.

Suddenly, a hope rose in her that had been missing before.

CHAPTER TWENTY-ONE

The lack of sleep began to tell on Ivy. She sat in the coffee shop and found it difficult to keep her eyes open. But closing her eyes meant the invasion of her dreams and nightmares, awake or asleep. It drove her mad. For the fifth time, she jerked awake from the partial doze and shivered.

It was always the same. The damned soft voice, promising so many things to Ursus. Things that involved her complacency, her taming. He believed. It was a very compelling voice. Ivy remembered it with a core-deep fear. She'd believed it, too.

She paced, wishing the rest would get back soon. She wanted to walk, to just walk fast. No, to run. Her body ached at the inactivity. This self-imposed prison wore on her. "I made the rule, I can break it," she muttered to herself. Snatching up her mug, she called out to Dave, "I'll bring it back!"

Before he could object, she tore out the door.

A fine morning greeted her. But the weather always cooperated for the Gathering. Glancing down the path, she saw a group of red robed Holy Rollers turning a corner and quickly began walking the opposite way. They were more interested in Helen and Emmett, but would badger her given a chance.

Dave's new croissant hadn't filled her belly. She headed for a favorite breakfast stop and took shelter until the rollers had passed. Once Duran returned to Dave's place and found her gone, he'd come searching for her. Of that she had no doubt. But she needed time and space. To think.

Once breakfast was done, she'd head down to the river.

———

Helen rose from Emmett's side as the door to their room opened. It surprised her that he continued to sleep. She reached out a hand to rouse him; sure it was Duran come to tell them of something ominous. But when it was Michael who met her gaze, she stopped.

He crooked a finger at her and she quickly gathered up a loose dress, hurried out to see him.

"If you're looking for Ivy, she and Duran billet above the coffee house," she softly said.

"I know. This is about you and your time infection. Helen, I don't see it...and I should. Will you come with me for one of our healers to examine you?" He held out his great hand, radiating comfort.

She swallowed, suddenly filled with both fear and hope. "Could Ivy have cured it when she..." Stopping, she shook her head. "No, it happened just before the valley opened to us. Damn it."

"Even though the valley would protect you from this infection, it should still be visible to us, Helen. I promise not to keep you long. He is on the roof."

She sighed, took his hand. The roof was only one flight of stairs above them. No building in the valley was over three stories tall, but this one had a very good view, being situated on a slight hill. She gazed out over the village as Michael approached a man she supposed was this healer.

The hills still painted much of the valley with shadows. But the high granite mountains surrounding the village were bright with the morning sun. A brilliant blue sky was already in evidence and she saw birds flitting about from tree to tree, where a small park lay at the end of the street.

"Helen, daughter of the warlord Ursus and the Cruz woman, Ivy? I am Aaron."

She turned to see that he was blind. His eyes were pure white, in a face of extreme age. He smiled, holding out a hand, so sure she would take it.

She did, without hesitation. One does not lean toward timidity in the household of a warlord. Aaron held her hand, turning it so it lay atop his, and enclosed it with his other hand. He sighed. "She is not infected by time."

"Then why do I age a year for every month?" she calmly asked, though a sudden rush of fear made her heart beat fast.

"You bear a Cruz mark?" He countered her question.

"Yes, though it is reversed." Her breath caught. No! It couldn't be...

"I am sorry, child..." as he continued to speak, Helen lost the strength in her legs. Aaron sank to the roof with her. This was not what she expected. But it was what she feared. Her Cruz curse truly was a curse.

After the tears, Helen wiped her face dry and straightened her back, "I can't...can't go back and tell Emmett about this. Michael? Is there somewhere I could just be by myself?"

"Aaron can take you to a place of sanctuary. I am sorry... I should not have offered hope." Michael helped her back to her feet. "What shall I tell Emmett?"

"That I'm with a healer. It won't be a lie, and it will give me time to decide what to do." She sighed.

"There is no decision, if you want to see the new baby born, you must take us up on staying." Aaron spoke matter-of-factly.

"What...baby?" Helen set a hand at her belly. "Why me? No one gets pregnant but me?" Her voice cracked.

"The Cruz alone carry the genetics to repopulate the world," Aaron took her hand, stroking it with soft, wrinkled fingers. "No one else appears to realize this. Those who rose above the time ribbon were untouched by the anomaly. Every child born since the change bears some Cruz blood. If you stay, the scientists will be pleased at the chance to add you to their study."

Helen blinked, stunned. "Why didn't you tell everyone? Why didn't you stop my father? How could you...?" She jerked her hand away from Aaron, rejecting his comfort. She spun to stare at Michael. "You all stayed away, and let him kill off the future?"

"We didn't realize how successful his campaign was until it was too late." Michael spread his hands. A feeble attempt to offer an excuse. "We did all we could to help the Cruz on Lina... We feared what the rest would do by then if we revealed the truth."

Helen strode to the edge of the roof, gazing down at the waking village below. If they knew, what would they do? The Cruz had always been seen as different, and different was frightening. Would they have done like her father? Taken Cruz women, held them captive, forced them to bear children?

Life with her father had left her no room for illusions regarding human behavior.

She stroked her belly. If Aaron was right, she had no choice. She would stay. The village would live with their decision. As complacent in the genocide as she had been. Her peace with his actions came at a steep price. Now she would lose the rest of her life.

What to tell Emmett...?

"I'm not stupid. I know what they would have done." She admitted, gestured out to the village. "Why has Ivy remained barren since I was born?"

"Her curse makes it difficult. Or it did." Aaron did it again; spoke of something stunning with no regard.

"She is...pregnant also?" Helen rushed to Aaron, grabbed his hand. "They can't put her on trial!"

"They must at this point," Michael explained. "It can't be stopped. Trust us, Helen. Gabriel is a fair man."

"Man? None of you are men. You're ciphers. Uncaring, removed, watchers..." She trembled, too much in her mind at once.

Her head suddenly hurt, her belly rumbled with anxiety. "I can't think. Please, just take me somewhere safe."

Aaron turned toward the roof door, urging her to accompany him. Helen paused, one last glance at Michael. "Michael, my father tricked her. Diva gave him a drug to use on her. She did nothing willingly. To put her on trial is a farce."

Michael took a deep breath. "It is suspected. Helen, the law is adamant. I will make sure Gabriel is told. You know this how?"

"I heard them, talking. They planned on using the same technique on her again. I can testify to what I heard, if needed."

"Diva of Orly has much to answer for. I go directly to Gabriel, make sure he knows." He nodded at her, brows knit and a frown on his face. It scared her, but it at least now they knew the depth of Diva's treachery.

She asked him one more question, "Will you tell Ivy? About the baby? Perhaps, she can let herself love this one and be at peace."

"Soon." He nodded. "Go with Aaron."

Sprawled on the grass, Ivy watched the sky above shift from early morning pale to the true blue of late morning. The sun warmed her bare skin and for once she dozed without the nightmares and memories haunting her. The scent of green grass, the soft burble of the river set her at ease.

Quietly and calmly, her mind slowly opened to the reality of all she'd heard and known from those weeks of captivity. Without awareness, tears trickled down the sides of her face. But she was ready and accepted, finally understood.

She'd been so tired. He'd been hammering her. She'd had one chance to kill him and missed. Weak with hunger, her body starved for water and crying for a release from the ropes holding her to the bed, open for his invasion. That voice promised rest. Promised her no more fighting. And it wouldn't be her surrender; it would be out of her control. All she had to do was swallow and believe.

So tempting! The drive to survive, to end this torture. Did she do it? Did she agree? She wanted to agree, that she remembered clearly. Did she nod?

Ivy opened her eyes in the meadow, shivering. She sat up, brushed at her face, took several deep breathes. Her heart hurt, a deep sadness anchored at her soul. She was going to lose this trial.

"Ivy." Duran squatted next to her. He reached out and touched the dampness at her hairline. "From never crying to this? Another nightmare?"

"No. Not this time, Duran. This time...this time I remember. Diva offered Ursus the chance to tame me for good. I heard her. Told him she had a drug that would stop my rebellion. I was so tired. So weak. I didn't want to die, Duran!" Her green eyes swam with more tears. "I wanted it. No more decisions to make. I'm guilty."

"Were you asked, Ivy?" Duran took her hands, twisting and tearing at each other. He held them still, tilted his head and watched her with his one eye. "Did Diva ask you? Did Ursus ask you? Did they even know you heard them?"

Her breath caught, she blinked, fighting to remember. Was there hope here? Closing her eyes, she returned to that ache and conjured the memory again.

Dark, fetid air. Cold. A woman in a black dress, standing a few feet away. Ursus, with an open robe. She stroked his chest, ran fingers down to his prick. Neither looked at the captive on the bed.

"No one will know. One dose will last a week. If you are content with her I will give the second and it will keep her complacent for as long as she lives..."

He'd chuckled, and agreed. Sold his soul to the devil.

Memories...how the woman had stepped toward the bed. Held up a vial. Ivy didn't fight as her head was lifted, tilted back, her mouth opened.

So tired...

Her eyes drifted to Ursus, naked, holding his prick as he watched.

"I fought!" Ivy suddenly remembered how it ended. "I bit her! She spilled the draught! I felt it trickle down my neck. Ursus... Ursus jumped at me, struck me and forced my mouth open. I spit most of it out!"

She gazed at Duran, astounded. The ache at her heart eased, and she fell at his chest. "Oh, God! I fought! I didn't agree! She still got some of it down me and I disappeared from my body. I lost control... He...! He...! He undid the ties and used me, moved me...posed me!"

With a sobbing wrench, she jerked from Duran's arms and threw up.

He waited.

She pounded on the ground. "I felt it! I felt all of it! I screamed and cursed and no one heard me. It was all inside my head!"

She raised her head, her body taut with tension. She howled into the sky, a sound of pure rage, pain and anger. It startled a group of starlings in a nearby tree and they took to flight. Several men turned toward them from the banks of the river but Duran waved them away.

Ivy stretched her arms to the sky, fists clenched. "He played with me! He laughed? He laughed and used things on me! He knew I heard him! She told him I could hear, that I was still there!"

Her eyes were wild when she turned again to Duran, hissed, "She was there...!?"

"This was a long time in planning, Ivy. I'm so sorry..." He held out his hands and she blinked at him.

"Duran? He said she'd promised him a baby. He thrust into me and chanted it. Said I'd never touch his child. I'd watch him raise it, teach it to hate me... I...! I...! I never had a chance with her, did I?" All at once, the anger disappeared and she sagged. "I let him destroy a mother's love."

"No, all you could do was listen, Ivy. Nothing is destroyed, just delayed. Mi corazón, you will survive this and you'll prove him wrong. You are stronger than he was." He brushed the bit of hair from her face and smiled slightly. "You are greater than him. He is gone and you remain. Listen to me, open your heart."

Her soul ached. But, at the bare center...where the dead past ruled, a seed sprouted. Could she actually love her daughter? Could she actually love this man? If she didn't try, if she didn't trust, Ursus would never leave, would keep killing her hope. She had to believe! To see that monster gone, along with his poisonous Diva, she would succeed! Drive a stake through Ursus, conjure a great wind and see him blow away.

The possibilities broke her heart open.

She gazed at Duran.

"Duran. I love you." She leaned closer and set her lips at his open shirt. Her shelter, her strength, her lover and her love. How amazing it was to accept that! His skin was so warm, all the warmth she missed. All the softness she denied herself lay there, at his heart.

"I know, chica. And I love you. And that is stronger than that black bitch and all her poisons, all her plans." He stroked her hair and gathered her slowly into her arms where they simply sat, in the sun. And all the silly words of praise he had spilled into her for years, returned to him.

An interlude of peace quickly interrupted as Emmett rushed to them, "Helen! She's gone! Michael told me the healers are with her, but something is wrong... Ivy?"

Ivy turned her head to look at Emmett, her keeper for too many years. There were times when she'd hated him. Because of him, she quit fighting and bore the baby. She shook her head. The baby. Helen.

"Wait, she is with healers? That's a good thing, Emmett. Why panic?" Ivy sighed, so tired. Emotions always tired her.

"Michael... I know when someone lies to me, Ivy." Emmett reached for her shirt and tossed it to her. "In one breath he said she was safe, in another he said the trial is starting early. This afternoon... He wouldn't tell me why. Just looked...guilty, and his eyes filled with tears!"

She caught the shirt and left the comfort of Duran's embrace. "I'm glad the trial is sooner. We'll find out what is going on with Helen, Emmett. I better go talk with Dave if things are coming to a head so quickly." Relief. Just plain old relief. Soon, this would be over and either she'd be dead or free. She wouldn't think beyond that.

Duran helped her dress, peppering Emmett for more impressions of Michael. At last he turned to Ivy. "Sounds like the remaining senior Guardians are back and ready to get this thing going. You go to Dave, I'll find Parrotte and alert them to the change in plans."

"I'm ready, Duran. I know the truth now." Ivy smiled slightly at Duran, turned and followed Emmett back to the coffee house.

"Michael didn't strike me as very emotional. You saw tears?" Ivy asked as they walked.

"Yes. And he wouldn't look me in the eyes."

They turned a corner to find a mass of red robed clergy blocking their way. Ivy stopped, rolled her eyes. Emmett growled.

One stepped forward. "We want to speak to Emmett. We swear words are all we will trade."

"No shit. One raised hand and you drop dead. Idiots!" Ivy sighed. "I don't have time for this. You want to talk to them?"

"I'll talk to them. But I won't be long," Emmett urged Ivy to move ahead. They parted so she could get through. And none of them said a word. It unnerved her. No cursing? No muttering or prayers? They didn't even avoid touching her. She wondered what had changed.

She turned, called out, "Emmett?"

"Go on! Talk to Michael!" he shouted.

"Damn it!" She shoved several of them out of her way and hurried, mouthing off to them as she went. "You hurt him and it isn't just the village curse that will haunt you!"

"He is in no danger." A tall man in a brown robe at the back of the group assured her.

"Right, you're reasonable, you get up there and make sure of it." She shoved him toward Emmett. He actually pushed past her shove and last she saw he was moving toward where she'd left Emmett.

"Talk to Michael, right. And Dave." Ivy left the group at her back and hurried.

Emmett took one step back. "I'm not going to denounce her and go with you."

"We know."

"Helen did nothing to her baby. Our child is safe and with family."

"We trust that."

Emmett examined the grey haired man. "Then what do you want from me?"

"To ask you questions regarding why the world changed, according to our separate dogmas." He sounded so reasonable, but the gleam in his eye didn't set well with Emmett.

"Your books don't speak about the world changing. None of them. It wasn't a gospel event. It was celestial. Live with it, the rest of us do."

"God uses the celestial heavens to do his will. Armageddon was promised and it was delivered. This is what we know. But the books do not address what is beyond." He took a step closer to Emmett. "Your knowledge is needed, to provide hope to the people. To offer comfort when the cold bites and there isn't enough food. That all of this suffering has a reason!"

A bit of spit landed on Emmett's cheek. He snarled, wiped it away.

"Wait, before you speak." A brown robed man gently pushed the zealot behind him. "We just want words."

"Words won't take the place of a full belly. They are just words! They mean nothing. Let me go, I have business to attend to."

The red robbed pushed forward. The threat was obvious.

A heavy sigh escaped from the brown-garbed man. "I am Brother Josiah. And I understand what you believe and why you believe it. But others truly do find comfort in the words from our ancient books. You were born with a gift of those words. There must be a reason for this! All we want is some time with you, as we seek clarity."

"This is useless. He has been poisoned by that witch! Hear me, boy. I am Cardinal Dinaro and I speak for the red robed. You will surrender yourself to us. To sit at our feet, to make proper absolution for your blasphemy. Or we will see your witch dead. We will find that baby and see it raised a true believer, if we must slaughter a thousand to do it!" He didn't raise a hand, he didn't even step closer. But his voice carried conviction.

"You're insane," Emmett whispered, even as the threat weighed heavily on his throat. He had a vision of Lina, crawling with the red robed, all the children caged.

Josiah moved up and stood next to Emmett. "This is wrong. We agreed to try my way."

"Your way is weak. She is right, the only way he'll ever convert is through the harder path." Dinaro stared at Emmett. "I speak nothing but the plain truth. The hard truth. At the end of Gathering, if you do not walk from this valley in our company, we will lose the dogs of war and find you."

Emmett took a deep breath, unsure of exactly what to say. A loud voice answered for him.

"Good luck, you bastards. Others have tried and failed." Duran linked his arm with Emmett. Behind him stood Parrett and a growing number of mercenaries.

Parrett chuckled and moved to Emmett's other side as Brother Josiah backed away. "You set yourself to hunt a mercenary in good standing with the guild and you forfeit all rights to protection. Your money will be useless. One hair of his son's head touched, one finger laid upon Ivy and we will strike against you."

"You are so few! What do we have to fear from the likes of

you?" Dinaro shouted, it seemed more for the benefit of his followers than anything else.

"A son? The babe was a boy?" Josiah smiled and slid to Emmett's front. "Bless him and his mother. I hope you will remember me with some charity." And he disappeared into the crowd.

Parrotte took one step toward Dinaro. "We are too few? But it takes so few to see those robes painted with more than simple dye. Leave off with the threats, Dinaro. I know you take pay from Diva and her general. All you believe in is your own well being, preacher!"

"And mercenaries believe in more?" Dinaro challenged.

"Mercenaries hold the honor of being upfront with our motivations. No hiding behind words or faith. The only faith we know is that of brotherhood and the oaths we keep to each other. Now, stand aside, this man has business to attend to, as do we." Parrotte simply pushed Dinaro aside and with one step forward, the crowd parted, all but stumbling to get away from the tall men and women who walked with purpose behind their leader.

"There are so few," Emmett whispered to Parrotte.

"The chaff are gone, those that remain are the best, Emmett. And we cannot afford to lose you or Ivy. Or this comedian here." He nodded at Duran. "I am sorry to spread the news of your son, but that will keep them busy, trying to fit that into their scripture."

Emmett nodded, unwilling to admit how much those words of threat had shaken him.

Ivy waited at the café. Dave stood behind the bar, speaking to a very tall woman. Ivy grimaced at Emmett. "You look pale. They get all angry and stupid again?"

"Yes, but none of them died this time." Emmett took a deep breath, pulled up a chair next to her. "Helen?"

"Dave either knows nothing or is just a better liar than Michael. We were talking when that skinny one showed up. Something is in the wind..." Her gaze transferred to Parrotte, and the group behind him. "This all that came?"

"The leaders are here, the rest will follow once they pin down where to go. I made it clear to the clergy, they attack any of you, here or outside the valley and we open vendetta against them." The room filled with mercenary leaders as Ivy blinked, the totally unexpected offer of support, so wholehearted, left her stunned. He'd all but declared war on the clergy? For her? For Emmett?

All of this spun around her head in a tangle. Duran took a seat across from her and smiled, winked.

That simple act broke through her shock. She shoved her chair back and stormed over to Dave. "What the fuck is going on? Who are you and where is my daughter?"

Wow, she didn't choke on claiming Helen as her daughter. She shook her head, pushing back that doubtful voice at the back of her head.

The tall woman set a hand on Dave's shoulder and nodded. Then she slipped away. Ivy took a step toward the back exit and Dave stood in her way. "Bela is one of the judges. Helen truly is with the healers. There is a complication regarding her rapid aging, but Bela didn't go into details. Aaron is the wisest and she is in his care."

Ivy snorted, discontent with what even she could read as partial truths. Which meant they also held lies.

Dave shrugged. "I can only tell you what I know."

Duran joined them. "Michael is also unnaturally tall. Is that what differentiates the elder Guardians?"

"Partially. They are Guardians; I am just a citizen of the valley. Most of us are. There are less than a dozen Guardians. And they've been traveling for more than a decade. This is the first Gathering I remember where so many are present." He wiped at the counter, something he must do a thousand times every week.

Ivy sighed. "Is this Aaron a guardian?"

"Yes."

"Where is the trial taking place, Dave?" Parrotte joined them, as did Emmett.

"The bowl near the meadow, in six hours. All the mercenaries will not fit, Parrotte. Chose representatives. The clergy have been told the same." Dave reached out and took Emmett's hand. "She is in good hands. The best."

Emmett nodded, but to Ivy's eyes, he obviously didn't trust what he heard. The lines on his face were deep...suddenly, she realized how much he'd grown. They'd been together for so long, from adolescent, to teenager, to adult. His shoulders were broad, his face filled out. Shit, she could barely see the eight-year-old thrust at her. And he held the worries of an adult, for his woman. And his child.

She sighed, proud of him and wanting to see him back on Lina, with his family. He'd grown more in those months on Lina than the years of wandering with her. It was time to let him totally go.

Helen, Helen deserved him. She made him happy. That was enough.

CHAPTER TWENTY-TWO

The waiting proved torturous. Ivy paced in the coffee house, growing more and more short-tempered. She snapped at Emmett, at Duran, and found herself avoiding Dave. She knew he meant to represent her, to offer defense. He'd been told everything they knew. Perhaps Emmett's concern for Helen was infecting her.

Finally, after two hours of bitching, she stood still and stated to the room, "I'm taking a walk. I need some air." To her surprise, no one objected. Duran huddled with Dave, and simple nodded.

"Good idea. Get that nastiness out of the way. Go beat up a post." He grinned slightly at her. "Just don't be late."

"Yeah, don't want to miss my own hanging." Ivy snorted and turned to the door.

Emmett stood in her way. "I'm going, too. But I'm looking for Michael."

"Fine. Let's get out of here." She brushed past him. It seemed too pleasant an afternoon to face a trial. Pausing in the path, she took a deep breath. Emmett stood at her side.

"You ever wonder where this fit into the world before it changed?" Ivy idly commented.

"No. This wasn't there or I'd see more ghosts." Emmett replied dryly. "You seem to be in a good mood suddenly."

"It's going to be over soon. I'm tired of waiting. Tired of hiding out. Either way, it will be over." She linked her arm with his. "You used to see ghosts here. Maybe they have finally faded." She tugged him down the path, toward an intersection.

"Ask one of the residents." Emmett sighed. "I miss her."

"She's only been gone a few hours!" Ivy rolled her eyes. "You saw less of her on Lina."

"And I missed her then, too." He tugged his arm free. "I know you care about her. This nonchalance doesn't fool me. Damn it, Ivy! Thought you were tired of hiding? Fuck, nothing but a bad habit you can't break, isn't it? Hide from her, hide from yourself. What is the difference if the trial is over, if Ursus is dead...if you run from yourself?"

Ivy's temper rose and she snarled at him. "Don't tell me how to feel, boy! You don't know anything about how I feel!" The good mood disappeared, just like that. She forgot, he didn't know what she knew.

Emmett stared at her a moment, then shook his head. "I sometimes think I know you better than you know yourself."

At her growl, he turned on his heel and strode away. She spun and went the other way. How dare he assume to know what she felt! She wasn't hiding from Helen, or from how she felt about the girl. She knew how she felt about her. Regretful, resigned. But Emmett couldn't understand that. He had no regrets. Men didn't regret, they just ignored the past. Said 'I'm sorry' and think that solved everything.

An apology wouldn't mend the chasm between her and Helen. It would take more. She'd find a way.

Ivy snorted. "Hell, maybe the men have it right. Just move on."

With a shrug, Ivy kept walking. She noticed how the people in the streets got out of her way. Some even stared and went silent. Who the fuck cared? What was she, dead woman walking? They afraid to be contaminated, struck down by the fucking Guardians?

She turned a corner and ran up against a group of Vallaeens. Lisle saw her and reached out, snagged an arm and pulled her close. "What you doing out? I thought they had you locked up until the trial!" A large laugh signaled what she actually thought of the rumor.

Ivy sighed. "No, I'm free to wander. A walking contagion."

"What are you talking about?" Lisle shook her head. "Most in this valley are on your side, woman. They're worried, that's all."

"My side? You have to be kidding. Why?" It didn't seem possible.

"They trust you, not Diva. And if charges are made that can reach back twenty years, and sustained? Lots of worried folks out there."

"Ah! That I understand. It isn't about me, it's about protecting themselves." Ivy shrugged.

Lisle lightly tapped Ivy on the top of the head. "Stubborn bitch. Sure, you're the one on trial, now. And they don't believe Diva. No one believes Diva. If the Guardians fuck this up, it means evil wins."

"Evil wins? Oh, that is funny? I'm on the side of good in a good vs. evil battle? I'm not good..."

"No, you're human. And that is what this is about. Don't be stupid, Ivy. These people know that you don't use drugs... What?" Lisle paused as Ivy shook her head. "You don't!"

"I didn't, but they were forced on me, Lisle. By Diva, who worked for Ursus when I was his captive. The Guardians have never cared why, just follow the evidence." Ivy met the Vallaeen's shocked eyes. "I may be found guilty, regardless of the why."

Suddenly, the Vallaeen nodded. "This is why Parrotte is calling us to witness. Why did you never speak of this?"

"I didn't remember, until recently." Ivy wrapped arms around her torso. "Still... No, I refuse to let it haunt me still!" She stood tall and looked around. "You on your way to the meadow arena? It's too early."

"No, we want to eat first. Join us? And tell me more of about this Diva bitch."

Ivy gladly took the distraction. Anything to avoid hearing Emmett's accusations. Nearly two hours later, she was still sitting next to Lisle when Michael hurried into the tavern and approached, agitation clear on his face.

"When did you last see Emmett?" He demanded.

Ivy blinked, wondering what the hell had happened. She stood, licked her lips, and tilted her head. "Not long after leaving the café. Why?"

"The valley sensors went off. He's left the valley." Michael paced. "Why? Why would he leave now?"

"He wouldn't. Not willingly. He was looking for you, worried about Helen. What route? I'll get him, find out what the fuck is going on!" Ivy grabbed her smallest ax from the tabletop, when Lisle's hand took hers.

"You can't. Your trial will start in less than an hour. There is no time."

Ivy snarled at Lisle. "He didn't go willingly! Something is wrong!"

Duran rushed in, followed by Dave. He studied Ivy's face for a moment. "You two argue? Bad enough for him to storm away?"

"No! Fucking idiots! He wouldn't leave without knowing what is going on with Helen! Let me go, Lisle! I have to find him! He's in trouble!" Ivy jerked her hand free. But now Duran blocked her progress.

"No, I'll find him. Trust me, Ivy. I will find him. You need to face the Guardians." He wouldn't let her pass. "You look like you're running and you'll never be able to stop. Ever."

She pounded on his chest, "Fuck the stupid trial! It's all a farce! They can reschedule it... I don't care. Emmett! Duran, Emmett is in trouble!"

"I'm sure you're right. And I'm sure I'm right. Go with Dave to the meadow, defend yourself. I'll get Emmett, Ivy." He snagged her hand, kissed the clenched knuckles. "I'll find him. Please, woman, trust me!"

Her breath caught at the plea in his voice. She looked into his remaining eye; saw how he studied her, pled with her. He kissed her knuckle again. "Mi corazón, trust me."

"I...I want to," she all but whispered. "Duran. I can't lose Emmett. Helen is gone, but I can't lose Emmett. She needs him!"

"I know." He lowered his head closer. "You have not lost Helen. You're just finding her."

Ivy trembled. She turned her face to one side and let Duran draw her into an embrace. Her eyes closed. "Dave? Can they postpone the trial?"

"No. They chose the time and place for a reason. And no, I don't know what the reason is." Dave sighed. "We need to start heading there."

"When did this alert let you know Emmett had left?" Ivy asked Michael, still in the shelter of Duran's arms.

"Nearly an hour ago. We've been searching for you." Michael sighed.

"So, he's been outside more than an hour..." Ivy pushed away from Duran. "You can find him?"

"I will find him. They are going to give me a fast horse. Right, Michael?" Duran's voice brooked no argument.

"I'll arrange it."

Lisle gestured at a woman across the table, "Terri? You go with Duran, provide some back up."

"I'm going, too." A voice from the back spoke up.

"Fine. Terri and Frenchie. We'll stay with Ivy. If someone aimed for Emmett, they aimed for her, too." Lisle turned to Dave. "You know when any of us leave?"

"No, just the Cruz." Michael answered instead of Dave.

Lisle tilted her head, prepared to ask another question. Duran interrupted, "Doesn't matter right now. Kiss me, Ivy..."

She held out her ax. "Take this. Bring back my boy, my girl needs him." Then she stood on her tiptoes and pressed a kiss to him. He wrapped arms about her and made it a good one. Then with a laugh, he backed away, snatched at Michael and hurried from the tavern. Terri and Frenchie followed.

Ivy turned to Dave. "The clergy? Or Diva?

"Diva and her general are already at the meadow. Most of the red robed are with her. I don't know, Ivy. We need to go, now." He held out his hand. With a resigned sigh, Ivy took it and followed him.

Duran ran just behind Michael. He could hear the two Vallaeens behind him, hoped they were the best Lisle had to offer. He would not let Ivy down. Michael led them down an alley to a stable. With several barked commands, three horses were led out. Great beasts, larger than any Duran had ever seen before.

Michael thrust him up onto a saddle. "They are fast, sure footed and know the valley well. Hurry. I will delay things as much as possible."

Duran simple nodded. "Where?"

"The Small River crevice." The Guardian stroked the horse's muscled neck. "Small River. Fast."

The horse surged with such strength, Duran had to fight to stay in the saddle. He heard a shout from one of the Vallaeens, and then the village all but blurred at they galloped forward.

He bent over the neck, remembering Ivy's kiss. The fear buried so deeply, she didn't acknowledge it. So close to breaking through, to being set free. He wanted that for her. Hell, he wanted that for him!

He doubted Diva stood behind this distraction. She had what she wanted. Ivy, brought before her as a prisoner, to a noose. The surprise would be on Diva, he was certain of that. If Ivy didn't break and run.

His horse took a sudden turn and Duran found the only way to stay on, was to concentrate. He'd find Emmett and bring the boy back to Ivy. Safe.

It took over thirty minutes to reach the Small River crevice. The horses slowed, as they carefully maneuvered over the rocks and narrow trail through a sliver of a ravine. He swore, he felt the valley's protection end. A cloud covered the sun and the air grew colder under the broken shade of a scraggly pine forest.

One of the Vallaeen jumped from her horse and studied the trail. "Four men..." She moved forward a hundred feet, then paused, tilted her head. "Hear that?"

Duran closed his eyes, then heard it. A grunt...

Damn it! He spun the horse and forced it down a game trail. The methodic pounding grew louder. Then he heard a voice he recognized.

"Done fighting, miracle? Good."

Duran drew the dagger and slid off the horse. He glanced behind and saw both Frenchie and Terri following his lead. He pointed one direction then the next. They faded away to circle what was ahead. Duran took care to be quiet.

It was that damned brown robed clergy. He should have known! The red robed were upfront, confrontational. Easy to face down. The browns sounded reasonable. Fuck!

He pushed some shrubs aside and paused. He could see Emmett's back. Strung up between to trees, his arms spread wide. His shirt was torn. His back covered with bruises and scrapes. His head hung lose.

Brother Jerome hit him one more time in the belly. Emmett didn't even grunt.

Duran saw the clergyman grin. He backed away and lifted a knapsack, rummaged about in it to pull out a long narrow skewer. "My grandfather collected books. He had this one that showed how to calm a troubled mind. And your mind is so terribly troubled, miracle. This will remove the doubt."

He stepped closer and stroked Emmett's hair. "Soon, all the pain will be done with. We'll take care of you, mend your hurts, dress you in robes and you will travel with us. I will be your mouth."

Duran froze as he heard a soft gasp from the other side of the circle of trees where Emmett and his tormentor danced their terrible dance. But Brother Jerome didn't seem to hear it. Slowly, Duran moved to one side. He could see Emmett's face, the eyes were swollen all but shut. His lip split and blood trailed down his nose. He'd fought. Good.

Brother Jerome stepped closer to Emmett, displaying the long skewer. "There is a part of your brain where doubt lives. I slide this past your eye, twirl it just right and all doubt will be gone. Brother Emmett, welcome to the order."

Duran surged forward, ax in hand. From the corner of his eye, he saw Terri and Frenchie taking down another of the monks. He growled. "You're a dead man, Brother Jerome Touching one of Ivy's people? Step away. I'll make this quick."

Jerome gripped Emmett's hair tightly, ignored Duran.

The hand holding the sharp prod moved closer to Emmett's eye. Duran charged, just as Emmett gave a twist and thrust a knee deeply into Brother Jerome's crotch. Duran kept moving, Ivy's ax sank into the monk's belly as he dropped the skewer and fell to one side. Duran jerked the ax, slicing open the sadistic bastard.

The Vallaeen darted forward and went to work on Emmett's bounds. Duran stood and caught the younger man as he sagged forward.

"Shit, Emmett. Ivy is gonna be pissed at your face." Duran sighed and propped him up. "How badly you hurt?"

"I'll live," Emmett whispered. "He..." licked his lips. Terri darted forward with a water skin and gently saw a few mouthfuls into the injured man. "Thanks. He said Helen was being taken by the Guardians."

"And you believed him?" Duran shook his head, then sighed. "I know, he appeared reasonable. Can't trust any of the religious. At least not their leaders!"

"Yeah. Should have known. Where's Ivy?" Emmett carefully

wiped at his face, grimaced at the blood as he carefully found his feet.

"On trial. We need to hurry back. You have to ride, Emmett. And we have to hurry."

"Yeah. I'll make it," Emmett shivered.

"You get up, we'll lift him to you. Either in front and you hold tight, or at your back and tie him to you," Frenchie spoke. "You're the better horseman, I nearly fell of a couple of times."

"Me, too." Terri admitted. They all glanced up with surprise as the three horses walked into the clearing, ready to return.

"Uncanny," Duran murmured.

"Damn." Emmett blinked at the horse, with a back easily two feet taller than his head. "You got a ladder?"

Duran snorted, grasped the horse's mane and hauled himself up to the saddle. The horse didn't flinch. The Vallaeens helped Emmett up to Duran's back. "Can you hold or you want your hands tied?"

"Tie them," Emmett murmured.

Carefully, his wrists were wrapped in a rag torn from his shirt, then tied around Duran's waist.

And then they were off. Fast.

CHAPTER TWENTY-THREE

The meadow amphitheater brimmed with onlookers. Ivy followed Dave through the crowds, all lined up at the edge. The benches ringing the small stage area held hundreds of people.

"Why are they all here? I thought the Guardians didn't want an audience." Ivy held tightly to Dave's hand as they skirted along the edge, heading for the steps.

"They want to be here. They won't riot. It worry you?" The dark haired barista glanced back at her.

"Last time I saw a crowd like this, a woman died on a flaming stake." Ivy shivered.

"It's Ivy!" A voice rose above the babble. Suddenly, those nearest them spun and grabbed at the woman. She lost Dave's hand as she was lifted high into the air. A hint of wood smoke drifted toward her. Her heartbeat soared, and she struggled, screaming. But she was being passed from hand to hand as the crowd pressed forward.

"Let me go! Fuck it! Let me go!" She struggled as a very large man suddenly took her in his arms. He took a moment to look down at her. She flailed; her nails gouged a red path down his arm.

"Ivy! Ivy...calm down! It's me... Ebain!"

Suddenly, she realized the crowd had backed away. Ebain grinned at her. “What you think, we were going to tear you apart?”

She went limp in his great arms. “Fuck it, Ebain. Scared the shit out of me... Sorry.”

“Nothing my woman at home hasn’t done to me before.” He shrugged and set her feet on the ground. “Just trying to get you down to the stage area. These people aren’t here to hurt you. They are here to support you.”

“Why?” Ivy rubbed at the beading scratch. “They don’t even know me.” She felt bad about marring the man’s arm, even if he didn’t see it worth flinching about.

“Ivy, Ursus was not a popular man. Diva is even less so. You may not be the sweetest thing to walk the Changed World, but you follow the merc code and can be trusted. Come on, people. Let her through. She wants to walk!” He roared out and the crowd parted.

“You show them, Ivy!”

“Don’t let them push you around!”

A chant suddenly built. “Ivy! Ivy! Ivy!”

She kept her head down, astounded at the support. An aisle opened for her and she began to walk down the steps. She could see Dave at the bottom, looking relieved. At one side she saw Lisle, with Parrotte and an impressive group of the mercenary captains. Glancing across the way, she saw a large contingent of red robed clergy.

They weren’t chanting. And beside them sat a silent wedge of military troops. Wearing a uniform of sort. She paused, staring. No one wore uniforms! But they wore the same black capes, red shirts...and no expression.

They were all huge.

Ivy swallowed. They looked like Diva’s general, Buckler. Al of them rippled with muscles; neck so thick they all but disappeared. What the hell was she doing to them? And where was Buckler?

A head swivel to the very outside of the arc revealed the general. And next to him stood Diva, maybe. Ivy stumbled as she tried to focus on what was wrong with Diva. She’d only had a glimpse of the woman when the valley opened. A moment later, Dave took her hand and urged her the rest of the way down the steps. Ivy couldn't take her eyes off of Diva.

Ursus' former counselor stood, very still. And she had also built her body up to level Ivy had never seen on a woman. Ivy shivered, trying to pinpoint why it bothered her so much. It was so unnatural. Then Diva turned her face toward Ivy.

"What the fuck?" Ivy spit out. "What is she wearing on her face? A shield? Some new bit of armament, damn. She already looks like a battle horse!"

"Ah, the half-mask?" Dave pointed her toward a seat directly opposite Diva and her contingent. "You marked her face, Ivy. She covers it with that black mask."

Ivy sat, blinking. A wry smile grew on her face, she looked up at Dave, standing at her side. "It's bad?"

"I haven't seen it, but I understand it is gruesome. She'd been thrown into a cell by Helen, so it remained untreated for some time." He glanced down at her. "Try not to gloat."

"Why the fuck not? Bitch planned on aborting my grandson, forcing Helen into her father's bed. I only wish I'd killed her. Thought I had at first," Ivy leaned back, crossed her arms. "Why are we early?"

"They worry the crowd could cause themselves harm."

She turned to her right and studied the crowd. "Seems peaceful enough."

Dave simply shrugged before kneeling in front of her. "Gabriel will speak first."

"And they'll all hear him?" she asked.

"If they shut up and listen. The acoustics here are excellent."

"I thought all of the Guardians would be here. So, where are they?"

"Waiting?" He took her hand. "Ivy, they already know all they need to know. We have spoken to them. Duran, Helen, even Emmett. Michael spoke to Bosun. This is a formality, they plan something more. I don't know what is going to happen."

She studied his face, suddenly incredible sad. She'd never have a chance to speak the truth. "A formality? I am already guilty, Dave. By the strict adherence to their rules. I hoped to say goodbye to Helen." She knew she should be feeling more. Where was the grief? There was nothing inside. There had never been anything inside. Ursus had killed it.

Dave shook his head and began to speak, "Ivy...it isn't..."

The crowd went silent. Ivy gazed beyond Dave, her eyes empty. He turned and together they stood up. The Guardians dominated the rear of the stage. Seven of them, each nearly seven feet tall. Ivy knew Michael. He looked pale as the tallest of them took several steps forward.

"Ivy of the Cruz, step forward."

Dave put a hand to her back and she moved forward until she stood in front of Gabriel, her neck tilted to meet the depth of eyes. She'd never been introduced to the head guardian, but it had to be him. The tallest, hair nearly to his knees, a vibrant blond and eyes that could carve glass. So blue it felt like she gazed into the sky. Or the merciless ocean...

This was it, her last moments. Regrets filled her head. Nothing mattered, nothing made a difference. She'd found Helen, she'd fallen in love with Duran, and she'd even met her grandfather. None of it mattered. Gabriel looked down at her.

"Ivy, your body speaks truth. A drug remnant is present."

She waited.

The crowd murmured.

"Do you deny this?"

"No." She whispered, the roar of hopelessness in her head stole all other words.

"Diva of Orly. You make the charge against Ivy, come forward."

Diva strode to the center of the stage full of confidence. Gabriel's hand drew Ivy slightly to his right side. Diva faced her now, a gloating gleam in her one good eye, and a smirk at the corner of her mouth.

"What would you say to this woman?"

Diva licked her lips before speaking, "You pay for violating the law of the Changed World. Stupid bitch."

Ivy's head cleared, a remnant from a nightmare Duran suffered from drove away the fear and replaced it with white-hot rage. He would rise from bed, bellowing. Told Ivy later how Diva would lick her lips just before administering some new bit of pain to him. He shivered as he related it.

"Ivy, what would you say to this woman?" Gabriel lightly squeezed her forearm. "Speak the truth."

Suddenly, she knew exactly what to say, "The truth! The truth of how Diva of Orly was there, in Ursus' bedchamber. She promised him my total subservience. She had a drug that would tame me. Brought it to the bed I lay on, held taut by rope, naked, tortured. She held my mouth open and I almost didn't fight her. I was so tired..." Ivy shook her head. "But I did! I bit her hand, tasted her blood, spit out her flesh! And so...only a small dose slid inside me. Enough for that one night."

She turned her face to look into Gabriel's eyes. "Yes. My body holds a drug. A drug she forced into me!"

"Hallucinations!" Diva snarled. "Easy to malign a dead man! I wasn't there!"

"Did you scar, Diva? Was that the first scar you suffered at my hands?" Ivy all but chuckled, watching the taller woman involuntarily reach toward her face. "I'd love to see it..."

"Show me your hands, Diva. Prove Ivy lies." Gabriel flatly demanded.

Diva held up her right hand, no scar. She dropped it, glaring at Ivy.

"Now your other hand."

Diva tried to take a step back, but Gabriel's left hand quickly grabbed at the woman, stopping her. "Your other hand."

Before Gabriel could move, Ivy darted forward, snatched at Diva's left hand and held it up. There was the pale crescent at the web between thumb and forefinger. A notch of missing flesh.

Diva stood perfectly still. "Means nothing."

"Oh, it means everything." Gabriel took a deep breath. "Ivy, step back."

Ivy dropped her hand and obeyed. She touched Gabriel's hand. "I didn't dream it...did I?"

How long has she feared it was all a dream?

"No, you remember true."

"Your own law dictates her death!" Diva hissed.

"That is true." Gabriel's voice carried over the amphitheater. Several voices shouted out, most for Ivy. A few for her death.

Ivy's breath sped up, her head ached. Did she deserve to die?

"But some allowances must be made for changed circumstances." Gabriel stared out at the crowd. "The law is the law."

"No!"

Ivy jumped at the shout, recognizing Duran's voice. She twisted to see him atop a huge horse. He eased an obviously wounded Emmett into the arms of a cousin and pushed the horse toward the stage.

"You will not kill her!" he bellowed as the horse built up speed. Ivy tried to take a step away, but Gabriel pulled her closer. He dropped Diva's hand and held it up toward Duran.

Ivy shoved at the Guardian. "No! Don't hurt him! It's me, not him!"

The horse abruptly stopped, and Duran fought to hold on. Ivy struggled in Gabriel's grip as Diva laughed.

The sound infuriated Ivy and she screamed, tore herself free from Gabriel and surged at Diva. Michael intersected her surge, holding tightly. He hissed at her, "Wait!"

"Duran of Losanglos, you interrupt these proceedings," Gabriel calmly stated.

Duran jumped from the horse, staggering a bit. He slowly straightened. "Ivy did nothing wrong. Please, don't condemn her. I need her." His face was lined, his body shone with sweat. But he stood forth as steadfast as the Guardian who blocked his way. "There would be no justice in condemning her. Just cold murder."

Gabriel simply nodded. “Your words are noted. Please, take a seat.”

“No. I stand with Ivy.” Duran waited a moment before Gabriel agreed and moved aside. He wrapped arms around her and took a step back, dragging her away from battling Diva. He whispered, “Emmett is hurt, but will recover.”

Ivy swallowed, her hands rose to touch Duran’s arms. She suddenly felt safe again. What was it about his man’s arms?

Gabriel turned again to Diva. Michael had shifted until he stood at Diva’s back.

She smiled, showing only confidence and amusement at the drama.

“It is true, Diva of Orly poisoned this child, and this child’s child. General Buckler? She has poisoned you, and your officers. Ursus’ cook has been questioned. The plot of kill Helen’s child has been uncovered. What do you have to say, Diva?”

The smile slowly faded.

A shout came from Buckler, “Poisoned?”

“One does not reach such physical proportions without assistance, General. What did she tell you?” Michael asked.

“Herbs! You bitch!”

Diva chuckled.

Ivy suddenly registered Gabriel’s charge. “She poisoned Helen? How is Helen poisoned? Where is she!?” Ivy gazed, wide-eyed, at Gabriel, while Duran held her tightly. “Helen?” Ivy shouted.

“Helen was never touched by time, Ivy. Her curse was twisted by Diva’s actions. From you, from Ursus. She ages due to a twisted Cruzan curse. I am sorry.” Gabriel answered Ivy.

“No. No.” Ivy felt herself grow weak. Now Duran’s arms kept her from falling to her knees. “No. That isn’t fair...she has a son!”

“She stays with us, and we will strive to temper this aberration. The truth was found in Salom, in Orly. We hope to restore her original gift. To spread fertility.” Helen’s healer spoke. “There is hope. If you will assist.”

“Anything. Everything for Helen,” Ivy whispered.

Duran groaned, "No, not everything."

"I owe her." Ivy kissed his arm. "I left her with him."

"You had no choice!" Duran squeezed her. "It was not your fault!"

Gabriel broke up the discussion, raising a hand. "Aaron will not ask for everything." He took a step toward Diva. "You have conspired with the province to the north."

"You're insane." Diva accused. "I left Orly long ago. Thrown out by the Guardians that attempt to govern."

"No, they sent you. To disrupt the defenses of Calif. They had foresight to recognize their mountains were returning to active volcanoes. Knew they would need territory. I have spoken with them, Diva. I know."

Diva tried to take a step back, but Michael was there.

Ivy heard Parrotte's sharp bark of laughter. He'd suspected as much, Ivy remembered. Her head still full of Helen's predicament, she almost missed Diva's reaction.

Diva took a deep breath and spit at Gabriel's face. "And I succeeded! No one here can withstand our occupation!"

"There will be no occupation. Oh, they were gathered, ready to advance...but volcanoes are very unpredictable. There is no force left, Diva. There may be survivors who struggle this way, but no military force." Gabriel wiped her spit from his cheek. "The Guardians of Orly are no more. Your mission doesn't matter."

If a black woman could grow pale, Diva did so. Ivy swore she saw the woman tremble. Doesn't matter, Ivy thought, her mind ignored the concept of an invasion. Helen had to stay? What of Emmett and their son?

"Diva of Orly, you are banished from Gathering Valley. Every man's hand will be raised against you, the length and breath of Calif. Your supply of illicit drugs are gone, there will be no more from your sources in Orly."

"You're going to let her go?" Duran objected. "No! She broke the law! With deliberation!"

"I'm not bound by your laws, fool." Diva hissed at Duran. "I will still see you dead, Cruz bitch."

"Like hell." Duran threw Ivy to the side, put a hand to his short sword and prepared to draw it. Ivy landed, spun and kicked out at Duran. He almost fell, but recovered. "No, Ivy. I don't care. She won't come at you again." He took another step and staggered.

Diva laughed.

"I'll just kill her now."

Duran went to his knees, the valley holding him from doing harm.

But Diva moved fast, drew a dagger and threw it. Ivy fell to her knees, the dagger embedded near her shoulder.

Duran bellowed and dove at Ivy.

Gabriel tilted his head at Diva. "Our laws hold you, woman. As you have done to her, to others..." A dozen daggers flew at Diva. They landed solidly and the woman stumbled back at the force. Her thighs were pierced; her belly took one, her arms. But none were immediately deadly.

While Duran cradled Ivy, hand pressed to her wound, Michael stepped forward. "This is done." He pulled another dagger and simple slit Diva's throat. It was over. Diva crumbled to the ground, dead.

Aaron knelt next to Ivy. "Let me." His fingers danced near the wound. "Her aim was off. She'll recover. And the baby will be fine."

Ivy was gazing at Duran as Aaron's words broke through. "Baby?"

"A son for Duran. Helen's is a girl." Aaron set about binding the wound, babbling all along. "We'll need blood from you, Ivy. She'll be staying at the village lab, and her genetic curse won't touch her there. Emmett can return to Lina and bring back their son. When the valley reopens, we hope to have stopped the rapid aging. You've broken your curse, so there is likely an answer to be found. Now, that is better!" He moved away.

Duran and Ivy held each other. The healer's words trickling over both of them.

"A son?" He smiled. "Ivy!"

"A baby? One I can keep?" Ivy could barely speak. Tears filled her eyes. Duran laughed suddenly, bent and kissed her.

Neither was aware of the exodus from the amphitheater. Diva's body was hauled away, a quick conference began between Buckler and Parrotte regarding whatever forces still needed to be dispatched. Aaron set about tending Emmett, who was told of his daughter. And when a cure would be ready.

"I didn't see it, at first. Thought she would simply have to remain in the valley. But Gabriel brought back evidence and now I know what to do. It's all going to be fine!" Aaron chuckled, and patted Emmett's hand.

Duran held her close, one hand at her belly. She covered his hand with hers.

"He will be safe," Duran murmured to her. "With his mother and his father."

"And in time, his sister..."

Shadows filled the empty arena. And they stayed, dreaming of each other and a life without running. And children.

SNEAK PEAK OF ESSENTIALLY HUMAN

CHAPTER 1

Federal Agent Sam Montgomery had seen amazing things in his career as a chief investigator for the Homeland Research and Security Department. He'd traveled across the world, met thousands of people, good and bad, and taken part in clandestine operations whose complexity would choke Einstein. But this was a first. Tilting his head, he studied the woman on the computer monitor. She certainly didn't appear to be dead. Despite the evidence of all available data.

In 2039, Rachel Inez Aster, at the admirable age of eighty three, committed suicide by jumping off the stern of a cruise ship, into the water off the Bahamas. Her body was never recovered. Now, twenty six years later, she was back, currently a resident of a security cell in Virginia. According to Dr. Drummond – Drum to his friends – she was forty three years old. DNA didn't lie, but he wondered, could it be fooled? According to the chief medical officer, no.

Sam tapped a few keys, bringing up a still from Ms. Aster's suicide video. With another keystroke, the video feed from the prison cell appeared next to the first image. He found another recording, of the author from the year 2000, and studied the three faces. According to the computer, they were the same woman.

She'd been striking at eighty three, good bone structure stood out from the lines on her face. He started the video from the beginning.

The laptop's autofocus took a moment to center on the woman as she sat down. She appeared to study herself on the screen, eyes darting from point to point. Then she settled and began to speak. Her voice was rough. She coughed, cleared her throat and began again.

"I, Rachel Inez Aster, know exactly what I've done. Or will do. My will is in the hands of Cardonza and Sons, San Francisco. My home is packed, everything ready for the estate brokers."

She gazed beyond the screen, the light reflecting in her light brown eyes. He noticed the white halo around the iris, a sign of her age. She looked fit, her color good and skin actually quite radiant. The reports he'd read said she'd been in good health when she made the recording. He turned the volume up.

"I have led a good life. Long and productive. Eight-three years is enough. I've made it quite clear, in the last two decades, of my general opinion regarding the direction my country and the rest of the world is heading. To be blunt, I don't want to live in this world. I don't want my DNA entered into some vast data bank, though I lost the argument on that one."

Sam found it ironic that she'd resisted having a sample taken, considering that tissue was now providing him with a baffling question regarding her identity. He took a deep breath and returned attention to the video.

"It doesn't matter at this point. I hope the crew of the ship will not waste time searching for me. And I apologize to any passenger who misses the next port because they insist on looking. At least you can brag that you were on the ship when that wacky romance author threw herself from the stern. I hope you can milk that for something once you're home."

She ran her hands through her short crop of silver hair and

took a sip from a martini glass, shivering as the bright green liquid slid past her lips. A smile lit her face and she tilted her head to study the glass. "Reynaldo, you made a wonderful drink. I hope the tip I left for you is sufficient. I don't know that I believe in the afterlife anymore, though I hope that what is left of me sinks to the seafloor and provides some comfort to the dying ocean. Sorry, another lost cause I embraced."

She upended the glass and let the last of it drain into her mouth, and then carefully set the glass down. He wondered if she'd been drunk.

"Ah. Now, the crux. Don't bother to look through my computers for bits and pieces of unfinished manuscripts. They are purged. Don't dig through my papers looking for unpolished stories to sell. They are gone. I wrote what I wrote and that is it. My agent has a final manifesto, but whether she finds a place to publish it, or is allowed to publish it...well, that isn't up to me, is it? Perhaps it is up to you. I don't know. This video will go live minutes after I have leapt from the stern of the boat. To my loyal readers, I hope I have brought you some light in the dark days."

He'd already done the search. She'd been quite thorough and nothing was published after her death. The manifesto had been posted, but ridiculed and torn to pieces by those who found her views unpatriotic. Officials had done an excellent job at suppressing any hints of validity regarding her observations.

At this point, the camera focus wavered, searching for the point to sharpen. All Sam could see was movement. Finally, she returned to center screen just in time to record her picking a full length black cape from her chair and settling the garment onto her shoulders with a theatrical flourish. She paused for a moment, gaze meeting the camera's unblinking eye. Then she began to remove her jewelry. Her earrings and necklace first, and then her rings, which seemed reluctant to leave her fingers. After a few struggles with the reticent bits of sparkle, nearly all her finery lay on the keyboard. She fingered a flashy charm bracelet and left it clasped on her left wrist. Then, with a wave at the camera, she hit a key.

The screen went black, the date, August 02, 2039, stark against the background.

Sam took a deep breath and played the recording again. He glanced at the image on the screen to the right, mounted on the massive wall shared by twelve different monitors, and back again at the woman in the cruise ship cabin.

Was it the same person? How could it be? He tapped a few keys and the frame froze at the point where she looked above the laptop and he studied her face. Another few keystrokes and he captured the image, transferred it to a special program and watched as the age fell away. He stopped it when he felt it was closest to the woman in the cell, a date and time continually blinked on that screen. *05/11/2065 02:45*.

He switched to a fresh keyboard and a moment later a montage from her funeral played across the screen. Photos of the author from younger days, some video, some stills, began to play. He listened as fans of her writing, along with friends and acquaintances, spoke of how much they would miss her, how her books influenced them to write, or to smile, laugh. She'd been beloved by her fans, that seemed obvious.

A politician spoke of her commitment to the restoration of individual freedom and how much the funds she'd left to the cause would be appreciated. Though he made it clear they would rather Ms. Aster had chosen a different path.

It all seemed terrible pointless. She'd killed herself.

Sam's focus swiveled from the frozen frames of the suicide video, the composite from the identity program and a still from the memorial service.

Damn. Whoever created her, did a good job of it.

Remove the cap of short, scrappy hair she'd worn in her *original* forties and replace it with five feet of wavy auburn curls and the woman could be the author's twin. According the DNA bank, they weren't twins, but the same woman.

Not a clone, reported Dr. Drum. At least not according to what they knew about current cloning techniques. After the international ban on cloning went into effect in 2020, rumors would rise of renegade labs in Sweden, or deep in Asia, making astonishing progress, but no scientific papers were published. The scare of the poultry plague killed off that branch of research. At least, the rest of the world assumed that.

Dr. Drummond's words from earlier in the day played across his mind. He'd known Drum for decades and could tell when the man was finding the entire puzzle much too amusing. His face betrayed the fascination, the curl of his lip and raised eyebrow illustrated excitement. Not to mention the near bounce as he gave his report

"She isn't a clone, Monty. Her DNA structure is much too stable and the radioactive trace in her skeletal structure, along with the mineral make up of her cells, indicate she didn't mature in a lab environment." Drum had met his eyes and smiled crookedly. "And why, in God's green acres, would scientists who could clone this perfectly choose a romance author from early in the century as a subject? It doesn't make any sense."

Drum had a point. It didn't make sense. Nothing about this mystery appeared simple. A clone of a terrorist, or a beloved politician or celebrity would make sense. Someone to win over the public, or rally the troops, fool the voters. But an author? She'd been well known, but not of superstar status. If this were a plot of some sort to win public sentiment, a more recent candidate would make more sense.

He glanced at the list of awards she'd won in her day. No, the *author* had won in her day. Something called a KATHY, four of them. She made the New York Times Bestseller list eight times, when it was still a print paper. There had been three television movies and an aborted big screen attempt to dramatize one of the best sellers. She'd been a popular speaker and only in the latter half of her career had her outspoken liberal politics impacted her sales. But even then, she remained a darling of the coastal populations, who embraced her Save the Seas Foundation.

She'd left most of her money to that effort. He'd been on the oceans most of his life, and to be truthful, totally agreed with her cause. Raised on the eastern coast, he loved to sail and took every opportunity to still find time on the water. Economic hardship hadn't done the waters covering most of the earth any favor. The big oil spill and fire off of San Diego had been an environmental catastrophe to rival every disaster of the century before. Millions had died.

With a sigh, he switched over to another screen and called up the reports from that charity. He pulled a chair out and sat to read. For over an hour he examined the news coverage after her death and, buried in the numerous stories, he caught something that made him smile. Evidently, Rachel Inez Aster had been partly responsible for the breakthrough in oil cleanup, since her foundation funded a scholarship for Angela Frederick, the scientist who would go on to patent the compound that neutralized spilled oil and turned it into benign chemicals.

He explored Dr. Frederick's background and read that she still worked in a lab on the west coast. And all the proceeds from her patent continued to fight for coastal waters.

Could she have covertly funded an effort to bring back Rachel Aster? It certainly didn't seem feasible.

He straightened his back and lifted his hands from the keyboard to stretch. A yawn threatened to break his concentration, but he shook it off.

Another cup of coffee would probably fry his brain, but he needed a breakthrough and something nibbled at the back of his head. Drum promised completed lab tests the next day, frowning as he studied the preliminary report. "Something isn't right, here. Might be a normal genetic abnormality, I'll send it in for further testing."

"What sort of abnormality?"

Drum had pointed to a series of lines running down the full body scan they'd done of the prisoner. "Might be scratches on the films, might not be. I'll get the Professor to analyze my equipment."

"She's busy looking over the video from the *Ballard*."

"Yes, but her imaging diagnostics are fully automated. She can let the program run while she works on the *Ballard*'s video feed." Drum had slapped him on the back. "You can't wave your hand and have all the answers. I know sixty-five sailors and scientists are missing. But you found no sign of violence, no ransom request, plus no group has gone online and claimed responsibility."

Sam didn't respond, his mind spinning with the horror of some new weapon that would cause the crew to throw themselves off the ship. He had a wicked imagination. She was the only clue regarding the crew's disappearance, if she'd only talk!

Monty pushed the chair away, stood and paced before the wall of monitors. After several minutes, he brought up the live feed from the cell where she sat. The subdued lighting mimicked night, but she didn't sleep. She sat on the cot, her arms wrapped around her knees. The bright yellow set of surgical scrubs came from Drum. A single ray of light, probably from a fault in the mirror, illuminated her bare foot and the vivid cuff of the pants.

When the Navy pulled her from that raft, floating four hundred miles from the South Carolina coast, she'd been naked. According to Drum, she must not have been there long. No sunburn, no dehydration.

He clicked another monitor on and loaded the video from the rescue. She'd been on her stomach, an impressive swath of hair providing some shelter from the sunlight across her back. When the Navy dingy reached her and one of the sailors slid onto the raft, she'd risen up, stared straight at him and then tried to throw herself into the water. It had taken three men to calm her down, get a blanket around her and one sailor had to hold her tight against his body as they sped back to the ship.

She'd tried to get away over and over again, never saying a word. She made no sound. Just attempted to escape. Finally, the medic declared her in shock and suffering from hysteria. They sedated her, locked her up in a quarantine area of medical bay and contacted the base. Three hours later, every electronic device on the ship failed, the video cameras and recorders stopped and seven minutes later, when they all returned to function, no one remained but the rescued female, still unconscious.

The Navy answered an emergency beacon, independent of the ship's power. In fact, it went off because the systems ceased so abruptly. After arriving and only finding the woman, they called his unit in and transferred her to the care of Homeland Research and Security Department for interrogation.

All during the recorded struggles to contain her, she'd said nothing. Forty eight hours later, and Sam had failed in getting her to talk. Drum found no physiological reason for her silence. The doctor's gentle manner won some trust from her, and she'd taken the clothing from him, dropping the back closing gown the *Ballard* crew had given her and slipping into the fresh outfit with no show of modesty.

Sam considered how fast Drum had spun to look away as she'd changed. No sense of manners kept Sam from studying her body. The past photos of the author showed a woman approaching obesity. Not this present incarnation. She was curvy, but not to an extreme. At one point, she'd glanced at the one way mirror, eyelids narrowing. He suspected she'd known someone was watching, but didn't care. He'd observed, poised to intercede if she tried to take advantage of Drum being a gentleman. She didn't. She'd allowed Drum to run a full series of tests, watching the medical expert closely. She'd only shied away when he plucked a few hairs from her head. Perfectly understandable.

When Drum took her back to the cell and sat next to her with a computer notebook, she'd listened to him intently. Sam almost refused Drum's request to see if she'd cooperate with a series of questionnaires. Right now, he thanked God his friend had convinced him.

"She knows what I'm doing. She's watching and she understands every question. She seems pleased that she's passing the tests. I don't think there is anything wrong with her brain. She may not speak English but reads it and knows it. Did you see her grin when Shep cracked a joke about all that hair and the MRI machine?"

He'd nodded. Lord knows, she'd basically ignored his interrogation. Other than to shrug her shoulders and sigh a great deal when he spoke about the missing crewmen.

He watched again as she examined the notebook, and then showed she understood what Drum wanted. The doctor left her with the device, a Marine on watch. And then she sped through test after test. The entire expanded Briggs and Meyer test took her four minutes, the standard IQ tests, twice that. The tests on moral compass made her grimace and she skipped a great many of the questions, rolling her eyes from time to time. At the end of three hours she set the device down, yawned then folded her arms on the table, set her head atop them and went to sleep.

The testing had surprised everyone.

He leaned back in his chair, closed his eyes and considered the episode. Once she'd settled into the notepad, Drum left and joined him in the observation room.

The doctor stood at his side, his mouth slightly agape. Her answers were analyzed as quickly as she entered them. Drum quit attempting to follow along on his linked notepad after thirty minutes. The screen blinked and the computer readings appeared when she'd finished.

Clearing his throat, Dr. Drum, read the results and shook his head. Then rubbed at his eyes and blinked. In all the time that Sam had known the man, he'd never seen him so rattled. "Well, her answers match what we know of the author. Her moral readings follow the liberal arts background. Her knowledge of modern history is non-existent. She has little religious opinion, neither an atheist or a believer. Ambivalent, I'd say." He'd let the notebook drop to his side. "I'm going to need time to understand this."

"She answered so quickly, did she even read the questions?"

"Yes, her answers show an understanding of what was asked."

“Could she have been coached on the standard tests?” It boggled the mind to consider that, but she’d seldom paused, her hands flying over the screen.

“Certainly, but the computer sets them in random order, no one could memorize a set of answers and spit them out that fast. Trust me, Monty. She answered from her first inclination.”

“Then why skip so many?”

“Because she simply didn’t like any of the answers. The option is left on the moral compass section, which are most of what she skipped. That test would be new to her, if she is the author.” Drum chuckled. “Quite a quandary. At least now we know, she can read and write.”

“She didn’t write anything.”

“Yes, she did.” He pointed to the final entry. “Under name she used the stylist to write *Ria*.”

“The initials of the author, Drum. Doesn’t mean anything.”

“But it does. She wrote without hesitation, after several hours. It was an automatic response. She considers Ria to be her name, period.” Drum slapped him on the back. “I’ll look this over tonight. Try not to stay here all night. Get home and get some sleep.”

“Yes, sir.” Sam spoke flatly.

“As if I could order you to do anything.” Drum chuckled and left the room. Sam stood and studied her sleeping form, then ordered her roused and taken to her cell.

Nine hours later, he was back to watching her, the monitors showing stills of her face from every conceivable angle. She sat, her face and most of her body hidden by the curtain of hair. A sudden thought occurred to him and he searched the data base for the MRI picture Drum had shown him before leaving. Could that be her hair? He shifted to a live view of the scan and noted that she did lie on the long strands. He magnified the picture and compared it with the scan. It shouldn’t pick up that mane, and hadn't in its entirety, but those seven lines directly matched that mass of wavy strands. She had something hidden!

He turned from the monitors and headed for the elevator. Just then, the discordant ringing of the building's alarm went off.

Ria glanced up as the bell began to ring. She held her hands to her ears, wincing. She doubted it sounded so loud to the rest, but she lived in a very quiet world and the clanging bell echoed inside her head, making her wince. She glanced up the corner of the cell. No doubt a camera watched her and recorded every move she made.

Damn, her body sagged with exhaustion, and her mind. They never stopped asking her questions. She didn't know where the sailors were. She suspected, but she didn't *know*. The tall man, with the striking blue eyes, seemed so worried about them. She sensed a patient and hiding anger behind those eyes. Hell, she hadn't snuck up while they napped in the sun, overpowered them, and forced them to board her raft! No doubt, he blamed her for their disappearance.

She couldn't tell Agent Montgomery what she didn't know. And she didn't dare speak. Once she opened her mouth, it would all spill forth and then they'd lock her away forever, convinced she'd gone insane. So, she kept silent.

At least that doctor trusted her to cooperate, without the constant battering. Fascinating to see how far notebook computing had come. That tablet had been no thicker than a standard magazine. It forwarded to the next page, or set of questions she supposed, without prompting. Some of those problems made her uncomfortable. Like a pebble dropped into her calm pool. Even now she found herself contemplating why they would want to know such invasive things or ask questions without better options.

One in particular filled her with an emotion she knew was rage, but she couldn't recall the last time she'd felt it.

You're on a lifeboat and three children cry out for help from a sinking raft. There is no room on your lifeboat unless an old man who is unconscious is thrown overboard. What do you do?

She'd looked for the option of getting out in place of the children and it wasn't offered. What sort of people were these?

The bell shut off and she sighed in relief. A moment later, she heard the locking mechanism to her cell click and the door flew open. Agent Montgomery shouted something to the guard and reached behind himself. He pulled forth something she did recognize. Handcuffs.

With a shriek, she shot to her feet and tried to back away from him, smacking into a wall. He followed, reaching for her right hand. She thrust her hands behind her back, tangling them in her hair and struggled with him. It proved useless, he overpowered her and strong-armed her to the floor, snagged her wrist and clicked one cuff closed. To her shock, the other closed around his left wrist. He hauled her up and thrust her at the door.

"No one is breaking you out of here! Might have worked aboard the *Ballard*, but not here!" He growled as the lights went out. "Not so silent anymore?" She felt him shove past her, then jerk her forward by the link on her wrist.

She stumbled and a moment later fell forward, pulled off balance. Reaching out she tried to figure out what she'd tripped on and found Agent Montgomery, sprawled on the floor. She felt around his body, searching for the key. But her hand slipped on something warm and wet. Lifting her hand she sniffed. Blood. He'd been hurt.

She left off looking for the key and ran her free hand up his body. She found a deep laceration at the side of his head. It had already soaked the short cropped hair. She tried to remember what to do with a head wound. If she tried to staunch the blood with fabric, would it act as a wick and increase blood loss or help the clotting process?

She couldn't remember!

So damned many things she couldn't remember.

A sound from the doorway made her turn a head. A soft glow approached. She could see the body of her guard, blocking the doorway. It was carefully eased to one side. She looked and relief filled her. "T'talin! Help me, he's hurt!" The familiar form of the present leader of the Aleena towered above her. He was strong, he could help her with Agent Montgomery.

"Ria, we must leave quickly."

"I know, but he's bleeding. Help him."

"His people will tend to him." T'talin slipped into the room and tried to help her stand. Despite the alien strength, the dead-weight of the unconscious man made it impossible. She glanced at the body and saw the blood pool spreading. Without hesitation she lied.

"I can't come without him. He chained me to him and I don't know how to free myself. He'll die before they can tend to him, and I'll be found with his body. They'll lock me away so deep you'll never find me." She didn't know where the lie came from, but she didn't correct herself. Some part of her needed this man to live.

T'talin leaned down and hefted him up. "Come. We'll see to him."

She grabbed the slim pillow off the cot, ripped its cover free and quickly wrapped it around Agent Montgomery's head before allowing him to lead the way from the complex.

ALSO BY MAUREEN O. BETITA

Book List

Alien Encounters

Essentially Human

The Alien Library

The Embrace Protocol

The Kraken's Caribbean Series

The Kraken's Mirror, book one

The Chameleon Goggles, book two

The Pirate Circus, book three

The Kraken's Promise, book four

The Dark Dreams of Davy Jones, book five

The Kraken's Caribbean Short Stories - in order

Rumsgiving - A Holiday for Emily

Silvestri's Unintended Consequences

The Founding of the Port

A Troubling Courtship

Keitran's Ascension

A Pirate's Vacation

Charlie's Big Catch

The Kraken's Caribbean Short Story Bundle

Forever A Pirate

A Caribbean Spell, book one

Red Sean's Revenge, book two

The French Gambit, book three

Magic's Hostage, book four

The Hard Choices, book five

Forever A Pirate, Boxed Set #1

The Spanish Challenge, book six

The Blood Tears, book seven

A Desperate Course, book eight

Summoned Home, book nine

The Lurking Menace, book ten

Forever A Pirate, Boxed Set #2

Ruby, book eleven

Something More Than This, book twelve

The Hunter's Trail, book thirteen

The Haunting, book fourteen

Upon the Bridge, book fifteen

Forever A Pirate, Boxed Set #3

The Magician's Pearl, book sixteen

The Nightmare Nest, book seventeen

The Night God, book eighteen

Soul Struggles, book nineteen

Miranda's Trial, book twenty

Forever A Pirate, Boxed Set #4

The Taste of Blood, book twenty-one

Lee's Gift, book twenty-two

The Rebel Plot, book twenty-three

Loose Ends, book twenty-four

More Is Asked, book twenty-five

Forever A Pirate, Boxed Set #5

Captured By A Past, book twenty-six

The Bitter Twist, book twenty-seven

Turning of the Tide, Book twenty-eight

Laughing Crows, book twenty-nine

The Divine Blossom, book thirty

Forever A Pirate, Boxed Set #6

Miranda's Passion - Poetry from Forever A Pirate

No Place Like Holmes

Born in Flight

Foxoddness

Four To A Bed

The Changed World

ABOUT THE AUTHOR

Maureen lives along the lovely Monterey Bay and finds great inspiration in being so near the Pacific Ocean. She shares her home with Stephen, her high school sweetheart, married for over 30 years and a cat named Isabeau. She travels miles and miles to attend pirate festivals, renaissance fairs, scifi/fantasy conventions, steampunk cons and writing conferences.

Join the mailing list and the news will come to you.

Visit Maureen
www.maureenobetita.com

www.ingramcontent.com/pod-product-compliance
Lightning Source LLC
Chambersburg PA
CBHW070841250626
47159CB00003B/870

* 9 7 8 1 9 3 9 9 1 4 9 7 2 *